'God v

So says Seamus Butler of his famous fall-goats, the result of the genetic strain which his father had inadvertently bred on this Settler family's farm. For these goats have an inborn fault which makes them worth their weight in gold: when startled, they keel over instantly in a dead faint. Thus a single fall-goat placed among a flock of sheep becomes the only prey when an enemy strikes, leaving the flock unharmed.

But it is these pathetic goats, with their mocking yellow eyes, which have given the Butlers wealth and influence in the Eastern Cape – an important factor in a time of great political upheaval, especially when oil is unexpectedly discovered right in the middle of the harbour town of Port Cecil. The discovery and its implications for the town bring into sharp focus the local black civic organisation's demand for a unified city council.

At the forefront of black aspirations is MaNdlovu Thandani, larger than life and seemingly indestructible. In opposition: Seamus Butler himself, a man whose dark moods and recurring depressions surge relentlessly through him like the seven deltas of the river which wind their way through Port Cecil and down to the sea.

And, while history dictates that these two separate worlds will inevitably converge, their families cannot remain unaffected, threatening to fall apart beneath the weight of their time. This is the backdrop to the story of the stud master of the farm known as Fata Morgana. It is a story which carves a path through the lives of the people of this Eastern Cape district, all of them inextricably involved, inescapably trapped in their heritage during a time where beauty and cruelty, violence and hope all become entangled.

Etienne van Heerden's short stories and novels, of which *Ancestral Voices* is the best known, have been translated into many languages. Amongst other awards, he has won the Hertzog Prize and was twice the recipient of the CNA Literary Award. *Leap Year* won Van Heerden his third AKTV Award. He is an associate professor at the University of Cape Town.

Other books by Etienne van Heerden:

Ancestral Voices
Mad Dog and Other Stories
Casspirs and Camparis

LEAP YEAR

A Novel

Etienne van Heerden

PENGUIN BOOKS

PENGUIN BOOKS

Published by the Penguin Group
27 Wrights Lane, London W8 5TZ, England
Viking Penguin, a division of Penguin Books USA Inc,
375 Hudson Street, New York, New York 10014, USA
Penguin Books Australia Ltd, Ringwood, Victoria, Australia
Penguin Books Canada Ltd, 10 Alcorn Avenue, Toronto, Ontario, Canada M4V 3B2
Penguin Books (NZ) Ltd, 182-190 Wairau Road, Auckland 10, New Zealand
Penguin Books South Africa (Pty) Ltd, Pallinghurst Road, Parktown, South Africa 2193

Penguin Books South Africa (Pty) Ltd,
Registered Offices: 20 Woodlands Drive, Woodmead, Sandton 2128

First published in Afrikaans as *Die Stoetmeester* by Tafelberg Publishers, 1993
First published in English by Penguin Books South Africa (Pty) Ltd, 1997

ISBN 0-140-262164

Typeset by Positive Proof cc in 10.5 on 13 pt Berkeley Book
Printed and bound by Color Graphic, Durban
Cover picture: The Image Bank

For Kaia

1

Something woke me. It could not have been the night sounds of the port – they are so familiar they form a kind of silence: the sighing of boats at anchor as the incoming tide disturbs their rest; the nightly barking of dogs in the fishermen's quarter; the hiss of steam escaping from the power station at Third Leg; and, if you listen carefully: fins cleaving the ocean depths, comets whistling through the firmament of heaven, the gentle rustle of a rose opening in the garden ...

And now I am back on that evening as it all begins: back with my sister Sarah, where she is standing alone on the stoep of the farmhouse, as she looks out over the veld awaiting the arrival of her guests.

This evening is yet another splendid occasion on the Butler estate. 'Not for the faint-hearted' runs the family motto, and in city clubs, on tennis courts and in noiseless Mercedeses speeding over farm roads there is general and admiring agreement: 'A dinner party at Seamus and Sarah Butler's on Fata Morgana is not to be undertaken lightly.'

Driving along the dusty road to the Butlers' farm, perhaps braking suddenly to avoid an unexpected lynx in the road, the dinner guests regard the moonlit veld with a measure of awe. After such a drive, the manor house with its wide verandas, open windows and flickering candles on the dinner table is a splendid sight.

The outside lamps have been switched on early and strings of little lights illuminate the garden even beyond the gates, now thrown open for the expected guests. In the electric light, against the fading background of the dusk, the aloes and cycads look prehistoric.

Perhaps I should add right here: In this part of the world one may never forget the impassive remoteness, the inscrutability of nature, the indifference in its giving and its taking. It is as though the God who conceived it all moves through the landscape like a majestic kudu bull, guileless, fattened and content after good rains, proudly carrying his magnificent horns.

Sarah sighs and looks out across the veld. At this evening hour the landscape grows gentler, more expansive. But it is deceptive. This is the time when jackals creep out of their dens and genets from their nests; when the few leopards still left in the kloofs come down from their ravines; when night adders glide swiftly through the dust in search of mice.

And people grow no gentler either as evening falls. Behind the house Sarah hears the slaughter-pulley being hauled up. The farm hands have just fetched a fat ewe from the slaughter pen, where Seamus keeps all the fall-goats destined for the table of the manor and the cooking pots of the farm hands.

Standing there on the stoep with a sherry in her hand, tensing and relaxing her shoulders, Sarah finds it all rather grisly. There is an unexpected chill in the evening air. Even while the labourers are making their way along the worn footpath across the kikuyu lawn towards the slaughter pen, already the slaughter goats are bunching together and growing light-headed. When the men push the gate open and the hinges groan, all the goats keel over as if they know what is coming.

Death comes swiftly. Before the selected goat can come to, one of the farm hands has thrown her over his shoulder and walked the short distance down the path to the slaughter-pole. There the jugular is quickly severed and the blood caught in a basin for the makwethas in their hessian tents up near the earth dam.

Before the animal has been properly skinned, its belly will have been slit open for the liver to be taken out warm and steaming, and one of the servants will be hurrying up to the kitchen with it. At Fata Morgana a tradition of many years' standing dictates that when the guests come to the table the starter has to be fall-goat liver. 'Slaughtered at sundown,' Seamus will announce proudly as he raises his glass. At moments like these, Sarah thinks with a shudder, with the yellow candlelight reflecting in his eyes, there is sometimes a disquieting resemblance between Seamus and one of his own fall-goats.

She shrugs her shoulders, irritated by her own thoughts, and goes over the seating plan again in her mind. Everything has to run smoothly. The guests invited over to Fata Morgana this evening will once again make up a typical Butler table.

There will be a few Afrikaners from the smallish Afrikaans-speaking community in the city. Their forefathers arrived in the area two centuries ago in oxwagons: these are the descendants of those who had not wanted to trek any farther.

The majority, of course, will be of Settler stock – the gentry of the region: the clans who have grown rich on pineapples and cattle, after slaves had piggybacked their ancestors ashore from the boats in Algoa Bay in 1820.

Usually – since the Butlers have always supported liberal principles – there will also be a Xhosa-speaking couple, or an Indian businessman and his wife. The Indians are among the wealthiest communities in the city; almost all live along First Leg, across the river from where I, Seer, have lived alone, ever since the death of our parents, in the ramshackle old family home where I grew up.

But the table will be incomplete without someone from the Afrikaans-speaking 'Coloured' community – tonight it will be the Bouwers, whose son has just been awarded his doctorate in ichthyology for his thesis on the coelacanth.

The sherry is helping Sarah relax some of the tension she always feels as she prepares for a large dinner party. Is she imagining it, or is there a smell of rain in the air? In this part of the country one can smell rain a day in advance even before any clouds appear on the horizon. Animals smell it even sooner, of course: earlier that evening she had been watching ants as they scurried across the back stoep.

She is worried about her guests. Most of them are city people and not always as aware as they ought to be of the danger of driving on farm roads after dark. Kudu bulls simply ignore fences, leaping them at will in search of females or better grazing. There isn't a single farmer hereabouts who has not lost at least one pick-up truck after colliding with one of the giant kudus of the region.

Especially when there is rain in the air, humans and beasts alike become very excitable. While the river always flows broad and full, the region through which it winds its way is the High Karoo, and trying to irrigate those parched plains is an impossible task. Every farmer has a couple of hundred morgen under spray irrigation, but for the rest they have to practise dry-land farming, and for that one has to depend on the grace of God.

But when it does rain, Sarah reminds herself as she pours a second sherry from the crystal decanter placed on the stoep table awaiting the arrival of the guests, even the highest fences cannot contain the kudu. Once the rain has passed over, the whole countryside smells fresh and clean, and rainbows hang like half-hoops over the ridges of the hills. As flying-ants billow out of their holes and pour down like rain showers onto the plains in shining silver swarms, antbears emerge from their drenched burrows, even though it is still light.

That, Sarah thinks, smiling as she looks out over the darkening plains, that is when the kudu take wing. That's how the old folks always put it. Then fathers will knock out their pipes and mothers will draw old tales from the depths of their aprons: about monkeys' weddings, when Mr Jackal ran off with Mrs Wolf; or Orphan Rockrabbit and his cruel stepfather; or Mr Fox who caught his tail in his mouth and cartwheeled all the way down the hills and away from the Hunting Hounds. At such a time, if you lay your ear to the trunk of a tree-aloe, you can hear the bitter sap within growing sweet. You can hear the cycads groaning as their prehistoric trunks struggle to wrest the water from the soil before it sinks away again. You can hear the subterranean groaning of the earth itself as deep roots suddenly come to life.

And then you know: it has rained.

'Kudu on the wing.'

Sarah is so startled that her sherry splashes onto the stoep. 'My frock ...!'

Seamus laughs. 'Don't worry, it's only on the stoep.' He wraps his arms around her from behind. She leans her head back against his chest. He smells of soap and after-shave, the same smell he'd had when they had first met, how long ago? Thirty, forty years?

'There's certainly a strong smell of rain in the air.' At her back she feels the voice vibrating in his chest. She nods. They know each other so well, each can read the other's mind. Perhaps that is why the chasms between them are so deep – because in so many other respects they are so much at one.

'Monkey's wedding,' she smiles.

'... Mr Jackal and Mrs Wolf.'

They stand together for a while, looking out over the landscape. In the last of the light they can see a flock of fall-goats making their way down the hillside. There is a bell wether a couple of paces ahead of the others. The rest of the flock are strung out in an irregular column of twos and threes for a good five hundred yards, as they make their way pensively down to the water for the night.

When darkness falls, suddenly, unexpectedly, they look like a white train sliding down the slope. Or like a snake, Sarah thinks, and shivers.

Seamus turns round to go into the house again. Sarah wants to call him back. That white file of goats fills her with a sense of foreboding, something which she has borne within her for months now: a vague premonition that there is something ominous in the air.

Her feelings are not simply the result of its being leap year, either. The winter months had given the district ample warning that nature was in an extraordinary mood. The June days had been unexpectedly warm. A meteor with a long yellow tail had passed over south-east of the Kei region, moving across the Tropic of Capricorn towards Madagascar.

One morning a silvery shoal of fish had swum up through the river mouth. With pots and buckets and watering cans clanking, the inhabitants of the town's squatter camps had come running down along the river, yelling. At Horseshoe Bend, at the junction where the seven legs of the delta diverged just above the estuary, the fish had hurled themselves against the sand banks.

'This is raging suicide,' people whispered. 'There must be a reason for it.' The university ordered its department of ichthyology to explain the phenomenon. After many seminars on the subject, the professors, all of whom had gained their doctorates for theses on the renowned coelacanth, formally agreed that they were not of one mind.

It was due to the turning of the moon, one suggested, and a light earth tremor (2,5 on the Richter scale) twenty miles out to sea. Another was of the opinion that the uncharted firepath of the meteor was responsible for the mass suicide of the fish. Or perhaps, suggested a third, the delicate ecological balance of the east coast of Africa had been disturbed by the sinking of the luxury pleasure liner, the Oceanos, off the Wild Coast, on that day when according to local gossip the Greek captain had jettisoned maritime tradition and gone ashore first.

Sarah takes another sip of sherry. The measured progress of the goats holds her spellbound. June, she remembers, had been followed by a July plagued by freak winds. The late winter winds, which traditionally do not start sweeping up dust across the landscape until August, had come early. There were falls of snow where none had ever before been recorded, even on the beach where the Dias cross commemorates the passage of the dauntless Portuguese seafarer in the fifteenth century. Up at Addo, too, the elephants wandered around through the underbrush for days wearing a white mantle of snow.

At Manley Flats, Sarah recalls with a shudder, a calf with two heads had survived its own birth to bellow at the astonished farmers from surrounding farms. She and Seamus had driven over to see it, and it was something she will never forget: the voice from one of the heads was melancholy and filled with unfathomable woe, while the other was cheerfully frivolous.

One day, so its owner Bill Heathcote said, the calf had taken a good hard look at itself and died. They had had it stuffed and it was now on view at the Settlers Museum, just round the corner from the glass cases in which wax dolls dressed in crinolines and top hats portrayed the arrival of the 1820 British Settlers.

All this had happened in the winter months – months when nature was usually at rest. Sarah is convinced: there is something untoward afoot.

When one of the kitchen maids comes out onto the stoep with the gravyboat and a little tasting spoon, she tastes delicately, holding her sherry in the other hand. 'Just a touch more salt,' she says, 'but just a whisper, see – be careful now.'

Perhaps the charm of this country lies in the unpredictability with which nature sometimes grows tender. Sarah walks across to one of the vases, takes out a wild rose and stands there dreamily holding it to her nose.

She will never be able to live anywhere except close to this city and the river with its seven streams running into the Indian Ocean. Ever since her childhood she has been in love with the sea-wrack restlessly bunching up against the quays, the barnacles clinging to the hulls of boats, the boulevards meandering through the wealthy areas, even the dirty, noisy squatter camps straggling out across the foothills round the delta. And most especially: the drive out through the milkwood trees to where, suddenly, the aloes begin and the inhospitable plains fan out.

It's a primeval world, she thinks, gently stroking the petals of the rose against her cheek. In the city museum one can view lizards and aloes, ancient fossils and dung beetles. As well as the habits and customs of the Khoi and San, displayed alongside the life styles of Xhosa, Boer and Briton. Also, since the Indian community of Port Cecil had put their heads together, there is now an exhibition area depicting their particular contribution to the turbulent history of the region.

There are exhibitions of fish and shells and starfish, too, and shark jaws big enough for a man to crawl through. And of course, stuffed and mounted on a pedestal beyond the reach of curious schoolboys: the Primeval Fish, Eldest of all fishes, the Coelacanth itself.

Illuminated with just the right play of light and shadow, it represents the primal wisdom of depths so vertiginous that museum visitors shiver at the sight of that primordial snout with its fringe of whiskers, its gash of a mouth, and its eyes. They shudder at the thought of the Indian Ocean Chasm only a couple of miles from the city centre, where the sea bed falls away into a gulf so profound that scientists are drawn to plumb its depths in inordinately expensive beetlecraft and deep-sea diving bells, the hesitant beams of their searchlights and video cameras groping to capture the teeming mystery of creation, for analysis later behind the ivy-covered walls of laboratories.

My sister wipes a hand across her forehead. I may be carried away a bit by my story here, but at this moment she feels equally overwhelmed by the landscape and what is moving beneath her feet. She places her empty sherry glass on the tray and chides herself lightly – never before has she had more than one sherry before her guests arrive.

The childhood which Sarah and I had spent in the oldest area of Port Cecil, in the rambling old ramshackle house half overhanging the river, had filled her with an instinct for the strange moods of this country. Her marriage to Seamus Butler and the fall-goat stud had taken her to the very boundary between the explicable and the mysterious ...

Perhaps I should now give a description of her home.

The Fata Morgana estate lies between the river and the mountain range. You approach the farm from Port Cecil by first crossing the graceful bridge across the broadest leg of the delta and then turning up along the river. When you take this road, you have to drive with caution, taking care to hoot at the women carrying long loads of firewood on their heads, at the children with home-made fishing rods and tins of earthworms on their way down to the mudflats at low tide, and at the donkey carts on their way to market loaded with pineapples or hand-made clay pots.

Then the road climbs steeply, leaving Port Cecil glistening on the seven mouths of its delta down below. In the distance the river becomes a silver snake twisting through dun coloured hills, and even farther away, in the haze which tourists take for mist but which is actually dust, the river becomes the indeterminate track of a snail. From there the road rises to the Manley Flats plateau and the renowned estate of the Butlers, the only breeders of fall-goats in the southern hemisphere.

Thousands of tourists visit Seamus's stud annually. The local agricultural adviser, officially in service of the department but actually the slave of the wealthy clans of Manley Flats, is then summoned to deliver a lecture on the breeding of fall-goats. The man is a victim of snow, frost, hail and every conceivable pestilence – from foot-and-mouth disease to scab, ringworm and rabies – and he makes sure that each presentation becomes something of an occasion.

Before the tourists leave the city en route for Fata Morgana, he sees to it that they first visit the tourist bureau on Cathedral Square where postcards showing the proud profile of the Fata Morgana goats are on sale. The insane yellow eyes, their expression playing somewhere between contempt and amusement, cause many a tourist to recoil instinctively from the rotary postcard rack.

They prefer to buy postcards showing one of Addo's elephants, or a blood-red aloe, or an aerial view of the delta with its seven legs, or the façade of the university behind its cloak of ivy, and the

Drostdy Arch where a century ago rebels were hanged in public.

After that the agricultural adviser leads the tourists silently through Seamus's fields. Quietly and respectfully they view the three-horned flocks and even run their hands gently over the backs of the oldest of the bell wethers.

For Sarah, too, it has become an almost daily routine, this waiting for the tourist buses and then serving pineapple beer under the pepper trees. That done, she will watch Seamus and the agricultural adviser taking up position in front of the double-storeyed Settler manor house. They are well placed for photographs and while the cameras click away, Sarah observes her husband with the eyes of a tourist: the bright blue eyes, the irritable hands, the large frame with the rather wide hips and when, lost in thought, his eyes wander for a moment, the peasant face from some back street in London just showing through beneath his imposing features.

Then the agricultural adviser tells the story of the Fata Morgana stud: how this is sheep country – from the little apartheid republic of Ciskei beyond the Fish River, inland to the High Karoo, and farther still to the even drier Murderous Karoo. Also farther to the south-west, past the salt pans to the Cango Caves and beyond to the feather palaces of Oudtshoorn where farmers in the old days had made fortunes out of ostrich feathers by pandering to the whims of Europe's fashion capitals. Northwards, too, beyond the Outer Snowrange, past the magical Toorberg, through the Camdeboo ... all of it is relentless sheep country.

Taming this part of the world had left the predators of the wild hungry. The farmers had shot out the game, so the jackals had begun to hunt down pregnant ewes and young lambs, and clumsy old stud rams.

At this point Seamus often interrupts the adviser: 'Balance of nature totally buggered by vast ecological tensions.' Strange, Sarah thinks, looking over her shoulder as though she senses Seamus's presence behind her, that he only ever swears when it is his stud that is under discussion.

Then Seamus will tell how his father had obtained a diploma in verminology from the Veterinary Research Institute at Onderstepoort. He had followed this up with further studies after he had spent years crawling through his fields with a magnifying glass researching the finest details of creation. Eventually he had gained a doctorate for his research on the dung beetles of the Addo Park, which live exclusively on elephant dung and which had served the Khoisan for centuries as a fertility symbol. But he was destined for greater things.

Seamus is swept away by the power of his own thunderous voice as he lists the outlying districts – Snowrange, Swaershoek, Klipplaat, Gamtoos, Katberg – where jackals had decimated the farmers' stock. Then by accident his father had left a lame boer goat ram and a pedigreed angora ewe locked up together in the same pen one night, and that was how, thanks to a recessive gene and an act of divine providence, the three-horned fall-goat species – Caper timidus – had been born.

The fainting goat of Fata Morgana was to achieve world renown and hit the headlines of agricultural journals on four continents. Farmers all over the world were intrigued by the hybridisation of the noble, gentle angora and the hardy, stinking boer goat, a hybrid bred in the mysterious landscape of Manley Flats, close to the city with its seven-mouthed delta. The goats are now exported to every continent – to Spain, Australia, Argentina, Tibet – wherever predators are a danger to flocks.

'The fall-goat,' Seamus will say, looking far out across the high plateau, where the late afternoon wind often bears the sound of the cathedral bells ringing for evensong, 'the fall-goat has one unique characteristic. A genetic defect, actually, which makes it the feeblest and most helpless species on earth. God would never have conceived of such a creature.' Seamus will look away. Only Sarah, who knows him so well, will notice the despondent expression round his eyes and the corners of his mouth. 'Only the crooked greed of man could think of such a species. It's actually a joke of a creature, but that is the very reason why it is so valuable.'

Here the agricultural adviser will resume his explanation. When the fall-goat is startled, it falls down in a dead faint. This loss of consciousness never lasts longer than ten minutes, though, and therein lies the goats' export potential. A farmer whose champion merinos are threatened by a predator needs only one fall-goat to graze in among his flock. When the jackal attacks, the sheep scatter, the fall-goat drops down unconscious in sheer fright and is eaten by the jackal. In this way the flock escapes the predators' habit of sowing death and maiming prize animals.

In the late afternoon sun the tourists will then look at the pens where the fall-goats are peacefully grazing. Wisps of mist will rise up from the direction of the delta, the cathedral bells will ring faintly and the sun will gleam in the yellow eyes of the goats.

At times like this, the Xhosa proverb says, you can see the other side of the moon.

Is she the only one who notices, Sarah often wonders, or do Seamus and the agricultural adviser also see the expression in the eyes of the tourists as they climb silently back into the tour bus after the lecture? What hovers in the glances of those foreigners, who understand nothing of the laws of Africa? Repugnance or fear? Contempt or reflection?

Sarah flexes her shoulder muscles again to rid herself of the goosebumps raised by her thoughts. Sometimes when she feels self-assured and good about herself – which is usually when Seamus's depression, too, is lighter – the breeding of the fall-goats seems to her a rather mysterious adventure.

At other times, like this evening, the whole business fills her with fear and a suspicion that the Butlers are wrongfully tampering with the genetic patterns of creation. And doing so, what is more, in a region where man has always been in submission to the natural order.

It was that file of goats moving as though they were walking on air that had set her thinking. She puts the rose down beside the empty sherry glass and folds her arms. For a summer evening it is unexpectedly chilly.

The flock of goats has disappeared now. There is the first gleam of headlights and the drone of an engine: the first guests are arriving. Sarah hurries into the kitchen to make sure that the liver dish is ready.

But not before stopping for a moment in the passage to telephone me down in my old ruin of a home beside the leg of the delta.

'Seer Wehmeyer.'

'Seer, what colour was the river tonight at sunset?' she asks, softly, so Seamus won't hear.

I answer, little knowing that my words are a prophecy, a prophecy about my own blood, too, and that barely two weeks later I will find myself here where I am today.

'First burgundy, just as the sun was setting,' I reply, 'the colour of old blood. But later, deep black, the colour of oil.' She makes no reply. Worried, I ask: 'Sarah?'

2

There's nothing in life that you can get a hold on.

We are carried along like flotsam when the river comes down in flood. We are like those dead, bloated donkeys, the trees ripped from the earth, the babies' prams, the spinning roofbeams.

Fearful of the banks moving past too swiftly, and too ashamed to admit it to one another, we don the uniforms of convention, conceal ourselves in professions and barter our lives away as though we were tourists on a pleasure cruise.

And all the while, relentlessly, the river is in flood; and we are nothing: mere debris, destined, ultimately, to be spewed out into the immensity of the ocean. And then you drift to where I am floating, dependent on the stream of memory; you come upon yourself tying an extra knot in your pyjama cord and sinking down on your knees and elbows. It is the morning after Sarah's phonecall and you're crouched over the miniature railway track which you have laid down on the floors in your house.

I hold the little steam engine in my large hands. The cylinders vibrate as the pressure builds up, and when I release the tiny lever for a moment, the pistons and wheels start moving impatiently.

I squint down the tracks. The line takes a wide curve in front of the sofa, accelerates under the legs of the coffee table, arches round a pile of National Geographics and shoots out into the open air through the veranda doors. With the river as a backdrop, the track stretches out across the stoep before dropping down in descending spirals into the garden, past the trunk of the purple bougainvillaea, through the rose garden with the sweet smell of rotting roses and then, slowly, back up the taxing slope to the kitchen door.

I am now lying with my cheek on the carpet. My face is close to the comforting smell of oil and steam. From here the toy station masters and conductors, despite their fixed smiles, look like real people. The miniature trees tower over the shade they cast and little women cycle to post offices while a small herd of cattle grazes in the distance.

Now comes the important moment: I release the tiny lever. Just for a moment the engine skids a little, but it soon gains a purchase on the tracks and busily tackles the distance ahead. It races past the cycling ladies, the dapper signalman with his flag, the herd of cattle. It steams along under the coffee table and then hurtles out onto the stoep, just scraping by the fronds of the ferns.

The silhouette of a hard-working little engine, steaming along past the backdrop of the river, is the most beautiful moment of my day.

I start all my days like this. An hour-long session with my toy trains gives me the heart to face the day ahead. I am a scientific collector and being a bachelor I have the whole house at my disposal. After the deaths of my parents, shortly before my sister's marriage to Seamus Butler of Fata Morgana, I simply allowed the contents of the steam-train room to take over the house.

Half the old house leans out over the water, gradually rotting away, smothered in ivy, climbing roses and river insects. I have covered one of the inner walls of the lounge with glass cases. That is where I display my steam engines. Some models date from the nineteenth century and are worth thousands of rands. Each stand has been provided with a card giving details of make, model size and capacity.

Other people begin their days with the newspaper and find themselves confronted with the regular ennui of political murders, kwela accidents, stock diseases, knifing statistics, pineapple and mohair prices – the endless squabbles and tragedies which occupy humanity's attention.

But I prefer to start each day with my beloved steam engines. Every one has its own personality, but their common factor is their complete commitment.

Nothing can match the charm of steam, except perhaps the compelling end of a novel, or an exceptional symphony concert. Or perhaps, I sometimes think, the sweet smell of one of the garden roses when you press your nose deep into it and find yourself overwhelmed by one of nature's narcotics.

It is an eccentric pastime, I suppose. People assume that I keep pets when they see the low arches sawn out at the base of my doors. Now I sit down on the sofa and wait for the engine to complete its trip through the garden and reappear through the hole in the kitchen door.

It is delightful sitting here. I do not feel at all lonely, for down in the garden the engine is hard at work striving to steam back into the lounge as soon as possible.

I am thinking of Sarah's anxious call last night, and of the cold, deep black colour the river took on. Sarah has many fears. We share the same genes, the same premonitions about approaching disasters or joys; and with them the need for security – which is why I, a man of forty, am still living in my parental home.

From where I sit I can see the river gliding by. This morning there is no sign of last evening's foreboding. The water is shining clear and blue. The first fishing boats are just setting out, their sterns deep in balls of white foam. Sea birds flap round the quays as the early hawkers with their donkey carts cross the arched bridge over First Delta.

For Sarah, I know, her premonitions are a nameless anxiety; rapids in a river which for the rest flows slowly through the mind, deep and depressive. It is as though in the course of years Seamus's depressions have leaked into Sarah's mind too. Whenever Sarah's anxiety gains momentum like this, she reaches for the telephone and, in imitation of a habit we had as children, enquires after the mood of the river.

If only we could turn our backs on the landscape we would find the world a more accommodating place. But that is quite impossible: as soon as you leave the city, the landscape closes round you; inside Port Cecil you are aware that the city plan itself is subject to the bends in the legs of the delta, the whims of high and low tide, the hills and dales, the inscrutability.

I put the engine aside. All at once I am disturbed by thoughts about my sister's call. Perhaps there really is something at hand? I get up stiffly and go to the bathroom. In my urine I can smell last night's asparagus pizza, which I made myself after declining Sarah and Seamus's invitation to dinner on the pretext that I had to work late.

Sarah accepted my refusal immediately. Since establishing my own attorney's practice, I find it easier to avoid social engagements. Previously Sarah would have put pressure on me. She has been trying for years to get Seamus and me to like each other.

Private practice has also provided an escape from the many business appointments which my partnership in one of the foremost legal firms in the city used to oblige me to attend. I have no desire to make big money. My parents left me quite comfortably off with the old house, the diesel-oil powered Mercedes and secure investments. 'Old money' is the term people use when referring to Sarah and me. I am at home with the possessions I have and avoid acquiring new things – this material self-confidence is something bequeathed me by my parents. One does not flaunt one's wealth, the old Afrikaners believed.

Disillusioned by the ways of the large practice, I rented the empty office between the butchery and Crown Shoes in Rhodes Street. The previous tenant was an African herbalist and I could never get rid of the smell of herbs and demons. Months after I had opened my practice there, sad souls from the most distant districts still kept arriving at my door.

Enveloped in blankets, often with a scarf tied over one eye or a bandage round a limb, and being led by the hand by a young boy, they would arrive seeking medical help. Carrying a barter chicken with its legs tied together, they would ask for the medicine man. Upon learning that the place now belonged to a law man, more often than not they decided not to turn away but to offload their woes on me instead.

For them, I often told myself, there was very little difference between the mystery of dried monkey heads, tortoise pee and the kidney stones of a genet on one hand and the arcana of the law and justice – the Roman-Dutch legal system – on the other.

Whichever remedy they chose, their underlying desire was always to get even with fate. That is what the poor were hoping for, worn out as they were by life in the slums and backward valleys, lost in the depths of the countryside. That is what was written on their faces whenever I admitted them to my office, feeling slightly absurd behind my huge desk, with the air conditioner in the window, the fan rotating under the ceiling, the framed degree certificates on the walls. What did these people think of me? Why could one always read fear in their eyes?

I'll never forget the day I moved into the empty premises. Outside, Rhodes Street was busy – lined with cheap shops and hawkers, it's one of the busiest streets in the city. There I stood, surrounded by cardboard boxes, starting to unpack: volumes of law reports, collections of poetry (Van Veldeke's love poems in Middle Dutch are an especial love of mine), concordances, the Koran, Xhosa dictionaries, encyclopaedias of herbs, the National Geographics for which there was hardly room in my house any more, cassette recordings of the complete Jimi Hendrix collection (after work, alone in the office, I would listen to this messiah of the electric guitar), useless files of notes and cuttings about the Xhosa prophetess Nongqawuse, books on haiku, the cultivation of bonsai, steam locomotives, the rose encyclopaedia ... and then the finalised wills, the details of claims, pleadings – documents inherited from my father's practice and retained as formal models.

The people mentioned in the court documents were long dead and gone, the goods listed were lost or worn out, the buildings referred to had been demolished to make way for new ones. There I stood, surrounded by all these things, hearing music blaring from a cheap clothing store across the street, getting the reek of baked sheep's head and sweetbreads from the butcher shop next door.

I positioned my desk in such a way that, through the buildings across the street, I could see the river flowing by. Whenever I looked up, there was the alley and the ceaseless flow of the water. Occasionally I caught a glimpse of a fishing boat heading out to sea, or a motor launch filled with holidaymakers skimming across the surface. Here, too, as at my home, the colour of the river was never constant – for the most part, however, it was a deep green, reptilian hue. It was possible to believe, looking over a client's shoulder, that you were watching a python gliding by.

In time the river became for me a symbol of my struggle on behalf of the poor. Here, far more than in the gleaming downtown practice, I was confronted with people corrupted by homelessness and violence, dishonest as a result of famine and deprivation, untrustworthy through loss of values and faith ... so poverty stricken!

Every day was like a maze for me to find small escape routes out of: to have a bail application granted, get an innocent client off the hook, help pin down a rapist. But then again: clients who, once acquitted, never returned to settle their accounts, visitors who carried off the waiting room's ashtrays, hawkers who came in just to rest in the air-conditioned coolness of the foyer and then to depart again unobtrusively, leaving the butts of their reefers ground into the carpet.

I could find no answer to my questions about the providence of a God who could allow so much misery to co-exist side by side with so much wealth in one city. And yet I found there something of a vocation – where once, in the downtown practice, I had occupied myself creating estate duty avoidance schemes and complicated trusts for the rich, now I was the executor for the destitution of the poorest of the poor.

And gained an insight, too: if a donkey broke out at night and ate the neighbour's laundry off the line, you could not sue the owner of the donkey. How does one sue the dispossessed? What recourse do you have against someone who owns nothing? In this part of the world, with its abundance of donkeys, a donkey is not worth anything anyway – you can buy them for a couple of rands apiece from the pound.

If you own nothing, no damages can be claimed from you. They can throw you in gaol, by way of civil imprisonment, but what if – like many of the poor – you find life there more sheltered than in the squatter camps?

I soon learnt that for this reason the poor were, in essence, elevated above the law. Free of accountability, the shack-dwellers celebrated their misery at night and over weekends with a fierce exuberance. Occasionally I was obliged to go into the squatter camps; I smelt the stench of the furrows and saw the piles of refuse and garbage, the emaciated mongrels and children.

God! I thought. Saviour, Jesus Christ!

But the river, the green python, went on gliding by.

I am now lying in a steaming hot bath. I realise that the little engine has stopped somewhere, its strength exhausted. There is some delicious Mozart on the turntable. I have sprinkled an aromatic preparation bought from a herbalist near my practice into my bathwater. The smell makes me almost light-headed.

Whatever happens, whatever the final outcome of Sarah's premonition – nothing will make any difference to the lot of the poor, to the salt of the earth.

Eventually I get up and start drying myself. I look with slight distaste at my hairy wet body in the mirror. No woman would ever be able to love me. The day is coming, mirror, when I shall unscrew you from the wall. I prefer to regard myself from within, rather than in such an indecently naked fashion from without.

I put on my suit and close the windows and patio doors. A last look out over the river. It is a beautiful, a perfect day. Nothing will come of Sarah's forebodings, I decide, smiling as I think of her. It's those fall-goats that disconcert one so. Imagine being involved in that sort of business all day long!

I decide to give her a ring at lunchtime, even if only to keep her talking on the telephone while that old goat Butler sits at the dinner table waiting for his wife ...

I draw the front door to behind me and wonder which clients are waiting at my office door this morning. It's two hundred yards to the street corner where I turn left. Within ten minutes I am in the bustle of the street and the fish market quarter near the mouth of First Delta. By this time of the morning the small fishermen have already moored their boats and the night's catch lies glittering on the tables.

A scant city block farther there is the wide open space where the minibus taxis have their terminus and the hawkers display their wares under the pepper trees. I weave my way through the tables and ground sheets, picking up something here and there, constantly astonished by the market: carved wooden walking sticks, masks, clay pots, balls of snuff, tree roots ... I try to look past the poverty of the hawkers sitting on their reed mats, waiting for buyers.

The body odours of the poor, their penury, their resignation to spending long days and nights here at the dusty market, eventually drives me onwards. Sometimes I enjoy the smell of prickly pears and freshly baked clay, of snuff and rhino dung, but at other times – like today – it catches me off balance.

I cross the street, occasionally nodding to acquaintances. I am gradually becoming known as an attorney who works here. I drop a shining coin into the hands of a crippled beggar near my office. Twenty yards on, I fit my key into the lock, assured once again that my decision to devote my skills to the people of this part of the city was the right one.

Already there is a bunch of clients hanging around on the pavement. Their body language betrays the smell of those who through their poverty and deprivation have fallen foul of the law – the smell of nervous sweat, glib lies, flight, a blade, and often, I suspect, the vicious, uncalled-for twist of the knife.

3

It is also the day of my first meeting with Ayanda Thandani. An attractive woman with high cheekbones, jet black eyes and a habit of wearing flamboyant headscarves. At first glance she appears poised, self-assured, but in the days which follow our unconventional meeting, I will get to know her better.

I seek her out at the old hospital in Port Cecil where she works in the building erected to accommodate the British wounded in the wars with the Xhosas. On its wide Victorian verandas the officers had whiled away the months playing bridge and smoking cigars while their wounds healed.

It was also used for a while as a fever hospital, and round the ivy, the old shade trees and tall palms, the broad corridors and wrought iron scrollwork, there still hangs an aura of the melancholy of white people brought here to die slowly, so far from Europe. It must have been dreadful, I could hear Ayanda thinking, having to sweat out your life in an African fever so far from home.

It was when she started work here as the first black doctor and a woman at that – that the gradual adaptation of the hospital to its environment started. It was as though her arrival made the superintendent and his staff realise that they could not go on offering medicine as though they were in the lavishly endowed south-west Cape.

Gradually the emphasis shifted from complicated, expensive operations on patients with medical insurance to community medicine, care of the poor, feeding programmes, Aids projects.

Yes, Ayanda thinks, watching the ambulance men under the trees, there are some things that never vary, and yet there are others which are changing, slowly but surely.

It is early morning, the night shift has just ended and the ambulance men are gathering up their sandwich boxes and coffee flasks. Wearily they walk away as a fresh team climbs in behind the wheels of the ambulances.

In Joza people are now streaming to work, their eyes fixed on the glitter of Port Cecil between the legs of the delta. They are walking away from the night, the darkness which had delivered its doleful load here at the steps of the Livingstone Hospital.

Like delivery vehicles from hell, the ambulances had arrived full of bloody gangsters with knife wounds, little girls holding their hands between their young legs as they tried to hide from the nurses behind the wheelchairs in Casualty, old folk robbed of their pension pay-outs by the mocking gangs in the squatter camps.

Bitterly, Ayanda had come out onto the veranda at about two o'clock in the morning. It was a humid night. A few lights were burning among the trees in the hospital garden. There were so many dead walking here – all those Colonial officers with their lame legs or amputated arms, and the fever-stricken exiles, worn out and emaciated, setting out on a last, sweaty walk ...

And still decades later, the violence rages on. It is as though we have never learnt our lesson. The affluent areas stretching out to the leg of the delta in front of her are peaceful enough. But the turmoil from Joza comes blowing across the water on the early morning breeze. She can see fires burning in among the squatter shacks of Sun City and the blue flicker of a police van weaving through the dark streets.

As always when she is distressed, she thinks of her brother Ncincilili who had been sent up north, after a protracted court case, to be hanged for a necklace murder.

To this day Ayanda's mother, MaNdlovu Thandani, refuses to believe that her eldest son has been hanged. It is the belief in Joza that the condemned are not sent to the Central Prison in the capital for execution at all, but that they are taken to the building on the hill behind Joza.

That building is not, so it is said, an ammunition store, as claimed by the military, but a Mint where prisoners spend the rest of their days smelting copper and nickel, pouring it into moulds, and hiding the head of the goat and the Dutch sailor Van Riebeeck, the first Dutch governor at the Cape, in the depths of the paper money.

Who else would put the watermark in the paper money? Only those who have been very near death would be able to create those ghostly images.

Frequently MaNdlovu's almost uncontrollable blood-pressure makes her faint, and whenever she comes to again, her mumblings are always about her handsome son, Ncincilili the necklace-murderer blowing watermarks in the Mint on the hill.

'Bring me a banknote,' she will say. 'A ten rand, a five rand, anything.' She will then hold the note to the light in an invariable ritual and say: 'That is what my youngster, the naughty little rascal, the gangster, my cleverest child, the brother-murderer, the Cain, is doing now.'

Ayanda sighs and watches one of the ambulance men washing down the sides of the ambulance with a bucket and an old rag.

Then a minibus arrives to take the night staff home.

They drive through the tree-lined streets to the arched bridge over First Delta. As they are driving over the bridge – against the stream of early traffic – the morning boats are bunched in the mouth as the fishermen wait for a lull in the tide so they can turn their boats' prows into the swirling turbulence.

She sighs as she pushes open the low front gate of the small red-brick bungalow she shares with her parents. Inside she has only just hung up her white coat and stethoscope behind her bedroom door when the telephone rings.

It is MaNdlovu, already on duty at the Civic this early in the morning. 'We've got to get a kwela-kwela, Ayanda. We've got to go up to Bisho. Once again your father has had too much to say about that cockerel of a tin-pot general. They've locked him up.'

Ayanda feels the nausea of an empty stomach and too little sleep rising within her. No, she wants to say, I can't, I've had to spend the whole night stitching up knife wounds, examining those little rape victims, looking into the eyes of the dying until there was nothing left, thumping up and down on chests trying to start hearts which had stopped. I am sick and tired of people and their transgressions. I want to have a bath and draw a sheet up over my head and forget that a human being is a bag of flesh and blood and water which can so easily break open and tear apart, in rage or by accident.

But she clamps the telephone between her cheek and shoulder and, in imitation of a ritual she has learnt from MaNdlovu, she takes off her bracelets. They tinkle on the table in front of her. In times of crisis, MaNdlovu always says, a Thandani woman's arms have to be bare so their grip will be firm.

Ayanda sighs. Pull yourself together, she thinks and asks: 'Oh no! What is my mama telling me now? Surely TaImbongi realised he had to watch what he said?'

'You know what a filthy big mouth he's got. It's that Section Twelve that the Ciskei is trying to zip up the mouths of the iimbongi with.'

'We'll have to get a lawyer.' Ayanda rubs her forearm. Where is the strength to come from, she thinks. Now I'll have to go down to the city. I'll have to face all that turmoil.

'There's no justice in the law,' sighs MaNdlovu. 'We don't need one of those rich lawmen who pretend they're on the side of the people, but the only people they know are the people in the building society.'

'There's a lawyer with a practice next door to the butcher where you always buy your meat, Mama. His name is Max Wehmeyer. The people call him Seer. They say he's supposed to be able to see deep into the law. And he's got a heart, too, I hear. One of my colleagues ...'

'Is he a Brit?' asks MaNdlovu. 'I don't want one of those Settler liberals. Get a Boer. They know how to fight. Even if they are always fighting for the wrong things.'

'Just forget what he is, Mama. He's a smart lawyer. And of course he'll do his very best if it's for the sake of the Kei's greatest imbongi.'

'Imbongi, my arse!' MaNdlovu explodes. 'If your father had only dropped his praise-singing and kept his family together, things would have been a lot better for us all. Then Ncincilili would not have been in the Mint, and then Mpho would not have wanted to go to the hospital to become a man. Then the traditions of our people would not have been in such a tattered and desperate state. God knows, this is the country where Cain beat the life out of his brother Abel. That's what I said to Father McDowell the other day. He said: No, MaNdlovu, you're wrong there, murdering your brother is not part of God's commands. I told him: Father, look at what's happening in the taxi war, and the Mandrax, and the Comrades. Which way is God looking then? The other way, or what? He said ...'

Ayanda sighs and rubs her arm again. 'Come now, my mama must rest now. Have you still got some of those blood-pressure tablets in your handbag? Take one and lie down for a while in the back room at the Civic.' Ayanda turns round to look at the alarm clock. 'You must lie down and rest now, MaNdlovu. I will go and speak to the lawyer. We'll get TaImbongi out.'

'That good-for-nothing,' sighs MaNdlovu. 'The old blabbermouth.'

Yes, Ayanda thinks as she pulls a clean dress over her head, there are plenty of people who'll be happy that TaImbongi has been picked up. They still resent the fact that earlier – even though it was years ago now – he had colluded with the rulers of the two homelands, the Ciskei and the Transkei.

TaImbongi simply cannot keep away from those in power. At the time he had been praise-singer to Kaizer Matanzima, first president of the Transkei.

In those days TaImbongi had been known as DeepVoice. He was a flashy fellow who would go down to the jazz clubs in the harbour with a bow-tie round his neck and a horse-tail switch in his hand to play ragtime. That was when the African Jazz Pioneers still played there regularly.

During work time TaImbongi dressed like an imbongi and drove around with Matanzima in the president's long, sleek Cadillac. 'That was a business for you,' MaNdlovu will often say. 'The chauffeur with his ice-cream seller's cap on, beside him TaImbongi-DeepVoice with his wilted ostrich-feather headdress, kudu-skin loincloth and leopard-tooth necklace. And behind them sat that old snake Matanzima in his black top hat. All of them enclosed in shaded, bullet-proof windows ...'

Ayanda sighs again and closes the door behind her. She starts walking towards the Civic, where the minibus taxis pick up passengers on the open piece of ground beside the Catholic church.

Matanzima's Cadillac used to be seen in the city often in those days. Ayanda recalls how as a young girl MaNdlovu had once sent her to the shop to buy paraffin. That was in the days when they were still living in a wood and iron shack on the edge of Joza and TaImbongi only came home from Umtata on Sundays.

A crowd of people had gathered at the petrol pumps beside the shop. She had gone closer and had had to crawl through a mass of legs to be able to see. The Cadillac was parked in front of one of the petrol pumps. Behind the tinted windows one could see Matanzima's top hat. While the chauffeur supervised the filling of the tank, TaImbongi – with bouncing feathers on his head and ostrich eggshell beads round his ankles – was cutting capers round and round the car.

One of Joza's favourite straight-arm dances, apart from the waltz and the tango, the limousine dance had its origin in that habit of TaImbongi's. And for Ayanda that same dance would later bring her a husband ...

Yes, these are painful memories for the Thandanis. Ayanda told me about them on two occasions, but it is only now, in hindsight, that I really understand them. The money which paid for her medical studies came from Matanzima's imbongi money.

That Sunday afternoon MaNdlovu had stuffed the ostrich-feather headdress into the rubbish bin and said: 'While you are prancing about around your chief, look what is happening to us here. Just look at this shack. At night I can see the stars through the nail holes in the iron. If you don't watch out, TaImbongi, I'll sell your headdress as a feather duster.'

Even now as she is walking to the bus terminus, Ayanda still catches a whiff of the paraffin she had been sent to buy that day at the shop with the petrol pumps. She can still hear the praise songs which TaImbongi had declaimed for Matanzima. There were songs about the president's eyes, with their unflinching gaze; his voice, which was the thunder that rolled across the villages and hills of the Kei; his hand, which held back the hail and lightning from the crops; and his foresight, which was going to build the Xhosas a shining republic where those stinging nettles, the Comrades of the Hammer and Sickle, would never be able to take root ...

In those days, Ayanda remembers, she and her little brothers, Ncincilili and Mpho, were mercilessly teased by the other children. At playtime the children had tied chicken feathers on their heads and capered around the playground singing in deep voices: 'DeepVoice! DeepVoice! Kaizer's choice! DeepVoice!'

Gradually TaImbongi had distanced himself from the homeland leaders. As the struggle against apartheid intensified and MaNdlovu urged him ever more strongly to throw in his weight behind the Movement, he was increasingly invited to perform for the trade unions down at the harbour.

The Thandanis could hold up their heads again. One day TaImbongi had returned from the shebeen and declared in a voice unsteady with brandy that he would never again permit the name DeepVoice anywhere near him.

'Wait and see,' was MaNdlovu's sober response. 'We'll see how long it lasts. My old man is like a tumbleweed on the plains. You never know which fence he's going to blow up against tomorrow.'

But the night-long quarrels in which MaNdlovu tried to convince TaImbongi of the merits of the Struggle had finally had some effect. TaImbongi's conversion was genuine and at last MaNdlovu had been able to announce: 'This is the beginning of a new time for the Thandanis. Your father's head has cleared.'

They had been dangerous times. One could smell burning flesh and rubber at night. The police began to use hard ammunition. Once two hundred soldiers with short, thick machine-guns jumped out of an aeroplane over Joza and landed in the dusty streets. One killed a dog which had flown at him as he landed.

'You must honour your traditions,' MaNdlovu had kept on saying, throughout those troubled years. 'Those history books from the Bantu Education Department teach you only about the Boer trekkers, and the British Settlers of 1820 with their little ships. But it's your own heritage that you must commemorate, and no one else is going to do it for you. You are descended from the Damaqua, the yellow people, the Khoi, and the Tinde, the blackest of the black people, the great cattle farmers. You must not think it's only the whites who walk around with a history behind them.

'Your history does not begin on the day when that sailor Van Riebeeck arrived at the Cape with his three little ships from Holland and marched ashore as though he had discovered Africa! As though Africa had not always existed with our foreblood living on it!'

Then MaNdlovu had explained the history of the clan. 'In your blood runs the blood of that first Khoi killed by Dias, the Portuguese captain, with his cross-bow on the day when white people from Europe and black people from Africa first came face to face to fight over a spring of water.

'That was the first black man killed by a white man's thirst. Don't ever forget him. He is blood of your blood.

'And the last Bushman artist shot like a dog here in the Zuurveld, with his little pots of paint in his belt – he's an ancestor; mark him in your thoughts.

'Dignity,' she said then, 'is something you inherit. You don't kick it up in the dust behind an ash-bush. And it's not something you can learn either.'

When Ayanda eventually reaches Zola Mtuze's minibus, she is feeling tired and dizzy. Night shifts have that effect on her – in the early morning hours when your biorhythms are thrown out of kilter by too little sleep, constant crises and exhaustion, then all the baggage of the past is suddenly exposed. You lose your structure, you bob about like a boat at the mouth of the river.

'I thought you were sleeping this morning,' says Zola. 'Aren't you on night shift?'

'I've got to go into the city, Zola.'

'Where?'

'First Delta. Past the market.'

Zola asks the passenger who had already sat down beside him to move to the back. 'MaNdlovu Thandani's daughter,' he says. 'Doctor Thandani.' The woman is not impressed and sighs. Ayanda is too tired to protest. In any case, there is no point in opposing Zola – from whom she has been divorced for several years – once he sits behind the wheel of his minibus.

Then, as they are pulling off, she notices the butt of an AK-47 sticking out under the seat at their feet. At first she says nothing, swallowing the stream of words that surges up inside her. Two nights ago she had had to try to save a young man whose body was hopelessly ripped apart by machine-gun bullets. She was at his side when he died, convulsively vomiting up blood and calling for his mother.

'What is going to happen if the police find this thing on you?' she asks at last.

He shrugs his shoulders and slides a cassette into the player. 'Miriam Makeba,' he says. 'Back out of exile. She's singing in the soccer stadium on Monday night.'

'Zola,' she counters. 'This is something you cannot be frivolous about.'

He looks out of the window and shakes his head.

'What if they suspect you of smuggling Mandrax, Zola?'

When he doesn't respond, she looks out of the window. The conversation has called up so many old memories: previous quarrels, misunderstandings. She, the ever-cautious, responsible one, and he, always straining to be out ahead.

They stop once more to pick up more passengers, and then drive into the city.

'How are things with MaNdlovu and the others?' Zola asks.

Ayanda looks down at the machine-gun which has slid forward during the bumpy ride along Joza's dirt roads and is now even more visible.

'What did you pay for this thing?' she asks, bitterness rising within her: violence, the ongoing civil war.

Men who cannot stop fighting.

'You can get them for as little as two hundred rands now. They come in through the Transkei from Zululand and Mozambique. This one belonged to a Renamo fighter. Look, there it is on the butt.'

Ayanda averts her eyes from the battered gun. She rolls her window down to smell the river and sea air.

'Or else you can hire one for twenty rands a night.'

She turns to him. 'You mustn't become part of this, Zola,' she says softly. 'Remember: there's Amanda. She's hardly grown up yet.'

He removes his dark glasses and says: 'It's for self-defence, Ayanda. You know how things are in the taxi business. Everyone wants to work on this route. The pirate taxis shoot their way clear.'

She looks out of the window again. A boat is trying to sail out under the bridge. In the distance, at the mouth, she can see white horses on the waves.

Then: 'TaImbongi has been arrested,' she says.

'What for?' Zola looks astonished.

'The general. TaImbongi opened his mouth too wide again.'

'So what now?'

'I'm going to see a lawyer. It's Section Twelve.'

'Section Twelve, is it!' Zola whistles through his teeth. 'Section Twelve, you say!'

Ayanda becomes aware that the other passengers in the minibus are now listening to her and Zola. It makes her happy; the hurts of the playground when her schoolfriends used to tease her about her father's collusion with the homelands go deep.

They have now reached the busy Market Street. People are dragging goats along on tethers, carrying fowls by the legs, balancing basins of fish or prickly pears on their heads.

Zola drops her at the door of my office. 'I hope he's not very pricey,' he says.

'Bring me a banknote,' they both say at once, in mocking imitation of MaNdlovu's ritual, 'a ten rand, a five rand, anything ...'

Ayanda walks in and waits after she has informed my secretary that her case is urgent.

She is surprised when I walk round to the front of the desk to give her an African handshake. I do not find her surprise unusual. My weight often surprises people, and my beard ...

'I am Max Wehmeyer. Do sit down, Doctor Thandani.'

Before I sit down I smooth a hand over my creased suit. If I could have known what was going to happen within the next few moments! She notices that my fingers are unexpectedly thin. They seem to taper down towards their fine pink fingernails. She does not consider my colour healthy. My cheeks have the pastiness of middle-aged men whose cholesterol is too high.

I sigh and clear a writing space among the papers on the desk in front of me.

'You are attached to the hospital?' I ask.

'Yes,' she answers. 'I have just come off night duty. I am feeling pretty drab.'

I smile. 'In the types of work which we do, you and I, exhaustion is a constant partner. But ...' I wipe my face, hesitate a moment and then say: 'Virginity was needed to trap the unicorn in every case.'

'Yes?' she asks.

'Auden, the poet.' I shrug my shoulders. 'Sometimes the work becomes so oppressive that one has to take refuge in poetry in order to stay alive.'

'It's an interesting coincidence that you should like poetry,' she says. 'I have actually come to see you in connection with a poet.'

I am surprised. 'A poet?'

'My father is a poet. An imbongi, a praise-singer.'

I lean back heavily and peel a thin new file from the pile behind me. I open it and slip a clean sheet of foolscap into it. I unscrew the top of my fountain pen and hold the nib to the white paper. I look up at her. 'And he's in trouble?'

'Yes,' she answers with sudden passion. 'He sold his soul to the homeland presidents for years and years. Now that he has raised his voice against them at last, they are hounding him. They are probably scared that the crowing of the old cock will wake folks up. Seeing just who is under whose bedclothes will frighten everyone.'

I sharpen a pencil, sweeping the shavings together carefully. I always do this when I sense that a client needs time to relax. 'Yes?'

'That bunch of fat, over-fed oafs in Bisho ...'

'Just a moment, Doctor Thandani,' I have to stop her. I light a cigarette. 'Do you smoke?' I ask, then, slightly embarrassed: 'You probably spend all day every day advising your patients not to smoke?'

'I have given up trying with smokers.'

I make a deprecatory gesture and then lean forward again. 'Well now. Who have you got anything against?'

'Against the general. And his henchmen.'

I smile and start writing at the top of the sheet of foolscap. 'Thandani versus the Republic of the Ciskei and Another,' I say in measured tones as my pen moves across the paper.

Ayanda shakes her head. She looks calmer. 'It's a disgrace, the way I am behaving,' she says. 'I always sit and allow my patients to get it all off their chests. That first flood of pent-up emotion! And I think: can't you control yourselves?' She shakes her head. 'And here I am, doing exactly the same thing!'

'Never mind!' I laugh. 'Wait till I come to you one day with a cold. I am such a hypochondriac that you'll never hear the end of it.' I stub out my half-smoked cigarette. 'Address to which I may refer?' She supplies her address while I get up to open the windows behind me.

'At this time of the day one does get the smell of offal from the butchery next door, but it's probably better than the smell of my cigarette smoke?'

I sit down again. 'You would like an urgent court order?'

'Whatever is necessary.'

'You do realise that there is an official state of emergency in the Ciskei and that he may be being held in terms of the emergency regulations?'

'Yes. But please see to it that he comes home as soon as possible. My mother's health is not very good. And his own heart, too, is not too hot. What's more ...' She waves her hand, searching for words.

'Yes?'

'What's more is that ... he's a compulsive talker.' She laughs in exoneration. 'They are my mother's words. He is always talking himself into trouble.'

I smile. 'We'll rescue him as soon as possible.'

I look her straight in the eye. She finds my eyes unexpectedly gentle.

We understand each other, she thinks.

An explosion shatters the half-open window, flinging me sideways across the desk. The wood creaks under the weight of my heavy body. Ayanda is hurled backwards against a filing cabinet. The top drawer shoots open and brandy begins to trickle down onto her face.

'Force majeure,' I groan. I prop myself up on one arm. 'It's the forces of nature.'

4

Determining incidents often have a kind of built-in comic quality. So forgive me if my tale sometimes yields to the temptation to be comical.

For I know now better than ever that the serious can grow out of the comic and that things tend to develop in ways that are both unpredictable and frightening.

Let's go back in time a little (this liberty is one of my privileges nowadays) and look at the events shortly before Ayanda and I were so unceremoniously flung to the floor.

After depositing Ayanda at my office, Zola Mtuze drives round the corner to the car dealer.

He hopes to buy a second-hand bakkie today. He will then hire a youngster to drive it – perhaps his brother-in-law, Mpho, when he comes back from the bush as a proper man.

Then the bakkie will drive up and down the streets of Joza late at night, stopping anywhere where people are having fun. There are very few stokvels or shebeens in Joza where the liquor does not run out at some stage in the small hours.

The driver will then have to open up the hatch at the rear and there, ready for business and at three times the retail price, will be the Castles and Amstels and Lions and Ship Sherries. It will not be necessary to keep them cold, for by that time of night Joza's respectable drinkers are all abed. The merrymakers who are still awake will be so far gone that no one will care how warm the beer is.

Zola parks his taxi carefully and makes absolutely sure that it is properly locked. When those buggers come through from the Ciskei and the Transkei the first vehicles they go for are HiAces. In back yards in Bisho and Umtata there are always guys with chain-saws at the ready. As the stolen minibuses arrive they are stripped down and sawn apart. This one's engine is fitted behind that one's nose, that one's backside finds itself perching on another one's rear axle, this one's seats are cut out and new ones fitted.

The whole lot is sanded down and repainted and in the space of five hours you have a bunch of brand new, patched-up kwelas. The old engine numbers are filed off and new ones engraved. All are ready for the long trip to Swaziland or Zimbabwe.

Zola gives his minibus a slap on the rump and strolls over to the canvas awnings sheltering a fleet of vehicles. The bakkie he had examined earlier is still in the same place. The salesman, with his Afro and his T-shirt proclaiming One Settler, One Bullet, comes up and greets him:

'Bra Zola.'

'Hi, Fikile,' says Zola, acknowledging the greeting. 'How's this horse today?' and kicks the front tyre.

'Full of fire. Ready for the road. Waiting for the wide open spaces.'

Zola runs his hand over the bodywork of the vehicle. 'Yeah, they're tough ...'

At some time this bakkie has come under machine-gun fire. Here and there an attempt has been made to patch the bullet holes, but you can stick your finger into others to feel the rust. Zola decides immediately that these bullet holes give the little van character.

'Why do you want to buy a bakkie?' asks Fikile. 'Why don't you rather look at that rebuilt minibus at the back there?'

Zola grins and shakes his head. 'Rebuilt minibus', he knows, means one of those cannibalised numbers whose welded joints will crack open the very first time you take a proper load of passengers on board.

At Peddie, one like this, with a driver and fourteen passengers racing at full tilt to a meeting, had split in half on a bend. The driver and seven of the passengers went on into the veld leaving their rear half behind. The backside of the kwela jolted to a halt and tipped out its load of humanity onto the tarmac. Like a tin falling off a shelf: all that mincemeat on the road.

That was the day the people started calling the kwelas Zola Budds and Mary Deckers, after the two athletes who had tripped over each other's feet at the Olympic Games.

'No,' Zola answers decidedly. 'This one's going to be my shebeen caravan.'

Fikile turns his head sideways. 'Your what, my bra?' he asks, laughing.

Zola makes no reply but creeps in underneath the bakkie. He looks at the springs, scrapes some mud off the brake drums and tries to determine whether the chassis is straight. He wants to know whether the bakkie has ever been rolled.

When he slides out from under the vehicle, Fikile is laughing till the tears run down his face. From where Zola is lying on his back, he looks up and repeats: 'My shebeen caravan! My shebeen on wheels.'

'But where have you ever heard of a shebeen on wheels!'

'Well, a train is a sort of hotel on wheels, isn't it?' Zola has got up and is dusting the seat of his trousers. He points to the river where the smoke from the tourist train is visible above the roofs as the engine steams across the arched bridge.

'That's true, I suppose ...' Fikile scratches his ear. 'But where are your customers going to sit, my bra?'

Zola loses patience. There are always people who call his entrepreneurial spirit into question. That was what had caused the break up with Ayanda. She was forever confronting him with her sober questions: Why? How? When?

'Where are they going to sit, Zola?'

'On their drunk arses.' Zola turns his back on Fikile and does some calculations. But the sudden irritation is still eating at him. 'Look,' he had always said to Ayanda when she had been trying to put a spoke in his wheel. 'I've got to move. My wheels have got to keep turning. I can't survive if my wheels don't spin. They're my life. Things may turn out well or they could turn out badly. But I've got to go on. That's why I'm not stuck in Donga Street any more. Do you remember what it was like there, Ayanda? Look at where I started from. Do you remember the hut down near the Ibayi salt pans? Do you remember my dad who spent his life raking salt? Wheelbarrow loads of fuck-all salt, do you remember, Ayanda, do you remember?'

Indeed. Ayanda once told me that shortly before his father's death – they were not married yet – Zola had taken her to meet the old man. Zola wanted to take her to the salt pans so she could see where he had grown up – those white plains stretching on as though they could have no end.

They had walked across the salt pans together, the salt grating under their feet. The wind was warm and dry against their skins. The salt drained all moisture out of the air. You could imagine the taste of salt in your throat, feel it stinging your eyes.

On the farthest pan, where the aloe ridges covered with rock and stunted shrubs began, they found him. There wasn't a tree or a shelter in sight. He was bending over his rake, working with slow rhythmical strokes.

He had not heard them coming. Twenty years of raking salt in the open winds of the Karoo had made him deaf to the footfalls of others. Like a tattered black scarecrow he stood there, working in the wind. Only when Zola tapped him on the shoulder did he spin round. He was about to lay into them with the rake from sheer fright, but gradually the small, dried-up eyes recognised Zola.

When they lowered him into his grave six months later, Zola remarked to Ayanda: 'That body will never decay. It's as thoroughly salted as a dried fish. He will lie in his grave forever incorruptible, that old fish biltong of a dad of mine. He could never leave the salt pans behind him.'

Caught in that white world of other men's commerce, Zola's father had believed that was all there was: this white expanse, this raking up salt for the dining tables of the rich in the hotels along Dick King Boulevard.

Zola turns round to Fikile. Just stay friendly, he thinks. Irritation is never good for business. 'What's the price?' he asks.

'Still the same.' Fikile points to the card hanging from the steering wheel. 'And it's guaranteed for two weeks.'

'Two weeks!' Now it is Zola's turn to laugh. 'Lord, but you're a bunch of sharks! What sort of service is that?' He shakes his head and looks Fikile up and down. 'Surely you couldn't rob your old uncle so shamelessly!'

'No, I would never treat my old uncle like a poor relation!'

'I'm an old customer,' Zola points out. 'I bought both my minibuses from you.'

'And is my old uncle still satisfied?'

'One's engine packed up.'

'But you did buy that one for spare parts.'

Zola draws at his cigarette and blows the smoke across the nose of the bakkie. 'Point conceded.'

'And Bra Zola's other kwela is still king of the open road.'

They stand smoking, not pursuing the conversation for a while.

'Right,' says Fikile. 'For my old uncle, I'll drop a hundred.'

'Drop two hundred,' says Zola immediately and takes a deep draw.

'One hundred and twenty discount.'

'That's no discount. One-ninety.'

Fikile shakes his head. 'Now my old uncle is talking like a pickpocket. Now it's you who is trying to rob me! Go and see what new cars cost!'

Zola walks round the bakkie. He kicks the tyres. 'These Dunlops are rotten,' he says. 'As soon as I drive out of here the speed cop is going to pull me off the bridge and try to hide a matchstick in the treads. Look at them – worn smooth! One-thirty.'

'One-seventy.'

'One-forty.'

'One-fifty and not a blessed cent less.'

'Bid accepted.' Zola stubs out his cigarette with a twist of his toe. Fikile rubs his hands together. They shake hands.

Zola drives off in his kwela once Fikile has promised to get the documents in order.

He is in a good mood. Perhaps he should go and play the horses later today; perhaps this is his lucky day. Or perhaps he should call on the old sangoma to throw the bones for him before the week's races.

The pressure on the taxi routes in Port Cecil is so intense nowadays that he has difficulty relaxing. You have to watch your step because there are more kwelas than ever before plying the route between the city and Joza. You have to keep on pushing – you can never relax.

He slips a jazz cassette into the player and drives up to Cathedral Square to pick up his first load. The bullet holes in the little van won't matter much – people will soon be saying: 'Here comes the holy shebeen!'

Zola knows: it is good talk, that – talk that makes the business roll in.

He stops in front of Get Lucky Fried Chicken, opposite the cathedral. He slides the door of the minibus wide open and decides to have a puff while he waits.

He watches the drilling machine struggling to sink a well on the open piece of ground beside the cathedral. The rig is set up between the dried-up fountain and a withered pepper tree. The city fathers and the cathedral clerics have been drilling for days in the hope of a decorative fountain and water for the cathedral gardens. Water from the river, so runs the grinning comment in Joza, is not pure enough for the paradisal gardens of Port Cecil's city fathers and priests.

Why don't they lay on taps in Sun City instead, thinks Zola. In the squatter areas of Joza the poorest of the poor have to walk long distances to draw water.

He rummages in his pocket for matches. The box must have fallen out when he was crawling around under the bakkie. Zola looks up and sees an old man standing beside the rig. The man often hangs around the tote on Saturday mornings.

Zola crosses the street and climbs over the fence round the drill site.

'Morning, uncle,' he greets the old man who has now pulled up the drill and is staring down into the hole. There are stripes of damp mud on the drill.

The old man nods. 'Dry, uncle?' Zola enquires politely, not wanting to bum a match straightaway.

The old man shakes his head. 'Craziness,' he says. 'When just down here there is a river with seven legs.'

Zola sticks the cigarette in his mouth and asks for a match. He feels satisfied: it has been a good day. Nice to have seen Ayanda again, too. And that shebeen caravan – he is going to paint it pink with snow white hub caps.

He strikes the match, exhales some smoke and looks at the old man shaking his head and saying: 'Craziness. Craziness.'

'A waste of time,' Zola agrees and in a gesture of solidarity flicks the burning match down into the dark borehole. So the old man can see precisely what he thinks.

The world explodes in fire and thunder.

Hot breath scorches Zola's face. He is vaguely aware of being flung through the air. I'm peeling, he thinks. The skin on the hand which flicked the match into the borehole is shrivelling up.

He lands bloodied and black with soot in the gleaming tiled foyer of Get Lucky Fried Chicken, in front of the glass cases where the roasting chickens are rotating on little spits.

Zola tries to retain his consciousness. He crawls on his elbows to the shattered glass window, trying to get away from the chickens.

Then he sees the black stream shooting up out of the borehole into the sky.

His last thought is: That just isn't possible.

5

Seamus Butler swings out of the saddle on his stallion. At the sound of a massive explosion surging out in waves from the direction of the city, all his fall-goats have fainted.

Seamus walks over to a ram lying senseless beside an antheap. He sighs, draws his cane from the horse's girth and prods the goat in the flank. Slowly an eye flickers open. The pupil narrows as it focuses on Seamus. Through the moist membrane the goat sees the huge nose, the blue eyes, the strong front teeth – so strongly reminiscent of those of the British royal family! – and the rust-red complexion which by now, over 170 years since slaves had piggybacked Seamus's forebears through the surf at Algoa Bay, has become part of their genetic heredity.

The conventional wisdom here at Manley Flats is that the first three generations of British Settlers had suffered from peeling sunburn. But now, in the last years of the twentieth century, even their babies born in the Livingstone Hospital are already a deep pink. It is as though the rose quartz of Africa, the pink flamingos of its lakes and the ruddy melancholy of its sunsets have all been infused into their pale British blood.

Even today descendants of the Settlers are still distinguishable from all the other boys in cheesecutters at Port Cecil's private schools – those grey stone institutions with their Anglican chapels, their resident chaplains, their Latin mottoes, their four-wheel-drive Range Rovers for natural history expeditions, and their Parents' Days with fleets of Mercedeses and Rolls Royces.

In rugger matches against the Afrikaans high school, his opponents used to call Seamus 'Turkey'. In the showers even his own pals called him 'Pinky'.

Not one of the Butlers can ever escape Africa's branding.

Slightly irritated, Seamus prods another goat with his stinkwood walking stick.

'Hey-hup!' he growls. The goat leaps up in fright and then trots off, gracefully releasing a shower of perfect little pellets. Gradually the other white bodies along the hillside also begin to stir. Some jump up alarmed and bleating; others simply get to their feet and calmly resume their grazing.

Perhaps he, Seamus, more than all the Butlers before him, has inherited the full hardship of this continent. When he turned forty – over twenty years ago now – his ghosts had caught up with him. And not only his own, but all his ancestors' demons, too.

Forty had always been the cut-off point against which he had measured his life. At forty his father – an overwrought but brilliant farmer, an unjust father, an unfaithful husband and a complex neighbour to the other farmers of Manley Flats – had committed suicide. At the time Seamus had still been at prep school, a boy who donned his basher on Friday afternoons and headed off down town for a soft drink in one of the city cafés.

In the years that followed, driven by the ghost of his father's suicide, Seamus had lived with an invisible stopwatch in his hand, sensing that in the prime of his life he, too, would come face to face with himself – his personal paradoxes, his own incapacities, his peculiar terrors.

The absent father was the cause of the most serious neuroses, the therapist told him in that office on the seventh floor of the Medical Centre. From where he sat in the psychologist's armchair, Seamus looked out over the seven-mouthed delta to the turbulent meeting of the inland water with the warm Mozambique current. My mind also has seven mouths, he thought, and all seven spew out their overflow here before this little monkey of a man with his professorial pince-nez.

In the course of years the therapist had laid bare Seamus's and the Butlers' family secrets with the perseverance of a terrier digging and wringing a jackal from its hole.

This image of his subconscious mind – a jackal, rancid with wickedness, being wrested from his hole by a bearded terrier in John Lennon glasses – is one Seamus cannot shake off. He mentioned it to the therapist one afternoon when the tides had subsided and the delta was flowing peacefully into the ocean.

'Imagine your father naked,' the therapist replied, and a week later, during their next session: 'Imagine your mother naked. What feelings do you experience?'

Beyond the doubt and the futility, beyond the lost chances gnawing away at the mind, beyond all this, wait the calm waterways of old age.

Or so Seamus would try to console himself, while this upstart terrier of a shrink was trying to establish all kinds of weird connections between his childhood experiences and his emotions during city council meetings; or his relationships with Cawood and Sarah and the influence which his breeding of fall-goats had had on them ...

Nevertheless, the therapist still made him wrestle and choke, and Seamus had the feeling of sitting on the branch of a tree high above the bend in the river, as he had so often done as a child, while beneath him the water flowed sluggishly through Fata Morgana's lowest gullies where the wet, black roots of the trees intertwined.

He would look down, knowing that he could jump right into it: his father had been even younger when he had first ventured to jump from that fork. But Seamus lacked the recklessness and daring to risk the leap.

'Imagine your father naked, there in the pool, as a small boy,' the therapist said, adjusting his glasses.

'Oh, bugger you!' Seamus answered, jumped up and stormed out. But the next week he was back again, humiliated now:

humiliated by his outburst of rage and his inability to accept things, to be philosophical and confident. He was looking down into the pool again now, as he had done, week after week, for months on end. Together with his therapist, Seamus sat there on the branch watching the dark waters of the river, and he knew: all are lost; in shame God has averted his eyes from creation; we are all the crippled children of imperfection.

One day he had had enough. He loaded a team of labourers onto the Range Rover and drove down to the bottom enclosure beside the river. Beside the black pool he showed them how to work the chain-saws and axes, and when the tree toppled over, leaving only a sawn-off, white stump, his relief was a kind of ecstasy. His men then set to work to dig out the stump, roots and all. All that was left of the tree eventually was a neatly piled stack of firewood, and that Seamus gave to his astonished workers, along with two old fall-goat ewes for them to grill. The remaining pile of green foliage he personally sprinkled with petrol. Then he set fire to it and left it to burn through the night: a dense, billowing pillar of smoke.

'Don't you feel you've made one hell of a mistake?' the therapist asked him at their next session. 'After all, in your mind the tree is still standing: its roots reach down into your earliest childhood experiences. That tree has a life of its own. It is rooted in your preconscious. It's the river flowing through your psyche that you have to jump into.'

'Oh, bugger you!' Seamus said, striding round the room, trembling uncontrollably. Demons had to be released; ghosts were leaping from branch to bough as chattering vervet monkeys blurted out his worst fears.

He lay there at the therapist's – as they had delved deeper into his psyche, he had transferred from armchair to couch – his father's packet of suicide letters on his chest. With each passing year, he explained to the therapist, the bloodstains had grown browner, until eventually they had turned almost black. Now they were fading – from rusty brown to dun.

And for the umpteenth time he told the therapist the tale of his father's suicide:

On yet another of his escapades, Seamus's father had been out late that night in the jazz clubs down by the harbour. Seamus's mother had been sitting in her dressing gown on the front veranda of Fata Morgana, the three-O-three across her lap. He remembers to this day the delicate pink of her nightgown, the perfume of her face cream, the movements of her hands as she kept the insects away, under the low roof of the Victorian veranda.

In his psyche she is permanently fixed there in the lamplight, with the dark veld in front of her: a pretty woman, alone and defenceless, waiting for her husband, who would return out of the unfamiliar darkness which she, as a woman and the wife of a farmer, had seldom experienced at all, and never – unlike her husband – on her own.

Seamus had felt an intense love for that lonely woman on the veranda that night. She had thought that he was in bed and fast asleep, while in fact he was lying on the floor of the drawing room behind the shuttered window, watching her. He would have loved to go out and give her a hug, but he knew that she would chase him back to bed.

When lights began to show in the distance on the farm road, first as no more than a gleam behind the hill and then suddenly bright and accompanied by the drone of an engine, he had suffered a sudden sense of loss in his heart – a loss borne within him ever afterwards and roused anew, according to his therapist, every time a fall-goat fell. 'The complex resurrection of the self,' the therapist explained, 'is repeatedly foiled by the fainting of your stud.'

Oh, stuff you, Seamus thought, but continued his story. There had been a terrible exchange of words between his parents on the front veranda that night. Seamus had not understood much of it at the time, and he had spent many excruciating quarter hours since then on the therapist's couch silently trying to dredge up from the muddy dam of his memory even a single sentence of that quarrel.

All he had been able to recall were the gestures of two people and their shadows between the mounted kudu horns on the veranda wall. Those gestures, he knew now, sprang from an intensity brought about by many decades of bonding and frustration.

Eventually his father had ripped off his wristwatch and ground it underfoot on the veranda. Then he strode into the house, his heavy footsteps thundering across the dark drawing room floor where Seamus lay on his stomach, unseen. He fetched the alarm clock from the bedroom, hurled it to the floor at his wife's feet and smashed it under the heel of his boot.

Seamus's mother had sat there with the rifle across her knees, waiting for him to fetch the kitchen clock and destroy that, too, at her feet. Her very silence, the adult Seamus thinks now, must have driven his dad demented.

His father then seized the grandfather clock in the drawing room and dragged it bodily out onto the veranda. Months later the drag marks were still visible on the polished floor of the passage. Then he seized the gun from Seamus's mother and sent a bullet through the face of the clock. In the drawing room Seamus had begun to cry. The grandfather clock with its dignified bearing and its solemn chiming of every quarter had always been like a human presence to him.

Then, gun in hand, his father walked off into the night.

Seamus was back in bed when the shot rang out. He and his mother burst out of their rooms simultaneously, nightclothes flapping. They raced across the veranda, but stopped suddenly at the outer edge of the circle of light on the lawn. Seamus wanted to push back the darkness, but the night was tough and impenetrable.

He followed his mother as she took the garden path down to the rondavel housing the generator. He recalled the rustle of the garden plants against her long nightgown, the smell of grass and night cream, the woman's hair blowing in the wind.

Sobbing, his mother had started swinging the crank-handle of the light engine, but he had taken over from her. The smell of diesel oil was overwhelming. The machine gulped a few times, stuttered into life and eventually started running powerfully. Diesel fuel had sprayed across his face: he was hardly as tall as the crank-handle.

Light flooded the manor house. Lights flickered on in the outbuildings, as did the strings of globes all the way down to the garden gate. In those days coloured bulbs were all the rage and the garden wore a carnival atmosphere as he and his mother began searching the yard.

His mother had moved wordlessly from building to building. She did not once call to her husband. Later Seamus realised that she had been expecting it; that there had probably been earlier suicide threats. After all, the suicide notes had already been written.

Beyond the farmyard fence the fall-goats that had fainted after the shot were coming to again. Their ghostly white shapes staggered up drunkenly. Suddenly his mother had swung round, grabbed him by the arm and dragged him back towards the house. So that he would not see. So that, Seamus thought as he sat tormenting himself at the therapist's, he would never, ever, see.

'If only your mother had let you look,' the therapist said, 'your healing would have been able to begin. It would have concretised the mourning process. Instead, all that is left in your mind now is your father's death, intangible, incomprehensible.'

Seamus sighs and prods one last goat in the belly with his stick. In those days the old folks believed in covering up and concealing – the less you knew and saw, the more carefree you were. He doesn't blame his mother. And in those days there weren't any clever terms for his father's problems either – people simply declared that Old Goat Butler's breeches were too deep for his own good; that he had tired of his stud and his wife; that he'd been consumed by the cantankerousness of a Briton in Africa.

And here Seamus is now, standing over his goats, looking ahead. Some days he simply shakes his head in disbelief that of all God's varied creatures the Butlers should have chosen to breed this particular species.

Certainly the flocks have profit potential, export merit, curiosity value – but they are so highly strung that breeding them sometimes degenerates into a nightmare.

That Caper timidus is intelligent has never been in doubt. You can read the intelligence in its eyes. It is an intelligence compounded of a kind of genial guilelessness and – the most disconcerting aspect of it – frivolity and irony.

Seamus swings back into the saddle and slaps the neck of his horse, 1820 – named for the arrival date of the British Settlers in this area – wondering about the explosion from the city a few minutes before. The shock wave had knocked out all his fall-goats at a single blow, just as though some giant hand had simply swept them away.

There is something in the air, something which makes you think of – how had Sarah put it the previous evening after all their guests had left and they were sitting alone on the veranda looking out over the moonlit veld, sipping a final liqueur? Oh, yes, the Xhosa proverb about seeing the other side of the moon ...

He rides back to the house. At such times his dreams at night are restless, feverish. He dreams of his doomed fainting goats grazing on five continents, destined to be victims of dingoes in the outback of Australia, pumas on the pampas of Argentina, hyenas on the savannahs of Zimbabwe ...

'God save our gracious Queen,' sings Seamus softly. In the deep promptings of his soul – according to his therapist – there is a genetic longing for green hedges, fields of daffodils and lanes winding through the English countryside. A longing for Big Ears and Noddy. For Wordsworth. For an English Rose. For marmalade.

And that is where one would like to leave the master-breeder: with his terrors and his yearnings. Let me be frank: my relationship with Seamus Butler has always been a complex one. It probably has something to do with the fact that we are brothers-in-law. We have to share our precious Sarah.

I must admit, though, that I understand him better now. Now that I am able to trace his thoughts – watch him carefully – even put words into his mouth.

I have to, since he is becoming part of the convulsion starting to rock Port Cecil. Let's follow his tracks as he rides back to the manor:

Seamus feels defenceless in the face of the reproachful stares of his fall-goats. Whenever they wake up, they fix those accusing eyes despairingly on him, the master-breeder.

As much as to say: you and your ancestors have bred into us so much fright that you must now reckon it to your own account. Our death, we know, will be bloody, a blood sacrifice made on some lonely plain somewhere in some godforsaken corner of the world. An oblation; suffering without reward.

It's those yellow eyes of yours that haunt me through the night, mutters Seamus. By our meddling with genetics we Butlers of Fata Morgana have thrust our hands unlawfully deep into the Divine Plan. God will not forgive us.

Back at the homestead Seamus hands the reins to a stablehand so 1820 can be led about to cool down. 'Currycomb him,' he orders, thinking: let's protect what we've got while we still can.

While he sits on the veranda waiting for his tea tray, he thinks with some irritation about Sarah's words this morning: 'You English won't allow anything British ever to be wiped out of your memory. Look how many of the liberals here in the city have British passports safely tucked away in their back pockets. Just that little back door which you always keep open prevents you from ever finally settling down like us Afrikaners, like the rocks on the veld.'

'Dull and ponderous and dour among the aloes ...' he had answered crossly. 'Stubborn as stoneheads.'

She had laughed. 'We have the reek of Africa on our hands, Seamus. It's the smell of poverty and deprivation. Of goat droppings and Karoo dust. We know where we are headed – back into this soil, to become once again dust of this earth. Not because we don't have any choice in the matter. This is what we ARE.'

'Well, you've made a fine mess of this country with your apartheid, haven't you?' He had swung his feet over the edge of the bed, angrily.

'Yes, and it was English capital that helped maintain apartheid, now wasn't it? Do you know who your English liberals voted for on the quiet in every election?'

'Sarah, who do you think kept the torch of liberalism burning through all the dark years? And who is going to have to keep that torch burning in the years to come?'

Sarah had pulled on her dressing gown angrily. 'My granddad used to say that the reason why the sun never set on the British Empire was that even God couldn't trust an Englishman in the dark.'

Sitting on the veranda Seamus gives a snort of indignation. It must have been something he had said at dinner last night that had upset Sarah so. That's the way she is: it is always the English-Afrikaans issue she digs up when she needs to defuse her other furies.

The telephone in the hallway behind him interrupts his thoughts. To save him from having to get up, a servant brings the telephone out to him on the extension cord.

The voice is shrill: 'Is that Mr Butler?' Seamus thinks he recognises the voice, but the hysterical tone makes certainty impossible. Besides, the man on the line is panting and out of breath.

'Yes, Butler here. Fata Morgana. Good morning.'

'It's the deputy town clerk here, Mr Butler.' The man takes a deep breath before blurting out: 'The statue of the angel in front of the city hall is covered with oil, Mr Butler! It's black oil, Mr Butler ... true oil, Mr Butler ...!'

'Tripe!' growls Seamus, gesturing crossly to the servant to pour him another cup of tea. 'Pull yourself together, young man. Now tell me: what cannon went off in the city just now? All my goats keeled over in fright.'

But the voice refuses to be calmed. Seamus knows the eager youngster – always on edge at council meetings, but with all that nervous energy he keeps impeccable minutes.

'I swear, Mr Butler. It's oil. True oil.'

'Listen, is there anyone there that I can have a proper conversation with?'

'Mr Butler, you are summoned ...'

'Summoned?'

'Yes, Mr Butler, the mayor has called an emergency meeting in ninety minutes' time ...'

'What hysterical nonsense is it this time?' Seamus frowns and looks out across his farm. Townsfolk are so quick to lose their bearings. And the younger generation are even worse – all atremble in their breeches.

He notices his neighbour's pick-up scurrying hastily over the hill. The man is a lazy veranda-farmer, but here he is, driving like a maniac. He grinds to a halt in front of the house, opening his door as his own swirling dust catches up with him. He must have taken his foot off the clutch while the vehicle was still in gear and the engine running, for the truck gives a comical lurch and hiccups twice.

But the farmer is already halfway up the garden path yelling: 'Jeepers, Sam!' Seamus presses the phone tighter against his ear: rather the babbling of the town clerk's little deputy than this idle Bill Heathcote. The fellow is so lazy he can't even be bothered to pronounce Seamus's name properly and calls him 'Sam' instead. Panting and sweating, Bill Heathcote stops in front of Seamus. 'Blimey, Sam!'

The clerk's voice rises another tone. 'Real oil!' By now he is shouting into Seamus's ear: 'Oil like you get in cars and things.'

Bill-the-Breathless is still standing in front of Seamus with his arms stretched out – as though inviting me to waltz, Seamus thinks irritably.

'Oil ...!' Soundlessly Bill mouths the word, but there is still an enormous exclamation mark behind the unuttered syllable. Excitedly Bill throws down his hat on the veranda floor beside Seamus's.

From its place in his shirt pocket, Seamus takes the little diary which the agricultural cooperative gives him each year, and notes down the starting time of the meeting. It is as the owner of a suburban villa in Port Cecil that he has gained a seat on the city council, and his portfolio lays upon him the responsibility of maintaining sound relations between the business sector of the city and the surrounding farming community. However, he also serves on the troublesome committee charged with compiling a report on the implications of a single unified municipality for white and black ratepayers.

'Jeepers, Sam! Just think of the money! Millions and millions!'

Angrily Seamus slams the telephone down on its cradle and signals to the servant to remove it. He looks up at the man who will not stop calling him 'Sam'.

'Even if all your hens lay golden eggs, Bill, you will never learn any manners.' Bill has to scuttle indoors after him, because Seamus is striding briskly down the passage. 'Sara-aa-h!' he bellows. There is no answer. She must be busy in the outside kitchen. Still trying to keep out of his way, just as she has all day since their quarrel early this morning. Has never understood his doubt and depression. Over-simplifies everything ...

'O-o-i-i-l-l!'

Halfway down the passage Seamus swings round so suddenly that Bill almost collides with him. 'Now look here, Bill. Fortunes were poured into the sea diving for alluvial diamonds in the estuary. Yield? Nothing! Then they were going to unearth the world's largest deposits of coal in the belly of the Camdeboo. What did they find? Sweet fanny. Then there was all that talk about gold reefs at Addo – do you remember that bunch heading off in among the aloes and the elephants? With their picks and tents and panning basins? And when all the money was spent, what then? Your millions fainted away like fall-goats. That's what.'

Seamus's resoluteness makes Bill waver slightly. 'But oo-ii-l-l!' he chortles in a suppressed whisper as his torso rolls in sympathy with that single round syllable.

You're a clown, Bill, thinks Seamus. You look like a noisy bustard flapping its absurd wings.

'Black gold!'

'Says who?' Seamus fills the wash basin with water, washes the dust and horse sweat off his hands and rinses his face. That the fellow should have the effrontery to follow me into my own bathroom. I've never been a person who could perform his ablutions in public. That's one thing about the Heathcotes – they've no breeding.

'They did discover the coelacanth hereabouts, Seamus ...'

'What ...?' Seamus swings round irritably.

'Well, you say discoveries aren't possible any more. Everyone said the fossil fish had died out along with the dinosaurs but then a trawler went and snared one in its nets just beyond the beach where you and your family always have your picnics. Sam ...'

'Seamus!' warns the voice behind the towel.

Bill Heathcote throws up his arms. 'But don't you understand, Sam?' he asks helplessly. 'Those drills have opened a gusher right beside the cathedral. It's oil, man, as in petrol and diesel fuel and paraffin. Oil, oil, oil!'

Seamus turns round to his neighbour. He has never seen Bill so beside himself before. He thinks of the huge oil rigs which had spent some months afloat in the deep water off shore opposite the estuary. Like giant jellyfish floating on the surface of the water, the great rigs had eventually moved on, westwards. The excitement – a rare enough commodity in this part of the world – had evaporated.

The old inhabitants of Kei used to say: 'There aren't any treasures under the earth's crust hereabouts. Here you've just got to make the best of what you can see with your naked eye: dust and rock and aloes and wind. That's all we've got to do our daily job with. That's the only way our children can keep on taming this continent.'

Then someone had struck natural gas farther to the west though the current gossip from those parts is that that well has now been exhausted. No, seeing is believing. I'll need to touch that oil first, thinks Seamus.

'So just calm down,' he tells the scarlet pineapple-beer complexion of Bill Heathcote. 'Your system won't stand it.'

He walks into the bedroom, pointedly closing the door in Bill Heathcote's face. Little Billygoat Gruff, he thinks. Your school nickname is still apt: you're still the stupid kid that will swallow anything you come across as though it was all sweet oats in springtime.

He puts on his newest suit and his old school tie. Ah, yes, The College, he thinks – those were the best years ...

He hears Bill's pick-up pulling away, wheels spinning over the gravel. A light tap on the door and Sarah appears, looking upset. 'There's been the strangest report on Radio Algoa,' she says. 'There was an enormous explosion in town, and instead of leaving the area altogether, thousands of people are apparently streaming into the city.'

It simply cannot be true, thinks Seamus. It will be impossible for prosperity to be visited upon us. 'Yes, I know,' he replies without looking at Sarah. Nowadays it seems to be taking longer and longer for his anger to drain away after he and Sarah have had words. 'The goats fainted. The whole bang shoot. In their thousands. The last time that happened was when those two air-force Impalas crashed into Stone's Hill.'

'Yes, but Seamus, what could it possibly be? And where are you off to in your suit?' Without waiting for his response she continues, worried, her hand on his arm: 'The radio said there will be further reports as soon as anything more is known.'

'I've got to go to an emergency meeting of the city council.' He walks past her without saying goodbye. 'It's about the explosion.' His long strides leave her standing in the bedroom. It gives him a certain satisfaction, leaving her despondent like that.

You'll never understand me, Sarah, he thinks as he speeds into town. I can get shot of it all: the fall-goat stud, Fata Morgana, you – the lot. Just like Dad did. To experience the feeling of nothingness, the mighty grasp of death itself.

I can do it with an inner inevitability that you do not even suspect. It will hit you just like the shock of Dad's suicide hit Mother and me at the time ...

Dust billows out from beneath his racing wheels. Seeing him coming, donkey carts and tractors with trailers draw aside from the road to let him pass unhindered. The temper of the master of Fata Morgana is well known throughout the region.

In the distance Seamus sees a thick column of smoke. If everything which the clerk and Bill Heathcote have had to say is true, everyone in the district will be wanting to dip their hands in that black gold. Urges suppressed by years of suffering lie fermenting within this community, waiting only for the right rain shower before they will surge to the surface like clouds of flying-ants billowing from their nests.

When he drives into the city and sees the dense cloud of smoke now being blown out to sea by the wind, he realises that the reports are true. His car is not the only vehicle coming into town covered in dust – others, too, have covered great distances on farm roads to get here. At the traffic lights motorists who normally would not have done so look enquiringly at one another.

We are so used to receiving nothing but hardship at the hands of nature, thinks Seamus as he drives towards Cathedral Square, we will find the advent of divine favour incomprehensible. After centuries of strife between Boer and Briton, black and white, rich and poor, we are deeply suspicious of anything even vaguely resembling salvation.

Ours are the cunning eyes of the mountain tortoise which only understands the rain once the showers are long past and the shrubs are already decked out in their fresh green leaves. We are the lynx that turns away from the guinea fowl and her brood of chicks struggling clumsily through the tussocks of grass because it all looks just too easy. Anything as available as that spells a trap.

Suspicion. And then they want to build a nation! After so many years of mistrust we recoil from peace and reconciliation, grace, mercy, redemption – even though that is what we most yearn for.

Because bloodletting and hardship are the only things we've learnt to trust.

Seamus smiles grimly. Perhaps excess was a greater risk to the system than want – as witness that Bill Heathcote who almost had a heart attack from sheer agitation.

In the city centre everyone, driving or walking, is heading in the same direction and soon Seamus lands up in a traffic jam. Angrily, he parks on a yellow line. Let the traffic cop write him a ticket: a telephone call from the city hall will soon have the fine set aside.

Perspiring in his woollen suit, he sets out to walk. Perhaps, though, his sweating is not due only to the heat. Although he stubbornly maintains his outward cynicism, in his chest a certain excitement is mounting. If there really has been an oil strike, it will provide confirmation of an ancient myth that the Kei is floating on a lake of subterranean oil.

He is completely surrounded by people, but he thrusts his way through them. Coming round the corner of one of the narrow winding alleyways here in the old part of the city he smells it: heavy, unmistakable, a stifling vapour that leaves an unpleasant taste in the mouth. Everyone who has ever entered a mechanic's workshop or bent over an open engine will recognise it instantly. It comes from deep within the belly of the earth. Something primal within Seamus reacts to it. It is a smell which rouses profound instincts.

'Greed,' he mumbles, as he begins to push and fight his way through the crowd. 'The urge to possess. The Great I Want.'

He suddenly notices that some people round him are carrying umbrellas, even wearing raincoats. But despite the cheerful colours of the sunshades and coats, there are no other signs of festivity. The way people are shoving speaks of an unwonted urgency.

Then he staggers round the last corner, only to be overwhelmed by the uproar on Cathedral Square. Linking arms and gritting their teeth against the assault of the crowd, police and firemen have thrown a cordon round the fountain of oil. Already their caps and uniforms are black with the stuff.

Seamus begins to tremble. Something subterranean jerks his body, making his teeth chatter. A stream of oil is spouting convulsively up into the air, as though some gigantic sphincter somewhere in the belly of the earth is controlling it. Oil is spurting up above the cathedral roof, sometimes even higher than the spire.

His skin feels sticky. He wipes his forehead and realises that an oily mist is sifting down on them, clouding their glasses and eyes. God have mercy upon us. This is a craze we'll never be able to cope with.

6

Sitting on the brightly lit veranda of Fata Morgana, waiting, Sarah is strongly conscious of the picture of which she forms a part: the dark, open plain which finds its focus in the radiance of the manor house, the coloured lights among the cycads and aloes in the garden, the woman sitting with her back to the open front door, watching the dull ribbon of the farm road beyond the farmyard gate.

It is no accident that she is sitting there. Sometimes that is the only way to reach Seamus: to torment him with his memory of the night of the clocks. That is why she is sitting there in her dressing gown, her face and hands already creamed. On the little table beside her is the alarm clock from her bedroom. The rifle lies across her lap, not only on account of the wave of terror gang attacks on lonely homesteads, but also because the scene will not be complete without it.

Not often, but sometimes, sometimes she simply has to jerk Seamus back out of that distant coolness of his. And when he returns home in the small hours, she knows that he will be able to see her sitting like this from a great distance away. Then everything inside him slips its moorings and she becomes his mother, here, alone, on guard, years ago.

And he is his father, that complex, obsessive man, racing along farm tracks, the man who had threatened all his life to use his capacity to take his own life.

Sarah sighs. She and Seamus are so cruel in love. They know each other's precipices so well that with only minor movements each can dress the stage for the most excruciating scenes, can call up the most hurtful dialogues.

To wreak vengeance, to cause pain, but also to call out: don't leave me behind; I am lonely without you; I don't love you; I love you.

As she sits there, a fall-goat ewe in the slaughter enclosure down near the vegetable garden gets to her feet. Something must have woken the ewe: perhaps some premonition or sound. The goat is going to turn round and stare at me now, thinks Sarah; she is going to force me into complicity with her.

But the goat only circles a couple of times, and then settles down again. Then, when the dogs on the veranda raise their heads, Sarah hears the car. As the radiance of the headlights fans out across the night sky, she draws her dressing gown tighter round her throat.

Shouldn't she just go inside after all? Shouldn't she just spare him today, the day of the oil? But remember, she reasons, remember how he left this morning without even saying goodbye properly, so distant in his suit, so calculated the manner in which the Mercedes took off at such a terrific speed that it hit the speed-hump so hard you could hear the toolbox rattling in the boot.

She had the radio at her side all day. The music programmes on the regional station were constantly interrupted by news flashes about the oil strike on Cathedral Square. There had been no discernible pattern in the bunches of opinions garnered by radio journalists from professors at the city's university, state geologists, local politicians or community activists.

Uncomfortable in the handling of good news, the radio station was covering the oil strike with the same anxiety index as the one with which they treated major disasters. The tone of the announcer's voice, the bleep of the emergency call to signal the news flashes, the clatter of a helicopter as radio journalists broadcast direct as they circled Cathedral Square, all reminded her of the similar coverage that time when the river had flowed upwards one night. Or the time when the Oceanos sank. And the year of the Great Flood.

We are an uncouth bunch, she thinks, as she watches Seamus stop in front of the farmyard gate, push it open in the bright lights of the Mercedes, drive in without shutting it again, and then come to a halt before the closed garage doors.

We have none of the cynical sophistication of people living close to the rich gold mines or in the wine country with its gentle natural splendour. We'll treat this oil bonanza like a jackal hunt, like a church fête, a gossip party, a clean-up operation in the township. We'll set up road blocks to impede the advance of progress and so give our suspiciousness full rein to examine everything. We'll appoint commissions and allow men in suits to chatter importantly and interminably. In our churches we'll thank God for His blessings and outside the church we'll allow the tumbleweeds of malice and envy to roll unhindered through our hearts and minds.

In our heart of hearts we carry around with us the semidesert, the Karoo, the godforsakenness. We want to rule by law and order, deny access with border fences, prevent ... Seamus stands before her, exhausted, desperately weary and confused.

Without a greeting, he stands looking at her. She, too, says nothing. She notices the oil stripes on his suit, the dirty smears across his face. Seamus has gone overboard at the advent of such grace and mercy.

As he stands there he is one great walking avarice. Sarah knows the Butlers. Seamus's constitution cannot stand the excitement straining his chest – which is why he looks so bewildered.

'You look like a goat that has got stuck in the river mud.' She gets up and turns her back on him. 'Please bring the gun and the alarm clock in with you when you come inside, Seamus.'

She goes into the house without looking back again.

She stands combing her hair in front of the mirror in the bedroom. Come in, just come and hold me tight. Assure me of your love. Even across the banked up debris, we can still reach out. We can still reach each other, Seamus.

She hears footsteps on the veranda. He is walking up and down.

Then she hears him going down the steps. She puts down the comb on the dressing table and stands holding her breath.

A shot rings out.

She rushes down the passage. 'Seamus!'

He is standing on the veranda, begrimed. The smell of the shot still hangs under the roof. He grins at her.

She sinks into a chair.

'I can also play games, Sarah.' He's been drinking. Where did he find liquor at this time of night?

'Have you heard about Seer?' he asks.

She looks up, brushing the hair away from her face. 'Seer?'

'Yes, Seer and the explosion.'

She clutches at her heart. 'Seer?'

'Blown right over his desk, apparently.'

'Seer!' She flies up, looks at the telephone in the hall behind her, then at Seamus. He nods his head and grins again. As he wipes his hand over his face it leaves grimy streaks on his nose and forehead.

'He only grazed his knee in the fall.' Seamus laughs, turns round and fires another shot into the night sky. Her body is trembling. She sits down again, her face in her hands. 'Go on, fall down, you goddamned goats! Castrates!' Another shot. 'Bastards!' A shot. 'Children of Satan!' Shot. Seamus's shoulders begin to jerk. He turns round to her. 'Curses, curses!' The last shot. It whistles through the roof of the veranda. The magazine is empty. She catches the rifle before it falls from his hands.

He lets her hold him. The oil on his suit rubs off on her dressing gown, her hands, her face.

'Sarah, God knows ...'

'Come now, Seamus, come now ...'

Later they sit at the kitchen table. He has taken off his jacket and she has helped him wash the worst of the oil off his hands and face. Sitting there with a glass of brandy, he looks up at her and says softly: 'I'm sorry.'

She takes his hand. 'So am I.'

They sit there in the quiet farmhouse. She looks up at the high ceiling. The house is too big for us. Now that Cawood can stand on his own feet – or can go clattering after herds of game in his own helicopter – all these empty, twilit rooms have suddenly become too much. We are going to grow old under this sky, two wizened grey heads in a gigantic Settler manor on the edge of the abyss.

As though he had read her thoughts, Seamus looks at her. 'We must sell Fata Morgana.' She makes no reply and asks for no further explanation. 'The game has changed,' he says. He gets up to pour himself another brandy. She listens to his footsteps going to the liquor cabinet in the lounge. 'Our city is going to become the economic heart of the region,' he says once he has sat down again.

'What has the sale of Fata Morgana got to do with it?'

His hand on the table contracts into a fist, the knuckles showing whitely through the skin. 'We must invest capital in the city centre. There's a fortune waiting to be made.'

'Seamus, Seamus. You can't ever get rid of Fata Morgana. There's your father's will. The entailment. You don't have the right to sell.'

'It's a ridiculous restriction. He wants to rule from beyond the grave. A court will help me. I'll ask Judge ...'

She interrupts him. 'You can invite as many judges as you like to come on your hunting expeditions. You and Cawood can take the judge wherever you like in the chopper. Your father's last wish remains.'

'His wish?' Seamus throws back his head. His lips are wet with brandy, his eyes shining. 'His wish!'

Sarah is resolute. 'Your father laid down in his will that the farm may not be sold. It has to remain in the family.'

'When he blew his brains out down among the vygies that

night ...' Seamus takes a deep breath. ' ... he left the world of the living behind. He forfeited his right to a hold over us. He cleared off ... for ever.' He sighs and looks round him, as though expecting help.

Sarah places her hand on his. 'I think it's time for bed,' she says gently.

'I'll never sleep now,' he says.

Seamus feels desperate: The demons emerge whenever the wind drops to this stillness over Fata Morgana; they are the ghosts of the ancestors emerging from ravines like lynxes and leopards and jackals and night adders. The hunt is on, and we – we ourselves – we are the prey.

'We must get some sleep.'

He takes his head in his hands. 'The fall-goats ... this whole enterprise ... Sarah ...'

'Come, Seamus.'

'There's something about it that is in conflict with creation itself, Sarah.'

'Come now ...' She comes to stand behind him, pressing his head to her chest, surrounding him with the perfume of her night cream, her femininity. She feels his shoulders relaxing.

'Mother,' he says.

7

Seamus is sitting on the edge of the bed, looking at his feet. He is brooding again. I listen, not without a certain sympathy. I'd actually have liked to sit down on the bed beside him, but I don't dare intrude. The tale has to continue.

What happens in a toppling-goat's psyche in those few minutes of unconsciousness? What fears are exorcised?

Seamus understands the twists in his own thinking well enough to know that today it is the turn of the decline-and-fall syndrome.

Which recessive gene, now dominant through inbreeding, is the one that carries the germ of self-destruction?

Who is the sacrifice for? Who profits from the penance?

Here is yesterday's experience still wrestling within him.

He has woken up feeling melancholy and is still just sitting there, staring at his white feet. Decades of wearing out boots up and down the gullies and over the plains of Fata Morgana have left his yellowing toenails bent upwards.

Since he started consulting that terrier of a therapist, he has spent a great deal of time agonising about his dreams. Eventually he has learnt that dreams are the currency which the subconscious uses in its commerce with the conscious.

If he concentrates on this rate of exchange, he can keep bankruptcy at bay; his mind remains clear; the murkiness in the pool subsides.

As he sits there waiting for Sarah to bring him his early morning coffee, snatches of his dreams surface again; nostalgic delights compounded of the smells of pendant pepper tree boughs, misty lucerne fields through which a small boy went racing on horseback with three white fox-terriers in pursuit, the smells of grass and sweat on the College rugby fields, the salty flavour of a fist in the mouth, and the sweetish flavour of ...

Yes, now the clearest memories are passing before his mind's eye again. Twilight at a farmhouse. Coloured lights strung between avenues of trees. It is New Year's Eve and he is a small boy, hesitating on the outer edge of the circle of light and adult merrymaking.

The hostess is wearing a pale blue dress. Her hair is caught up in a bun on the top of her head. Adults are talking of an imminent war. There is a desperate romanticism in the air. As he slowly revolves (holding with one hand onto a rough, low branch above his head while boring a hole in the Karoo dust with his toe), he senses the muffled movements of cows in an enclosure, and farther off the melancholy rippling of plains in the moonlight.

But he remains entranced by the circle of light on the clay tennis court, now temporarily converted into a dance-floor. There is a band playing: piano, guitar and accordion. The hostess opens the dancing with Seamus's father. They are young and vital and the lively dance is modern and uninhibited.

Before long the whole floor is covered with dancing couples. From time to time farm hands weave between the dancers with watering cans, keeping the clay surface damp and laying the dust. Young farmers with rolled-up sleeves are holding women with bright, open faces and strong calves slimming down into neat ankles. The air is redolent with the faintly sour smell of antheap-clay, perfume and beer.

Seamus walks away from the pepper tree, easily finding his way to the goat shed by moonlight. Yes, he remembers, yes, he recognises it now. It is Fata Morgana, before the garden was remodelled, before the old goat shed was demolished to make way for Mother's rose nursery.

So the woman in blue could not have been the hostess. But where was his mother then? Why had his father opened the dancing with that other woman? Who was she? All answers are lost in dreams and wisps of memory.

He pushes open the door of the shed and goes inside. It is dark but a cleft of moonlight as white as the neck of that dancing woman cuts across one wall and reflects light into the room.

He is standing before the pen of the very first successfully bred fall-goat ram. The half-light is sufficient to catch the gleam in the goat's yellow eyes. As Seamus approaches he catches the sharp smell of fright given off by the three-horned beast.

They stare at each other. From outside comes the laughter of partygoers. Someone calls out a request to the band. The accordion starts up provocatively, falters, begins again: a tango rhythm.

The moment seems to last impossibly long, but the goat does not waver in the face of the boy's gaze. Slowly, imitating the brief demonstrations which his father proudly put on for visiting stockbreeding experts, the boy holds his hands out in front of him. Then he stretches out his arms, turning his palms inward.

The goat stares at him unblinking. Is he imagining it, or is there a brief flicker in the animal's eyes – a subtle change of colour in the irises?

Sharply, he claps his hands together. The sound rings out in the silence of the shed. The goat's eyes roll over whitely as its legs give way. It collapses and lies inert.

The boy flees. Outside, he races across the yard, hares past the tennis court. The dancers glance in surprise at the shadow scuttling by beyond the wire mesh of the fence before it disappears from sight among the branches of the pepper trees. Their last impression of him is of an iridescence of coloured lights spattering across a small body.

He feels he is running right through the curtain of merriment, cutting through the aura of pineapple beer and jokes, leaving behind him forever the smell of women's perfume and men's hair oil. He has to get through, through, through ...

Nobody follows him, for the farmers believe that a youngster has to find his own way through the veld, and through the wide open spaces of his own mind, too. In this open country there are things which you have to settle with yourself, early on – or else there is something lacking in you.

He runs through the orchard with the sweet smell of peaches. Nettles sting his legs and little night creatures flee before him in the grass. He is crying, and his breath is panting in his throat by the time he leaves the orchard. He stumbles through a ditch and then he is out on the open veld, bathed in moonlight. He runs and runs as though he will never be able to stop; through moonlight and splendour; through silence and timelessness.

In his flight the boy foresees the suicide of his father; he prophesies the night of the clocks, that night a year later when he and his mother will stumble across the yard with a flashlight, searching for the body of his father ...

A profound sadness overcomes Seamus as he sits there on the bed. Some things there are which will never be. There are incompletenesses which live with you and yet somehow, in their own macabre fashion, fulfil themselves, though never in the way they should. There are moonlit nights and young people self-confident of their own strength resolutely celebrating the successful harvests of the old year and facing up to the prospect of a terrible war. And the prospect not only of war, but also of their own impending mortality, their own ageing and unfulfilment and imperfection, stretching out ahead.

There is the romance of vast open plains, of an isolated homestead where people come from all over the countryside to dance and make merry in a circle of light and to copy the dances of another continent. There is the dark outside the circle of light; and there is that madness, so unexpected, in a corner of the shed.

Seamus smells the dark water of the pool. But even in the midst of this dizzy anguish – his melancholy sometimes makes him quite light-headed – he realises that what he is smelling is the aroma of coffee; and, Sarah, cup in hand, standing before him, deeply concerned.

She rests her hand on his bowed neck. 'Seamus,' she says. When he looks up, he realises that there are tears on his face. If she only knew how many tears he has shed on that silly little man's couch in the Medical Centre!

And the tears, too, on the back of 1820 sometimes, when he is overcome by the sense of his own mortality.

The reckoning that awaits us all.

The penance that is so integral a part of this landscape.

'Seamus!' Instead of fetching him a handkerchief from the tallboy, she throws open the curtains and allows the morning sunlight to stream into the room. He tries to turn away, ashamed of his tears.

'You men should learn to cry,' she says, and goes out again. At the door she hesitates for a moment. 'Though we know that you do cry in other ways – with your whiskies, your hunting rifles, your jackal hunts, your affairs ...'

'Yes, Sarah,' he answers. He dries his tears on the sheet and cautiously sips the coffee. The scene beneath his window reminds him of the reason for his waking up so early.

Farm hands are leading horses out of stables and currycombing them. The early morning sunshine gleams on the quivering flanks of the mounts. Then, like a shining dragonfly in the distance, growing gradually louder until its noise is quite deafening, Cawood's helicopter comes skimming over the plain.

Oh, that son of mine, sighs Seamus – just look at those exhibitionist swerves across the landscape, perfectly unnecessary arcs and crescents executed above the fields by the shining chopper merely to tease the fall-goats before landing in a cloud of swirling dust.

And yet there is something about the arrival of young Cawood – game-trapper and safari leader, whose principal clients are, of course, super-rich Americans – which makes all the old excitement of the hunt tingle in Seamus's breast once more.

I am, after all, the Master of the Hunt, he thinks, and the time has come for the greatest sporting event in the Kei. Even the oil strike will not keep the farmers from turning out for the annual Hunt. It is a greater event than even the summer cricket tournaments when family teams drawn from the Settler clans, owners of the largest tracts of land at Manley Flats, compete against one another, clan against clan.

The Hunt compels respect; it is an affirmation of breeding and male exuberance; a tribute to the forefathers and – not least! – also great fun.

The Hunt is suffused with tradition – including the mutual agreement that no boundary fence should be allowed to check it. In the chase, which can last for up to nine or ten hours, fences get short shrift.

If the sinuous jackal manages to slip through a fence which then halts the dogs and horses in their tracks, mounted farm hands move in with wirecutters, snip through the fences and drag the wires aside, droppers and all, to allow the dusty, cheering huntsmen to charge through.

Seamus hears vehicles stopping in the yard. With all the noise of Cawood's escapades in the chopper above the manor house, their arrival has been unheard. Then Seamus hears the yapping and baying of the hounds and the clatter of tailgates and side railings.

He dresses quickly: the riding boots, the leather belt he inherited from his father, the hunting horn which tradition requires should be blown by the eldest son of the Master of the Hunt. From behind his handkerchiefs (where he also keeps all the gold-filled molars which he had to have pulled), he withdraws the little silver whisky flask.

He tightens the belt of his holster, rejoicing in the smell of the leather, the smell of copper rising from the bugle, the whiff of whisky from the flask in his shirt pocket.

And now, he thinks, there will be the added smells of horse sweat, gun oil, male armpits, dogs' breath and, ultimately, the smell of the fulfilment of the Hunt ...

He shudders at his own thoughts and strides down the passage. As he appears on the veranda, there is spontaneous applause from the nearly forty farmers already gathered in the yard. Sarah and the servants are bringing out trays of coffee, horses are being led up, hounds are straining at the leash.

Seamus closes his eyes for a moment. Now, he thinks, for the most delicious hours in the Kei ... galloping horses, baying hounds ... Without touching the coffee he hands the horn to Cawood and passes through the assembled men.

He mounts 1820 and tugs the horse round, feeling the excitement rippling through the animal's frame. Over the heads of the farmers, Seamus looks straight into the eyes of Sarah, the gentle eyes of the woman he loves; the concerned eyes of the person who knows too much about him, who has had to share and bear too much already, who is now standing there, transfixed for a moment in her worry with her lightly reproachful air. Then she smiles sadly, waves and serves someone a final cup of coffee.

Cawood brings the horn to his lips, the company of huntsmen set off and soon they have left the homestead far behind. Eventually they swing off the farm road and fan out across one of Fata Morgana's largest enclosures where in the course of the past month farm labourers have frequently noticed a jackal. The horsemen are now led straight to the animal's den.

When the jackal leaps out at once and streaks across the veld all the huntsmen, vaguely disappointed, crouch low over the horses' necks. Standing upright in his stirrups, Cawood sounds the traditional mournful halloo over the heads of the Hunt.

Just as swiftly, and equally disappointingly, the jackal disappears again and soon the horses and hounds are clustered around an antbear hole. This is too easy, Seamus thinks. No Hunt ever moved into the action phase so early.

Yet the silence so characteristic of this stage of the hunt is still a challenge. The dust round the antbear's burrow smothers the restless hooves of the horses. It is the hushed moment before the Hunt's final act. The air bears the smells of horse sweat and whisky from the small flasks which the riders hold ready.

But the experienced huntsman, Seamus thinks, can smell something else, too. It is not a smell emanating from hounds or horses or men. It is the smell breathed out by the Hunt itself. It rises out of the togetherness of man and animal; out of the appointment between huntsman and prey; out of the twilight where life and death lose their boundary fences ...

'Fetch the terriers!' Seamus's order is a bark. The Hunt servants pull the hounds away from the hole and the pack of terriers are brought up.

The huntsmen sick on the dauntless terriers. Their cocky little hips pushing and scrabbling away at the earth, they force their way into the hole. Yes, Seamus thinks, that is just what happens to me on the couch of that little fellow with his granny-glasses and his short, cocky little legs. That's just the way he winkles me out; the way he hunts me down remorselessly till I, too, am exposed, belly up and defenceless.

The horsemen, holding their breath in order to listen better, hear an initial growling yap and know that one of the terriers has made contact. The underground tunnel has led the terriers to right underneath the horses. The desperate fight now beginning under their hooves starts them trippling about uneasily.

Then it is quiet again. The hounds sink down onto their bellies, eyes glued to the hole. The farmers have their flasks at the ready. The first terrier creeps out of the hole, bloodied, its body covered in dust, one ear hanging by only a scrap of skin. One of the servants springs out of the saddle, grips the terrier between his legs and, before the dog has even had time to snap at him, slices off the ear flap with a single stroke of his pocket knife. He throws the ear to the hounds and, crazed with bloodlust, they begin to fight over it.

The last terrier – the one which had apparently settled the fight – creeps out and the rest of the terriers and the hounds all cock their legs at the entrance to the hole. The farmers are disappointed that the terriers have not brought out the jackal.

Cawood surmises: 'Perhaps he's playing possum.'

'These terriers are still young,' affirms Bill Heathcote. 'Perhaps he's got them fooled.'

Seamus gestures for the wirehook to be fetched. We'll get you yet, he thinks, you pestilence, out of your den, you hunter in darkness ...

The old Hunt servant, Boesman Plaatjies, with his thirty years and more of experience in the Hunt, pushes the end of the long piece of wire into the mouth of the hole. Lying on his stomach with his ear to the ground, he gently starts feeding the wire down the tunnel. From time to time he draws it back slightly, indicating that it has caught on a snag or run into a bend.

At last he looks up at Seamus and nods. The huntsmen know that the end of the wire has pressed against the soft body of the jackal. A less experienced man would have mistaken it either for soft earth or else for the end of the tunnel.

'He's still alive, Huntmaster,' says Boesman Plaatjies.

'Bring him in then,' commands Seamus, undoing the flap of the holster at his hip.

A thrust and a twist and the fur is caught at the end of the wire. Boesman starts sweating; he needs to concentrate if he is not to lose his prey. He begins to pull.

'He's coming,' he says, with his cheek to the ground. 'I can feel his heartbeat in the wire.'

The huntsmen bend over the necks of their mounts and watch – truly, there is a definite rhythmical vibration in the wire.

The circle of horses narrows. The servants keep a firm grip on the leashes of the hounds.

With a sudden jerk the jackal is out. It lies there, mauled but motionless on the trampled earth at the entrance to its den.

'Just look at the skelm,' says Boesman. 'Watch him playing dead.'

Seamus draws out his pistol, bends down out of the saddle and with a single shot shatters the jackal's skull.

The farmers raise a cheer as the horses rear from the unexpected report. The sun glitters on the silver whisky flasks as the traditional triple toast is proposed: to the British Empire and the Queen, to the Republic and the State President, and then, laughing and exuberant, to the Minister of Agriculture, beleaguered on all sides by drought and pestilence.

To ensure that the terriers maintain their bloodlust for the hunt to come, Boesman Plaatjies slits the jackal's belly open and cuts out the little liver. He chops it into tiny pieces and throws it to the terriers.

Seamus gestures for the Hunt to proceed and the company now heads up the hill which runs parallel to the river, the hounds fanning out ahead of the huntsmen, weaving their way between prickly pear bushes and tall aloes. By now the sun is quite high in the sky and the heat is blazing down.

For a solid two hours they comb one pasture after another. At last, Seamus thinks, this is becoming a real hunt: protracted expectation, tension alternating with boredom – but unceasing, relentless, inexorable.

As they move up yet another hill, the company is electrified by a sudden bark. The next moment Seamus catches a glimpse of a rust-red jackal haring downhill, with the hound which had picked up its scent a good hundred yards behind.

Seamus fires his pistol into the air to indicate that the chase has begun. Cawood's horn echoes mournfully across the tableland, a lowing sound which drives the hounds frantic.

The company, which had been heading up the hill, is now forced to wheel round and regroup: the Master of the Hunt way out in front, followed by the horn, then the hardened riders and behind them the young catchers, with the bunch of servants whose task it is to control the hounds and cut fences bringing up the rear.

The hounds string out ahead of Seamus, pursued by a rearguard of shortlegged terriers struggling to keep up.

When the slope becomes too steep, the jackal takes its tail between its teeth and rolls downhill like a hoop, head over heels. Then it loses its balance and ends up in a cloud of dust in a dry watercourse.

The huntsmen cheer. 'Bravo, Reynard!' Bill Heathcote yells. A sight like this is rare. Seamus, unable to control his excitement, fires a couple of shots into the air.

Down in the hollow the horses set off at a comfortable gallop. Now they are in the relentlessly leisurely stage of the hunt. At the first fence hound and huntsman alike are dammed up in their impatience. One of the hounds is stuck halfway through the narrow hole in the mesh that the jackal had squeezed through. Cunning beggar, Seamus thinks – leads us to this boundary fence where he knows the size of the hole.

Impatiently Seamus shouts at the hunt servants, who are struggling with the wirecutters. Eventually they drag the fence aside and the horsemen bunch their way through. They chase along a watercourse and up a slope, to the wailing accompaniment of the horn. The huntsmen are startled to see the city in the distance – that they should have ridden as far as this already today! The jackal is now lost to view, the hounds have lost the track and are milling around in circles on the wide, flat stone slabs. 'He's taken to stone!' Cawood calls out.

'He's circling!'

'Bloody fox!'

'He's doubling back on his tracks,' predicts Seamus, from long experience. He calls some of the hounds back, and the company has to wait while they find their direction again. It is time for a swig from the flasks. The farmers confer on horseback while the servants jeer at the hounds.

Then the hounds pick up the scent again, the huntsmen stow their flasks and dig their heels into the horses' flanks. They string out across the plain again, whistling. It has become one of the most extensive hunts the clans have ever undertaken. The jackal keeps a good distance between himself and the leading hounds, running in wide circles across the plain, leading them across flat rocky outcrops where his scent is not as readily absorbed by the hot stone. From time to time he looses a spray of urine, ensuring that the hounds will all congregate to urinate on the same spot, and so gain precious time. The horsemen begin to fear that their prey will escape them – evidently a really sly customer, probably one of the major culprits when it comes to sheep stealing.

Seamus speaks to the hounds and his men. The time has come for them to put their all into it. The Hunt has to be fulfilled.

The farms grow smaller as the Hunt approaches Port Cecil. The boundary fences draw closer and closer to one another. The company comes to the first smallholdings.

There is no agreement about jackal hunting between the Hunt and the owners of these small farms, as there is with the proprietors of the large estates of Manley Flats. But now the company is in a reckless mood and so inflamed by sun and whisky and dust that it would be unthinkable for the Master to call the hunt off.

Seamus is a little concerned – he is an alderman, after all, and this can lead to all kinds of trouble – but at the same time, like all his fellow-huntsmen, he has a hearty disrespect for these smallholding farmers.

So the company charges on regardless, through vegetable patches and across pastures, scattering terrified sheep in their wake. The jackal is tiring now and is trying all sorts of cunning tricks: swimming short distances down irrigation furrows, trotting across the low roofs of pigsties, trying to keep to enclosures where many animals are grazing so as to confuse the hounds with the multiplicity of smells.

But systematically the Hunt is gaining on the jackal. A recklessness such as Seamus has seldom seen on a hunt takes possession of the group. The fence of the final smallholding has now been cut and the jackal is sprinting across the patch of open veld between this last smallholding and the first huts in the squatter settlement. He sways his brush from side to side, confusing the hounds about which direction he is going to take.

Seamus wavers for a moment when the horses struggle to get through an erosion gully and have to pick their way carefully through the dangerous rubbish which litters it, but there is no way he can hold back the younger men now: Cawood, red in the face, his eyes shining, is wearing the same expression he has when playing with his helicopter. And after all the jackal is a worthy opponent – the Master of the Hunt cannot insult his prey by simply allowing him to escape.

Bloodlust knows no logic: Seamus himself leads the Hunt through the gullies. Forty yards ahead he can see Sun City, the poorest of Joza's squatter settlements. At this sight some of the older farmers hesitate. Worried, Bill Heathcote looks at Seamus and shakes his head vigorously, but the young turks push past them, raucously urging the hounds on.

Through the first squatter huts the hounds pursue the jackal. The astonished shack-dwellers shrink back before the great horses. They have not seen the jackal – all they see before them are the pack of hounds and the riders.

The jackal ducks underneath donkey carts, springs nimbly over hen-coops and flashes past tethered mongrels. Curs untied or unrestrained by their owners fall in in a noisy pack behind the hunt terriers.

There is no possibility of turning back now, Seamus realises, as they charge through the most poverty-stricken part of Joza and indignant shack-dwellers try to pelt them with stones. There is no end to these huts, Seamus thinks on the back of 1820, looking at the way these people live. It is hard to believe that so much filth and deprivation can be human habitations.

The jackal flashes out onto an open piece of veld beyond the last of the shacks. The Hunt charges across a tarred road and through a depression of stunted bushes festooned with wind blown plastic shopping bags.

At the industrial area beside the river the jackal leads them down along factory walls, then past abandoned locomotives standing rusting amid rank kikuyu grass. As they go sloshing through the muddy marsh at the bottom of the valley, the jackal heads for the bridge that arches across First Delta.

Traffic dams up and some motorists even get out of their cars to watch the spectacle of a horse commando with hunting hounds charging across the trussed arch bridge. There are more foreign registration numbers than usual: people have driven great distances to see the oil.

Beyond First Delta the jackal keeps to the stormwater drain beside the main road until he reaches the university quarter where he swerves into the narrow alleys. Students drinking wine and playing cards on their balconies yell abuse at the great huntsmen chasing the tiny animal.

There is a strong Green movement on the campus and Seamus has to dodge the rulers, fruit and balls of scrunched up paper hurled at him.

'Shame!' pouts a pretty young woman.

Seamus looks at them in irritation. What do you know of the battle against nature in Africa? Of the demands made by this continent? Here you sit, your purses stuffed with your parents' money, and you imagine that you are lords of all you survey.

But we, the farmers of Manley Flats, are the ones who form the real front line; who understand the inevitabilities of this place; who play the game according to the rules of wind and weather, of survival and death, of hunter and prey ...

The horses, already nervous because of the traffic and the yelling students, now have to struggle to keep their balance on the uneven cobbles that are laid like the scales of a fish in this old quarter of the city so close to the cathedral.

Cathedral Square lies ahead. But there is no time to bring the Hunt to a halt now. In their haste the hounds knock down a couple of patrolling soldiers and send their rifles clattering on the cobbles. The soldiers scrabble out of the way on all fours to escape the hooves of horses in full cry.

1820's chest snaps straight through a cross-bar and braziers go flying. Like a man possessed, Cawood raises the horn to his lips and sounds the note usually reserved to mark the successful conclusion of the hunt. But there is no time for the Master of the Hunt to reprimand his son now for they are already bursting out into the open on Cathedral Square.

Seamus catches the glint of sunlight on the fountain of oil gushing forth on the far side of the cathedral. Here the commando encounters another line, of firemen and soldiers this time, but these immediately give way before them. Somewhere a siren goes off.

Seamus looks across the square to the city hall and closes his eyes for a few moments. This is a municipal disgrace, a public scandal. I shall lose my seat on the city council; also the respect of my fellow councillors.

The jackal takes fright at the siren and the soldiers and heads straight for the dark cave of the cathedral doors.

He slips inside.

Seamus rises upright in his stirrups and holds up his hand. Breathless and sweating, the flanks of the horses white with saltpetre, the bunch of huntsmen come to a halt. Fortunately there is no oil on this part of the square. How the horses would have slipped and slithered!

Above their heads a helicopter hovers with a television cameraman trying to film the highly improbable scene. The farmers raise their hats and wave up at him while the baying hounds mill round the entrance to the cathedral. Trembling with excitement they cock their legs against the stone arches anchoring the massive doors to the earth.

The hounds do not enter the cathedral, which surprises the riders, who look at one another uneasily. A crowd of soldiers has gathered round them – clearly relieved that the commando is not intent upon the oil-fountain, but apparently also uncertain as to what is expected of them now.

Seamus looks up at the stained-glass windows; saints in their golden haloes; expressionless, quiet faces in the glass.

More pressmen have now come running up. The commando is a welcome diversion, a bonus added to the oddity of the oil-happening. Seamus is aware of the picture they make: his own bearded figure beside his magnificent stallion, the blond-haired, suntanned Cawood with the copper horn, the riders loudly emptying their silver whisky flasks, the hunt servants with their weather-beaten faces and farm clothes.

'Shall I have a look?' Cawood asks, pointing to the cathedral doors.

'For heaven's sake, Cawood, NO! You're quite capable of shooting it under the very rood.'

'Dad!' But Seamus takes no notice of his son's indignation. He turns on his heel and strides into the cathedral. The porch is cool and smells of polished wood and old stone. Also, more subtly, of incense and wax candles.

Stretched out on its side against the rear wall of the sanctuary, close by the organ pipes, lies the jackal.

Seamus regards the scene for a long time. A bitterness wells up within him – why he cannot tell. Overcome, he swings round, and is caught off-side again by the intensity of the glare of the sunlight outside.

'It's playing dead,' he announces.

The Hunt stands around irresolute.

'He's as sly as Satan himself!' exclaims Bill Heathcote. The whisky and the day's exertion have not agreed with Bill. Seamus observes how red and puffed up his neighbour's face is and how the thin, sweaty hair is sticking to his forehead.

As Seamus turns round again towards the cathedral doors a shadow falls. A priest has emerged from within. The man looks quite disconcerted at the sight of the Hunt. For a moment there is panic in his eyes; but then he pulls himself together and folds his hands before his chest.

'Yes, my children?' he enquires. Seamus gives a slight cough, aware suddenly once again of his status as an alderman. It is a dangerous situation that has now arisen. He knows the Manley Flats farmers well enough to know that when their hunting blood is up, as it is now, any reasonableness becomes well-nigh impossible. In all the years of the Hunt's existence it has never once happened that the prey has been willingly and consciously abandoned.

And in any event, these people are not accustomed to limitations. If you have farmed all your life on your own soil, on property so large that its boundaries are not visible to the naked eye, you do not easily accept the imposition of limits.

'This vermin, Father ...' Seamus removes his hat. The man is, after all, a priest. And the press is here, too – this event will have repercussions.

'Vermin?'

'Inside.' Seamus coughs again. 'A jackal. We,' he gestures needlessly, 'are huntsmen.'

'One moment, please.'

The priest disappears inside and reappears straightaway.

'Who are you?' he asks Seamus.

'Seamus Butler of Fata Morgana.'

A flash of recognition shines in the priest's eyes. 'Oh yes, Mr Butler, the fall-goat breeder.'

'The same.'

The priest hides his hands behind the folds of his white cassock, as though ashamed of their pallid whiteness in the presence of so many sweating, suntanned men.

'And you have chased the jackal to here?'

Seamus nods.

Cawood steps forward. 'These brutes are killing our stock,' he says sullenly.

'And the little creature has fled to the Church for sanctuary ...'

Seamus realises that they are already losing the battle. As an experienced municipal politician and a veteran of many a community meeting he can sense that the sympathy of the crowd now congregated round them is solidly behind the priest and the jackal.

Over the past few years the Greens have increased their militancy, something of which the city council is fully conscious. And the farmers, in their ceaseless struggle against jackals, eagles, skunks and monkeys, are only too well aware of the new Chair in Eco-education which has now been created at the university.

That bunch of middle-aged hippies – Seamus has heard people say at farmers' meetings – the tired-eyed flotsam and jetsam of the era of flower-power who now occupy chairs at the university and still go around dressed in sandals and worn jeans: you couldn't expect them to have any understanding whatever of the farmer's struggle against nature.

The oil strike, too, has brought many of the eco-activists together here today. Seamus looks around him. They've got us surrounded now, he thinks, with all their moral self-righteousness, and in the front line, of course, the press. If only young Cawood – who hasn't the faintest idea of tact – will keep his mouth shut.

'It is a necessary ritual, Father,' Seamus tries to explain. 'The farming community needs to hunt to defend its flocks and herds against the wild beasts of the field and the birds of the air. Today is the annual jackal hunt; it is a symbolic day for us – symbolic of the charge laid upon man in Genesis to subdue the earth and have dominion over all creeping things ...'

'And yet, my son, is it not man that has disturbed the balance of nature?' Like Seamus, the priest – also a hardened manipulator of people – has sensed public support on his side. 'To the extent that that little animal no longer has any natural prey left?'

Seamus sighs. The hunter has now become the prey. How unexpectedly labels can be switched! New times, new demands. But we, we still have to fight the good fight, for we have no defence against wind and weather, against sun and earth.

'Father ...' At the same time Seamus is irritated that this man with his weedy physique, so obviously many years Seamus's junior, should have the power to intimidate him – and with him an entire commando of huntsmen. 'Father ...'

Cawood thrusts himself forward. 'We demand the brute!'

The priest looks straight at Cawood. 'And I say to you that this is the house of the Lord. That creature has sought sanctuary here.'

Cawood is indignant and ignores Seamus's hand on his shoulder. 'But it's vermin!' He looks as if he is going to strike the priest. 'The only reason it ran in here was because it thought the cathedral doors were the entrance to a cave!'

'How are we to know?' replies the priest softly, and smiles slowly. 'Perhaps the jackal has led you, the hunters, to this place ...'

This thought is so improbable that the farmers scowl and begin to grumble. Voices in the crowd jeer at them.

'Go home, yokels!'

'Hairybacks!'

'Hillbillies!'

'Murderers!'

Seamus draws himself up to his full length. Round him the farmers in turn are shouting at the city dwellers: 'What do you know about farming? About the bloody hard life we have to live?'

Seamus lifts his hand and the farmers fall silent. He is the Master of the Hunt and they are under his command. All at once one of the pressmen, who has sneaked into the cathedral unobserved to photograph the jackal, reappears. 'It's gone,' he shouts. 'The jackal has disappeared!'

Spontaneous applause breaks out. The priest smiles. 'Sometimes there is a miracle hidden in the tiniest incident,' he says. 'God may command the least of His creatures to call His congregation to their senses.'

Seamus decides against replying. 'To saddle!' he orders the Hunt. 'The hounds!' he commands the hunt servants. All the huntsmen mount their horses and the hounds are leashed.

As they turn away from the cathedral the bells ring out. When Seamus turns to take a last, humiliated look over his shoulder, he sees the fluttering cassock of the priest against the inside wall of the porch. The man is swinging on the bell rope, his shadow flapping like a bat.

Seamus guides 1820 carefully through the curious throng. The oil strike has given everyone an overdose of courage. Priests, businessmen, farmers – we've all had a shot of adrenalin. We think we are destined for greatness; that want is a thing of the past; that at last we shall be able to realise all our hopes boldly and energetically.

We have forgotten which continent we are living on.

Seamus deliberately leads his commando away from the university quarter. They ride to the nearest hotel in the business district, a building that is a remnant of the British colonial era, its walls decorated with photographs of fighter planes from the Second World War.

While the hunt servants are left under the command of Boesman Plaatjies to wait outside in the shade of the pavement trees, the huntsmen invade the bar. They toast the unfinished business of the hunt, the element of surprise so characteristic of this part of the world, and the power of the unforeseen.

And also the triple toast, once again, despite their second prey having eluded them, to the Empire and the Queen, the State President, and finally, in the midst of wolf-whistles and catcalls, to the Nationalist government's Minister of Agriculture, currently involved in tense negotiations at the constitutional conference at which the country's future will be decided.

8

We enter MaNdlovu's house quietly – so that she will remain unaware of our presence. She is sitting in her favourite chair in the dining room. In her left hand she is holding the large white man's handkerchief that she always has with her, while her right hand is rubbing the arm-rest of the chair. It has been rubbed quite smooth from all the years she has sat here and talked when times were hard.

She is not speaking to anyone in particular; she is alone.

'Women like us,' MaNdlovu says, 'know how to take care of our families. Our funeral policies are always up to date – ten rands to the Metropolitan every month. A visit to the sangoma every full moon to have the bones thrown and read. In church every Sunday, in the front pews where you can smell the incense properly.

'On the great days we are first with a slaughter animal. When it is a really important day we slaughter one of the Butlers' fainting-goats for an extra sweet morsel of meat. And when Christmas comes, I am the one who has been knotting a coin or two in the sheet every week of the year so that we can afford those shining new school uniforms for the children.

'Even for that great loudmouth Zola, there is always something – a soft cushion for his taxi, because the whole family knows he suffers from piles. Or a next year, the talons of a kestrel, the best talisman in all the Kei, to hang on his rear-view mirror for protection on the open road.

'To get hold of those kestrel talons last Christmas I had to swop three fainting-goat skulls, boiled clean and wind dried. And I had to make everyone promise not to say anything about it to Ayanda, she gets so angry about our old beliefs. And for TaImbongi the year before, it was framed portraits of Mandela and Tambo, in those thick gilt frames the Indian used to sell, when such photos were still forbidden ...

'But it is in times of plenty like these now, when the hunger of the whole world descends on us, that my wisdom fails me. Actually we Thandani women have been raised to suffering and want – that's when we know how to scrimp and save, to encourage the faint-hearted, to render the oil out of the same fat again and again.

'But in times of plenty, our legs go lame.

'Plenty,' says MaNdlovu, and her eyes fill with tears. She gets that look on her face that she always has when talking about the old days. 'Plenty makes me think of the days when I was still a young girl on the threadbare plains of Struggle Kei, when the pedlar's wagon would turn aside up the track to our huts and his axles would be bending under the weight of the load of bottles – huge great jars of sweet wine for the men of our village.

'To keep them tame, to befuddle their heads while our land was sold out from under us and we were forced to shift aside, farther aside, constantly farther aside. Wherever white men saw a black person farming, they said: shift aside, farther aside, constantly farther aside ... That's how the Forced Removals robbed us, rendered us landless, Jesusss ...!'

She takes out her handkerchief and wipes her forehead. 'That pedlar's wine made the men reckless and made them sign papers for long terms on the mines in the north. There they went to dig, and once a year they came home for a fortnight and poked us women raw. There was no stopping those men with their city habits and their bragging, imagining that every woman was dying to open her legs for a Western Deep cowboy.

'Once the bellies were swelling, off the men went again. All they left behind was a tawdry OK Bazaars radio, and when its batteries were flat, the thing just lay like a piece of junk in the hut, because the red Jew at the General Dealer's said he wouldn't sell transistor batteries to kaffirs. They would just listen to the radio and think they were clever and turn into communists.

'Feeling remorseful and guilty doesn't help, Tata, my mama always told my dad. You go jackrolling strange women all year in those mine compounds and once a year you come back here strutting like a cock ostrich in your Jet Stores clothes and when I complain, you come up with glittery trinkets for my arms and ears, or a coolie kerchief for my head, but Tata – yes, that's what my mama would say – Tata, she said ...'

MaNdlovu sniffs and shifts on her chair. 'Tata, you bring back everything except what we need. What we need in these days of loss and removals is pride, and strength, Tata, and our traditions. You men have left us to face the no man's land alone. I hear the government wants to call it a homeland. But we've all known for a long time there's no home for us. Never will our children or grandchildren be able to call this country home ...

'Then that year my mama lifted up her head – I was a big girl already – and my mama said: I'm shaking the dust of this place off my feet; I'm saying to hell with this little patch of mealies with its coarse soil and stones; I'm turning my back on this village without men, this place of forgotten women and snotty-nosed children, deserted by men who have gone to dig riches for Anglo-American; and I'm taking my children and my bundle on my back and help me Lord God, I'm walking to the city, to that big place; and I'm either going to make myself confused or decent again, so help me God.

'Yes, my mama.' MaNdlovu blows her nose. She is silent for a spell, lost in thought. 'I'll never forget that walking. There were five of us children. Mama's money lasted only from the first station to the second. Our little pail of milk was soon emptied. I was still carrying forty prickly pears, wrapped up in a cloth. We sold them to the station master and bought two loaves of bread.

'We sat at the station for two days. There was a water tap, there was shade and also a knot of other people travelling. It was a pretty little station, with flower beds. My mama comforted us, saying: Children, we're going to get a house with flower beds just like this. We'll plant flowers. Forget those weedy mealies. We'll look at the pretty flowers in front of our house and we'll forget all about the jackrollers and the Western Deep cowboys.

'On the night of the second day Mama said to each of us: you will sow the red flowers, and you will sow the yellow flowers, and you ...' MaNdlovu takes out her handkerchief again. Eventually she continues: 'Yes, it was a pretty little station. It was just that there were so many trains. The engines ran back and forth and we couldn't read and we couldn't find out where the trains were running to.

'Were they going to the towns where there was land and work? Or were they heading for poverty, for yet another place of prickly pears and mangy animals and crooked pedlars?

'Yes, and not one of us could read,' says MaNdlovu. For a while she says nothing. The room is filled with her silence.

'That station master with his beer belly looked slyly at our mama and that night when we were all lying bunched together under the pepper trees beside the tap, our bodies stinking and our stomachs hollow, when we children had even stopped wriggling and arguing, that shows how dog tired we were ... then ... Mama must have thought we were asleep, but I peeped out from under the blanket ...

'Later Mama came back and the station master was standing on the gravel under the light in front of his office buttoning up his fly and watching Mama walk away. I hid my face under the blanket and Mama came back ...'

MaNdlovu starts folding her handkerchief. First this side over, then that side over. Her big hands work lightly, gently with the material.

'The next morning Mama took the station master's money and bought us all third-class tickets to Port Cecil. There was just enough money for tickets, two loaves of bread and a tin of fish.

'Yes, Mama ...'

MaNdlovu struggles to get up. It isn't easy. She has to push to get out of the chair. For a brief moment I forget where I am, wanting to go forward to help her. She looks up as though she has seen me. We hesitate for a moment, then I draw back. I must let her be. I can't do anything else. She is leaning on her stick. The black-rimmed glasses steam up. The glasses are an old pair of TaImbongi's. They help her eyes when her blood-pressure is raised.

After a while she feels steady again and her light-headedness disappears. I am relieved. Slowly she walks towards the dining room table and stands there for a while, leaning with her hand on the table top. Then she walks back to her chair and sinks down into it again.

'Of all my brothers and sisters I probably turned out the most respectable. We were railway children. Mama built a shack out of corrugated iron and saplings near the Joza station. That was before they named the place Sun City – we just called it The Ditch. We were too scared to go farther in, closer to the white town ... In the daytime we used to sit and look down on the legs of the delta, the ships coming and going, the horse carts ...

'We ran all over the railway tracks, picking up coal that had fallen from the engines and selling it by the bucket in Joza: a tickey a time, tickey, tickey, tickey. That's how we ate.

'Where they all are now – my brothers and sisters – I don't know. The lorries broke down our shack and loaded up the pieces and off we went again, away, onwards, I don't know where, the places don't even have names. Settle, they told us. Settle here. Homeland ...

'Mama slowly died. Of hopelessness. Of guilt that she should have left Tata like that in her anger, but also of the knowledge that she could not go back. Of longing, yes, longing for a place to call her own, a place she could tame with spade and broom ...

'A place she could call home. For us Xhosas, this country has never been a place like that.

'That's why I say: cling to our traditions. We Thandani women have got to keep our arms ready to seize. You don't get a second chance. Life gives you one chance and if you make a mess of it, it's over and done with. Before you can wipe your eyes, you are old and useless, you've got scales on your eyes, and as soon as you get a bit worked up you keel over.

'Yes ...' MaNdlovu unfolds the handkerchief again and wipes the sweat from her forehead. The clock on the sideboard points to half-past seven. The street outside the house is quiet. At this time of the morning those who are going to work have already left to catch the taxis. And those who are not working have gone down into the city to hang around like sheep gawking at the oil fountain. 'Riches ...' MaNdlovu says softly. 'The question is what we are going to do with our wealth, we who were raised for want and drought.'

She laughs softly. 'Would you believe it, Mama, a house with a dining room table, a sideboard, a television. A microwave oven even. A child and a grandchild with degrees. A husband with a bakkie, would you believe it, Mama ...

'You didn't sacrifice your body in vain, my mama, at the station with the pepper trees.

'And only you and I, your eldest daughter, knew about that white usana, born limp and still slippery from your womb, that you buried that summer afternoon in the sandy ditch. The next rain storm, you said, would wash everything around here clean again.'

MaNdlovu starts to get up again. She struggles, her jowls trembling from the exertion. Eventually on her feet again, she moves towards the kitchen.

There she stops in front of a photograph of her three children: Ncincilili, Mpho, Ayanda. I go closer to look over her shoulder. Ayanda, particularly, interests me. 'You can read, you spoilt brats,' she grumbles. 'Unlike my mama, I shall see to it that you honour our traditions. That much I owe her.'

She sighs. It is getting late. She has to get down to the Civic. There is work to be done. Soon everyone will be asking: What should we do now, Great Mother? MaNdlovu pulls the front door to behind her and walks down the street. It is not far, and as she walks she thinks again about Ncincilili. 'We have lost a lot, our family. Lord knows, we are thinly sown when it comes to men.'

At the Civic she goes into her workroom. As she walks in, she orders: 'Get that box of clothes to the convent in Peddie. I thought it left here two days ago.'

She sits and rests for a while in the overfilled room. On the wall behind her hangs a painting of Christ with piously folded hands bending over a little boy holding a lamb. Next to it hangs the framed piece of black cloth which MaNdlovu had hung there when Mandela was still on the Island and his portrait was banned, to remind visitors to the Civic about the fate of the detainees.

The desk in front of her is piled high with pamphlets about workers' rights, breast feeding, ante-natal exercises, safe sex, instructions on how to bridle donkeys so as to protect the animals from chafing and injury.

My wretched congregation, my poorest of the poor. You're all so timid and miserable out there in Sun City. Just like a bunch of children and their mother at a strange station years ago.

But hang on, MaNdlovu, she reminds herself, now you're getting sentimental. It's pointless your hankering after the old days, the days when you started the Civic in this old nuns' home.

And indeed that really was one of MaNdlovu's major achievements. In those days the church next to the Civic had one of the largest congregations in the Kei.

Now the priest seldom has more than thirty or forty souls to preach to. The tsotsis paint their slogans on the walls of the church. When you walk out of the front door of the Civic building you run straight into Mongrels Rule. Mandrax is King. One Settler One Bullet. Impimpi Necklace.

At night the smugglers meet the dagga-crazies here, in the safety of the church grounds. When morning comes there will still be teenagers lying on the verandas. All the verandas are streaked with the slime that dribbles from the mouths of the white-pipe smokers in their ecstasy. Then MaNdlovu will grab hold of a garden hose and squirt the children awake, and swish the spit off the verandas. Also the tiny heaps of ash where the white pipes have been knocked out, and the pee marks against the pillars.

'For shame, shame, shame!' she will exclaim, till the children stagger out through the gate.

Now MaNdlovu gets up and goes into the room next door. She sees to it that everyone is working. They have to pack food parcels with meal, dried fish and bread – for taking out to Sun City later.

Then, very quietly, she goes out through the front door, taking care not to touch the floor with her stick. Outside she pushes her glasses straight and starts to walk. She is greeted by faces that remain hazy. As she progresses upwards, she begins to perspire. It is in the heat of the day.

She keeps close to the garden fences, hoping that the minibuses that usually go hurtling past here will see her in time. Once she feels dizzy and has to stop and rest a while. Standing there, she gradually becomes aware that she is almost leaning against a harnessed donkey. With the coir-like fur under her hands she pushes herself away from the beast and struggles on again. As the slope gets steeper, the houses grow sparser.

Now, MaNdlovu knows, they will start searching down at the Civic. They will phone Ayanda; if they do not get her, they will send a messenger to the taxi terminus to track down Zola. Eventually they will hear from someone who has seen her walking away. And then they will say: If that is where she is going, who are we to stop her?

She stops when she hears the sound of horses' hooves. Or is it gunfire in the distance? But then she hears a pack of dogs barking as they bound along beside the horses. As the noise draws nearer she throws herself against a hedge. People start screaming in their front gardens, mothers call their children and doors slam shut.

The dogs come by first – all she can see is a hazy movement, but she smells their breath – then there is the overwhelming smell of horse sweat. She clings to the fence and has to hold on tight to keep her balance in the dust and the thunder of hooves.

She hears a bugle. Soldiers! Is the army now bringing in mounted troops to suppress us? Have we not suffered enough under the Casspirs and the police vans?

When the dust has settled, she struggles on again. Eventually she is past the last houses. Under the sparse thorn trees here on the edge of the squatter settlement is the place where families without even pit toilets come to squat. Only the rain ever washes this place clean.

MaNdlovu shudders when she catches the sweetish stench of rotting ordure. She wishes she were better able to pick her way between the little mounds that lie around here like small veld tortoises. But she presses on, telling herself that the sweet smell comes from prickly pear blossoms.

Once past the clump of trees, she stops to catch her breath, and waits till her heart slows down a little. The footpath now leads steeply up the slope, but she sighs, lifts her skirts and starts to climb.

A mother can be pushed only so far, she tells herself, as she heaves her body up the steep path, yard by yard. Only so far, she pants. And then no further. My old body is too weary, my eyes too blind, my head too dizzy. But I have to press on. I am MaNdlovu Thandani the Xhosa mama, the mother elephant. Just this far. Just this far. Just this far.

She stops to rest again and turns to face into the cool breeze. If her eyes were better she would be able to look out over the city now. She would be able to see the river fanning out into the seven legs of its delta, the arched bridges which link up the islands, the boats sailing under the bridges with sea birds circling their masts, and the city spread out across the islands with the squatter settlements like a rusty fungus growing on the slopes.

She hears the city noises quite clearly. They form a hum, the buzzing of a swarm of bees. Is that what we sound like to God, she wonders. Does He ever distinguish between the praying of a prisoner, an axe chopping, a car door banging, the tinkle of a cup in a saucer?

Behind her something is banging in the wind. It sounds like a door swinging on its hinges, higher up, above her. Her feet slipping, she inches upwards on all fours, grazing her knees, her temples throbbing. She loses her handkerchief and cannot find it again. Her glasses slip off, but them she recovers. She crawls on, smelling the dusty earth and the Karoo bushes.

The fence smells of rust and sun. Up against the fence the earth is baked hard. Water dams up here when it rains. Then it evaporates, leaving the earth harder than ever. She lies with her cheek to the ground. Smooth as a child's skin, she thinks. Smooth and warm and alive.

Again she hears the banging, gets up onto all fours and creeps along the fence. She has to go round the anchor post at the corner and then along the other side. Broken bottles and rusty beer cans she sweeps aside with her knees. The noise grows louder. She cannot find any break in the fence. She sits up and starts banging on the wire mesh with an old beer can. The rust flakes off to reveal shining metal underneath. She twists it, feeling the steel cutting into her hands.

MaNdlovu bites through the wire. She kicks open a hole, pushes and shoves. She feels the salt taste of blood. That's from biting the wire, she thinks, and from a stroke coming on. It's blood of my blood.

She creeps through and waddles across the clean raked gravel to the wall fifteen yards farther. Then she attacks the wall, noticing the trowel marks in the coarse plaster, feels her way along its length. The banging must be coming from round the corner, she thinks, there's an open door, banging in the wind.

Ncincilili comes round the corner. He is wearing those gold-rimmed spectacles which she had hated so, and a neat jacket and tie. He smiles at her and she sees his lips forming her name. He holds out his arms to her and she smells his body.

She has forgotten how handsome he is, how strong, how lovely.

9

When I arrive home Ayanda Thandani is sitting in the dilapidated minibus in front of my house.

'Doctor Thandani!'

'Lawyer Wehmeyer.' She looks tired. 'I couldn't get hold of you at the office. I've been trying all day to ...'

The keys of the old diesel Mercedes tinkle in my hand as I make a gesture. 'I was in court. Will you come in?' The case was an interminable wrangle for damages after two fishing trawlers had collided in the estuary.

The Butlers' car is also parked in front of the house. That would be Sarah – she has never surrendered her key to the house after the deaths of our parents and I have never thought of asking her to. The house is as much hers as mine. It is our shared past.

'No, thanks. I can't come in now. I came by on my way to the hospital. Everyone knows this riverside house is yours. I saw you stopping.'

'You are worried about your father.'

'Yes. Our family is all in a muddle again, about all sorts of things ...'

'I am still struggling to find out why and where he is being held. I may have to drive through to Bisho tomorrow if my correspondent there cannot come up with anything.'

'You would do that ...?'

'Of course. It's my duty.' I sigh. 'We'll get him out.'

'Thanks.' She climbs back into the kwela. 'And to crown it all, my own car was stolen last week, so now I have to drive around in this borrowed wreck.'

'Try not to be too worried.'

I turn round. In the growing dusk the ramshackle old house looms up dark and large. When Sarah comes visiting, things seem to fall back into an old pattern. The house looks to me as it did when I was a child: dark and mysterious, an endless labyrinth of rooms and passages, balconies and outbuildings, fright-spots and dark dens.

Sarah often comes for a visit at the end of the day and then waits down at the bottom of the garden until I get home. I know these moods of hers, when she feels rejected by Seamus, excluded while he fights his private battles with himself and his past, but also tired of the goat stud and the routine of the homestead.

At such times I will leave her alone and get on with cooking, or service my locomotives. Meanwhile she will sit there, motionless, beside the water, giving no indication that she is aware of my having come home. I recognise this ritual – even participate in it. For Sarah it is a repetition of our childhood: our parents are busy inside the house; she is daydreaming out across the river; I am playing somewhere. There is life and security, a sense of being nurtured, in the smells of evening, the calm river, the small lights flickering on, and inside the brightly lit house the sounds of dishes and people.

Ayanda drives off and I walk up to the house. The paving on the garden path is overgrown with moss. I take a deep breath of its moist smell. Before going through the front door I stroke the thick, rough bark of the grapevine over the pergola. I remember quite clearly the day our parents planted that vine.

I walk through the dark house and stand on the back patio. It is already so dark that I cannot see her. 'Sarah?' There is a lazy splash of someone – probably one of the neighbours – slowly rowing a skiff out across the river. Suddenly, there she is behind me. She had been in the dark kitchen.

'Here I am.'

'Oh.'

We stand in silence, looking out across the river. On the opposite bank the lights are like a glittering diamond necklace.

We don't need to talk when we are alone together – particularly not when we are here. Then all the barriers sink away. We know each other's anxieties and doubts so intimately that words are unnecessary.

It is so different from when Seamus is with us. That restless energy of his, his quick, sure movements, that self-confident body which never betrays his depression, the words which spring so readily to his tongue. Although Sarah has repeatedly assured me that Seamus is consumed by anxiety and self-doubt, all I ever see is the inexplicable, self-assured fury so typical of the spoilt Butlers.

'I shall wait for the day,' I once told Sarah, 'when Seamus reveals his weakness and humanity. Until then I am not prepared to give him the benefit of the doubt.'

'That day will never come,' Sarah had answered. 'If you are waiting for Seamus to show you his weak underside, you will wait for ever.'

If only Seamus will admit to me, just once, that he is defenceless, that he is human – our relationship will be able to continue in a different tone. That is what I always tell Sarah when she goes on about Seamus and me needing to try to understand each other.

Then Sarah shakes her head. 'It will never happen. He won't let anybody get near him. Even I, his own wife, am excluded.'

In hindsight, now that it's all over, I confess that I actually understand Seamus better than I have ever been prepared to admit, even there in the ramshackle old house during my conversation with Sarah. I know that he is running through the dew-wet kikuyu, following the muffled sound of his mother's feet as they stumble along the narrow garden pathways, with the terrible torchlight bouncing across the empty yard ...

Perhaps I have always been envious of the relationship between Seamus and Sarah. It has always fascinated me. Possibly because I have not had the experience of a lasting relationship myself, this devotion between people who could identify so many flaws in their relationship is to me mysterious – sometimes even slightly crazy.

And Sarah's next words confirm my preconceptions: 'When people have been together so very long, it's like an osmosis: his fears become your own; his incidents yours; and yours – hopefully – his. There's a whole chunk of living between you. In a sense you are both sitting on the edge of it, looking at it, and just occasionally genuinely meeting each other on that shared terrain. But you cannot break away from it ... it becomes ...' She is searching for an image. 'It becomes ... like this house ... for you and me, Seer. How does one express it in words ...?'

I take her hand. 'I understand.'

She shakes her head. She looks close to tears. 'It's just that ... at some stage Seamus crossed a boundary. It's as though ...'

'Yes?'

Sarah looks up and swallows her tears. 'How shall we ever know,' she asks, 'what the mirror tells someone else; what another person's relationship with his own shadow is; what you are thinking in those determining moments in your life; moments perhaps only seconds long – which remain with you your whole life long and strangle you ... strangle you, Seer, because that's what is happening to Seamus ... he is being squeezed out of his own body by terrors that are too big for him ... and where can he go to? How can he escape except by ... like ...' She begins to weep and I take her in my arms. 'Except by taking ... like his father ...'

'Sarah ...'

'Oh, Seer, I can't burden you with all this ...'

I say nothing, waiting till she has dried her eyes and regains her composure.

'A whole life cannot feed on a single incident,' I say cautiously.

'One's life builds on from a single incident,' is her clever reply.

'When we think carefully, there is always one determining moment, a moment which is constantly repeated, which establishes the pattern. And we always pursue that repetition, even if it contains within it our own destruction. We all have one theme that we're devoted to – it is our germ cell. It may be good, it may be evil. It can be heaven or hell. In Seamus's case it's hell. A pebble falls into the pool and every spreading ripple owes its origin to that one pebble ...'

'Well ...' What else can I say? Our devotion to another – so often an opposite – is a form of self-destruction, a compulsive urge of the ego to be cancelled out. After all, what does a lifetime together mean? How many people actually succeed in living with dignity within such a relationship and in avoiding all the temptations to wound each other? Forgive me my rhetorical questions (it's my nature, I'm afraid), but who survives the battlefield of love? Is it only the utterly stupid? Isn't the price too high? Isn't the measure of blindness required simply too large?

'Well ...' Yes, that is all that I, the bachelor, can reply. Because her words so often confront me with myself. Where is my theme? If I think carefully – and I have often thought about this – all I find is loneliness. No incident, no trauma – only an inexorable conviction of otherness, of aloneness. A sense of self-evident eccentricity and isolation for which this old house, so far from bourgeois suburbia, and so exposed to the river's damp and temperature fluctuations, and all the insects and weeds which they attract, is such a satisfying metaphor.

That's why I can never leave here – not even in death. Perhaps, perhaps this house is my lover. Perhaps my most enduring relationship – apart from my connection with Sarah – is with this ramshackle old house. Perhaps I don't need another person, since I find all kinds of moods in this house, and whims and caprices, and seasons and terrors and comfort, and excitement, too ...

But let's forget about my ruminations (I can be such an old woman!) and watch me turn round to Sarah. She is still looking out over the river. I hear her swallowing softly from the glass in her hands.

'What is it, Sarah?'

'You know loneliness, Seer,' she says. 'I sense it when I walk in and you're not here. The old house is silent. It has something of a grave about it.' I am ready to protest, but she turns towards me. 'But the loneliness of someone who lives alone like you is nothing compared to the loneliness one can experience within a relationship.' She takes a sip from the glass. 'To live with someone day after day and still to have no part of him. You are the rejected prisoner ... That is what I have become on Fata Morgana ...'

We sit down. I light the little buchu-lamp to drive away the mosquitoes. The tiny flame casts shadows over her face, making her eyes look deep and dark ringed.

'Sarah ...'

She shakes her head. 'I'm sorry.' She sniffs. 'I love him very deeply. He can't live without me. He worships the ground I tread on. We are devoted to each other. And yet everything which I always say about our relationship is valid. How is one to understand it?'

I shrug my shoulders. 'One cannot comprehend it.'

She turns on me angrily. 'But why not, Seer? What game is being played with us? Sometimes when I look at those goats and I see their eyes, I think we are just as ridiculous and absurd as they are. We are certainly just as much victims as they are. Imagine the humiliation of swooning away like that every time you have a shock. What is the difference between them and us?' She spreads her hand across her face. 'God is demonically cruel.'

'Sarah ...'

'You can Sarah me, Seer, you can go on Sarahing me, but I'm telling you: you come and spend just one night with Seamus when he's having one of his terror-attacks. You find yourself leaning over the edge of hell, Seer. You look down into something which you did not know could even exist in the mind of man ... so much desolation, such intensity, it's so overwhelming, it's almost a kind of ecstasy, Seer, you can ...'

'He'll recover, Sarah.'

She nods. 'Yes, he'll recover,' she says. 'He'll recover. He'll die, probably by his own hand. And he'll become a cycad or an aloe out there on the plain. He'll stand there for decades, possibly for a century. He'll stand there in sun and wind and frost and snow. He's beyond the reach of time. He's a plant or an animal. A fall-goat, or a leopard. He's a vygie or a weed ...' Through her tears, she begins to laugh. 'It's no accident that they call him Old Goat Butler, Seer. He'll drown in his own blood, like a goat ...'

'Sarah ...' I have to hold her tight. 'Oh ...'

What would Father and Mother have to say if they could see us like this, so different from what they had probably hoped for, from what they had worked for through all those years of careful education: this middle-aged, melancholy bachelor, their daughter who had married so well and wealthily but who is now being dragged through the depths by her neurotic husband?

Both having to face what Father and Mother surely also had to wrestle with, what every human being enters into disputes about: the cliché of living, of surviving, of off-setting expectations against frustrations, and ideals against failures, and possibilities against limitations?

How – and when – do you calculate these things? When do you allow yourself to admit – to yourself – that the possibilities have been exhausted, that there are boundaries to pull you up short: incapacities which eventually become part of your personal baggage ...?

'It's the oil, too.' Sarah turns away. 'Seamus is oil-crazy. He wants to sell the estate and put all his capital into property in the city. He has smelt money, in a way quite unnecessary for the Butlers. I mean, theirs is old money. They have always had money.'

'He's not the only one, Sarah. You should see the way people are streaming in here. Did you drive past the caravan park today? They are pitching hundreds of tents. I hear all the hotels are chock-a-block.'

'But we're not fortune hunters, Seer. We are the ...' She

hesitates, then goes on: 'All right, let me say it, even though I know you don't like it: We are the Butlers. We have a rich tradition. We cannot simply sell it all up ...'

'You have become more attached to the estate and the Butler name than you would like to admit,' I scold her lightly. She shrugs her shoulders. 'Not that I blame you,' I add hastily. 'There is that splendid Fata Morgana, with the allure of tradition and dynastic history, the lunatic charm of the fall-goat stud ...'

She interrupts me. 'You're wrong, Seer. It's much simpler than that. I enjoy farm life. I revel in the smell of the landscape when I throw open my windows in the morning and smell the veld and the dew. I enjoy watching the sun set that one, still moment before it sinks away sadly into its own redness, as it can only do in the Kei. And the nights: the stars so sharp.'

I sigh. 'Oh, I guess I'm just jealous ...'

She thinks for a moment. 'This oil is going to call down something dreadful on our heads, Seer. I know it. Do you remember my phoning you the night before leap year? When you said the river was the colour of old blood ...'

I look at her in surprise. 'And old oil. I used the word oil!'

She smiles. 'Exactly. I've been telling you for years that we were both born with a caul.'

I laugh. 'Remarkable! But coincidence.'

'If you say so.'

'This doesn't mean the oil is going to last, Sarah. Do you remember, years ago, when fortune hunters descended on the delta in search of alluvial diamonds? One or two found something in their pans and then suddenly it was all over and the whole bunch cleared off to the north again.'

'Exactly.'

'Seamus had better be careful. He could lose everything.'

'There's another reason,' she says softly. 'He's telling himself that he has to get rid of Fata Morgana for commercial reasons. But I think what he wants is to free himself from his memories. The older Seamus gets, the more intense becomes the reality of his father's suicide. He thinks he will slip it off his shoulders like an old jacket that you dispose of. It's craziness.'

We sit watching a brightly lit boat sailing by, its lights reflecting in the black water.

'I am constantly surprised by how beautiful it is here,' she says. 'Even after all these years.'

'Yes, I am lucky to be able to live here.'

'Do you still remember, Seer,' she says a little while later, and her voice takes on an almost childish tone, 'how we used to sit here with Mom and Dad watching the fireflies? How they used to swarm up out of the garden and turn in front of us and then fly out over the water?'

My eyes grow misty. Then: 'That was a very long time ago,' I reply.

'Do they still come?'

'Occasionally, in summer. But less and less nowadays. They're supposed to be very sensitive to pollution.'

'That's a pity. But do you still sit and watch them?'

'Yes, I still watch. Then I remember the smell of Mom and Dad. Dad smelt of pipe tobacco and faintly of sweat. It's a strange smell. Last year for the first time I smelt that same smell on my own body. I think a man begins to smell that way once he's past forty. It's an odd smell,' I say absent-mindedly.

'And Mom smelt of frangipani. When the fireflies came she always went and picked a frangipani blossom for her hair.'

'I think they were very fond of each other,' I murmur. 'Caruso, on the old record-player.'

'And Callas. The dark veranda; in each other's arms.'

All at once I get up. 'What they had, neither you nor I will ever have. The country has disintegrated around us. The endless droughts have made us narrow-minded and grasping. My whole life is a struggle against my one basic instinct, and that is to withdraw into this old house and never to go out again. But I have to go out, otherwise ...'

'Seer ...'

'Then I think of them ... about Mom and Dad ... about what they had here, and I realise it could be sufficient for me to relive their lives again through my memories. That's enough for me ...'

'Seer ...'

I turn my back on her. Without looking at her I say: 'Seamus isn't the only reason for your coming here tonight.'

She gives an uncomfortable little cough. 'No, it isn't, Seer.'

'Well?'

'I peeped out just now, when I heard your car stop. That woman in the minibus ...?'

'It was Ayanda Thandani.'

'She's a client of yours?' It is a statement, not a question.

I hesitate. 'Yes, she is.'

She gets up and joins me at the railing. We look out into the night. 'I came to warn you.'

'Oh?' I ask in surprise. I look at her, but cannot make out her expression in the dark.

'And just then she arrived here.'

'What is it, Sarah?'

'Do you know who that minibus belongs to?'

'No?'

She turns towards me. 'Zola Mtuze. The Thandani woman was once married to him. Her mother is one of the ringleaders agitating for a single municipality.'

'Yes?'

'He's a taxi owner. Seer, the last lawyer to act for one of the families in the taxi war ended up a corpse in the boot of his own burnt-out car. Keep out of the taxi war.'

I sigh. 'Is that one of Seamus's stories?' She says nothing. 'I'm asking you again, Sarah, is this another tale from the city council?'

She clears her throat uncomfortably again. 'The taxi war and Mandrax smuggling are so intertwined, Seer.'

'Why not throw in the liberation struggle, too, just for good measure ...' I snap.

'Seer ...'

But I continue angrily: 'Seamus only considers it unhealthy when I, his brother-in-law, act for interests in the township. He reckons it might damage his good name in the city council. And in any case, how did he come to hear that I was acting on behalf of Ayanda Thandani?'

'Seer, you are always so quick to distrust Seamus.'

I turn to her. 'Sarah, the Thandanis are my clients. They approached me on a perfectly legitimate matter. What it is is confidential. But I am their attorney and I shall act on their behalf. And fight to the death for their rights.'

'Seer, the Thandanis are a well-known family. That old MaNdlovu has been causing trouble for years with that Civic of hers. Seamus says ...'

'You go and tell Seamus, instead, that I derive a thousand times more satisfaction acting for the people of Joza than for the fat-cats from swanky suburbia.'

'Oh, Seer. Now you're cross with Seamus. Don't you two have a difficult enough time just getting on with each other?'

'It's typical of the English, Sarah. They talk liberal, but if you step too far over their colonial fences, then they're quite as bad as Afrikaners any day.'

'Now you are really being unfair, Seer.'

'Oh, tripe! Tripe, Sarah! Seamus had better not come near me with any of his holier-than-thou liberalism again.'

'Let's just stop it.'

I take a deep breath. 'I'm sorry.'

She puts her arm through mine. 'Just be careful, Seer. You're my brother, you know.'

'Save your concern for Seamus.'

'Stop it now, Seer.'

'Right. I'm sorry about my outburst.'

'Let's go and make coffee.'

'Coffee? Yes, sure.'

'And then I must go. Kudus are leaping in front of every possible car these nights.'

Once we have had our coffee, I accompany her to her car. She looks so small and alone in the great big Mercedes when she says goodbye. As I watch her driving out of my tale now, I wish I could call out to her, ask her to stay a little longer. I am even tempted to walk over to the figure standing there such a long time in the empty street as though lost in thought, or perhaps afraid to go back into the empty house. I could warn him about what is going to happen to him.

But he is not actually me. Not yet. And I may not.

10

Leaving me in front of my ramshackle old house, Ayanda drives off to the hospital in Zola's minibus.

She is in a sentimental mood – about remembered loves: those whose hands have left their traces on your face and whose words still waver in your ears, half-forgotten, whispered somewhere (where could it have been?), whose mouths you still taste – all the beautiful young men of Joza who have disappeared in teargas and longing. Young men so much less complex than her brother Mpho who is now in the bush-lodge to be circumcised.

We're wavering, Ayanda thinks, between past and present, between the old and the new. When Mpho let slip at home that he would prefer to be circumcised in the clinic because he had heard that a man could pick up Aids when the incibi's assegai slid so swiftly from man to man, MaNdlovu put her foot down.

'Now you are ditching every tradition we have!'

That was not a day the Thandanis will forget in a hurry. Ayanda wanted to support Mpho: there were indeed many dangers attached to bush circumcisions, especially since the incibis nowadays were no longer as scrupulous in their observance of the careful customs of old.

At the same time, she could understand MaNdlovu's fear that customs once allowed to slip away might never again be retrieved.

Mpho sat on the stoep with his back against the wall. He was waiting for the neighbours' daughter to pass by, her legs rubbed shiny with Vaseline, in that immorally short school gym of hers.

He was also waiting for TaImbongi to go off to the shebeen so that he could pinch a little tobacco from the old man's bedside cabinet. That was where TaImbongi kept his pipe tobacco, beside the old copy of the Freedom Charter, once clipped from a newspaper and now brittle from all the folding and unfolding.

That was also where TaImbongi kept his old dompas, even though the pass laws had been rescinded and despite MaNdlovu's threats on account of the painful memories evoked by that document.

In the house she and MaNdlovu sat talking, while TaImbongi listened, as he usually did, though he pretended his thoughts were elsewhere.

'Mpho has gone wild,' MaNdlovu said. 'Ever since Ncincilili went up to the Mint, Mpho has got out of hand. He lies in wait up there in the hollow for every schoolgirl in town, and when they come by with their loads of wood, he slavers like a hyena. Who does he think he is? King of the Swazis, or what? And I'm tired of hearing about the way he hangs around the doorways of the shebeens. Every empty that flies out the door he grabs and sucks out the last few drops as though it was his mama's tit.' MaNdlovu sighed heavily, knowing that Mpho out on the stoep would hear her. 'What is going to become of Mpho? Another hopeless Thandani male?'

Ayanda tried to argue. 'But Mama, hardly a day goes by at the hospital that we don't see young men who have picked up trouble as a result of the bush-lodges. More and more men are going to clinics nowadays. It's much quicker and it's also more hygienic ...'

Mpho had come in from outside and was leaning against the doorjamb. 'What?' exclaimed MaNdlovu and grabbed for her walking stick. It was bright day outside, but the television was on so that MaNdlovu could sit and look at the test pattern. 'It keeps my eyes clear,' she would say. 'In this family of bullshitters there's got to be someone who's clearsighted.'

The varicose veins in MaNdlovu's calves trembled as she struggled to rise. She glanced at the television and commanded: 'Switch off that rainbow rubbish.' TaImbongi, who had been sitting silently at the dining room table behind Ayanda and MaNdlovu, reached for his hat.

'No, TaImbongi, you sit down.' MaNdlovu's shadow against the wall wobbled slightly. Without her headscarf her hair was a wild bush.

'Ayanda, go and call Mpho in.'

Ayanda waited for Mpho, standing at the door, to answer for himself. 'I'm here, Mama.'

MaNdlovu turned to look at Mpho. 'You're going to have yourself cut properly.'

Ayanda sighs. It is difficult guiding the minibus through the heavy traffic, particularly near the city centre. That day Mpho felt the weight of MaNdlovu's foot on his stomach: when the old elephant cow put her foot down, people always said, she squashed your insides out.

In the old days it had been a tradition that a man with an assegai would stand behind the incibi-surgeon as the young men lined up to be circumcised. If the incibi made a slip, the man wielding the assegai would spear him. That showed the importance attached to the surgery.

But times have changed. Any old Tom, Dick or Harry is hired, and the hospital often sees cases where it is quite clear that a dirty assegai has been used.

With Mpho in the doorway and TaImbongi with his hand on his hat, Ayanda tried again.

'There's the danger of Aids, Mama, the silent disease. It can be transmitted by blood on the assegai if they cut one man soon after the last.'

'Silent disease my arse!' thundered MaNdlovu. She glared at Mpho again with her myopic eyes. 'You'll pick up all the silent disease you want from the loose women at that shebeen where you and your dad hang around at night. Your dad has been having his ragtime down there at the harbour all his life. He thinks I don't know about it.'

MaNdlovu turned round and pointed her stick at TaImbongi. 'It's been going on for years. Every month when I was on the rag in my redtime, you would clear off down to the harbour with your cronies and go flirting with all the harbour whores and listening to jazz with the sailors and egging one another on to sin, telling each other: We've got the right because our wives can't receive us tonight anyway. They're on the rag; it's ragtime. Do you think this is New Orleans or what? This is the Kei, this is ...

'This is the Struggle Kei and it's no place for cheating or coming unstuck. It's a place which demands that we stand together and observe our traditions. Otherwise we'll all fall apart, the lot of us.'

TaImbongi gave his nervous little cough and stood up. He did not wish to hear any more. Ayanda tried to argue: 'Mama ...'

But MaNdlovu took no notice of the fact that TaImbongi had stood up. 'I shall send a message for them to get an incibi from Addo or the Bay. They say that one from Addo cuts very well. It's elephant country, that. They still know about traditions there. Yes, he's the man we must get to come.'

MaNdlovu wiped her face with her white handkerchief. 'No, by heaven, it's time we had a man in this house. We've been without a man for long enough. Ever since Ncincilili went up to the Mint ...'

'Mama ...' Ayanda wanted to grab her father by the arm and her mother, too. She wanted to force them together, make them both sit down.

But TaImbongi took his hat and before he was out the door it was already on his head. MaNdlovu sat down again. She was finished with the men. She had hung her walking stick over the back of the Morris chair and tears were coursing down her cheeks.

'It's a terrible trial keeping you all together, my wild children ... a terrible trial ... my wild old man ... this mess of a country ...'

Ayanda and Mpho kept still, because MaNdlovu did not like people touching her while she was weeping. She was someone who wept a great deal, and was proud of it. The snow white men's handkerchief went to bed with her at night, too. That was where, she said, she wept her great weepings.

Ayanda stops at a stop street. Even in her weeping MaNdlovu was strong – stronger than the cousins and uncles and brothers and TaImbongi. She explained the men's suffering to them and then wept it so thoroughly clean that grown men hung their heads in shame in the face of such candour.

Ayanda sighs. Here in the tourist part of the city there is a remarkable increase in the number of cars and pedestrians tonight. The restaurant terraces are crowded. Everywhere newspaper sellers are touting the local paper emblazoned with the front-page news of the oil strike.

The old customs would have it that a particularly naughty or rebellious youngster should be driven out into the bush by the women because only there would he find peace and dignity.

When Mpho's time came, MaNdlovu struggled up the dusty street, waddling along with her stick. She was determined that her younger son would take the place of her eldest, Ncincilili, that he would also have to fill the place which TaImbongi, the folk artist, had never filled.

'Hamba! Hamba!' MaNdlovu screamed. 'Go! Go!' She stamped her feet in the dust and rocked her body back and forth. In her rhythm and movement she was a young woman again. 'Hamba! Hamba!' she drove Mpho to the street corner. 'Hamba! Hamba!' at the start of the footpath, and right up the hill.

The bystanders stood watching in respectful silence because they knew of MaNdlovu and TaImbongi's difficulties, and of the sadness of MaNdlovu's visits to the Mint when her longing for her dead Ncincilili became too much for her.

They knew that the prison authorities had never sent MaNdlovu a body to mourn over – only a grave number marking a nameless mound of soil in the state cemetery.

Ayanda sighs and bites her nails as she waits in a traffic jam. Cars with foreign registration numbers and tired travellers are damming up, the drivers evidently have no idea where to go. Even on sidewalks there are cars parked.

Ayanda doesn't even want to look at Cathedral Square. She knows instinctively that something is happening for which there is no cure. Instead of being glad because of the oil, everyone is afraid.

Yes, these days we all know instinctively: the city will never be able to withstand this influx; the political tensions which have been mounting for months as a result of Joza inhabitants' demand for a unified municipality – with the Civic in the van – will only become sharper now that the rich municipal business district, traditionally a white preserve, has the addition of the oil gusher to fill its coffers from.

So Ayanda is also aware of the many realities of the country. You can drive through the rich tourist district here, with holidaymakers in gaudy shirts wandering about between aquariums and merry-go-rounds, and think that you are somewhere in Europe.

And then there was that day in Joza which changed the lives of the Thandanis for ever, the day when the difficulties with Ncincilili began.

That was a day none of them will ever be able to forget, the day when the constable's burning head exploded and his boiling brains burst out and spread across the road together with the molten rubber of the tyre. When the crackling flames began to lick up the oil of the brains the bystanders held their hands over their noses.

She, too, veteran of so many anatomy classes and post mortems, had had no idea that the head of a living person could stink as much as that when it burst open in fire.

The township taxis never use that part of the street as a loading zone any more. The police washed away the pieces of rubber and charred bones with fire hoses, but they were not able to get the pattern of the man's body out of the tarmac.

The fire-shadow with its crooked arms, twisted legs and head is still visible there.

After the necklace murder the stench of the exploded head hung over the township for the whole afternoon. When it grew dark army patrols came in and shot flares over Joza. People shut their windows and drew their curtains against the reek.

'It's the policeman's treachery that stinks like that,' said the Comrades, and that night they, the young lions, paraded through the streets of Joza. 'It's his impimpi-tokkeloshe soul that smells so bad. It's his own fault for wanting to wear the Boere uniform!'

The people of Joza got out of their way, because in those days you never knew who was a Comrade and who was a tsotsi. And the Third Force intervened as well, bribing tsotsis to pretend they were Comrades and get up to all sorts of things in order to discredit the Movement.

It was a muddled mess of a time. You never knew whether your neighbour was denouncing you to the Security Branch; you didn't know who belonged to which organisation ...

'It's our people's blood on his hands that stinks so,' said the Comrades about the impimpi constable. The stench was so bad that people had to call their dogs into their yards – the animals were going mad because of the strange smell.

Behind closed doors people prayed that the Comrades would not start a march to burn down houses, and that the Casspirs would not come to kick in doors or overturn furniture in search of weapons.

You could taste the stench of the man's burning right down into your throat; his terror; his writhing.

As the people stood watching with their shopping bags full of bread and samp and soup bones and Sunlight soap, the man's bladder broke. The Comrades were wrestling with him to force the tyre round his neck and to pour petrol over his head. Then his stomach started working and someone in the crowd yelled: 'He's trying to piss out the fire!'

The flames leapt up all over his body and he began to crawl round and round in frantic circles with wet streaks running down his buttocks. He sat bolt upright, rocking back and forth, till he toppled over, and eventually all that was left were bits of charred flesh.

Ayanda is trembling so violently that she has to pull the minibus off the road. She stops opposite a hotel and drops her head into her hands. She is shaking uncontrollably. May God forgive me for just standing there, me, the healer, who has taken the oath of service and selfless duty, that I should have stood there mutely watching, petrified, in a state of total fright.

May God forgive me for not going forward to prevent it, in the name of compassion and healing.

What is happening to us in this country? Why have we been caught up by forces too powerful for us? That first overwhelm us and then leave us confused and lost?

She breathes in deeply and leans back with her head against the seat. Fortunately she has not stopped near a street light. No one will see the shining tears on her face.

I have betrayed medicine; and if I had acted, then Ncincilili would still be with us today. But I remember the fear; it was a flaming necklace round my throat; round the neck of everyone who stood watching.

But more round mine, because there was Ncincilili, in the background but still involved: a Comrade. It was his peers who had grabbed the policeman and he, Ncincilili, had not dared to run away.

That's what the times were like.

And afterwards there were MaNdlovu's questions: 'Why didn't you stop Ncincilili, Ayanda? Why didn't you protect your brother? Why didn't you stand up and say: Yes, we are the Thandanis of Joza, this young man and I, and we are furious, we are mad with rage about apartheid and the oppression of our people, but God knows, we wouldn't roast a poor man and make his death a spectacle in front of our wives and children. Where were you, Ayanda?'

And in court the questions did not stop either. Was Ncincilili the one who threw the stones or was he the one who had jerked the constable around by his collar right at the start? Or had he emptied the petrol can over the man's head? Was he the one who had taken out the dagga zol and first pretended to give it to the constable to smoke, but then shoved it into his pocket and shot the burning match at the petrol-soaked man?

Was he the one who picked up the limestone boulder and dropped it on the defecating man's chest so that you could hear his ribcage crack? Or was he the one who had rolled the tyre nearer? Was he the one who had merely stood at the edge shouting 'Impimpi! Impimpi!'? Or was he only involved at the start and when he saw which way things were developing, did he move right to the back?

Because there was no escape from a necklacing. You had to watch, otherwise you had to face the Comrades and be asked what was the matter with you. Whose side were you on then?

All this, Ayanda recalls in the midst of the hooting traffic, was what the judge had to decide on.

He was a strict man and acting on the legal tenet of common purpose he sentenced Ncincilili to the gallows, despite Ayanda's evidence that he had only jerked the constable around at the very beginning and had then disappeared into the back of the crowd.

And now, according to MaNdlovu, he is working in the Mint. And his name has eventually come true, because 'ncincilili' – I disappear – is the word with which the Kei's imbongis conclude their praise songs.

'I'll disappear,' murmurs Ayanda, and looks unseeingly at the cheerful chatting groups entering or leaving the hotel. How can one ever measure complicity?

She smiles wryly. But I can't disappear, she thinks. I have to be present.

TaImbongi will never stop his tricks. Mpho is not made of Ncincilili's stuff. And MaNdlovu – she wants to see strength around her, energy, work, industry. Soft as her heart is towards the poor, she can be as hard as flint if those nearest to her do not measure up to her expectations.

And the only one who can even remotely satisfy MaNdlovu is herself, Ayanda.

She turns on the ignition and weaves into the stream of traffic: I who betrayed everything that day the constable was executed.

I who broke my oath.

11

It is only a year or two since black people have been allowed to use the front entrance to the hospital. And even now, as though the news had never reached them or merely because old habits die hard, most of Joza's inhabitants still go round to the back, to sit there patiently waiting for the overworked doctors to help them. Or perhaps, being poor, they simply feel more at home there, pushed aside but together.

But tonight the three Thandani women – Ayanda, her daughter Amanda and MaNdlovu – walk in through the main entrance.

'I can already hear what they are going to say in the council chamber of the city hall,' pants MaNdlovu. 'They're already saying it was that drilling company that discovered the oil.'

She extends her elbows so they can help her up the stairs. 'Canaan, if you don't mind – Canaan Drillers. Another bunch of Boers who think they're the children of Israel. Oh, give me a hand up this last step, my children. Think they're in the promised land. Still don't realise we're living in this mess of a Kei.'

At the head of the stairs MaNdlovu wants to stop and catch her breath. Ayanda closes her eyes tight for the sake of patience. If Mama will only stop talking for a minute, she won't get winded so quickly. We're always being told how much TaImbongi talks, but MaNdlovu!

'And just like they twisted our whole history to suit their pockets, now they're lying Zola Mtuze clear out of his discovery of the oil well.'

They are standing on the hospital veranda while MaNdlovu catches her breath.

Over the city flares are arcing up into the sky, popping and flickering and bathing the buildings in a weird white light.

'Just look at those flares,' MaNdlovu continues. 'The year before last, night after night it was anti-aircraft searchlights left over from the Second World War. Then there were the police torches, and – as though that wasn't enough – we had to put up with the missionaries' talk about The Light. And we Xhosas had to live with all these lights in our eyes. We were dazzled, like springhares caught in a car's headlights.'

'Us, the denizens of darkest Africa,' Amanda adds sarcastically. Ayanda looks at her daughter. Every time I see you, she thinks, I am amazed that that old Dunlop Zola and I could have produced you. You're a love-child – one can tell by your strong, healthy body, your open face, your bright eyes. And you're well cared for, too: the delicate plaited twists clinging close to your head, the little round granny-glasses that give you such a scholarly air. Protect your body, my child, from the tsotsis of Joza and from those smooth-talking city slickers from the Bay ...

But her thoughts are interrupted by MaNdlovu's indicating that they can go on again. 'Yes, they're lying old Zola out of his rights. But Joza will remember: if Zola had not thrown a match into the borehole, there would never have been an explosion.' MaNdlovu sniffs. 'And now they want to light up the sky with their flares, as though we didn't know that light is just a kind of shadow in which you can commit all sorts of sins ...'

'Come now, Mama, come, don't upset yourself again.' Ayanda shakes her head vigorously at Amanda without MaNdlovu's noticing – if the girl goes on and on agreeing and affirming MaNdlovu will make herself dizzy with her own volubility. It is better, experience has taught Ayanda, to keep quiet and simply let MaNdlovu go her own way.

At the reception desk they find out which ward Zola is in. The nurse leans over to Ayanda and asks: 'Pardon my asking, doctor, but is he the taxi driver that planted the bomb on Cathedral Square?'

Before Ayanda can respond, MaNdlovu snorts: 'He hasn't got enough bomb in him to frighten a spider in a lavatory, my child.'

'Mother!' Angrily Ayanda turns her back on her mother. She looks crossly at the nurse. 'Is that the story they're telling now?'

The nurse is alarmed at Ayanda's aggressiveness. 'I ... I, doctor, I only heard that ...'

Ayanda shakes her finger at the girl. 'If you nurses gossiped less and did your work better, this hospital wouldn't be in the mess it's in now.'

Then she turns on MaNdlovu: 'And you should realise, Mama, that this is the place where I work. You can't just come in here and ... and ...' Angrily she gropes for words.

Amanda takes them by their elbows and steers them down the corridor. 'Come now, surely you two mamas have not forgotten how this town can gossip? It's all just talk ...'

'He wasn't actually hurt, Doctor Thandani,' the nurse calls after them, trying to cancel her transgression. 'Only his arm got burned.'

Thank God, thinks Ayanda.

'He's so thick-skinned, no fire will burn him,' growls MaNdlovu.

Ayanda takes a deep breath. What is the use? Ever since she and Zola have known each other, MaNdlovu has been difficult about the relationship.

They had hardly fallen in love before the warnings began. 'Ayanda, you mustn't take on that old Dunlop Zola just because you like the way he tickles you in the dark,' MaNdlovu said.

In those days Zola was still a fork-lift driver at the Dunlop factory in the harbour. He was full of stories about the Jazz Palace down beside the pier where, despite the Liquor Act which forbade the consumption of strong drink by whites and blacks together under the same roof, the police turned a blind eye after midnight if white people and black people wanted to listen to jazz, or – as Zola put it – 'just felt like some fast and loose tricks and never mind the Immorality Act.'

And even though she and Zola have long been divorced, he is still the first man she turns to when things start going wrong. First she takes off her bangles – she is, after all, a Thandani. Then she tells herself: You're a Thandani from Joza.

And then she sees to it that she gets to Zola as quickly as possible.

As they are walking down the corridor, MaNdlovu resumes with a vengeance: 'I swear they're going to send those Third Force balaclavas in here one of these days to take Zola out. Then we'll lose the genuine evidence about the discovery of oil on the ancestral lands of the Xhosas. My child, we'll have to get that lawyer-fellow of yours to have Zola put under armed guard in here.'

'Oh, come on, Mama. Now you really are letting your imagination run away with you.'

Ayanda looks at the dilapidated wheelchairs against the wall. The linoleum on the floors is worn through. The walls bear the marks of cripples who have shuffled along them down the years.

You don't notice things like that when you're on duty, she thinks. You're too busy. But just look at the place; money is tight ...

'Our history has gone to hell because nobody ever writes it down.' MaNdlovu has jerked her arm free of Ayanda's grip and taken Amanda's hand. 'That's why I'm always telling you, my child, you students are the young people who must set things to rights. This praise-singing of TaImbongi's is all very well, but it's only pretty noise. It doesn't turn any wheels. The wheels of history are only going to turn if we set that history to rights ...'

'You should tell that to TaImbongi, Granny,' grins Amanda. 'Then we'll certainly hear it.'

MaNdlovu is so carried away by her own thoughts that she stops short.

'Come on, you two.' Ayanda has to breathe deeply to keep a

rein on the impatience rising up inside her. For all she knows, MaNdlovu may have forgotten what they have come here for.

'Yes, Amanda, I did confront TaImbongi the other day. I told him: "You imbongis are just a bunch of clowns. You carry on like secretary birds that smell rain, but when your tongues have had their way with you and everyone has gone home again, you haven't even got a scrap of paper left to show for it."'

MaNdlovu halts again. She stops a passing nurse. 'Where are our records? Where is our history?'

Confused, the nurse stands still, greets Ayanda and says: 'Medical Records is shut at this time of night, Doctor Thandani ...'

'Oh for goodness' sake.' Ayanda rubs a hand over her eyes.

'Where is our history? Where are our libraries? Our archives? The stories of our people?'

Ayanda stands looking at her mother. It's true, she thinks. My mother is right. Here we are, three Thandani women, but only two of us have papers of our own. Amanda and I have certificates and diaries and documents, but MaNdlovu's got virtually nothing: no birth certificate, no record of her parents, nothing. There is nothing but TaImbongi's dompas and the Freedom Charter in the drawer of the bedside cabinet.

'The Afrikaners and the Settlers have put up buildings bigger than the Mint for themselves to keep their papers in. Anyone can go and scratch in them and find evidence of their great-grandfathers' or -mothers' existence. You get deeds of sale and purchase, you get baptism certificates, you get letters and diplomas and marriage contracts.' MaNdlovu sniffs. 'We've got nothing. Nothing, child – not even a little snapshot of my mama or my mine-captain papa. They're dust, and their sufferings are blown about the Kei on the whirlwind. Gone. Gone!'

MaNdlovu begins to sob. 'And now my old bugger's stuck in gaol, too. What could he have got up to?'

Amanda shakes her head. 'You're wrong, Granny,' she says. 'History doesn't just disappear when it isn't written down on paper.'

'There's nothing, my child.' MaNdlovu shakes her head. 'What do you know? When your life began, mine was already almost over. You don't know about that huge open space before your birth. I close my eyes, and I see nothing but wind and blood and dust and thorns.'

'Granny ...'

'I see people trampled on by the British, walked over by the Boers.'

'Mama ...' Ayanda takes MaNdlovu in her arms. Feel the flutter in her old heart, she thinks. She'll have a coronary yet. These violent currents of thinking will mean the end of her. I must try and persuade her to take a tranquilliser. But she always refuses. She'd rather struggle up the hill to the sangoma who will give her a tree-root to chew.

Amanda pulls them apart. 'You're wrong!' she says. 'MaNdlovu herself says that the paper history we learn at school is worthless. But here's history all round us. Granny with the Civic. That's history. Mama here as a doctor in the hospital. That's history. Daddy and the oil.' Her eyes are shining. 'It's all history. It's always with us. We're never without it. We are history!'

MaNdlovu takes a deep breath and looks up at the fluorescent tubes against the ceiling. 'Evaporated in the heat of the sun?' she asks. 'Trodden into forgetfulness by passing feet? In one ear while the imbongi declaims it, and out the other as soon as the imbongi goes off to get drunk with the rest of them? Lost in the lazy ears of our dumb people, destroyed by the greedy white people who always want everything, who just want to grab and grab. Oh Jesus, sweet Jesussss!'

Ayanda looks round. The nurse is still watching them. When the girl sees that Ayanda is looking at her, she swings round and hurries away. Ayanda seizes MaNdlovu and pushes her into one of the wheelchairs against the wall.

'Now sit down, Mama. Oh God, Mama, must your head always go on spinning?'

MaNdlovu sinks down onto the chair, sweating and panting for breath. 'Take the handles, child,' she orders firmly. 'Let's go and take a look at that old rubberface Zola. I hope the rascal's as well grilled as a Get Lucky Fried Chicken.'

They turn to the left. Ayanda pushes MaNdlovu into the ward in the wheelchair. There are rows and rows of beds. 'Just look for the whisky bottle on the bedside locker,' she pants. 'That's where you'll find the old rascal.'

'Hush, MaNdlovu!'

The hand he lifts to attract their attention is the one with the bandage on.

MaNdlovu struggles up out of the wheelchair. 'There the old Dunlop is ...'

Amanda, too, draws nearer, feeling as uncomfortable as she always does when expected to approach Zola.

'All the Thandani ladies!' says Zola. 'I am a lucky man!' He turns his head to look at MaNdlovu. 'And the great mama, too.'

'Zola, my boy,' says MaNdlovu, taking his bandaged hand gently in hers. 'No man deserves this. To be blown up like this, and now they want to write you out of history too.'

'What's that you're saying, MaNdlovu?' asks Zola, but Ayanda shakes her head to indicate to him: rather keep quiet.

'We Thandani women are fond of you, Zola,' says MaNdlovu. 'We honour you as a man with an enterprising spirit. You should never forget that.'

Ayanda also comes closer. She takes Zola's hand. There is no need to say anything.

'So where's your big mouth now, Zola?' she asks.

Before he can reply, MaNdlovu says: 'Snapped shut from the fright, I reckon. Is there anything for an old person to sit down on?' She looks round as Zola indicates to Ayanda with his unbandaged hand.

'What ...?' asks Ayanda.

She notices that MaNdlovu has sunk into a chair but is trying to get up again.

The old woman has stretched out one arm in front of her, the index finger trembling.

'Mama?'

It is Amanda who reacts first. 'Uncle Mpho!'

'Mpho!' MaNdlovu jerks aside the partly drawn curtain round Mpho's bed.

'Mpho ...' murmurs Ayanda, thinking: I forgot to bring MaNdlovu's blood-pressure tablets.

'MaNdlovu. Ayanda. Amanda.' Mpho sits up in bed, the sheet pulled up to his chin.

'But you're in the bush ...' Ayanda looks at Zola, then at Amanda.

MaNdlovu has now risen right out of the chair. She takes a deep breath. 'Is this you, Mpho? Are you the son of MaNdlovu and TaImbongi of Joza?'

'MaNdlovu ...' Mpho's voice cracks.

'Are you the brother of Ayanda and Ncincilili Thandani?'

Ayanda wants to stop her but feels paralysed.

'Are you the one who went to the bush to become a man?'

Now MaNdlovu begins to pant, rocking from side to side on her thick legs, her words following the rhythm of her body.

In the other beds men start laughing.

Ayanda looks at them, humiliated. The days on the playground at school are suddenly immediate – the children teasing: DeepVoice, DeepVoice, Kaizer's choice ...

'Are you the one I hamba'ed out of the house, along the street, through the ravine, past the thorn tree, up the road to the bush ...?'

'Mama ...' Ayanda takes MaNdlovu's arm. We don't need a spectacle here now, she thinks, not in the middle of the hospital. By tomorrow the stories will have spread down every corridor and ward. Why must the Thandanis and those close to them always make a spectacle of themselves?

Amanda pushes the wheelchair closer. Ayanda indicates that she must push it in from behind so that MaNdlovu will only need to fall backwards to find her seat.

'Are you the one the incibi ran towards, brandishing his assegai?'

'MaNdlovu ...'

'Are you the one our household slaughtered a fainting-goat for?'

At every sentence of MaNdlovu's the other patients laugh louder and louder. Two nurses appear in the doorway. Seeing Ayanda, they hesitate for a moment, but come in anyway, looking as though they know something is required of them but don't know what it is.

'Are you the one who was going to uphold our traditions?'

Ayanda could weep for the humiliated Mpho. Behind her she hears Zola pleading: 'Please, Mama. MaNdlovu, please ...'

MaNdlovu rips the curtain away from the bed altogether. The bar holding up the curtain clatters onto the floor. MaNdlovu jerks her arm free of Ayanda's grip and moves up to Mpho.

'Have you been cut? Are you a man?' She tugs at the sheet, but Mpho clutches it tight.

'MaNdlovu!' he pleads.

'Show me! Are you a man? Are you a man? Are you a man?' When MaNdlovu jerks the sheet again, it tears. The two nurses take hold of her and thrust her firmly into the wheelchair. While the men in the other beds whistle and shout 'MaNdlovu!', the nurses push her out through the swing-doors.

Ayanda looks at Mpho, weeping under the torn sheet.

She walks out, and notices one of the nurses giving MaNdlovu an injection in the corridor.

'Ncincilili ... Ncincilili ... bring me a banknote, a ten rand, a five rand, any one ...'

MaNdlovu faints, but she is too heavy for the grasping hands to be able to keep her in the wheelchair.

She slides down onto the floor.

12

Watching myself writing 2 March at the top of the first file I am getting ready early this morning, I can hardly believe that I'm meeting those last days so imperturbably.

Or perhaps I am simply confused. Because as I am sitting there writing, Leap Year's Day is not yet forty-eight hours past, yet it feels as though the oil has always been with us.

And that the oil should have chosen to arrive on that most eccentric of all the days on the calendar!

A little while later, and quite unexpectedly, Seamus marches into my waiting room. My brother-in-law, in his smart city council suit, fills the whole room with his presence. The other clients in the waiting room – the poor of Joza and those who have travelled far from outlying areas – shrink into their chairs.

The Mercedes is parked outside, on the yellow barrier-line in front of the office, its flanks covered in farm road dust. There is a dent in the bodywork where a half-brick apparently struck the car a while back when Seamus had gone into Joza to have discussions with the black town councillors about their 'One City, One Municipality' concept.

'Most welcome.' I would prefer my brother-in-law to wait his turn, but I think of Sarah. We shake hands and go through to my office.

We are about equally tall, but in the presence of Seamus I am always conscious of the fact that he, although older, is fitter and more spirited than I am. Beside Seamus's swift, powerful movements, I always feel, my body moves slowly and hesitantly.

Now, after the event, it is quite different, of course: the delight of mobility! To be able to move around my story so nimbly! Mind you, that's not completely true. I realise now, during this re-visit, that I am altogether too heavy hearted (melodramatic, even) to feel footloose ... As though my old body ...

We sit down. I make a half-hearted attempt to clear away the dirty ashtray, the collection of unwashed coffee cups, the pile of poetry books (how many clients will not wonder what Yeats and Eliot are doing in a lawyer's office?). I know that Seamus consults only the smart practice on which I turned my back and in any case Seamus is privileged enough to be a personal client of old Mr Prinsloo's, the senior partner with his silver hair, his bow-tie, his imported Mercedes Sport and his quicksilver tongue.

Seamus's father had been a client of Prinsloo's principal in the days when Prinsloo was still an articled clerk. Traditions die hard in the conservative English community of the city, so I am surprised when Seamus says: 'I've got a commission for you.'

Even during our very first meeting, the tension between Seamus and me hung heavy in the air – like cigar smoke from the cigars which we smoked as we sized each other up, while Sarah, young and flattered by the attentions of the young laird of Fata Morgana, was making tea in the kitchen of the dilapidated old house.

This rivalry for Sarah's love and attention was there from the beginning. Perhaps Seamus sensed instinctively, at the first meeting, the bond between the two children who had grown up together in the rickety old villa beside the river, isolated from the suburbs where their peers were playing.

In all the years I have known Seamus, there has been only one occasion when something like a unanimity of soul flickered up between us. It lasted no more than a couple of hours, but there was something of a relief in it, for both of us. And especially for Sarah.

Perhaps I can be more honest now than I could then. Perhaps Seamus and I had more points of correspondence than I was prepared to admit. On one side there was me – who never felt properly at home in any structure – the overweight old jurist who passed his time in his decrepit old house on the river bank, playing with his steam engines. Who felt that the world had rejected him with his eccentric combination of interests.

And then Seamus, with his resolute affirmation of his Britishness in the midst of post-colonial Africa with its corrupt governments, its despots with Swiss bank accounts, its civil wars, its Aids epidemic and famine. It was also a form of loneliness, of depression – an inability to discover his true identity here in Africa.

Our moment of identity occurred in the year the white meteor passed over us. It was on the evening when the whole district was ready to flee in terror because the river was flowing upwards. Yet it was this strange event that drew Seamus and me to hare through the mud like two schoolboys, to witness it.

I was visiting Seamus and Sarah on Fata Morgana. It was Sarah's birthday; Cawood was at boarding school at the private school in the city and could not be home that evening. He had to play the bugle when the school band performed on Cathedral Square at the wreath-laying ceremony in honour of the fallen.

Seamus and I were trying to make the evening as pleasant as possible. We were just tucking into the fall-goat liver hors d'oeuvre when we suddenly saw an intensely bright light outside. We ran out. The landscape was bathed in a fell, chill radiance, flickering at first, then in a frightful white brightness. We looked at one another, and at the pallid, sickly glow of our skin.

Sarah's chief cook also came running out, with a dishcloth over her arm. In contrast to the ashen sickliness of our skins, her black body gleamed in that strange light with the glow of ebony.

'It's a sign,' we heard her whisper, before she summarily dropped her dishcloth onto the potted geraniums on the stoep and ran off to the labourers' cottages, yelling 'National liberation!

National liberation!' Her shouts were smothered by the hissing of the meteor which tore across the estate from behind the manor house – a fiery ball with a furious head and a tail of sparks. In the valley, the fall-goats looked up and keeled over.

Suddenly the light was gone. Dumbfounded we went back into the house and Seamus immediately switched on the wireless to hear whether there might be a news flash. There was only a symphony concert. Shortly afterwards the telephone rang. It was Seamus's neighbour, Bill Heathcote. 'The river has turned, Sam!' Bill yelled into the phone – so loud that Sarah and I could hear it too. 'I've just seen one of the jetties from Third Leg floating up past me. People are evacuating the city!'

I could see the gleam in Seamus's eyes before he had even replaced the earpiece. I, too, began to tremble, and then I realised that the sparks of the meteor had ignited something deep within us, something which we shared but which I could not put my finger on.

That fire would go on burning in our hearts for weeks with the exciting conviction that – as I later scribbled on the back of one of my office files – 'the world might still turn a complete somersault'.

Nonplussed, Sarah was left standing on the stoep that night while Seamus and I leaped into the Mercedes and raced down to the water to witness the weird phenomenon of a river running the wrong way.

We listened to the current groaning over its own bed in its Herculean attempt to challenge the natural order. Seamus switched on the headlights of the Mercedes, and his hunting torch, too. We saw chattering monkeys clinging to floating tree stumps. A deep-sea trawler appeared, stately and grave, revolving slowly on the surface of the water like the hand of a giant clock.

The crew stood on the deck with arms upraised, their bonewhite faces turned in the direction where the meteor had vanished. When neon boards began drifting by, advertising agricultural implements, hairdressing salons, bookshops and cafés, we realised that the river was dragging whole sections of the harbour city inland. We watched mailboxes, lamp posts, drowned pets, street signs bearing the names of forgotten politicians from the apartheid era, all floating upstream.

Seamus commented: 'It's probably a sign that the old order is giving way. A new world is going to be born.'

Suddenly I remembered my house: my irreplaceable library of books! My postage stamps! My coin collection! My autograph signatures of the first founding father Jan van Riebeeck, the architect of apartheid Hendrik Verwoerd, the Portuguese explorer Bartholomew Diaz, and the cross made by the Zulu king Dingaan! My steam engines! My rose garden! The bonsai trees on my sun porch!

But before terror took complete hold of me, one of the farm labourers arrived bearing a message from the ever considerate Sarah. The old home was still standing – the force of the upthrusting water had made the water overflow at the bend on the opposite bank. The house had been spared, though many families on the opposite side had lost everything – and they were mainly out-of-work whites, unemployed since the large motor manufacturers had withdrawn from the city as part of the international sanctions campaign.

Seamus and I returned from the river bank that night like two brothers. It was as though something sublime had happened to us, a fresh baptism or a conversion experience.

Our shoes were thick with mud, our knees were covered with grazes and streaks of slime. While Sarah, still in a state of shock, served mugs of hot coffee, we couldn't wait to tell her our stories: of how an entire city, helplessly caught in the power of nature and with all the elements wrenched out of their normal patterns, had come drifting past our eyes.

The evening was spoilt when Seamus's fellow city councillor, the dean of the Science faculty at the university, telephoned to say that the scientists were agreed that the reversal in the river's flow was not in any way related to the passing of the comet overhead.

Rather, it was the fault of the Nationalist government which had carried out a nuclear test far out at sea. It was an acknowledged fact, the dean said, and the dean of Social Science had corroborated it, that the government was not yet aware that a new world order had come into being with the fall of the Berlin Wall and the crumbling of the USSR. It was still trying to play a part in the Cold War.

With a start I wake up out of my thoughts. Seamus is sitting opposite me, talking about his father's will. 'It's pathetic,' he says, 'that anyone should be able to rule from beyond the grave like this.'

'A will is the expression of the deceased's final wishes. That is why our courts show such respect for it,' I answer cautiously.

Seamus mentioned to me years ago that he was keen to sell the southern portion of Fata Morgana, the level section between the farmstead and the smallholdings on the outskirts of the city.

In the meantime Seamus's commercial interests in the city had developed to such an extent that he needed more and more capital to run them. Besides, he is so active in the city council, on the board of directors of various businesses and on the council of the university – not to mention the Freemasons and the divisional executive of the Democratic Party, on which he serves as an influential citizen – that he really does not have the time to attend to other farming activities besides his flourishing fall-goat stud.

Seamus is explaining why the oil is going to bring unheard of wealth to Port Cecil. 'Property prices in the city are going to shoot through the ceiling. One of these fine days you won't be able to buy a single plot of ground anywhere between First and Seventh Delta. You won't be able to turn your car in the high street. I need capital right now – I must invest in the city. It's almost too late already. We must have that piece of dead ground cut off straightaway.'

I observe that Seamus is looking slightly guilty. He turns his imposing profile on me and looks out of the window. 'It's a pity that I have to turn against my father's will, but I don't have any option.'

Ever cautious, I suggest: 'We could possibly petition the court. I don't want to discourage you, but I really must warn you that it will be extremely difficult.' I move the dirty coffee cups further in among the piles of papers. 'You don't need me to remind you,' I continue, not without deliberate intent, 'that the dead do not have the privilege of locus standi. Your late father cannot testify in court on his own behalf as to his precise reasons for specifying that you should inherit Fata Morgana on condition that you never subdivide it. That fidei commissum was his last wish.'

'But the court would surely take current economic realities into account?' asks Seamus, his voice a tone or so higher. I notice once again that hint of the spoilt brat, the rich man's son who can't get his own way – a headstrong self-indulgence which finds adult expression in Seamus's formidable powers of persuasion in the numerous organisations to which he belongs.

'The court must also take into account the wishes of the deceased. What would become of the dignity of our final dispositions if courts were simply to ignore the intentions of the testator and summarily set wills aside? It is for that reason that the Master of the Supreme Court is there as the institutional guardian of the last wishes of the deceased.'

'Crap,' says Seamus with the curt arrogance with which he customarily dismisses opposition he regards as unworthy.

'Testatory law,' I continue, 'is one of the few bridges between the living and the dead.'

'Seer.' Seamus gets up, irritated. 'Skip the philosophical claptrap and get my father's will set aside. You go and tell the Master of the Supreme Court: Seamus Butler says that will is null and void and of no consequence.' He turns to leave. At the door he tosses over his shoulder: 'It's high time I put my foot down and told my father to get stuffed.'

Before I can even heave myself up out of my chair to see Seamus out, he is gone, leaving me standing there behind my desk.

I look at my watch and sigh heavily. In an hour's time I will have to leave for Bisho, in pursuit of that TaImbongi. I see them sitting there in the waiting room with their helpless eyes.

Philosophical claptrap ... can you believe it?

'Next!'

13

Unseen, I am at Sarah's side as she stands on the stoep of Fata Morgana looking out over the landscape. Wisps of early morning mist are lying in the hollows as two herons, heavy wingbeats propelling their ungainly bodies, fly slowly along the course of a dried up spruit.

She folds her arms. The scene before her looks tranquil enough, but nature here is too temperamental, too intractable, for our European memories.

She is awaiting the arrival of the tourist bus. It looks odd, droning through the veld with its gleaming nose and large windows, the travel agent's logo painted on its sides. How will the scene strike the tourists, she wonders: the dirt road meandering away across the plain, the flocks of goats watching nervously, and in the distance a double-storeyed house where a woman with folded arms stands waiting?

What photographs will they be taking back with them to Europe and America, or Japan and Singapore? How will they explain the vagaries of Africa, the grim white tribe, the pathologically sick continent?

She shudders. If some enthusiastic tourist trains his video camera on me again today, I'll lose it – I'll scream, or run away. Or tell them the rules that apply here: the suddenness, the unpredictability, our impotence when it comes to trying to love.

And how we mould our hate according to nature's patterns: the jackal and the guinea fowl, the puffadder and the mouse, the spider and the butterfly.

Or shall I tell them how we idealise their civilisations: their plenty, their assurance, their self-sufficiency.

Or about my husband: patriarch, fall-goat breeder, neuropath, and occasional lunatic?

Fortunately Cawood has indicated that – in Seamus's absence – he will come round to help with the guided tour. Cawood is preparing to take a party of American big game hunters up the course of the Kei, to tour the game farms so that they can eventually return to their homes in triumph with their stuffed and mounted kudu and buffalo heads.

The glass eyes of those stuffed victims, thinks Sarah, they are the greatest indictment of all.

And the district scandal: that game farm at the headwaters of the Kei which, they say, buys up tired old lions from the unsuspecting Boswell Wilkie circus and keeps them in small camps for eager American tourists to shoot, at ten thousand dollars a head.

The game rangers feed up the male lions in advance and then make a great show of leading gullible Americans along a taxing detour through the bush.

When they spot one of the tame, friendly old males, they have to shoot quickly before the lion can come up and lick its master's hand. And yet, so the story runs, this trick fools one American after another. And everyone is happy: the game farmer who makes a handsome profit, and the American who goes home to show off his stuffed trophy and photographs of himself with his foot on the dead lion's shoulder, behind him the wide open spaces of Africa.

Only the SPCA and, of course, the environmentalists, are upset. And the circus people would be too, if they only knew.

For a while another rumour did the rounds, too: that on Cawood's farm the leopards are wearing radio-collars – to speed up the hunt.

And us? What do we care? Is there room for morality in this place? We are so weary and spoilt; so tatterdemalion and inbred. Our disgraces haunt us through the nights; our phantoms seize their guns and obliterate themselves; we wander about with our depressions and our terrors. And so we muddle on. What do we deserve? Oblivion?

Sarah and I; always the same questions.

Just as the bus drives in through the gates, Cawood arrives in his helicopter. Irritated, Sarah watches Cawood performing circles over the goat camps. She realises what he is doing: deliberately making the goats nervous so that when the time comes for him to address the tourists he can demonstrate with a single crack of his whip just how sensitive Caper timidus is.

The arrival of the helicopter is a bonus for the tourists. Tumbling out of the tour bus they kneel with their polaroids and video cameras to record the scene for their family albums back home.

Sarah turns her back and goes into the house. Behind her, she knows, Cawood in his khaki clothes and his big game hunter hat is climbing out of the chopper. His tanned legs and forearms are perfect photographic material – as is the contrast between the high-tech helicopter and the farm labourers in their overalls, the slaughter goats milling around uneasily in the slaughter camp, the farmyard dogs barking and urinating all round the chopper.

In the kitchen she sees to it that the game biltong sandwiches are ready for serving with the pineapple beer. Each tourist also receives a watch strap made of fall-goat skin, a porcupine quill or two, and an indigenous, highly polished semi-precious stone, all tied up in a little genet-skin bag from a muti-man.

They are also free to wander round the tourist rondavel to buy souvenirs: antelope horns, postcards of fall-goats and hadedas, pottery made by labourers' wives on Fata Morgana, reed mats woven in the Ciskei, tanned lynx skins, little glass bottles of elephant dung from Addo, dried samples of Addo's unique dung beetle which lives entirely on elephant droppings.

She goes outside again, after checking her make-up in the hall mirror. Cawood is already surrounded by cameras: he has to take off his hat, then put it back on again; he has to pose with his big game hunter's rifle across his shoulders, then with it in front of his chest.

Then one of the farm labourers has to come and crouch at his feet – the archetypal photograph, thinks Sarah with repugnance, of the colonial farmer with his kneeling serf.

She appears on the stoep, friendly and cheerful. She sees to it that the sandwiches are served and that every tourist tastes the pineapple beer. Those wanting more commercial potables are obliged, too. She answers questions about the stud, mystifying her hearers, hinting at things unknown – as Seamus often says, she is Fata Morgana's best salesperson.

She tells about the British Settlers and the Afrikaans Voortrekkers, the Xhosas and the Khoi, the small bands of San, and the Jews who had made fortunes out of ostrich feathers, particularly on the Parisian fashion market.

While being photographed under the stuffed kudu heads, she calmly strokes her dogs, all the while wanting to scream: My husband is going out of his mind because he cannot keep up the charade any longer; everything is collapsing; we are not even sure of our farm any more; the ANC is talking about nationalising private property; are we going to lose everything? And what will you find for your cameras to photograph then? Will it be the spectacle of poor whites living in hovels again, as it was decades ago?

She feels faint and dizzy and is glad when the attention shifts to Cawood and the agricultural extension officer giving a lecture on the fall-goat stud under the pepper tree beside the engine room. I am the victim and you are voyeurs: you, the well-meaning, privileged innocents from the First World; you, without sin or transgression; you, who will never understand nor forgive an isolated white tribe on a dying continent.

Am I asking for pardon? Watching Cawood playing to the audience, she feels helpless and weary there on the stoep. No, nothing will ever excuse our madness. I know the depth of our transgressions; I know the remorselessness of our selfishness. I would rather you did not come. Yes, that is what it is. Keep away. Disintegrate in your high civilisation. Just leave us alone – leave us finally to confront our selves.

Let us complete our penance on our own. Stop watching us. Our shame is too great. Our corruption too pervasive.

She wipes her sweaty forehead, sighs and gets up. She observes Cawood playing quite unconscionably on the gullibility of his hearers. My son. In a way, you have escaped. In a way, you have worked out a modus vivendi. You are not, in the final analysis, a member of the species Caper timidus.

Perhaps it is a compliment to me, your mother. Or perhaps it's a moral failure on my part. Perhaps I did not succeed in making you aware of the sins of your fathers. And your mothers. Or perhaps you just don't care. Perhaps you are the new, polished South African – the one who knows how to make a profit out of his conversion, out of his volte-face, out of his squeaky new conscience.

Cawood, don't become so guileless, so smooth. Keep the ability to look your past in the eye and say: this is what I have inherited; I am part of it; I am sorry; I shall arise with fresh intentions and try to be human.

Cawood ... keep your nerve. Keep your reason, in a country which has lost its reason; where blood is cheap; where life is small change and the economists of power are minting a different rate of exchange.

Cawood, I love you; I wish you success and peace of mind. But I as an Afrikaner woman know that peace of mind will not dawn on this continent for your generation. Perhaps for your grandchildren; perhaps for them there will be freedom. But we, we are the scapegoats; the goats for sacrifice. And we have so much to sacrifice for; and to sacrifice ...

She folds her arms as the agricultural extension officer starts telling the story of the Butler ancestor whose research into the life and death of the Addo dung beetle eventually bored him so thoroughly that he started experimenting with the genetics of angora and boer goats.

There was something in the air, said the extension officer, which made breeding in those days a risky undertaking. Everyone involved in stud farming – whether it was merinos or hunting dogs or angoras – could sense that there were strange forces stirring.

And that was the time when grandfather Butler bred his first fall-goat ram – Caper timidus primus – even though it happened by accident. Being so extraordinarily nervous, the little kid was regarded as a sickly hybrid between a boer goat ram and a pedigreed angora ewe which had accidentally ended up together in the same camp. But eventually the little ram had grown to reveal a mind of his own, a pride and a sense of humour which earned him affection on Fata Morgana and characterised him as a freak of nature.

When he eventually mated with a hand-reared young boer goat ewe, nobody took any particular notice – except old Seamus Butler, who with the instinct of a stud farmer, the cunning of a British Settler and the scientific methodical way of his forefathers noted down every movement, every bleat, every breath of the new arrival.

When one day his notebook fell out of his hand and landed with a clap on the floor of the ram shed, the young kid looked at him, rolled its eyes and fainted.

Old Seamus Butler could not believe his eyes. Something in him realised straightaway what he was seeing – a freak of nature: a goat with a God given fear so deeply inbred that no one would ever be able to breed it out again ...

'Caper timidus!' he shouted aloud, Latinist that he was, and spent the next three days in the bars of Port Cecil getting drunk. He knew he had discovered the answer to the jackal plague, and he saw continents opening up before him – farmers from tens of countries pleading with him for aid against all the vermin in creation.

That, alas, is how the Butlers lost their way – in the blood of a hybrid species, on the dubious terrain of fear and vulnerability, they lost themselves irredeemably.

You Butlers, thinks Sarah as she listens to Cawood's speech under the pepper tree, have bartered away your strength. You forfeited all certainty when you decided to start a fall-goat stud for gain, for the sake of your own profit.

If this continent denies you – if Africa rejects you as being too timid and too thoughtful, too nervous, too lacking in force – you have only yourselves to blame.

You made your own choices.

God chose to look the other way.

And the worst is: you didn't even notice.

Worse still: you are now bartering your new-found repentance and intentions as though they are able to buy you a new right to subsistence here. As for me, I don't know. I doubt. I will admire you, despite everything within me, if you really can rise again. Your capacity for survival, your adaptability, are formidable. But I remain cynical. Until then, I reserve judgement. And I, an Afrikaner woman, suffer with you.

Because I am one of you.

Sarah sits down in Seamus's chair and watches the workers dragging along a couple of fall-goat rams by their horns. The tourists bunch together, cameras at the ready. The agricultural officer has his hands full keeping order.

Cawood walks across to the helicopter and comes back dramatically brandishing his stockwhip. It is an old whip which Fata Morgana's old jackal-catcher plaited for him when he was a boy.

Sarah gets up. It will always be a strange phenomenon. Cawood stops, facing a semicircle of tourists. Behind him the workers are holding the goats by their horns. Cawood looks into the cameras, lifts the whip, and the ten-metre length of plaited kudu thong flashes through the air, the bushbuck whiplash cracks and the fall-goats collapse.

May God forgive us, thinks Sarah, and flees indoors.

14

I buckle my safety belt.

We are driving in Zola Mtuze's minibus, still half wrecked from the explosion. My unreliable old Mercedes is not suitable for the open road. Ayanda's stolen car is still missing, and her father's bakkie, parked idly at home, is far too small for both Ayanda and the two heavyweights, MaNdlovu and me. And in any case, Ayanda said, TaImbongi is quite extraordinarily particular about his bakkie.

The kwela does still have four wheels, I console myself, even if it does not look like the safest means of transport on earth. The roof and windscreen are covered in sticky oil spray. The only view of the road is through the two halfmoons which the windscreen wipers have swept clean.

But Ayanda resolutely slides in behind the steering wheel. MaNdlovu, too, with the full weight of her convictions, groans into the back, wearing a broad-brimmed hat against the pitiless sun.

I sigh as the minibus, the wind howling through its shattered side windows, crosses the arched bridge over First Delta and starts up the hill past Joza.

I bend down and lift my briefcase onto my lap. I page through Thandani vs. The Minister of Law and Order, Ciskei. It is going to be a long day, with these two determined women in the windowless, oil-begrimed kwela. We will have to rely on grace, for the sun is already baking down and sweat is trickling down the small of our backs.

'Look at all those church spires,' MaNdlovu says as we reach the highest point and look out over the city. Because of her eye problems (cataracts? high blood-pressure? glaucoma? I have not yet been able to establish the cause), MaNdlovu cannot see that far. The city lives only in her mind's eye.

'I'm telling you,' MaNdlovu continues, 'that there aren't five converted souls for each of those spires.' Her hat begins to flap in the wind, so she holds onto the brim. 'The whites call themselves Christians, don't they? The missionaries had already come to convert our souls in my great-grandfather's day, but for their own pleasure they took yellow women and they prayed and bred and schemed the Church into growth, until they'd got hold of enough money and power to make our people cart the stones to build those forts which they call Houses of God.

'As though God had not set up house here in the dongas and ditches and plains of the Kei long before they arrived with their boats and wagons ...

'When that English governor Harry Smith made the Xhosas kiss his boots, we knew for sure: this lot knew nothing at all about the love of God which the missionaries preached. My mother used to say that our ancestors died with the taste of shoe leather on their lips. In the very moment of their death, that was the flavour they tasted.

'It started when the very first Captain Portuguese dropped anchor in the Mouth and made that slave woman that he'd captured in West Africa swim out to the Khoi on the beach. She couldn't speak the Khois' language. The poor woman hadn't any idea where in the world she was. But the cowardly Portuguese, who were too scared to come ashore themselves, wanted her to tell the people of the Kei about the power of the king of Portugal and she was to tell them they were seeking a route to Prester John's silver mines.

'Sometimes when I look out over the Mouth, I feel that woman's blood in my veins ...'

We have crossed the ridge at the top of the hill and are driving along the open plain. The minibus begins to gather speed, shuddering and complaining, but Ayanda Thandani clenches her teeth and crouches over the steering wheel as though trying to urge the vehicle on by the weight of her body. MaNdlovu has now placed her arms on the back of Ayanda's seat so that she will still be audible above the rushing of the wind. Glass splinters still sticking in the window frames blow loose and tinkle down into the back.

'And our people told the Boers,' MaNdlovu drones on, 'and we told the British garrison, too, we said: You bastards, you with your blunderbusses in one hand and your horse whips in the other and the Christian cross in your back pocket, and with that towed cannon of yours that blows our handsome warriors to bits ... We say to you: You graze here and we'll graze there. Keep your guns this side of the river and we'll keep our assegais that side. Let us live in peace.'

MaNdlovu leans forward with the result that her hat is now flapping between Ayanda and Seer.

'Take that thing off, Mama,' says Ayanda without taking her eyes off the road. 'You can always put it back on again when we get to Bisho.'

But MaNdlovu continues undeterred. 'You know how human greed works. This one wants to farm more smartly and on a grander scale than that one. That was when the Butlers of Fata Morgana – she's your sister, isn't she, Lawyer Wehmeyer? – also began to get big ideas.'

MaNdlovu sniffs. 'The fanciest of the ideas the Butlers got was the one that made them think they were good. Nobody lays claim to as much righteousness as the farmers of Manley Flats – or the Zuurveld, as we always used to call it. But we Xhosas were never bluffed by the Butlers' righteousness ... not to mention their missionaries and the liberals' Rule of Law. We just say: different fires, same smoke. Greed and big business. Paternalism – ag shame, see what noble savages ... that sort of thing. Show me a poor Butler and I'll tell you apartheid was a picnic.'

'Mama ...' Ayanda warns.

'No, child, if our lawyer's going to stand up in court for us, he's got to know our history. He's got to put our case. How can he defend us if he doesn't know what we're like?

'And you Afrikaners,' MaNdlovu says to me, 'are wickedness incarnate.' She waits for me to react, but I am staring out across the plains. 'It's a wickedness as obvious as those stones,' she continues.

MaNdlovu is now sweating so profusely she keeps holding the large white handkerchief to her face. I notice Ayanda keeping a concerned eye on her mother in the rear-view mirror.

'You should sit back and rest a little now, Mama,' she says. 'There's a long, hot road ahead still.'

'How are we ever going to build a nation?' asks MaNdlovu. She wipes her face and takes off her hat. 'There's only one thing binding us together, and do you know what that is? It's our rages and our jealousies. What use are our leaders' fancy-women to us? All they teach us are the latest fashions in headscarves which they pick up at conferences up there in North Africa. Just look at Ayanda today with that Christmas cake on her head! Why doesn't she wear her doctor's coat instead – then at least they'd let us through the road blocks.'

'Oh, come now, Mama!' Ayanda protests, laughing.

'And in any case those northerners are not our people,' MaNdlovu continues. 'We are southern people; our people don't go messing about beyond the equator.'

'Speaking about beyond the equator,' I say, 'there's oil for you! In Nigeria, for instance ...'

But MaNdlovu is not to be diverted. 'Perhaps what we ought to find is some craze that we could all share. If only all our hopes would meet in one spot, then we could become a real people.' She sighs. 'But on the other hand: what a crippled old people that would be. Imagine a whole nation rooted in greediness.'

I do not want to reply that I am too cynical to respond to words like 'nation building'. What hasn't the Afrikaner already done in the name of big words? How has history not been distorted to serve that idea! And see where it has landed us. Life, I would have told MaNdlovu if the wind was not competing so disturbingly with the words in my head, consists of those who have and those who have not. Beauty versus insignificance; those with a roof over their heads against those who wander; people with someone to love, as opposed to those without ...

But I let MaNdlovu have her say. Her idealism shames me. My weary cynicism! I, who had grown up in the midst of the Afrikaners' attempt to build a white volk, now watching them doing egg-dances as their ideology disintegrates – and this old woman, after a lifetime of suffering and struggle: on the brink of fresh possibilities.

And yet: what assurances are there that the expectations of a new black generation will not also lead to corruption? Africa is crawling with instances of it: the dictatorships in Uganda, the Congo, Liberia, wherever you care to look. The rulers had snatched up for themselves and their favourites and their extended families everything which the departing colonials had dropped, while the rest of the population were left in dire poverty.

How would MaNdlovu understand the excesses of twelve partners who pocketed over ten million rands annually? How well I remember the monthly partnership meetings of Prinsloo and Meyer.

First the fee-book lists were compared. Each attorney had a green fee book at his elbow in which every telephone call, every incoming letter, legal paper or document, each brief drafted, had to be recorded according to the prescribed fee.

At the end of the day the secretaries came and sorted all these fees into the relevant files, and at the end of the month each attorney's total fees were calculated. The yield per partner was then laid before the partnership meeting.

And after each partner's earnings had been held up to the meeting, and those lagging behind had been raked over the coals and those who had most efficiently milked their clients had been praised, there followed the discussion of how to split or invest the profit.

As a young attorney who spent the last days of each month scared that my fees would not be up to scratch, I milked my files for every conceivable fee that could still be levied: here I would send a not really necessary letter, but one that would at least bring in a few rands; there I would claim to have had to read a particular document, or that I had had to research certain court reports; or I would hurriedly telephone someone on the file, to bring in a further rand or three ...

And the partners' interminable conversations about the profits. Should they buy each partner a time-share on the sub-tropical north coast? Or did the partners already own enough of them in game reserves and holiday resorts along the coast?

Should they throw another party on the river boat and take their guests up the main stream, under the arches of the delta bridges and past the fishermen's quarter? Later the hovels of Sun City would also glide by, and bushes would start to fringe the river banks. Then the trees would grow denser and the sides would narrow in, making the channel dark and icy, where monkeys chattered in the undergrowth along the edges and waterfowl sheared low across the surface of the river.

The guests would be the city's merchant princes, the vice-chancellor and the registrar of the university and their senior buying officer, the headmasters of the city's private schools, the commander from the military base, some advocates and a couple of judges who, despite the danger of compromising themselves, had nevertheless yielded to temptation at the prospect of such pleasure.

Far upstream, where the riverine bush grew sparser and they could see the land stretching away on either side in the twilight, the captain would switch on the strings of little coloured lights all round the boat and up the masts, and the boat would be transformed into a twinkling nightclub on a silent silver river lost in a deserted landscape: a boat floating on its own glittering mirror image.

How would I explain to MaNdlovu the delight of an exclusive boat trip like this: the luxury of a river and a stretch of landscape possessed only by those on board at that moment, to the exclusion of ordinary people – or plebeians, as the classically trained jurists would remark as they sailed past the fishermen's quarter and the slum areas; the exclusivity of a party of merrymakers in a silent landscape?

How should I, as a privileged member of the property owning class, speak to this woman about nation building? Suppose she was to ask me to throw open my home and share it with four families from the squatter camp – I, the bachelor living in a dilapidated old villa with five bedrooms, two bathrooms, a living room, a family room, a lounge, a study ... Would they understand if I were to try to explain what privacy was? That I lived in each of these rooms with a different facet of my being? That I couldn't exist without a variety of spaces in which I could be completely and utterly private?

And my garden? That rose garden which doesn't bring in a cent and whose roses serve only to accompany greeting cards to lonely folk in the city on birthdays or festivals? How would the sweet aesthetics of my rose growing measure up to the possibilities of a vegetable patch which could be planted in its place so that water could be pumped up out of the river at night against municipal regulations by a clandestine pump?

How could I explain that I would not be able to endure a house full of people, chattering children, the smells of other people's food cooking and their body odours, the continual assault of voices, echoes, feet moving, toilets being flushed, the awareness of so many bodies close to mine?

Would MaNdlovu understand this vulgar insistence on privacy and space, which is part of the privileged class's genetic make-up?

Ayanda slows down and pulls off the road. I am so deep in thought, I get out and listen to the silence. MaNdlovu remains sitting in the minibus. Ayanda comes and stands beside me, indicating in a whisper that she can see that MaNdlovu is overwrought and that all her ceaseless talking is building up to a fainting fit. We should just leave her alone for a minute or two, to allow her to calm down.

We are standing on a hilltop with the hard-baked landscape stretching out below us. In the distance a river bed meanders away in the dusty haze. On either side dongas have eaten gullies down the hillsides, the dongas widening out as they approach the watercourse. I point, so that Ayanda can see them too: if you look carefully there is a vast swarm of locusts drifting over. Like a gigantic dust cloud the swarm moves over the plain, and behind the flying locusts lies nothing but bare veld, eaten clean by the insects.

I imagine that I can hear the rustle of the swarm, their frenetic munching mandibles, their scrabbling feet, the shirr of their wings. Their primal hunger.

'Listen,' I say to Ayanda. It feels as though we are the only people alive. In the kwela MaNdlovu has lain her head sideways across the back of the seat and is dozing with her hat over her eyes.

'There are millions of them,' Ayanda whispers. 'You can hear their hunger all the way to here.' So I have not been deceiving myself. For a moment – was the wind turning? – the rustle is deafening. But then it disappears again and we smell the sun-baked stones under our feet, the scattered, parched grass, the smell of our own bodies steaming in the heat.

The silence all round us and the sense of being dependent on each other make me feel uncomfortable.

We turn away from the scene as the swarm blots out the sun, forming a huge shadow which gradually moves across to the farthest range of hills. The shadow climbs like a thing with a will of its own and then, suddenly, it is gone.

We climb back into the kwela and, without waking MaNdlovu, drive on.

Eventually the road runs through an area where the locusts have stripped the veld so bare that the red-brown earth itself is exposed. A strange insect smell hangs in the air.

Ayanda shudders. 'The Kei knows no mercy,' she says softly. I nod, thinking of the poor in my waiting room, of their hands taking worn documents from bags, opening them and fearfully and carefully moving them across the surface of my desk. I can see their desperate eyes before me: the terror because of lost identity books, births never registered or unknown dates of birth, their unrecorded years lying in tatters. And bulldozers wanting to flatten their shacks, clinics wanting to send their children away for incomprehensible operations, social workers wanting to split up their families ...

I nod again. 'Yes,' I say.

'The people are all in tatters,' says Ayanda, as though reading my thoughts. 'The struggle against apartheid has eaten holes into our community. In the worst times you couldn't tell who was friend or foe. You would find that your uncle was an impimpi and your brother a Comrade, and the two would be living under the same roof. The father was a policeman and the son would be picked up and tortured by the security police.

'We would lie awake at night under the blankets with all the lights out and listen to what was going on outside. First the soldiers' boots on the gravel and their rifle butts thudding against the doors. Afterwards, once the Casspirs had driven off, tsotsis would come, calling themselves Comrades but having nothing to do with the Struggle, and they would burn down and rape and grab whatever they could lay their hands on. Then came the young lions, the Comrades, and they would clean up what had been defiled ...

'But the worst was not the tsotsis who stole our goods. It wasn't about furniture or clothing or whatever. The worst theft was the robbing us of our dignity, our sense of family, of belonging together and caring for one another. That was what was taken away from us in the days of the Struggle. That's why we call it the

Struggle and that is why you white people will never understand the word. I know you've had enough of the word, because for you it is only a slogan. But we know the meaning of that word.'

I give a slight cough, not knowing how to respond. The landscape round us is growing even more inhospitable. Dust-laden winds hang over the plains. Around clusters of huts the earth is grazed bare, while beside the huts and their lopsided hen-coops children with swollen bellies stand waving to us.

'This is apartheid's rubbish dump, this Ciskei,' says Ayanda. 'They were removed from the white areas in their thousands and dumped here on the bare earth to live as best they could. Look at those kwashiorkor children.'

'Yes,' I reply, 'there doesn't seem to be any industry or factory in sight.'

She shakes her head. 'And if we do manage to get an industry going, things don't improve.' She sighs. 'Look at the taxi war. There are the different groups and each of them is split into splinter groups. Then there are the pirate taxis trying to break into the established routes. The shootings at the taxi ranks are an almost daily occurrence. Poor old Zola, he ...'

'That is who exactly?' I shift about on my seat. Sweat is making my trousers stick to my legs.

'Oh, I'm sorry, don't you know him? Zola Mtuze. He was my husband.'

'No, I know the name ...'

Embarrassed, Ayanda looks out of the window, rubbing her hand across her cheek.

'Yes, you would have heard it from your clients. He's the man who threw the match down the borehole. He was always the one that the weirdest things happened to.'

'At least he's still alive,' I say, 'and apparently he's not too badly burned.'

Ayanda smiles. 'Imagine it,' she says. 'You toss a match into a dry old borehole and the world bursts open all around you ...'

She giggles. 'You have to know Zola to appreciate it.' I laugh and wipe my face.

'See what a sight his old kwela still is as a result of the explosion.' Ayanda bends over the steering wheel and shakes her head, giggling. 'His flagship!' she laughs. 'The pride of his fleet!'

15

We are an odd bunch who arrive in Bisho that day. I have to smile now when I see myself sitting there in the front of the minibus, dripping with sweat and worn out by MaNdlovu's chatter. Circumstances have delivered me up to two really extraordinary women! And these two do not easily allow words to be placed into their mouths, as is the case with Seamus and Sarah ...

When we stop in front of the Palace of Justice MaNdlovu screws up her eyes to ward off her dizziness. Passers-by look curiously at the minibus which has been so badly shot to pieces but quickly turn their eyes away again. Either they are used to such sights, MaNdlovu thinks, or else they are fearful for some reason or other of appearing inquisitive.

'There's a lot of fear about in this toy republic,' MaNdlovu says as she climbs down and puts her hat on. She watches Ayanda locking all the doors of the little bus, whose every window (barring the front windscreen) is shattered, and thinks: my dutiful daughter – always doing everything so correctly.

'Straighten your dress, Ayanda,' she says, then turns to me: 'You, too, lawyer Wehmeyer – your tie is crooked.'

I offer to carry the basket but she refuses. Inside it is TaImbongi's birth certificate, his Gideon's pocket Bible, six sandwiches spread with goat fat and peanut butter, a small flask of whisky, a cake of soap and a tube of ointment for the prison vermin.

Ayanda too – as she had shown MaNdlovu earlier – has a little packet for TaImbongi. Hers contains vitamins, a wide-spectrum antibiotic, adhesive plasters and painkillers. Also, some washing powder and a few clothes pegs.

'Come, children.' We set off. MaNdlovu notes with satisfaction that I am carrying my briefcase and looking professional. She is still one of the old sort: an important man has to walk slowly and not allow his glance to flit about. These smooth, modern youngsters with their rapid movements find no favour with her. Ncincilili had it – the ability to move slowly and with dignity like the old men, even though he was so young.

'Stop rummaging in your handbag, Ayanda.' We walk up the path to the front entrance. I clear my throat and MaNdlovu divines that I have something to say. 'Yes, lawyer Wehmeyer?' I cough again uncomfortably. (So very careful not to hurt her!) 'You'd better say what you have to say, lawyer.'

I glance at her and she notices my sad eyes. To her I always look half mournful. What is it that this loner carries about inside him? Why doesn't he get married and fill that old house of his with children?

It's as well that, walking there, I do not know what is going on in her mind, else I would not be able to act professionally!

'It won't help if we all speak at once in there, Mrs Thandani.' The bushy eyebrows knit together above my earnest blue eyes. The man doesn't get enough sleep, MaNdlovu thinks, looking at me. Or is it that he doesn't eat healthily? What does a man who lives alone like that eat and drink? Café take-aways? Whisky? 'We shall have to come to an agreement that I do all the talking.'

'I won't interrupt you,' MaNdlovu says. 'And Ayanda is a woman of the modern world. She always knows when to keep quiet. The chatterbox is in there behind bars.'

I smile and walk ahead. MaNdlovu looks at the way my trouser legs, being too long, wrinkle above my shoes. Poor man, she thinks, he really needs the firm hand of a woman.

In front of the building a security guard salutes us.

'Good afternoon, my boy,' MaNdlovu greets him, but the soldier does not bat an eyelid. To Ayanda she says: 'See how smartly his shoes shine. That's just what the Ciskei is like – shiny without, rotten within.'

Before we can cross the threshold we first have to pass through a security checkpoint. As I go through the alarm goes off. I have to turn out all my pockets before trying once more. It is my bunch of keys, explain the men sitting there in dark glasses. They then unpack MaNdlovu's basket, all in a row: the ointment, the Bible, the whisky.

Perhaps they heard what she said about the Ciskei, MaNdlovu thinks. When they have packed everything except the whisky back into the basket, MaNdlovu goes nearer. 'You ...' she starts, but I take her arm and gently draw her away.

'No liquor allowed in a government building,' announces one of the men in dark glasses, grinning as he slips the flask under the counter.

'Scoundrel ...' growls MaNdlovu. In her youth no pipsqueak like this one would ever have dared to address his elders and betters in such a manner. Nowadays, however ...

She takes Ayanda by the elbow and walks down the long corridor, fighting against her dizziness. Her sudden fury with the security guard has brought on the old dull headache that she has learnt to live with. 'Do you know where we go now, lawyer Wehmeyer?' she asks. She has learnt: keep talking, moving, living, and the dizziness remains at bay – you shove it aside.

'Hush, Mama ...' Ayanda whispers. 'You're not in Joza now ...' MaNdlovu realises that her voice is echoing down the empty corridor.

'Your mama is the same wherever she is, my girl. In gentle Jesus's heaven I'll carry on just as I do in Joza. You know I've taught you from childhood on not to dissemble, like your father does. Just be yourself and all the world will respect you.'

'Mrs Thandani ...' I have stopped, pointing to a bench along the wall of the corridor. 'You will have to wait here. I have to go into this office alone ...'

'What for, lawyer Wehmeyer?' MaNdlovu holds the white handkerchief to her face as Ayanda helps remove her hat and hangs it over the handle of the basket.

'I have to make representations,' I say. 'To find out where he is being held. And to establish whether he was detained under the emergency regulations.' MaNdlovu feels herself coming over dizzy again. For a moment she sees TaImbongi sitting in a prison cell. 'My brief was to bring you with me so that you can appear before an official in person if need be.'

'Tell them he's an old blabbermouth, lawyer Wehmeyer,' says MaNdlovu. She is feeling suffocated. Her heart is pounding. She is thinking of how TaImbongi's small face puckers up whenever he feels oppressed and trapped. 'Tell them he's harmless. He's just an old clown. The only republic whose downfall he could cause would be the republic of the shebeen.'

I smile. 'I'll do my best. Won't you sit down and rest?' I nod to Ayanda. 'Are you comfortable, Doctor Thandani?' Then I go through the door.

MaNdlovu feels the walls turning. The hat on the basket – it is the hat she bought for Ayanda and Zola's wedding – grows hazy. She gropes for Ayanda, who makes her lie down on her back on the bench. Turning and turning through MaNdlovu's mind goes the refrain: I want a ten-rand note, a five-rand – anything ... 'Ncincilili!'

Then Ayanda is gone and MaNdlovu can hear her heels clicking away across the floor. 'Ayanda!'

Images of Joza go spinning past her eyes: the iron sheets of the Mint knocking against the walls, the dagga-loonies lying slobbering on the veranda of the clinic in the morning. 'My poor little Mandrax-lambs ...'

Then Ayanda is back. 'Mama ...' The cloth is cool against MaNdlovu's face. 'Would you believe it! I asked those two baboons for your whisky to help bring you round and they just laughed! Can you believe it ...'

'Did you tell them you're in medicine, my child?'

'It wasn't necessary, Mama. Come now ...'

'You're always so shy, Ayanda. You should listen to your ma: it's not for nothing that you've got a title.'

'Oh, Mama.'

'I'm better, my child.' MaNdlovu sighs. 'It's just the tension and the longing. Your precious father is a mess of a man.'

'Hush, Mama ... just calm down a bit.'

They wait in the empty corridor. From time to time MaNdlovu hears a door banging and footsteps. But no one, she thinks, comes up to find out what is happening to the two women – one of them flat on her back. It is a cold place, this.

'Listen ...' whispers Ayanda. From behind a door comes the sound of loud voices. Then the door flies open and she sees me storming out. I look like a bull. MaNdlovu struggles up into a sitting position, seeing a lawyer Wehmeyer she doesn't know. His head is hunched into his shoulders, the briefcase clamped under one arm. 'Lawyer Wehmeyer,' she begins, but then I spin round and storm in through the door again. When it bangs behind me, again they hear raised voices.

Ayanda's eyes grow wide. 'He's fighting,' she says to MaNdlovu. 'They say he's like a pit bull terrier in court.'

'He's a fighter,' replies MaNdlovu. 'I see that now.' She feels better immediately. 'Oh my girl, that puts the heart back into me. We'll have our old TaImbongi home again tonight.'

'You mustn't hope for too much, Mama. These people don't know the meaning of mercy. They've picked up their airs and graces from the white government.'

'Here you never know which hole has a snake sleeping in it. Or in which old tree stump there's a honeycomb.'

'What's that, Mama?'

But then the door opens again and I emerge, shaking my head. I stop in front of them.

'It's worse here than ever the state of emergency was with us, even at its worst. They don't give a damn about the law, any law.'

'Jungle justice,' says MaNdlovu. 'But we've known that all along.'

'Mr Wehmeyer?' asks Ayanda.

I sigh. 'We'll have to leave,' I say. 'They think – notice: they think – that he may be being held up north somewhere. They say we'll just have to go from place to place searching. There is no central record of detainees.'

'No ...' MaNdlovu holds her handkerchief to her mouth. I put my hand on her shoulder. As I tell it now, I would like to reach out to her again, to give her brave old shoulder a squeeze. But I remind myself that my comrade-in-spirit is there. (It's only days since this happened, but he looks so much younger! So inexperienced!) He does his best to mix empathy and professionalism. But of course we know which of the two tells most with old Seer ...

'It's not going to be easy, Mrs Thandani. But there's nothing else we can do.'

'They're animals,' whispers MaNdlovu. 'They're nothing better than beasts. If this is the way they treat their own people, what are they going to be like when they have power over other people?'

'Come, Mama.' Ayanda helps to get her moving.

They have to pass the two men again.

'Give back the confiscated whisky,' I growl.

The men sit back and laugh. MaNdlovu is surprised when I go right up to the counter, my shoulders heaving as I pant.

I lunge in under the counter, feel around, and before the men realise what is happening I have the flask in my hand.

'Come!' I push MaNdlovu and Ayanda out ahead of me and we burst out into the sunlight. MaNdlovu's eyes blink in the glare. The soldier salutes.

'Puppet,' hisses MaNdlovu. 'Hyena.'

Then we are out in the open. When MaNdlovu looks round, she sees one of the security men in the doorway, his dark glasses glinting in the sunlight.

'Lawyer,' she says, when we are back in the kwela again and

Ayanda, still trembling with fright, is struggling with the gears: 'You're the kind of man closest to my heart.'

We drive out of Bisho. When we are on the open plain again, we all feel better. I had made a list of police stations before the official and I started quarrelling in his office.

We stop in several villages and in each the same procedure repeats itself: we drive up and down a couple of streets, find the police station, stand calling at the locked gates until a constable appears, and then explain in full and tiresome detail.

At the first two police posts an irritated station commander runs his finger down the list of detainees in the cells behind the charge office. But the farther we get from Bisho, the sparser grow the circumstances.

At the next station we are asked to come along to the cells, since there isn't any list of detainees. We will have to accompany the warder and identify TaImbongi if he is being held there. We stand for a long time in front of the large, overcrowded cells, the men staring at us unseeingly.

'Dagga,' whispers Ayanda.

'Scum,' growls MaNdlovu. 'What would TaImbongi be doing among such creatures?'

'Perhaps there are men of substance among them too, Mama.'

'They're bandits. You can see it.'

At the fifth police station MaNdlovu's sight begins to grow dim again. Ayanda has to lead her and the prison bars are all a haze before her eyes. She can detect the movement of bodies behind the bars but no more.

'Are you there, TaImbongi? TaImbongi, are you there?'

Eventually we decide to turn back. We have to be home before dark – at night the roads can be very dangerous.

We drive back, the veld growing softer and gentler as the afternoon wears on. MaNdlovu feels herself driving farther and farther away from TaImbongi.

Land of desolation, she thinks.

I am with them there on the open plain, accompanying the

vehicle, so minuscule against the surrounding landscape. But I feel at peace, for I know that everything has an end. I feel free, because I realise that every imprisonment – life included – ends in wider spaces.

But even though I am consumed with eagerness to do so, I may not mention a word about it to them.

Even my kind of freedom has its conditions.

16

Tired after the long trip to the Ciskei and back I sit fiddling with the old radiogram which my father imported from England at great expense in the time of Prime Minister D F Malan.

That was soon after 1948, when the National Party, in the days after their first victory at the polls, was beginning to implement apartheid with one law after another: the Group Areas Act, the Population Registration Act, the Separate Voters Rolls Act ...

When the Indian family, who had extensive business interests in the city and lived in the old colonial villa diagonally opposite our ramshackle home, were forced to move out to a black residential area, my dad decided to send for the radiogram – an old Philips – so that he would be able to listen to the news programmes on the Africa Service of the BBC.

'We've got to know what is happening in our country,' he said.

He had a huge aerial welded together and fixed high above the roof of the house. Through the years it became something of a landmark for small fishing craft sailing out down the river at night, for in a defiant gesture my father had fitted a light to the tip of the antenna.

Left burning day and night, that little bulb was regarded by the Wehmeyers of the right bank as the symbol of our enlightenment.

The old radiogram, which has been subjected to all kinds of exorbitantly expensive electronic adjustments down the years, still stands in the lounge. For far less money I would long since have been able to buy a brand new hi-fi set with a much stronger transmitter, but the hissing and the static crackle of the old 'gram are so much a part of my life that I do not really want to change.

Also, the hissing and the fluctuating volume heighten the romance of hearing distant voices from a different, better world where tolerance reigns and opinions can be openly weighed and measured.

There is an oppressive feeling in the air. I have already checked the barometer on the patio. If you look out across the river, there is a layer of mist over the water, which is moving sluggishly, almost stickily – as though the sun is baking the steam out of the water. Only occasionally is the surface broken by the quick flash of a fish after the mosquitoes swarming above the water. The fish have to compete with twittering swallows darting to trap the insects in flight.

When there is a knock at the front door, I turn off the 'gram in irritation. The crackle and hiss over the ether always makes me suspect that all sorts of things are happening over Africa: they are the bad vibrations of famines and civil wars, plague and malaria, dictators and the primitive, sultry tropics.

I am surprised when I open the door to find Cawood standing there. It is not often that my nephew comes to visit me, particularly not this late in the afternoon when the young people of the district are playing tennis, or gathered round a swimming pool, or perhaps out in their jeeps and four-wheel-drive Toyotas – even in the closed season – hunting buck up in the kloofs.

It is a district full of macho young men. For the young people of Manley Flats pleasure is a matter of the body: it is found in the movement of a horse between their thighs, in the kick of a rifle butt against their shoulders, in dizzying spins in Cawood's helicopter, or in tempting fate by hang-gliding down from the heights of the Hogsback even in the most unfavourable weather conditions.

I always regard this generation with a degree of envy. Even in the time of war on the Border and strife at home, they have succeeded in growing up with enormous self-confidence, so sure of the strength of their bodies, of their abilities within their small world of whose limitations they are simply unaware. They are so guilelessly dependent on one another too: young men having beer parties, competing in cricket matches, arranging clay-pigeon shooting tournaments, racing from one event to the next in their off-road vehicles – always accompanied by energetic young women ready to deal with game carcasses brought in from the veld on the backs of bakkies, or else to sit chatting and crocheting while their young farmers are shooting or kicking or wrestling or competitively comparing their crops and other conquests.

It is an enticing way of life, disturbed neither by ever picking up a book, nor by hearing any contrary opinion, nor by travelling outside the safe routes of organised touring parties and tourist attractions.

Yet within the stuffiness of the confined spaces in which these people live and move and have their being, there is a physicalness, a virility, which never fail to surprise me whenever I encounter them. They have an inviolate naiveté untouched by the men's vulgar jokes, which are always on the same subjects: the arrogance of the bank manager, sex with black women, Botha and Mandela ...

The innocence of this world – whose whole existence depends on the pain and deprivation of so many other lives – gives it the appearance of eternal youth. It is a limited district where everyone knows the codes and in which everyone therefore moves comfortably, always ready with a joke which everyone will catch, a reference to someone whom everybody knows, some gossip about mutual enemies.

It is a tribal bond, and against the background of the realities of Africa, there is something about it that I can sense but not name – just as I could sense the atmosphere on the river a short while ago.

It is the scent under a large stone overturned in a damp watercourse, the odour of a cement-lined dam drained for the first time in decades, the smell of a newly shot buck's intestines when the butcher's knife cleaves it from breastbone to pizzle.

'Cawood!'

'Hullo, Seer.' I have insisted, since Cawood's earliest years, on his not calling me 'Uncle' as local custom demanded. In the teeth of Seamus and Sarah's objections, I stuck to my guns: why should the young man have to use a title to address me?

'May I come in?'

'Yes, of course ... sorry! I am just surprised ... Sure, come inside, do come in ...' I open the door and walk ahead of Cawood.

As always happens when I receive an unexpected caller, I wonder in alarm what may be lying around in my lounge to betray my privacy: perhaps an unusual book that I was reading, a model engine imported from Scotland and only just unpacked, a new record that I wanted to listen to ...

I am not used to visitors. I always feel exposed when strange eyes fall on the things I busy myself with. But then I remember with relief that there are no half-completed sonnets or open volumes of poetry lying around. In the presence of Seamus or the young Cawood I am always especially conscious of the things which fascinate me but which to them will probably seem totally eccentric.

'Come ... let's go out on to the back veranda. It's so stuffy this afternoon.'

'Stinking hot.' Cawood sits down in one of the deck chairs, a little surprised by the depth of the seat. For a moment he doesn't quite know how to fold his legs and evidently feels slightly ridiculous and uncomfortable.

Noticing this, I ask: 'Wouldn't you rather we sat on those cane chairs beside the water? There might be a slight breeze down there.'

'Yes, it's really stuffy.'

'I'll get us something to drink. Beer?'

'A long one, please!' Cawood smiles. 'A man picks up a long thirst on a farm road when it's as hot as this.'

While I fetch the beer and glasses from the kitchen, I wonder about the reason for Cawood's visit.

'Where are your pals this afternoon?' I ask as I carry the tray of beers down the grassed slope to the cane chairs beside the old jetty. 'You and the others are always out having fun on summer afternoons.'

'They're swimming at the Settlers' Inn pool,' Cawood replies. 'There was a champagne breakfast there this morning and an auction of Persian carpets and kelims. It was that old Malay from Cape Town who goes off to Turkey every year and then comes back here to hawk his purchases.'

I caution my nephew: 'There are still rumours that the goods are stolen.' I can't resist adding: 'And the champagne makes you chaps bid far too high for carpets that, so I've heard, are sometimes complete and utter fakes ...'

Cawood shrugs his shoulders. 'Oh, it's good fun,' he says. 'And in any case, it's not hunting season and ...'

I interrupt him, irritably. 'Come! Your health! It's not every day that I have the pleasure of entertaining my young nephew. It's a privilege. Particularly when there are sure to be so many young girls lying around the Settlers' Inn pool in bikinis.'

Cawood raises his glass. We take long, greedy gulps. 'Hell,' he says, 'only now do I realise how dry my throat was. And look at the river – placid as a dam.'

'Yes, it moves very unobtrusively. But you'd be surprised how strong the current is when you swim out ten or fifteen yards.'

'Have you swum here?'

'Well, of course!' I laugh. 'Your mother and I lived in the water. We were like otters, always wet and in and out of the river. There's our little skiff, still drawn up on the bank, over there ...'

'Oh ...' Cawood laughs absent-mindedly.

After a while he says carefully: 'I can't actually imagine my mother here swimming. Laughing ...'

'She's a very cheerful person.' I take a sip of beer, look out across the water, but decide against saying anything more. That terrain is too dangerous. Once before I mentioned to Cawood something about Seamus and Sarah, and years later it surfaced again in the course of a conversation with Sarah. Young Cawood, so guileless and snide, is not to be trusted.

Cawood clears his throat. I can see he has something on his mind, but decide to wait for him to make the first move. Could it be a paternity suit? Maintenance? Or has he run someone down in his bakkie? Is it his everlasting shooting? A shooting accident perhaps?

'I could do with a swim myself now,' Cawood says slowly. Then he looks at me suddenly and says: 'Seer, I hear my dad's a client of yours nowadays?'

The question comes from an angle I have not foreseen. 'Your dad?' I ask unnecessarily, playing for time.

'He wants to split up Fata Morgana. To sell off part of it.'

'And who told you that, Cawood?'

'You don't need to be so cautious. My mother told me. Dad was present.'

'And what was your father's reaction?'

Cawood snorts. He bangs his empty beer glass down on the tray and unties his bootlaces. He pulls off his socks and starts running his toes through the thick grass. On his insteps I notice marks where the boots have pinched him.

'Well?'

'You know my dad.'

'And what is that supposed to mean?'

'He didn't say a thing. Absolutely nothing. Don't you know he doesn't need to say anything to anyone. He's Seamus Butler!'

'I see.' I sip my beer. I have to be careful here. This is an explosive situation. I will bend the tree while it is still pliable. 'But you know I cannot discuss my clients' affairs with you, Cawood. It would be unethical.'

Cawood looks at me indignantly. 'But these are family matters. You're my uncle!'

I smile. 'And your mother's brother. And your father's attorney.'

Cawood looks me straight in the eye, and then grins. His facial expressions can change so quickly – from the charming blond boy to this calculating, selfish opponent.

'You're always so cautious, my Uncle Seer,' Cawood says slowly. 'You're always so ethical. You don't care whether I lose my farm, my inheritance. Provided you can act correctly. Provided you can stay clean.'

Cawood is now on his feet, unbuttoning his shirt. 'Provided you can keep yourself pure.' He peels off his shirt. I catch a whiff of sweat. Cawood's torso is stronger than I would have expected – with his shirt on he looks thinner. Now the deep chest is bare, the shoulder muscles in clearly visible relief, the belly stretched firm and flat below the ribcage, with a track of hair disappearing downwards under the belt.

'I'll tell you what your nephew thinks, Uncle Seer.' Cawood starts undoing his belt. I hold my breath. 'Your nephew thinks you have never dared to live. Your nephew ...' He peels off his trousers and with a swift movement throws them across the back of the chair. 'Your nephew thinks you have always avoided the things that matter.'

With his thumbs Cawood then pulls down his underpants, steps out of them and stands there suddenly naked, against the background of the green garden and the river. He turns round and with four strides of his powerful legs, a leap and a single graceful movement he dives into the river.

It can't be happening. It is impossible. I look at the river, at the bubbles breaking the surface as Cawood moves along under water. The shining, slowly moving water, the little lights now beginning to flicker on the opposite bank – the familiar scene is being ripped apart by the young body gliding across under the surface.

Farther up along the bank a fish eagle lets go of its perch and skims across the water with wings flapping. Cawood shoots up, breaks the surface and emerges up to his waist. He laughs, swimming deeper in until the current begins to tug at him. Then he turns round and with an easy backstroke swims back to the bank.

In the shallows he straightens up, staggers, laughing, half out of the water, unsure on the uneven bottom. Then he comes fully erect and I notice shining droplets of river water collecting in his bush.

With a shout Cawood throws his body over backwards, arms spread wide, the dark tufts in his armpits showing. His strong young body stretches out, the muscles between the ribs tauten, the nipples contract against the water, and his pert member, shrunken from the cold, bobs up and down in the air before Cawood glides away again in the water like a dolphin.

It is the first time I have ever seen a fully grown man naked in the flesh. I had missed the draft, never joined the army, and never took part in those team sports where everyone showered together in communal showers after matches.

All I know is my own body, sadly overweight and lazy, morning and evening in the mirror. And recollections from my childhood of small boys' bodies playing in the shallows of the delta alongside my own: that was all water and grass and exuberant smells of summer and excitement.

But it is different now, with this young man so boldly challenging me.

I rise, gather up the glasses and take the tray up to the veranda. In the kitchen I stand at the sink for a long time, leaning over, feeling faint.

And so the river drags its slow length along.

17

Seamus and I always agree about the long-winded academics whom one frequently encounters in Port Cecil. With the coming of the oil, these armchair commentators are of course in their element. Now I'm enjoying looking over Seamus's shoulder where he and a couple of professors are sitting in the private lounge of the Dick King Hotel. The walls are panelled in dark wood and muted photographs of the 1947 Royal Visit to South Africa are the only decoration.

'It is as though our entire history is being funnelled together in these days,' the old history professor tells Seamus. 'In these days I note all the great motifs: the mythology of discovery, of Monomotapa and the Kruger millions, the ambition of Rhodes and the gold rushes of the previous century, the natural disasters and the devastation of the earth ...'

'The El Niño phenomenon,' interjects the professor of geography, leaning forward and tapping the ash off his cigar into an Indian ashtray.

'... the unbalanced scales of rich and poor, the tribal wars, the ...' The historian makes a gesture as if to imply that he is being overwhelmed by the multiplicity of phenomena.

'Perhaps God is launching an experiment in our city,' suggests the dean of divinity. 'We are being tried: how will we deal with this sudden blessing?'

'Oh, tripe,' growls Seamus, shoving his glass towards the centre of the table with an irritable squeak of glass against wood. These people can make such a fuss about things. He beckons to a waiter. 'A double,' he says. 'On the rocks.' He wipes his brow and has second thoughts. To the theologian he admits: 'I have also considered the matter from that angle. In fact, that was my first reaction. When one is confronted with anything as unexpected, as sublime, as brutal as this, one searches instinctively for the hand of God behind it.'

He shifts forward in his chair. 'But the more I think about it, the more I am forced to the conclusion that that black gold comes directly from the dark angel. From Satan.' He sits back, his challenge directed at the theologian.

'Oh, hardly,' counters the professor of philosophy, trying to prevent a confrontation. 'I really don't care much for your paradigm. You are both mystifying matters, and you,' he says, pointing to the historian, 'are mythologising them. All we have here is a challenge to reason and ethics. What we as citizens of the city have to do is simply to reason the case to its conclusion – how are we to act justly and apportion the wealth fairly?'

'But that is surely also the province of ecology,' interrupts the occupant of the ecology chair. That, after all, is the great challenge of the turn of the century – the utilisation of the resources of Mother Earth ...'

'That I concede,' affirms the philosopher. 'Our task here on the river with seven mouths forms a kind of model for the country's most pressing priority: how are we to give to those who have not, to those who have remained poverty-stricken as a result of the policies of the past, how are we to give to them without depriving, in an immoral manner, those who have?'

'It's a hell of a question,' adds the historian.

'That's exactly what I said,' exclaims Seamus. 'It's the devil!' He gives the waiter a generous tip and sits back in his chair.

He always finds it interesting spending an evening with the academics. He has never felt that they, learned as they are, know any more about life than he, a farmer, does. On the contrary, few things which he has seen in the university community through the years have led him even to suspect that their theories could make a scrap of difference to the struggle between one human being and another, or between humans and animals, or between people and the earth. Or for that matter between man and God, man and the devil, or God and Satan.

And anyway, he thinks, this university – named for a British imperialist – has spent too long right in the lap of a victimised landscape without taking any notice at all of its surroundings. Behind the ivy-clad walls generations of academics – with certain notable exceptions – have spent their time thinking the hours away and repeating the same lectures year after year without apparently ever looking out of the window at the growing slum settlements on the slopes of First Delta.

And once they have had a couple of tots, like now, when the third or fourth whisky is coursing in their veins, all their colonial longwindedness comes to the fore and they will brag about their Oxford degrees and grow melancholy as they discourse on the collapse of standards. Look at them sitting there like fall-goat rams, boasting about their whatsitsnames, their paradigms ...

'You townies don't know anything,' he says. 'City folk can't plumb the world. You sit with your noses in books. You're a bunch of fishmoths.'

They laugh. 'There speaks an agricultural tycoon who serves on the Council of the University and sponsors a chair in animal husbandry!' teases the ecologist.

Seamus makes a gesture, enjoying the attention. At times like this, among people like these who don't have a single foot on the ground, he too can forget about ... he shakes his head; shakes away the thoughts which bunch up like impatient goats at a gate. 'You'll see: the oil is going to bring the Kei tragedy rather than prosperity. I feel it in my bones. And my animals in the highly nervous state they're in nowadays sense it too ...'

The professor of drama, who has so far been content to stare silently into his drink, now lifts his glass to Seamus as though he is about to propose a toast. 'The concept of tragedy comes of course from the concepts "tragos" meaning goat ...' He winks at Seamus and continues: 'and "oida": song.'

He says nothing more, but his slit eyes keep watching Seamus. Seamus listens to the others' conversation for a while, but keeps feeling the man's eyes on him and remains aware of their faintly mocking expression.

He's watching me, he thinks, with the expectation of a director who has just confronted his actors with an unexpected mixture of elements and is waiting for their reaction.

Again the image of a herd of goats milling round at a gate comes into his mind. He can even smell the droppings and the dust. He looks up but the man is chatting to the colleague beside him. Seamus tries to catch what the two professors opposite him are saying but he has lost track of the conversation.

He feels himself growing light-headed. His mouth goes dry and fright grips him. He wipes his nose, but cannot rid himself of the smell of crowding goats. He hears their hooves drumming on the hard earth, and their demented bleating.

His heart is beating wildly. Whenever his anxiety overtakes him as unexpectedly as this, he can put up no resistance. Ahead of him stretches the endless plain. It is the Karoo at its worst: dry, repellent, mean.

He tastes the dust on his palate. From the trunk of his brain the oil branches out to overwhelm his mind. It is the black plasma of despair welling up in his spirit and smothering him.

'Excuse me ...' He pushes back his chair quickly, brings his napkin to his lips and tries to rise. He feels the eyes of all on him. They know. They know that I, Seamus Butler of Fata Morgana, have lost all purchase on reality, that I ...

He turns away and hardly makes it to the door. He gropes his way along the wall of the passage and pushes open the door of the gents' toilet. From the row of mirrors above the wash basins a series of images leaps out at him: Caper timidus with its three horns and yellow goat eyes, its demented realisation of doom, its melancholy ears ... the goat driven out into the Judean wilderness to atone for the sins of the people. The scapegoat ...

He reaches a toilet and sinks down dizzily onto the seat, leaning his head and one shoulder against the wall beside him. His dizziness keeps coming and going. He rummages in his pocket for the box of pills he carries for emergencies.

He places the little pink pill under his tongue and tries to breathe deeply and rhythmically. Out of the corner of his eye he notices beside his head a crude pen sketch of the horns and nose of a goat. The goat's nose bulges hairily out of its forehead. Seamus shudders and jerks his head away from the wall he has been leaning against.

With his eyes farther away from the drawing, he sees that it is not a goat's head at all, but a scrotum with the penis semi-erect. Written above the curve of the genital organ there is a telephone number.

Good God, Seamus thinks, where am I? At this time, when that bunch inside are talking about the future of our city – I must get back, I've got to keep their feet on the ground. The University Council is a powerful organ and its influence reaches deep into the community. The members of the Senate serve on the boards of many of the city's businesses; the network of loans and obligations and family ties which the bunch of professors in that private lounge form part of is a web of power-relations which could be the deciding factor in the politicking round this oil gusher.

I've got to get out of here, he pants. I've got to pull myself together. The pill is beginning to take effect: a pleasant sleepiness is spreading in him. The lava is cooling. He is becoming human again.

Well done. But what those good-luck tablets, as Sarah calls them, actually contain is a dose of deceit. You feel the relaxation of tension coming over you, but it is actually an illusory lameness: beneath the soporific mood there is still the vague suspicion of terror and dementia; beneath the goodwill there are still voices trying to outbid one another like the sounds coming from deep under water that he remembers from his days as a keen diver off the coast.

The muted wailing of demons; the smothered cries of terror of a thousand goats.

He sits with his face in his hands, recalling the story which a priest had once told him: that the animal used for sacrifice in the Old Testament was a sheep, not a goat, although in antiquity it was a goat that was actually the sacrificial beast.

'The lamb was chosen in preference to the goat kid,' the priest said, 'because a sheep dies without a sound. Like most other animals a goat screams when the sacrificial knife begins to saw through its throat and the blood spurts out ...'

'Why are you telling me this, Father?' asked Seamus. It was during one of his deep depressions. Sarah, desperate that after ten weeks the pills prescribed by the psychiatrist had still been unable to assuage Seamus's despair, had summoned the priest to Fata Morgana.

Seamus was lying in the bedroom where he spent most of his days at that time. The priest sat down on the double bed and took Seamus's hand in his, unselfconsciously, with tenderness and understanding.

'Because the image of our Saviour, Mr Butler, is that of the lamb. The Lamb of God, led out without protest to the Cross, there to die in dignified silence for our sins ...'

'And did He not call out to God, Father? Did He not ask: My God, why hast thou forsaken me?'

The priest smiled. 'God never forsakes us, Mr Butler. God is forsaken by us.'

'Christ felt godforsaken, Father. It says so in the Bible.'

'That, my son, is because at that moment Christ had taken upon His shoulders all the godforsakenness of all sinners through all ages. In that one moment He took the desolation of the whole world upon His shoulders. He bore your pain, too, Mr Butler, that day on Calvary.

'That is why He is your personal Saviour.'

'The sacrificial goat,' murmured Seamus.

The priest looked away. 'God be merciful to you,' he said softly.

'I am not blaspheming, Father,' Seamus said. 'I hear what you are saying.'

'You cannot rely on Satan, Mr Butler. He is the dark angel.'

'We who take issue with the hard earth, Father, we who wrestle with the elements and earn our living in the seasonal cycles of life and death, seedtime and harvest, deprivation and plenty, punishment and reward – we recognise the hoofprints of that old tokkeloshe when we see them.

'I think he and God are partners.'

A sigh escaped the priest's lips. He began to murmur softly and touched the cross on his chest. The hand in which he was still holding Seamus's hand began to sweat.

'No other footprint resembles Satan's, Father. Even my best hounds turn tail when we're out hunting and their noses detect a trace of the great goat.'

'No, my son ... no ...' the priest whispered and crossed himself. He looked up at the wall of the room where a photograph of Seamus and his late father hung. They were at an agricultural show and were holding two fall-goats by the horns.

'Yes, you may look at my father there on the wall,' Seamus said. He tried to give a cynical laugh, but something like a sob caught in his throat. 'He was the old goat himself; out there in the garden his blood grew black on the vygies. Long after the funeral everyone was frightened to go near that spot in the garden where he had blown his own brains out. But I, as a little boy, went there daily and touched the blood with my fingertips. It grew blacker and blacker and crumbled, and ants began to carry it off. I sat there fascinated, watching how ants carried away the last remains of my father. I picked up a little crust of blood hardly the size of my pinkie nail and took it home. I hid it in my room inside an old book. I've still got it.'

Seamus began to weep softly. I, a grown man, lying here in my bedroom in broad daylight, in front of a priest, crying. But he continued: 'The bullet blew my father's head open, Father. There was just blood and slime and brain marrow. I didn't see any soul soaring upwards, Father. No dove ascended to heaven.'

The priest freed his hand from Seamus's grip and drew it across his forehead, his fingers trembling. Seamus leant upright against the pillows. 'I saw the goats lying there prone as a result of hearing the death shot of their breeder-father. No lamb, Father, no forgiveness, no Calvary. Just a lump of flesh lying there: my father.'

The priest closed his eyes and prayed in a soft murmur. They sat there together for a long time. At last the priest opened his eyes. He looked calmer. 'You are descending into hell, my son,' he said gently. 'God is leading you into the valley of the shadow; He is revealing to you the temptation of Satan. But He disposes. He has a purpose for your suffering. He will bring you back again at last, like the prodigal son. And He will prepare a banquet for you.'

The priest rose to his feet. 'I shall pray for you,' were his final words.

Seamus smiled a crooked smile. 'Light a candle near the altar for me, Father. And another for my late father. The Butlers do not wish to reject the Church.' The priest looked at him intently, hesitating. He seemed about to ask something. 'That's not a joke, Father. It's a request.' The priest nodded.

When the man had left, Seamus slid down deeper into the bed again. The priest had left a little tract entitled 'God is love'. Seamus slid it under the ashtray. Love! How could anyone travelling through this country, anyone who was prepared to think for a moment about the history of this region, about all the dead and the suffering, all the blood and the shit, the pain and despair, the fraud and adultery – how could anyone still think that God was a sweet old Patience Strong father with a flowing white beard, watching over everything in a fatherly fashion with only one emotion in his heart: love?

Wherefore this confounded muddle that was humanity? Was God incapable of pulling His mess of a creation together? Any farmer, if his farm was in such a bad way, would realise that matters had reached a terminal stage and intervene.

Any farmer who did not, could not – or else he was absent and had forgotten about his farm. Perhaps he had other business in some other district. Or he was sitting back, enjoying the encroachment of weeds: thorns and nettles growing rank in the vegetable gardens, wild animals leaping the fences at night and gobbling up the haystacks, the gradual invasion of the homestead by bats and owls and stray curs, rusting fodder cribs, lands being washed away, dongas ripping open ...

'Oh God ...' Sitting on the toilet, Seamus breathes deeply. Memories account for a large proportion of the milling herd at the closed gate, and if the gate is to give way, they with their sharp hooves and stinking breath would be the first to burst into the camp. 'Oh God ...'

Seamus suddenly realises where he is. The goat smell disappears and he catches the odours of urine and toilet cleaner. He struggles to his feet. Round him the walls are gyrating. Gradually they stabilise enough for him to slide aside the latch on the door.

He stops in front of one of the mirrors and straightens his tie. Combing his hair, he thinks: that's a fine head of hair for a man well into his fifties.

He walks out into the passage and takes a deep breath of air. On his left the Settlers' Bar is a noisy fug of dense cigarette smoke, huddles of bodies, laughter and cheering. And audible above it all is the thunder of a TV set: for the first time in years, after the sport boycotts, an overseas rugby team – New Zealand's All Blacks – are playing against the Springboks.

He turns in the direction of the private lounge where their meeting is taking place and starts walking towards it. Then he feels himself swaying again: there is something floating before his eyes, he is not sure what – a flickering on the edge of consciousness. Seamus thinks: it's a figure. It's something ...

But he shakes his head, straightens his shoulders and strides back into the lounge. The men are just raising their glasses. The professor of history calls out the traditional toast of Settler descendants: '1820!'

'1820!' the rest respond. With crystalline clarity the elusive image drifts into Seamus's consciousness. It is a telephone number, and he does not even need to repeat the figures with his lips.

The graffiti number in the toilet is the number of Cawood's house.

18

Zola Mtuze and Ayanda Thandani met at the annual Ball Room Dancing Entertainment in Joza. That was years ago, before Ayanda started her medical studies and when he, Zola, was still a poor fork-lift operator down at the harbour.

Zola had taken another girl to the ball, but from early on in the evening he had eyes for Ayanda alone, Ayanda with her proud head tilted to one side as she danced the tango, her skin gleaming against the mauve luxuriance of her ballgown, her strong calves kicking the seam of the dress outwards as she whirled round, the sinews of her ankles rocking and retreating, and just for an instant: her knees with their dimples, her muscular thighs, and a hint – just a suggestion of a quivering of fat ...

He knew then, Zola thinks as he sits drinking whisky on the stoep of his pink palace, that there were more luxuriant delights in store higher up – the wide hips of a woman who would bear many children and not recoil from mischief in bed either.

He left his other girl – who was she again? – at the cooldrink table, straightened his bow-tie, wiped away the worst of the perspiration of the dance from his brow with his sleeve, and made a beeline through the dancers. The band struck up 'That's All Right Mama' – that playful, simple song full of fun and twist and rock-and-roll and kwela – and full of comfort and warning at the same time: 'This woman you got, son, ain't no frien' o' you ...'

He bumped into bodies whirling in the dance but pressed on.

'... But that's all right ...' When the vocalist started 'deedeedee' and bent over backwards, that jazz-belly with the buttons taut to bursting – nobody was dancing any more as they stood in their tuxedos and ballgowns clapping their hands to encourage the singer – he reached her.

The man at her side looked wilted. Later Ayanda would tell him that her friend had had too much cane spirit. 'Excuse me ...' ('ain't no frien' o' you ... ') She looked up and he said: 'I'm Dunlop Mtuze, fork-lift operator from the factory on Fourth Quay.'

There were so many things he wanted to add: I've got a good job, he'd have liked to say; I'm not just a nobody like that clamp on your arm; I'm a respectable Mtuze; I've got good contacts with the councillors, I'll soon be able to get a house ...

But it took all he had to get up enough courage to ask: 'Next time the band plays a tango, may I ...'

She gave him that slow, searching look of hers. He would discover later that she had inherited that look from MaNdlovu. Eventually she smiled, slowly, and sang softly in imitation of the band: 'Ain't no frien' o' you ...' Then, as though it was the most natural thing in the world: 'Yes, Dunlop Mtuze. You may dance with me. But don't you tread on my toes.'

When the band struck up the limousine dance – the township tango – he consoled his girl with another lemonade and crossed the dance floor to where Ayanda was waiting for him. He was blessedly unaware that the limousine dance had originated with TaImbongi. Now she was no longer the self-assured young girl of a moment ago – years later she would admit that she had been terribly nervous, that she had sensed that this was going to be the most important tango of her life ...

Zola sighed and looked out towards the city. From the heights he could see the floodlights round the cathedral tower. When she was in his arms for the first time, he could feel the spring in her tread and the heat of her breath on his cheek, and when they took the floor, it was as though they had been practising together for years ...

God made men and women to play on each other like lightning over a plain, Zola thought, to overflow each other's dry dongas like floodwaters ... Hallelujah, the start of the tango, the backing and advancing, the flight: under their heavy lids her eyes were slightly open as she threw her head backwards and lay against his arm, a faint layer of spittle between her upper teeth and her lip. And with the spin around: that delicious, light odour of woman's sweat from a strong young woman who held back nothing on the dance floor ...

Zola sighs. That is where I fell in love with her, he thinks, in that old school hall which the children later burnt down in the Liberation Before Education campaign during the emergency. That was where he felt the desire for her burning in his throat and decided that he had to have her.

'Get lost,' she told him late that night on the veranda of the hall when her cane drinker was already dead to the world and his lemonade drinker had disappeared in a huff. He had pulled Ayanda close to try to kiss her, shoving his hips indecently close to hers for her to feel the strength of his lust. 'Get lost,' she said firmly. 'I'm a decent girl.'

With those words she swept out and disappeared into the night. As he walked home it stayed with him, all of it: the shiny mauve of the smooth dress beneath his fingers, the dampness of her open back in the exertion of the dance, the bounce of her hips ...

Dizzy with love, he walked through the smoky, noisy streets of Sun City – past the tin shacks with drunk men shouting at children, past shebeens with drunks throwing up in the street, past a gang fight with seven pairs of men wrestling in the shadows without a word.

He walked on, while knobkerries laid into human flesh and footsteps fled off into the night. He just went on walking and whistling as though he'd won a million rands on the horses. He sniffed his hands, breathing in the sweet intoxication of her. He imagined again the swell and splendour of her body. 'We were created for each other, Ayanda Thandani,' he said aloud to himself as he walked across an opening between the shanties where the stormwater rushed through when it rained.

Whistling, he walked along the footpath between the wrecked cars and other junk which people threw there for the rain to sweep away some day. Where it was darkest, down in the hollow out of range of the great floodlights on their tall masts which cast their beams all over Joza, tsotsis attacked him.

They beat him up and robbed him at knife-point, their pangas gleaming under his nose in the moonlight. They stripped him of the hired bow-tie and tuxedo and let him run home practically naked. But Hallelujah! He'd met the most desirable maiden in Joza: Ayanda Thandani of Seventeenth Street, Extension Seven, Joza Township, the daughter of MaNdlovu Thandani of the Civic and old SpeakEasy, as the people then used to call TaImbongi behind his back.

Zola sighs as he pours himself another whisky. He is sitting alone on the second-storey stoep of his pink palace, the house that towers above the little squat boxes of the squatters' shacks, all constructed of rust-brown iron sheets.

Once his house, too, had been a two-roomed shack, but as he gradually made money with his minibus taxi, so he has systematically been able to add on rooms, until he eventually ventured the second storey.

Now the house is a maze of rooms that open unexpectedly into one another, passages that turn corners or simply come to an end where he still intends to add further extensions, drive-in lean-tos for the kwelas, stairs up to little balconies which allow a view across the sea of iron roofing sheets on the horizonless shantytown.

Inside, each room is lined with wallpaper. The two lounges have wooden panelling on the walls. Proper doorjambs and doors have been built in and the ceilings look like those of brick houses, except that they are a little lower. There are also TV aerials on the roof, because he is soccer-crazy, and two hot-water geysers.

Electricity has not yet been laid on in Joza, but one night a friend who worked for Eskom helped him connect a pirate cable to the Eskom powerline, which runs to the farms at Manley Flats, at a distance of about three hundred yards from the township. The pirate cable was hidden underground and by daybreak Zola was able to sit and watch 'Good Morning South Africa' while eating bacon and eggs with his friends.

At night his house is brilliantly lit – a beacon for that section of Joza. 'A Christmas cake!' MaNdlovu always scolds him. 'And on stolen government batteries, too. It's high time that a unified municipality saw to the provision of power to Sun City.'

For Zola the house is a sign of prosperity and hope in the midst of the dark, poverty-stricken squatter shacks.

He will certainly be able to slip a bribe to the councillors and get a serviced plot up there on the slope near the Mint. That's where the township's supermarket tycoons, the foremost shebeen queens and the trade union leaders live – just like the whites – behind high fences and guarded by Rottweilers.

But he likes his palace here, in this human place, where the noise and activity of humanity is never stilled, and where terror and joy do not select an individual here or there but settle like a swarm of locusts on everyone at once.

The Thandanis will never fully understand why he wants to live here. Those who can, get out of Sun City to the better areas of Joza or, now that the Group Areas Act had been rescinded, to the suburbs between the legs of the Delta where formerly only whites could live.

In her own way MaNdlovu can be obdurate, too. As long as you agree with her she will do anything for you, but beware your soul if ever you cross her ...

Poor Mpho was chased out to the bush with a great hamba; he had no choice. But then the drunken incibi's knife slipped and he cut so badly that they had to carry Mpho, faint from loss of blood, to where an ambulance could pick him up.

The poor young man did not know where to hide his head when he landed in the hospital bed opposite Zola's. He was still semiconscious from blood loss and the injection which the ambulance officer had given him. 'I'm a man! I'm a man!' he shouted and shook his head from side to side on the pillow.

Zola looks at his watch. He has to get some sleep, it is an exhausting time. Earlier Ayanda had fetched him and Mpho from the hospital and they dropped Mpho at the footpath which led up to the bush so that he could rejoin the other abakwethas. They sat there for a long time, even after the boy had disappeared from sight behind the thorn trees. They felt sorry for him, not knowing what awaited him when he tried to rejoin his fellows.

Occasionally Zola is greeted by people passing in the street in front of his house. Some stop, to make their voices audible above the jazz blaring from the open windows. It is a miracle, they say, that he had brought so much wealth to the Kei and still emerged virtually unscathed.

The old muti-man who lives a little way farther up comes walking down the street. He has closed early tonight. Usually he remains open till just after midnight.

'Hi, Bra Muti,' Zola hails him from the balcony. 'Got any ointment for my naughty thoughts?'

'All you need is a monkey's balls, you stinking rich bastard!' the old man snarls jokingly up at him.

'Oh voetsak, old timer,' he mumbles under his breath. 'Go and chase your baboons, old pig-ears ... spunkbuster ... fuckin' tokkeloshe-hawker ...' Zola doesn't like people to call him rich, but he is a little apprehensive of the old man.

Not that the old man has any room to talk of wealth – the manager of one of the branches of Lewis Stores in the city had personally come to furnish his house for him – all spanking new furniture with fancy names like Regency Suite and Diana's Lounge ... every bit of it brand new.

Zola watches the old man walk away and pours another whisky. He is getting sentimental, thinking of the days when he and Ayanda were still young.

They would often visit the Summertime Club in the harbour. In love, they would wander through the anchor ropes and look up at the great ships groaning at anchor. The twinkling harbour lights would reflect off the water and in a dark corner he would take her in his arms and kiss her.

Then the suffering of Joza, the laws of the land, the horrors of famine and unemployment would fade far away and they would be in an interspace, between the city and the open sea, beside these vast old ships which could take you across the sea to other, more peaceful countries.

Zola sighs and takes another sip. If only I could just have her back, he thinks sadly. Can't we just pretend that everything that drove us apart no longer exists?

But he shakes his head. He knows the Thandani women. All of them – from MaNdlovu right down to little Amanda – are now going without their bangles. All the bangles are lying there on the cabinet in the dining room so that all their arms can be clean for the setting free of TaImbongi, for the marches to the oil gusher, for the continuing struggle that MaNdlovu simply can't live without.

Perhaps later, though? When everything is more peaceful ...

Drunk and lonesome in the dark night, Zola practises saying: 'Ayanda, lovey ...'

He stretches his right leg out in front of him. It still feels stiff from the fall in Get Lucky Fried Chicken. The humiliation!

'Ayanda, my darling ...'

The minibus coming round the corner bears no number plates. As if in a dream Zola sees the pink walls of his house reflected in the windscreen. He sees the man in the balaclava, and when the kwela hurtles past his house at full speed he sees the second balaclava-head leaning out with the AK-47.

The rifle stutters. Bullets tattoo the pink walls and time stops as Zola waits for the clattering bullets to come his way. The whisky bottle explodes. When the minibus is past and gone, vanishing into the darkness of the slum, Zola is left lying among shattered glass.

He groans. What a waste. Of life. Of good whisky.

19

The house is dark and stuffy. For some reason or other my radiogram has lost the BBC's Africa Service signal. All that is left is a hissing noise, sometimes louder, sometimes softer. I sink deep into the sofa, breathing in the familiar smells that make me feel relaxed and at home: the steam and benzine of my locomotives, my own sweat, the olives and onions I had so liberally scattered on the homemade pizza I have just eaten.

The patio doors are wide open. Closing my eyes, I see Cawood's tanned body, arms flung wide, dive into the river. To think that the human frame can possess so much natural grace, that such a movement can be executed as though it has been endlessly rehearsed!

And that one body can play so mercilessly with the vulnerability of another – perhaps that is where Cawood's true acrobatic skill lies. In his high school years he had represented the Eastern Province on the horizontal bars, vault, the trampoline and the rings.

Seamus and Sarah were so proud of their athletic young miracle. He was driven in the Mercedes from tournament to tournament (travelling in the school bus with the other children was not good enough) and only the very best of equipment was bought for him.

He was going to be a Springbok, Seamus vowed. I heard from

Sarah that Seamus reckoned Cawood had escaped the qualities which so hamstrung him and which had driven his father to suicide.

In his tenderest moments, Sarah told me, Seamus thanked her that his son favoured her, rather than the morose Butlers.

But Cawood was not destined to gain anything beyond his provincial colours. The international sports boycott had prohibited any possibility of participation overseas. And in any case his attention span was too short for the protracted, disciplined practice sessions required of the sport.

He eventually graduated to guns, bakkies, motorcycles and the young folk clustered around him who shifted their parties like nomads from one farm homestead to another. And eventually there was his military service, which he spent in southern Angola during the bush wars and which he would never talk about afterwards.

The safari enterprise matched his temperament to a t. The rapid change of parties, the brief intensity of the hunting expeditions, the outdoor life, the machismo and the opportunity to be a khaki-clad big game hunter, all the while earning American dollars or Japanese yen in the process, was just what Cawood's personality had been waiting for.

His turnover was soon large enough to pay off a helicopter in instalments. Seamus bought Cawood a farm deep in Manley Flats, to the south-west, not too far from the sea, where the rugged hills and the densely forested kloofs would be just the right terrain for such an enterprise.

Overnight Monomotapa Safaris and Cawood became the focal point of social life for young people in the district. Every hunting party from Munich or Washington, from Tokyo or Montreal has to be introduced to typical Eastern Cape folk, the inhabitants of the Kei and descendants of the famous Settlers of 1820.

Great barbecues are held at Monomotapa, antelopes are roasted whole on spits, groups of tribal dancers are brought in from the Ciskei and the Transkei and traditional dances are performed against the backdrop of the illuminated swimming pool, the manicured lawns, the blazing fires and the full moon reflecting off the glass cabin of the gleaming chopper.

The homestead had been rebuilt. Broad stone terraces lead up to wide verandas with kudu horns on the walls and comfortable chairs draped with leopard skins. The vast sitting room has no ceiling, so that the thick wooden beams supporting the woven thatch roof are clearly visible. On the walls there are mounted animal heads: kudu, leopard, buffalo and gemsbok. On the grand piano a stuffed eagle spreads its wings and clutching talons. In front of the hearth lies a lion skin, with a stuffed head and bared teeth.

A gun rack holds some of the best hunting rifles in the world, and in another corner stands a liquor cabinet with the country's best red and white wines, KWV brandy, bushveld mampoer and peach brandy from the farthest corners of the country.

Magazines like Flying Springbok and Garden & Home are starting to publish photo-articles on Cawood's safari dwelling: there are photographs of Cawood with an orphaned baby baboon born without arms; of Cawood playfully wrestling with two young lion cubs; Cawood in safari dress between two models promoting the summer range of a leading Cape fashion house.

In the master bedroom there is a huge double bed with a lion skin as a coverlet and draped mosquito nets. Walking past the room once during a party, I noticed the bed and imagined Cawood and a pretty young girl romping on it like leopards ... Now I am not so sure ...

I sigh and shake my head. And yourself? You who have lived here all these years, so isolated and apart from those who are alive, away from the dramas of family life and the selflessness which that requires, from clubs with their attendant risks of night life and casual sex, from hard-bitten business circles with their merciless ambition, from the inbred university community, from the farmers with their obsessions about weather conditions and Providence ... You turned your back on all that. You live as though there are only you and your trains, your books, your radio and your music. And the few model train enthusiasts overseas with whom you correspond are all, for the most part, bachelors like yourself, loners, casualties who have never been able to give up the games of their childhood.

You deny your yearnings and your incompletenesses; there are so many possibilities that you decline; you reject love; you reject your own body; you reject life itself.

Are these not also talents given to you – just like your sharp brain, your facility with words, your gentleness and compassion? Do you not deliberately avoid the fullness which it is your duty to achieve?

What happened to you, Seer, that you hide yourself away here?

I sink down deeper into the sofa, and feel the tears welling up inside. My stomach is shaking as they trickle down into my beard and I lick the saltiness out of the corners of my mouth but refuse to wipe my eyes with my hand. Fortunately the lights are off.

But there isn't anyone there to see me anyway. There is nobody nearby. The adjacent plots are overgrown and the old villas in the neighbourhood all deserted. It is far from being a decent neighbourhood any more. The affluent have moved to one of the other deltas where they will not have to see the squatter shacks of Joza. Even the young – the city's yuppies – are not buying here, preferring to purchase doublestorey houses round the old city and then restore them and fit them out with jacuzzis, home gymnasiums and glass atriums.

All that is left here are the ghosts of a bygone era, the voices of my childhood when all the gracious old homes were filled with cosmopolitan families, and children from every branch of the country's multiple cultures romped and played in the streets and on the river banks.

With the advent of the Separate Residential Areas Act the houses emptied. Some families emigrated to Canada or Australia. Some of the older folk died. Now there is just the decay of once glorious gardens: bougainvillaeas, roses, palms, cycads and ferns.

I am lonely. So lonely that I am not always even aware of it. So when I saw the young body of my nephew I suddenly realised just how much I longed for the smell of another body, for tenderness and cherishing, for the breathing and needs of another person. Just for the nearness, just for the caressing words, just the breath of a human being.

I sit there for a long time. Eventually I consider telephoning Sarah. But I know she will be alarmed and drive the Mercedes straight into town. For her to take those farm roads alone after dark in these times will be perilous. No, I have to get out, rather – close the front door behind me and go into the city.

I have to admit and exorcise my loneliness. In rising excitement I begin to dress. I lock the patio doors and first go by the liquor cabinet for a couple of quick whiskies. I hesitate at first but then do it anyway: slip the small flask of whisky into my jacket pocket. I draw the front door to behind me and take a deep breath of the night air.

I switch on the ignition of the old Mercedes and drive down the street. The exhaust, which has a rust hole in it that I am always forgetting to have seen to, makes a stuttering noise that echoes off the walls of the deserted houses. Not until it has driven half a block does the old engine get into its stride. It is a disgrace that I can no longer transport my clients in my own car – even that blown-up kwela of the Thandanis' looked more reliable for the trip to the Ciskei the other day!

I don't quite know which way to go at first, so I head for the part of the city I know best – the market district where my practice is.

It is a little disconcerting to find the area cold and deserted – so different from the daytime bustle when I walk through it to work.

The marketplace is dark, almost without any lighting. Papers, ghost white and floating over the tarmac, are being whirled about in the spaces between low trees where daylight will see blankets and canvas sheets spread and on them merchandise laid out for sale. A minibus with four men in it is parked under a tree. They turn their heads in my direction as I slowly drive by. I shiver, accelerate quickly, and with a shudder running down my spine, turn into the street where my office is.

As I drive past my practice I barely recognise the area. The shops have their shutters closed. Some businesses have heavy steel doors rolled down to hide their faces at night.

Port Cecil, a city with so many faces, so many moods. If you were to drive through Joza, you would never be able to imagine the discos and their flickering strobe lights that amuse the tourists in the hotel quarter. Or if you stand in the old city beside the cathedral, the nouveau riche suburbs on the hills of Fourth Delta with their Vibracrete garden walls and their Biggie Best interior decoration would be unthinkable.

And if you move through the university campus where some dons still deliver their lectures with academic gowns hanging from their shoulders, you would not be able to conceive of police and army barracks where riot police and troops stand ready to charge into Sun City or Joza with Casspirs and sneeze machines at the first signs of insurrection.

Feeling even lonelier now, after the disillusionment of a deserted quarter which I associate with life and activity, I decide to head for the city centre: there will be life there.

I take the long boulevard past the tourist hotels – here the nightlife is bustling. There are also several cars with foreign registration plates – clearly not holidaymakers. These are the cockroaches that have crawled out of the cracks and scurried across the country towards the puddle of oil in the Kei.

There is a commissionaire on duty on the brightly lit porch of every hotel. Each hotel management, competing to attract tourists, dresses its doorkeepers even more absurdly than its rivals: one is kitted out as a Xhosa chieftain, with shield and spear and leopard skin draped over the shoulder; another, at a hotel behind a phalanx of Mercedeses, BMWs and a single natty Porsche, is arrayed like an Oriental potentate, complete with handlebar moustache, a sabre hanging from his sword-belt.

At the next hotel a touring bus has just stopped and the tourists are alighting, to be received immediately by tour guides clad in khaki shirts and shorts and wide-brimmed bush hats with leopard skin bands round the crowns.

I pull up against the sidewalk. There is so much activity here that no one will notice me. I watch the tour guides – strapping young men and women with tanned legs – shaking hands with each tourist and snapping their fingers to the porters at the hotel entrance.

I turn on the ignition and wait a moment for a merry string of people to cross the road to the boat restaurant moored beside the river bank opposite the hotel, its lights glittering in the water. I decide to wait for the boat to leave – it is always a beautiful sight. Also because I don't really know what to do next anyway.

I watch the gangplank rising. The band begins to play and the guests, drinks in hand, lean on the rail to watch the boat slowly drawing away from the bank. It shudders as the engines build up power and then, amidst a flickering of lights in the water and the gleaming brass of the band's instruments, slowly glides into the darkness of the midstream.

Soon they will be out of the delta and sailing up into the lonely Karoo without the passengers being able to form any idea of where they are. Naive tourists from abroad will believe the stewards who tell them that the river they are sailing on is crawling with Africa's largest crocodiles and hippopotamuses, and that there are hungry lions lying in wait in the dark forests on either side.

Later, when the revels reach a climax and empty champagne bottles are floating in the dark water round the boat, now riding at anchor deep inland in the middle of the river, a skilful whistler will trumpet 'My Sarie Marais' on the ship's siren. And if Cawood and his cronies are making merry at a farmstead within earshot, the young men will reply by shooting off their hunting rifles into the air.

I shake my head and smile. Then I pull away from the kerb again, more relaxed now, and decide to take a turn round the nightclub quarter. I drive slowly down the street, looking at the flashing neon lights advertising the clubs. Perhaps I should risk parking the car and going into one of them?

The street grows darker. This is an older part of the city, close to the industrial workshops between Second and Third Delta. It is the prostitutes' quarter and there are all kinds of figures walking up and down in pairs, looking round at the approach of a car, flashing smiles or hand signals.

I drive more slowly and realise that I have no idea of how the naked body of a woman would feel against mine: what do breasts, those bulbs of flesh, feel like against your chest? Or the moist warm pudendum if you lay your hand on it? The rapid movements of two bodies – wouldn't it make you shudder? Or burst out laughing?

All at once a slim figure with blonde hair and red lips comes into the path of the car's lights. I realise that I had seen her just moments before – I had inadvertently (or perhaps deliberately?) driven round the block, and this time she catches my attention. I pull up.

I am breaking the law, but there are so many of my own laws that I have to transgress if I want to live. I indicate to her to come to the passenger's side. She gets in and I am about to pull off, nervous and alarmed, when she restrains me by putting her hand on my leg. I take my foot off the accelerator. I realise that she wants to talk business first. I feel my shirt, wet with sweat, clinging to my chest. It is fright – terror of another body – anxiety about my own body and what she will think of it, about my clumsiness and being exposed, about the criminal unknown.

Fear of the prospect of darkness ahead, the dark pierced only by the car's headlights.

'We must go,' I say hoarsely. She shakes her head. I start to panic. We are close to a street light and I am convinced that passers-by will recognise me. There are not too many of these old-model Mercedeses in the city. 'I'm going now,' I say, but then her grip on my leg tightens again.

Surprised by the strength in her fingers, I look down at the prominent knuckles on the hand, and when I look up I know instinctively what is hidden behind the powder, the wig and the fluttering eyelashes.

'You're a man!' I shout. 'You're no woman!'

I start trembling. God, that it should happen this way.

'Get out!'

In the rear-view mirror I see the man gesturing at me, flashing an obscene sign. Then I turn the corner, pushing the Mercedes to its utmost.

I pull down the sun visor to hide my face and speed out of the area as fast as I can. Avoiding the busy streets, I now race farther and farther, through suburbs and silent shopping areas, where to I do not know.

Later I find myself on the bridge across First Delta. I will drive farther, out into open country. In this city with all its people there is no companion for me tonight. It was a mistake to have risked reaching out like that; I should have stuck to the familiar company of my trains, my pizzas and my magazines.

One is born this way, so clumsy and alone, so indecisive, without the capacity for surrendering oneself to another. There is nothing that can be done about it.

The Mercedes is hurtling along the silent road. The city is eventually no more than a faint glow in the rear-view mirror. I swing out along the turn-off to Manley Flats, and soon the gravel road is rumbling along under the belly of the car. I roll up the window to keep out the dust.

Where am I driving to, at half-past midnight, on a lonely farm road leading nowhere? Then I realise that I have taken the road to Fata Morgana. I have already passed the farm's first camp, on my way to the only person who will understand me: Sarah.

I look at my watch and realise that for me to pitch up at Fata Morgana at this hour would be totally weird. I do not want to burden Sarah any further, traumatised as she is already by Seamus's seizures. I will just drive past Fata Morgana, just to see the lights round the homestead, the silhouette of the trees and the windmills, the house and the outbuildings. Perhaps there will still be one last, comforting light left burning in the house. A little way farther I will turn round again and drive back to town where I'll knock myself out with whisky and a sleeping tablet.

I strike the fall-goat ewe that suddenly appears in my headlights full in the flank. The blow catapults the goat onto the bonnet of the Mercedes. As I jam on brakes and skid across the gravel road, the goat slithers off, leaving a bloody stripe on the nose of the car.

I stop and in the red glow of my brake lights see the goat lying in the swirling dust behind me. Murmuring something, I shift into reverse and drive round the goat so that my headlights shine on where she is lying, one front leg pumping as though in a final desperate attempt to flee.

'Oh, Father almighty ...' I get out and kneel beside the shuddering animal. She lies on her side. She is dying. I sit down in the road. Her yellow eyes, demented with fear, watch me. She does not faint; she knows what is coming. She realises she is dying, I can see it in her eyes.

'Goat ...' The animal's sides tremble and she groans. It is the expiring moan of the Kei.

The goat jerks. I smell blood. Then her flanks begin to heave peristaltically and slowly a little goat kid is born, in the dust of the road, while I tug clumsily at the limp body of the ewe to get her to lie straight.

When eventually the kid is out and I press the slimy little body against me, feeling the trembling of life against my own body, the mother goat dies.

The dust settles. The Mercedes's lights burn a dull, flickering yellow.

20

After an episode like that anyone deserves some comfort! But it is Sarah that I am thinking of particularly – she who has had to learn to live in a climate of longing. She is not a person of very strong likes or dislikes. What she asks for is happiness, that is all. Watching her now, working in the kitchen on Fata Morgana, I would have liked to talk to her. At any rate it will be a kind of comfort – even if only for me that I can be close to her as I tell my story.

It is already almost half-past one in the morning and Seamus, who came home tired and dejected after his meeting in the city, has only just fallen asleep.

She had to let him soak for an hour in a hot bath and then gave him an extra sleeping pill.

How she longs for a husband whom she does not constantly have to entice back from the brink of the abyss with words of comfort and encouragement ... Seamus's medication does not really work. He will switch from one family of pills to the next – while one type relieves his depression, it will not blunt the edge of his anxiety; another dulls his fears, but leaves him so stupefied that he is not able to deal with everyday routines and so wanders aimlessly about the estate. Sometimes he is so bad that she is afraid to let him drive into town on his own and has to use all her tact to persuade him not to go.

A third kind of pill numbs both the fears and the depression to quite a considerable extent and is not as paralysing in its effects, but it excites him so much that no sleeping pill can knock him out. In his manic mood he will stride up and down in the house, fiddle with the goat stud's records, toy with family trees and plan all kinds of cross-breeding strategies with a view to producing goats which will be able to experience terror selectively: to faint only in the face of predators, and not at every crack of a whip or gunshot or thunderclap.

Their nights become long, protracted conversations about his parents, guilt, Cawood, Fata Morgana, the white man in Africa, colonialism and apartheid.

Sarah sighs. My toppling-goat. How I betray you with my longing for simplicity and optimism. She is standing with her hands on the cool kudu flesh she is working with. In her eyes, Seamus's persistent depression lends him a certain stature: he is a man confronting his own demons.

In one of his rare gestures of affection Cawood had dropped off the kudu here and Sarah is slicing up the fillets for biltong with skilled, sure strokes. Surrounded by the smells of fresh meat, coriander seeds and salt, she thinks: you should thank God for what you have; for this secure life with its comfortable rhythms, its familiar demands, its rituals and its bond with the earth which you understand so well.

She often sees Seamus in the company of other men – men of his own generation – but beside him they seem frivolous and superficial. His large stature, the troubled eyes, the irascibility round the eyebrows, the deep furrows in his cheeks, the measured movements so typical of a depressive personality all lend him an aura of experience, of lived-through suffering, which she does not sense in other men.

I do love him, this dignified, tormented husband of mine. Even though the medication leaves him impotent and unaware of the needs of others for long periods, and even if he does live so distant from me, so sealed into his own thoughts. He bears so much more within him than that Bill Heathcote and the other whisky-swilling farmers of Manley Flats.

At least Seamus is prepared to look into the abyss that we all carry about inside us.

She sighs: if you have to live your life where I have to live mine, trapped inside your husband's problems, overwhelmed by his pain, then all there is is hope, hope, and again: hope.

I come right up to Sarah. Yes, I want to say, cling to hope like hope for a good crop of lambs, for good rains ... There isn't actually anything else you can do.

She breathes deeply, taking in the scents of thyme and coriander, and the smell of fresh blood. The familiar kitchen environment with its heavy basins of meat and the muted hum of the freezers makes her feel secure and at home. When she stops working she can hear Seamus snoring in the bedroom. At last, at last he is asleep.

When she thinks she hears a vehicle, she keeps her hands still. But no, it is probably the fridges having to work extra hard to chill the fresh load of meat. But then she hears it again: there is undoubtedly a car turning off the through road onto the private farm road that leads up to the homestead.

I wish she won't, but she takes fright. Seamus is in one of those deep sleeps of his out of which nothing will wake him. She quickly rinses her hands under the tap, dries them and stands for a moment with the crumpled towel against her chin. The droning grows louder.

Outside the dogs start barking and the flock of geese kept in the house camp as an early-warning system sets up a raucous squawking. Sarah can't help thinking of the recent wave of attacks on isolated farmsteads. Almost every day a farmer and his wife, or farmers' wives living on their own, or isolated old folks are attacked by vagabond bands of robbers. Farmers believe that the attacks are part of an organised campaign to disrupt the farming community – a first step towards the ultimate takeover of white farmers' large stock farms by black peasants.

The paranoia is exacerbated by pyromaniacs who are systematically destroying the best grazing on farms along the Fish River on the Ciskei border by setting fire to large tracts of veld.

Seamus and Sarah shook their heads when unnerved farmers started talking of mustering commando forces to patrol the border. Some even erected electrified fences round their homesteads.

Now she is the one hurrying past me to her bedroom to fetch the thirty-O-six from the locked wardrobe. She does not even consider waking Seamus – he will not be in a fit state for eight or nine hours yet.

The rifle fits snugly in her hands and she feels stronger. Whoever you are, I'll blast your heads off. She is thankful that she has regularly attended the shooting practices arranged by the Civil Defence for farmers' wives. She is one of the best shots in the district among them.

With the gun in her hands she switches off the passage and lounge lights and peers cautiously through the curtains. The car comes slowly up the drive. The dogs congregate at the gate to the farmyard, barking. The geese bunch up in a corner of the camp in alarm.

The car stops at the gate and remains there, idling. No one gets out. Sarah strains her ears as she stares into the headlights. One or two of them are approaching the house from behind, she thinks suddenly, and they're busy at the back door while the dogs and I are being decoyed by the car at the gate. They have already cut the telephone wires. The servants have revealed that old Seamus Butler of Fata Morgana, the toppling-goat, has taken his sleeping pills early tonight and fallen into a coma from which nothing will wake him. There's only the white woman left. Alone.

She points the rifle barrel through the open window of the lounge and lets it rest on the crossbar of the burglar proofing. I am beside her and now I simply have to do something. A figure is moving round the car. Sarah takes aim across the sights. The man stands looking at the house for a long time, but against the strong headlights Sarah cannot make out who it is. She will fire a warning shot.

She licks the droplets of sweat off her top lip, expecting at any moment to hear wood creaking, glass shattering, a sheet of roofing iron being bent back above her head.

Sarah! Before I can stop her, she fires a shot.

She takes fright as the man jerks, hesitates and appears in the light of the headlamps. It is my untidy, overweight body she sees struggling with the gate, looking uncertainly up towards the homestead and then down at my hands.

Standing here in the house behind Sarah I look at myself down the black barrel of the gun. I watch myself battling with the gate, not succeeding. 'Seer,' Sarah's lips move as relief drains the tension from her body. She remembers to slide the rifle's safety catch up, then switches the lounge lights on again as she hurries to the front door to wait for me, the gun still in her hands. She is trembling with relief.

'Seer?'

I'm here, dammit! I want to say. Heavens, how you frightened me, Sarah. But I am already guiding my car through the gate, closing the gate behind me and driving up to the veranda. I get out, stop at the open door of the car and look at her standing on the stoep. I shrug my shoulders and then shake my head.

'I'm still awake,' she says softly. 'Come in now, come on up.' She beckons me up the steps. We remain standing opposite each other on the half-lit veranda.

Then she reaches out a hand to my cheek. I jerk my head away and point to my car, so she will see the blood streaks on the bonnet.

'You've hit ... killed ... someone ...'

I shake my head. 'Sarah,' I say.

I look tired and she takes my arm.

'Seamus is asleep already,' she says. 'Shall I make my old brother some coffee?'

'I was driving past when I saw all the lights still burning, so ...'

'Don't worry,' she interrupts. 'It's wonderful to see you. I was feeling so alone too. And I got such a fright when I heard the car.'

She wants to lead me indoors, but I am hesitant.

Standing in front of me, she wants to give me a hug, but our relationship has never depended on any excessive physical contact, there is always too much embarrassment involved. How I regret that now, afterwards! How I long for her touch!

'Sarah ...'

'Seer?'

I shake my head and go into the house. She follows, but in the passage I turn round. 'I've got something in the car,' I say.

'Oh?'

She follows me outside and stands behind me as I open the back door and lean inwards. I lift the newborn kid out and stand there with a wry, sad smile, holding it clumsily.

'But Seer!'

'Sarah ...' I come up close to her. The kid is still bloody, so she realises that it is newly born.

'Seer? But what is this all about, Seer?'

'Sarah, do you know that I ...'

'Yes?'

I look at her, then avoid her eyes. I look round me with a helpless gesture, the kid held tightly to my chest with one hand.

'Seer?'

I stride past her. 'He's got to get some food,' I say in a matter-of-fact tone. 'Milk, or whatever it is one gives an orphan kid. And I want to buy him from you.

'He's mine.'

21

Oh Seer, Seer – that you could have made such a fool of yourself! For a moment you really were afraid that Sarah, fine shot that she is, would summarily blast you out of the web of your own spinning! Ham-handed ... as always.

Well, let me now avenge myself on him who was sleeping off his self-indulgence during the near-showdown between Sarah and me. The master-breeder, who can be so snide about the professors' pomposity, is not above flights of bombast himself. Listen:

Meetings of the city council normally take place in a stately manner. The rituals belong to a municipal memory that harks back to England, so the council chamber where Seamus and the other aldermen usually meet is a dignified, elegant room.

Today, however, the mayor has decided that the councillors should use the smaller committee room overlooking Cathedral Square. From there they can keep an eye on the oil fountain and developments on the square.

The reality of the pulsating stream of oil and the thousands of people now constantly milling around it prevent them from withdrawing into the traditional council chamber with its splendid wood panelling and green leather seats.

As the aldermen debate, the activity beneath is in full view: technical teams trying to decide how to cap the gusher – it is the first such find on the entire subcontinent and the technology to deal with it has not yet been developed – but finding their attempts thwarted by the magnitude of the pressure; geologists taking soil samples and examining the drill samples taken during Canaan Drillers' search for water and still shaking their heads in disbelief days after the discovery; a police contingent and a line of troops keeping the curious at a safe distance and, particularly, ensuring that inhabitants of the squatter camp with their tins and other containers do not get close enough to the well to scoop up fresh oil.

As the squatter population burgeoned in recent years firewood became increasingly scarce and women have to walk for miles every day with long loads of cut saplings on their heads. The oil was quickly seen as a substitute.

Seamus Butler, with one eye on his notes and the other on the scene outside – the begrimed cathedral walls! – is addressing the councillors.

'It is not every day that an event of this nature occurs behind the aloe curtain,' he says. 'If we do not approach this like a properly planned logistic operation, that black angel down there will become more than an oil-smeared statue – it will be the harbinger of evil tidings, the herald of the decline of all that is commendable and orderly. It will become the angel of iniquity, the black angel flying batlike over our city ...'

He pauses in silence for a moment as he looks out across Cathedral Square. 'Joy and happiness,' he continues, 'excitement and ecstasy ...' he takes a deep breath and draws himself up to his full height, 'must necessarily yield for a time to practicalities, which I shall list for you:

'Firstly: security.' He points to the window. 'If that black fountain catches fire, it could send the entire city up in flames.' He looks down at the astonished faces round him. 'This is not some far-fetched notion. London has had the experience of being burnt to the ground. I need not remind you that was the fate that befell that city of all cities ...'

The imaginary spectacle of a world capital burning, one also situated on the banks of a river, makes the councillors listen to him with renewed attention, Seamus notices.

'Our fire brigade is no match for such an eventuality. And because we are so isolated, we shall not be able to rely on the assistance of other large fire brigades. Can you imagine us calling in the help of Alicedale's little red Ford with its single watertank and hand-pump and then waiting half a day for them to come bumping along the dirt road to our aid?'

Some of the councillors chuckle at this prospect. 'Or Bedford, or Salem, or Bathurst? They can hardly manage more than a pick-up with a 44-gallon drum on the back. No, I am afraid we shall have to rely on ourselves.'

Suddenly the councillors realise once again just how vast the plain is that stretches out round the city. Now, Seamus notices with considerable satisfaction, they are thinking of more than just our isolation – let them too share his overwhelming attacks of agoraphobia! – but there is also their terror of being exposed to the stark barrenness of a natural world aloof from the concerns of humanity.

Seamus exploits their anxious attentiveness. 'We shall have to pay attention to our emergency teams. The police, the army, civil defence ...'. It is becoming a battle. Seduced by his own metaphors of conflict, he continues: 'Pollution. Our city has always been a delightful oasis in a parched semidesert. What is the aim of this attack of oil? For, yes, it is indeed an attack which nature, as it were, has launched upon itself. I wish to ask: is nature here attempting suicide? The oil is creeping into the drainage channels and ditches and relentlessly stalking the estuary. Take a look at Fourth Delta: it is a quagmire of oil and mud and dead sea birds. Anglers are pulling in dead fish as far up as Horse-shoe Bend already. We are facing an ecological disaster – and you know as well as I do that the ecology is the challenge of our time. It is about pollution, the rape of our Mother, but it also raises questions about the possession of the earth: how should her assets be distributed?

'There are thousands of students at our university who are fit and ready. We must enlist them as recruits for the Green Branch.' The councillors all nod. 'And now that ...' Seamus sighs and looks out of the window again, 'now that we agree that the concept of ecology is something which includes the compulsive struggle for ownership of land and possession of power over the earth, now we come to our black brethren and sisters ... our neighbours in Joza ...'

He leans forward and takes a sip of water. He can feel the tense attention of the councillors fixed upon him. These are the only times when his depression really lifts, when he is here among the others and his loneliness is subsumed and he can give his words free rein – when he can combine his sense of civic responsibility with his love of rhetoric and ritual.

'Now that apartheid is being systematically eradicated from the statute book, the attacks from Joza for a single unified municipality are – as you are aware – becoming more intense than ever. And from now on those attacks are going to achieve an unprecedented degree of militancy. I say militancy, Mr Mayor, because Joza knows that wealth has been struck here, great wealth. Black gold, your worship, nothing less. Black gold.

'Passions will be released in our city which we shall almost certainly be unable to contain on our own. The black angel of chaos is on the wing above our heads. My fellow councillors, this is crisis time ...

'And we who have been placed here in the south-east by Providence to embody the best of British values here in Africa, we shall have to be strong. Our forefathers came ashore here in the wilderness. The year 1820 flashes like a burning torch of light in the historical consciousness of this whole region, for that was when the finest liberal values took root here ...

'We,' Seamus slams his fist on the table in front of him, 'we, as descendants of the Settlers, will once again, as so often in the past, have to be the torch-bearers in a dark time. And then, your worship, I have not yet referred to the rush of usurers and gamblers and streetwalkers since the oil strike. Our city will lose its character as an historical seat. Tents are even being pitched on school rugby fields. I am told that the stables at the pony club have been converted into a hostel for speculators and brokers of all kinds. Every spendthrift and wastrel in the country, every pickpocket and bag-snatcher, cheque-forger, confidence trickster, stock thief and gaolbird is now going to make our fair city his prime destination ...

'Mr Mayor, if we do not act swiftly and resolutely, we shall become the Sodom of the Kei. Thank you.'

I am quite out of breath when Seamus – likewise breathless – resumes his seat. I had to struggle to keep up! And, I confess, I smuggled in a few big words of my own here, in amongst all the ones he chose himself.

The councillors, caught up by the emotion of his speech, start beating their palms on the table in front of them. He rises once more and shouts: 'Down with the Sodomites!' and sits down to loud applause.

During the tea break he sits in the small office set aside for his use here. Now that the energy of public speaking has drained away, his spirit is growing heavy again.

Seamus wipes a hand across his eyes. There is no connection between our hollow rhetoric and what happens to us – either within or outside our minds. Committee work like this, public office, municipal politics, community service are all rituals of evasion. They create constructs in which the participants protect themselves. Reality is without form and void. It stinks. It is filthy. It cannot be defined.

In front of Seamus stands the Fall-Goat Trophy, which is to be awarded again in two days' time. He strokes the back of the bronze goat. It is a beautiful statue. On its base are the names and dates of previous winners.

Seamus sighs. If I do not have this, what is there left of me? Cawood has no inkling about me – we have never yet had a single, serious conversation. Sarah tries to support me, but there are so many chasms between us, so many bitternesses built up over the years. They are like flotsam in a dam – if one was to open the sluices now, they would clog the outflow. One may as well leave them where they are – and rely on the little that there is.

Seamus looks at his diary. He will still need to call in at my practice, later. He has to fetch a new battery for the John Deere tractor from the agricultural cooperative. Post the therapist his cheque. Perhaps down a quick whisky in the bar with the World War II fighter planes.

He shuts his eyes again: I have to hold on, I may not let go now ...

22

'Now they're making Zola the scapegoat,' sighs MaNdlovu. 'First they burn him pink like a sewer rat in the street; now they shoot him to pieces, him and his house both.'

At first from behind my desk I want to interrupt her and protest that Zola has suffered a mere flesh wound in the attack. But my attention is distracted when the little orphaned kid lying on a reed mat in a corner of the office makes a sudden movement. The desk top between MaNdlovu and me is piled high with papers and books.

'When he went and built that castle of his three storeys high and then painted it bright pink, I told him, I said: You can't just go and put up a thing like that and think people are not going to notice everything you do. Wherever you go in the squatter camp, you see that pink palace sticking up at you like a prickly pear. No wonder it's become a target.'

'Mrs Thandani ...'

'That's the way it's been ever since they started casting our traditions aside like tattered old rags. Look where my Ncincilili has ended up, look where TaImbongi has landed, look how I had to hamba-hamba Mpho to get him out into the bush. I don't think my poor nerves can take it any more. Our men have drunk themselves sodden and beaten each other to pulp. It's only the women who've got any strength left. Lawyer Wehmeyer, you ...'

'No, hang on now, MaNdlovu ...' This is the first time since I met her that I have dropped the formal mode of address. For a moment I actually lose the thread of what I am saying. The woman in front of me reminds me of black women from my childhood: the huge Missus Madyibi who always came to our old home collecting clothes for the church. In those days she was the only Xhosa woman who did not come round to the back door – she knocked on the front door and sat down at her ease in the lounge.

And the Sunday afternoons round the antheap tennis courts of the district – I don't remember on which farms any more – when the adults in their white togs would play interminable sets, and then doubles, and then swop over and play again; when the Christmas beetles would screech dementedly and Sarah and I, beside the cars in the shade of a pepper tree, would wait for the matches to end at last, and then the picnic baskets and glass jugs of lemonade would be brought out ...

Throughout, a black woman had to sit beside us and patiently keep us in check to see that we didn't crawl or, later, waddle out on unsure little legs to the fence round the tennis court and break the players' concentration. I can still smell the sour odour of antheap clay rising as the farm labourer on tennis duty moved across the court with a watering can to keep it slightly damp.

'Yes, Lawyer Seer, you can call me MaNdlovu. It's my name and everyone in Joza calls me that. And anyway you are doing so much work for our family nowadays that soon you and that orphan kid of yours are going to be Thandanis yourselves ...' MaNdlovu laughs, her huge chest heaving, till eventually she is shaken by a coughing fit.

'I don't guarantee success.' I get up, stroke the sleeping kid's back, and stand at the window with my back to MaNdlovu. I remember, I want to tell her, the patience and motherliness of women like you. And I also remember the self-confidence and strength of others who, with scant resources and by way of great sacrifice, had to fight for their families, just like you.

Behind me, MaNdlovu is weeping quietly. I do not turn round.

Not only do I have the events of the previous night to digest, but now MaNdlovu is here, too, with the full force of her personality. I have to get TaImbongi released as soon as possible – and in the middle of a state of emergency in the Ciskei at that, and amidst rumours of an imminent coup d'état in that homeland. Apart from that I have also just been asked by MaNdlovu to consult the prison services about – as she put it – the whereabouts of Ncincilili.

She marched in and announced: 'Lawyer Wehmeyer, I've got a whereabouts-case for you.' And when I peeled a fresh file off the pile behind me and asked: Yes, whose? Who is it we are trying to trace? she began to tremble, took out her white handkerchief, and could not manage a single word for a couple of minutes. I had to ask my secretary to moisten her handkerchief with a little water and to serve us coffee.

And the third case I had to take on, she explained, was the Zola affair. I was to get to the bottom of – to the chopping of the axe – of the taxi war. Why should it have been Zola who was shot at? Was there any connection with the fountain of oil? Was it the shebeen owners who wanted him taken out because he was proposing to run a mobile shebeen in his bakkie? Was he being punished because he was clever? Was it, as always, a case of people who were incapable of coming up with original ideas of their own trying to prevent others from doing so? Or was Zola implicated in Mandrax smuggling, as he had been that summer when he and Ayanda had separated and people whispered that he had got involved with the Chinese contraband tycoons of the harbour area?

I tried in vain to persuade MaNdlovu that there were no legal grounds for action – she would do better to approach a private detective. She persisted. For MaNdlovu, justice was an all-embracing concept. 'Officers of the law – like me – had to exemplify that concept. This she informed me with the force of such conviction that I felt obliged to do something.

'I'll go up the Ciskei again tomorrow,' I say. 'I'll try again to see if I can trace your husband.'

She crumples up her handkerchief and pushes it into her pocket. 'I'm coming, too. We must warn Ayanda, so she can put in for leave.'

I shake my head. 'No, I'm sorry. I shall be more mobile on my own. I'd much rather you stayed at home. The journey would only exhaust you.'

She looks at me and tilts her head on one side, all at once looking much calmer. 'Sit down, Lawyer Seer. There's another matter.'

I sit down. It is late in the afternoon; she is the last client of the day – I do not need to hurry. All that there is at home is just the unapproachable river, the roses tired after a day of wind, the shining noses of the steam engines, the large deserted rooms, the nest smell of a lonesome house closed up all day and inhabited by only one person.

'Take down a new folder,' MaNdlovu commands, pointing to the pile behind me.

I lean over backwards, taking down another file. 'It seems that MaNdlovu is preparing to take on the whole world.'

She does not laugh, but takes the white handkerchief out of her pocket again. She bunches it up, clenching it tightly in her fist. She knocks her knuckles on the desk top, emphasising each word with a loud knock-knock: 'Prosecute the church.'

I sit back and take a deep breath. With my limited medical knowledge I have to draw the inference that MaNdlovu is suffering from high blood-pressure and that her fainting spells and sudden urges are a prelude to a brain haemorrhage. Too much emotion will exert pressure on the capillaries in her brain, and either she will feel faint or – as now – her thoughts will flit about electrically.

'What is it you are saying now, MaNdlovu?'

She takes a deep breath. 'That ground that the cathedral stands on and that the oil is spouting out of, is Xhosa soil. Our ancestors lie buried there. Their bones are still there under the foundations. My people tried to stop it at the time, but the cathedral was built over the graves of the ancestors.'

She sits back and folds her arms.

'We want the ground back,' she says. 'We were here first before those silly Settler ships with their loads of pink Brits, and before the oxwagons brought the damned Boers in here, too.'

'MaNdlovu ...'

'Our ground.'

'But MaNdlovu, the church ...'

'No two ways about it.'

I close my eyes. There are pinpoints of light behind my eyelids. A dustdevil in which the tail-lights of the Mercedes glow red; the ewe lying jerking in the road. The whole firmament of heaven is in my brain. A galaxy is spinning in my blood. When I open my eyes, she is on her feet already.

'You can pray if you like, Lawyer Seer, but the time has come for the Thandanis to stop taking shit.'

23

Ayanda is standing on the veranda at the hospital. The death of Ncincilili weighs heavily on her conscience, and she does not know how much longer she will be able to bear that weight.

Within the space of a few horrific moments – when that policeman thrashed about on the tarmac in flames – she was saddled with a burden that was too heavy for her to carry.

Often, when pressure of work in the hospital permits, she will spend a little while at the bedside of a dying patient. The desperation she feels as she looks into eyes that are slowly glazing over has never diminished from that time years and years ago when as a young doctor she first witnessed a death.

You try in vain to resuscitate the body in front of you, for you know it is not just a piece of flesh and blood that you are trying to keep alive – it is a whole unfathomable world of experiences, a lifetime of seeing and hearing and feeling, of trying and failing – all this seeps away as you sit there, powerless. And at last, when you draw the sheet up over the face, a part of the world itself seems to have been lost, a private history just as important – perhaps even more important – than the histories shaped by wars, earthquakes and battles.

You, Ncincilili, Ayanda thinks as she drinks her coffee on the hospital veranda at the end of a long stint on duty, you did not die in front of me, but I cannot banish your last hours from my mind.

How were your last moments at the gallows? Were you silent or did you scream, as some do? Did they have to drag you to the execution chamber, or did you march in singing, your fist clenched, like many freedom fighters? Has death brought you freedom?

The teaspoon tinkles in her saucer. She feels light-headed. It has been a long stint; she lost three patients. The advent of the oil and the superficial jollity that accompanied it has led to a series of attempted suicides.

And you just don't have the time to sit with these people, she thinks, because the intercom is calling for you to attend to an emergency somewhere, ambulances are constantly disgorging bleeding bodies at Casualty, ward sisters are striking for improved working conditions, there are shortages of certain essential medicines.

Ayanda is haunted by the aged, struggling figure of MaNdlovu battling her way up the path to the Mint. Each has her own way of dealing with tension. I lose myself in my work and imagine that the task of bringing complete healing to everyone rests on my shoulders and mine alone. TaImbongi heads for the shebeen and there practises his praise songs before a grateful audience. And MaNdlovu slips away from the Civic – where the staff watch her very closely ever since the disappearance of civic activists, and assassinations among them, became commonplace – and climbs the hill to the Mint.

Quite recently MaNdlovu disappeared again and it was Ayanda who had to struggle up the track in search of her. She found her mother covered in dust and blood, with her back to the wall of the old warehouse, weeping.

Ayanda said nothing, she simply sat down beside MaNdlovu. They spent a long time there waiting for emotions to subside, for the wind to stop howling round the building, for the rusted sheet of roofing iron beating against the plastered wall to fall silent.

Then Ayanda helped MaNdlovu to her feet and took her home, stumbling down the footpath, as the city, shining and cold, lay spreadeagled across the seven legs of the delta. A helicopter was circling lazily above the city centre.

Ayanda takes her cup indoors. Today there is none of that sense of liberation at the end of a long shift – she still has to visit Zola to ask how his shoulder wound is getting on and to try to establish whether he has any idea of who had fired at him.

For the police are slow to investigate such attacks. Violence spills over from the homelands and attackers flee back to the Ciskei and the Transkei. Often the struggle between political factions is bound up with taxi wars and Mandrax smuggling, which leaves the truth concealed so deep that no amount of detective work can trace it.

The army, too, is out of control, utterly corrupt, with special units devising and carrying out their own operations against activists. And black pressure groups have declared war on whites. All the perpetrators of violence believe that a general amnesty will be proclaimed which will absolve them of all their crimes.

It is quite possible that Zola, with his love of money and his impulsive way of doing things, may have become involved somehow. The machine-gun under the seat of the minibus is a first indication.

She walks resolutely down to the male ward. It is not my duty to act as your keeper, Zola. It's not my task to try to keep everyone everywhere together. But if I let go, the whole lot of you will burst apart. The oil has only made everything worse: it is almost as though the whole city has gone into spasm like a muscle.

When she walks into the ward he is lying on his side. He's waiting for me, she observes. 'Ayanda,' he greets her, 'you look tired.'

'It's been a long shift. Is your pain any easier?'

He nods, and sits up against his pillows with a painful expression on his face. He sighs, and she follows his eyes. Patients in the other beds lie looking at them wordlessly. Irritated, Ayanda gets up and draws the curtains round the bed.

'They're watching me because they know about me and the oil well,' Zola says softly. 'They don't know who shot me, but they are afraid that friendship with me is somehow going to annoy "them". They don't know whether I'm an impimpi or a hero – they're expecting those balaclavas to burst in here and shoot up the whole ward ...'

'Never mind now ... hush now ...'

'Ayanda, I've got to get out of here. I know ...'

'Zola, we've got guards outside on the verandas. For months now every vehicle has been stopped and searched at the hospital gates. No one can harm you here. All you need to do is relax and get well again.'

'Where is Amanda?'

'She's busy. You know Amanda: if it's not the literacy project in Sun City, then it's the night shelter for street children on Cathedral Square, or the youth league, or heaven knows what else.'

'She's forgotten about me.'

'Oh, nonsense, Zola.'

'An old taximan father isn't good enough for my educated daughter ...' He looks despondent.

Ayanda sighs: No, I am not going to carry this, too, today. 'Come now, Zola, we've got to try and find out who shot you.'

He sighs. 'Tsotsis.'

'Rubbish. Tsotsis aren't professionals. This was a well-planned operation. In that busy street. They got away and no one can point a finger.'

'Probably the Third Force then.'

'Everybody's talking about a Third Force, Zola – but why should they go for you? And who are they?'

He shakes his head and looks away.

She takes his hand. 'Zola?'

'Yes?'

'You haven't been couriering Mandrax for those harbour captains, have you?'

He shakes his head. 'No, Ayanda, and I don't smuggle AK-47s either. And I'm not an impimpi. I'm just what you see here in front of you: Zola Mtuze, the taximan.'

'Someone must have thought you were more than just an ordinary taxi driver.'

'There are people in Joza who can't stomach my prosperity,' he says. 'They want to pull me down to their level, to clump about in the mud with them. They can't bear ...'

'There are people who say it has to do with the oil,' she interrupts. 'They say the white business community is refusing to admit that you detected the oil. They think the people of Joza will want more of the oil if they think you were the one who discovered it.'

'Oh, I don't know.'

'We've got to find out, Zola! Perhaps it's because of the Civic.' She feels helpless – never before has she seen Zola so tired, so listless. 'They'll be shooting at MaNdlovu next!'

'No bullet could penetrate that thick hide.'

Ayanda gets up angrily. 'All you lot can do is quarrel among yourselves. And I am the one who always has to be the peacemaker!'

'Just get me out of here,' Zola answers. 'Bring my kwela. I can drive with one arm.'

'You're not going anywhere. You're safest here.'

Both annoyed, they look at each other. 'And when is the march on the oil well?' Zola asks. Ayanda throws up her arms. That, too, now! MaNdlovu and her Civic are planning the city's biggest march ever. The people of Joza, MaNdlovu said, would stand in a solid phalanx right round the oil well and demand what was theirs.

'The day after tomorrow,' she says. 'And if MaNdlovu's dreams come true TaImbongi will be marching right up front like a general in shining armour ...'

'And Mpho?'

'No word of him. They must have accepted him back into the bush.'

Ayanda shakes her head and closes her eyes to stop the room spinning. I need to rest; I must get into a cool bed and forget the failures of my day, forget the patients who died on my hands, forget my divorced husband, my frenetic, absent daughter, my mother's illusions, my ...

She leaves without greeting Zola.

She passes by me – without even a nod of recognition. I watch her go: the only dead man under my hands, Ayanda, is myself. So lifeless, but so light-footed, so free! At last, I have left my nature behind. Naturally.

24

'Tragos is a freak of nature,' I tell Seamus as we sit in my office. 'He is hardly one day old and you can tell that he is a goat of extraordinary potential.'

While we are going through the documents on the desk between us the kid lies on his straw mat in the corner. Every now and again he will get up and reveal the pitch-black birthmark staining his chest.

'This is the first fall-goat with red eyes that I have ever bred,' says Seamus. 'It's disturbing. I'll have to keep an eye on this year's crop of kids. I hope it isn't some germ that's got into the genes. You never can tell what is going to come out in the breeding these days. You know what influence that oil pollution is already having on the delta and the coral reef. I wonder whether the red eyes mightn't somehow be connected with that other freak of nature ...'

'The oil is a good long way from Fata Morgana,' I counter, surprised at the strength of my emotion. And with a surge of loyalty towards the little kid: 'And anyway the foetus was already pretty well developed by the time the oil was discovered. It couldn't have had any influence at all.'

'When the wind blows from the city,' Seamus replies irritably, 'my leading goats lift their heads and sniff the air. I've seen them do it. You can smell that oil, Seer. You people here in the city are so used to the pollution that you can't smell anything any more. It's the first time since the government banned Dieldrin and DDT that I have noticed this toxic restlessness in my animals again. And that little kid ...' Seamus turns to look straight at the baby goat, 'I'm quite certain that kid is the first of a deviant generation of stud animals which this district is going to bring forth now that that Black Evil is oozing up out of the earth like molasses.'

The kid gets up and starts out delicately walking across the polished wooden floor towards us. I smile fondly. 'See how gingerly he steps,' I say. 'He followed me to work this morning. He's like my shadow. And he's bright, too – he knows how to duck out of the way of the kwela taxis when we're crossing a street. When the hawkers at the market grab at him playfully and offer to buy him from me – apparently his red eyes will make strong muti, he sticks close to my legs ...'

'I went through his mother's records this morning after Sarah told me about his eyes,' Seamus says. 'She comes of one of my best bloodlines. And now suddenly there's this freak with his birthmark and his red eyes.' He shudders. To my amazement I notice goosebumps on his hairy forearms. 'You have no idea what this does to a stud breeder. It's like that calf with two heads – Bill Heathcote wasn't the same person for months afterwards. Even though he invited the whole district to come and see it. As though that would lessen his disgrace ...'

I look straight at Seamus. Go on: I challenge you. But Seamus hurriedly looks away. The kid so peacefully, cautiously, circling the desk unnerves him. We sit there for a while after Seamus has quickly dropped his gaze before the challenge in my eyes.

Then he sighs, rubs his hands together and thrusts his shoulders back. 'I've got to get that piece of ground alienated now,' he says. 'I've got to shift the weight of my interests towards the city. If this sort of thing' – he points at the goat kid – 'is going to start happening on Fata Morgana now, it is all the more essential for me to invest in the city.'

'Yes,' I reply, now more businesslike. 'Read through the sworn affidavit. It's very important as support for your application. Do take your time.'

I get up and go into the waiting room. There are no more clients – it is past six already. My secretary has gone home and the doors are closed. I was just packing up when Seamus arrived.

Strange that I should have more self-confidence in Seamus's company today. It must be because of what Sarah told me the other night about Seamus's terrors. Old Goat Butler – also sometimes known as the Toppling Goat (the nickname which the envious and the gossipmongers had given his father) – is only human after all. See how little Tragos has unnerved him. He's actually come out in goosebumps ...

'Tragos, Tragos ...' I call softly as I take the feeding bottle with the teat from the small fridge behind the secretary's desk. The preparation is a mixture of goat's milk and allergy-free powdered milk for babies. 'I don't want a goat with colic,' I joked when Sarah and I were sitting in the kitchen in the wee small hours discussing the orphan kid's nutrition. (Even the gunshot had not woken Seamus!) Sarah promised to send a small can of goat's milk from Fata Morgana into town every day for the 'Wehmeyer orphan'.

I sit in one of the waiting room chairs holding the bottle for him and Tragos happily waggles his bum, enthusiastically drinking his milk.

Seamus's shadow suddenly falls across us. 'One of these days he's going to stand as tall as your waist,' he says disapprovingly, the documents in his hand. 'Are you going to give him the teat then too?'

As though you are not giving your young Cawood the teat, and him well over twenty! I would have liked to reply. But I say nothing – the line between family and business in situations like this is a very fine one. I prefer to keep things on a professional level – even though I am sitting in such an undignified position, feeding bottle in hand ...

'Are you satisfied?'

'Yes. I have made slight amendments here and here,' Seamus replies as he riffles through the documents with characteristic haste. 'But they're minor matters. Have a look at them and phone me. I'll come in later and sign. Have we got a court date yet?'

'Things don't happen that fast,' I reply. 'The registrar of the court will only let us know later. But I must warn you again the courts are overflowing with cases in the aftermath of the discovery of the oil. If there is one group that is celebrating, it's the legal profession. You'd be amazed at the variety of cases: from the Greens' urgent interdicts on oil pollution to the fishing community's applications on fish quotas, and of course the world and his wife are applying for liquor and business licences. What with crayfish smugglers and dagga growers and nightclub tycoons, the crime rate has rocketed two hundred per cent. Every pickpocket and conman in the country is heading for here.'

'Nobody can claim innocence,' Seamus says, dropping the documents on a chair and – with a last annoyed glance at the milk-drinking kid – strides out.

'Goodbye, Seamus.' I try to twist the teat out of Tragos's mouth, but Seamus is already in the Mercedes and swerving away in the direction of the big hotels.

I stand on the pavement watching him. Probably going off to the pub again. Once more Sarah will be sitting up late tonight in that isolated farmhouse.

I go back inside, only to find Tragos nibbling the corner of the reed mat. 'Hey, you little hell!'

I finish off a couple of things and then lock the door behind us. The dusk is already deepening as I slowly walk home, the kid at my heels. The streets are quiet. At the taxi rank on the marketplace domestic servants and shop assistants are queuing up for the last minibuses.

I greet those who recognise me, smiling at all the remarks about the kid with red eyes. When we reach the street that runs along beside the river I look appreciatively at the tranquil water. The river flows in a broad stream here, the sinking sun reflected redly in the water. Down at the mouth in the distance there are foaming white horses at the meeting of inland water and sea.

Such excitement when a boat leaves the calm waterway of the river and crosses the bar! I recall myself as a youth, smelling the salt wind, licking the sea spray off my lips, seeing the white of my knuckles clutching the edge of the boat.

It is true what Cawood said – I have lost the capacity to live. Or perhaps I have never acquired it. Perhaps I am too much the unsporty, overweight child, enamoured at too early an age of the things one does alone: music (opera at age ten!); reading; looking out across the water to fathom the moods of the river; stalking birds with field glasses; collecting the insects which crawl all over the river banks and the garden of the old home; the ancient Greek myths and – always – my model trains ...

One of these days I really must beg a boat trip off someone again and sail out through the mouth. I would like to know what my reactions will be in the face of such a challenge, in the face of mortal danger – yes, it will have to happen in the teeth of the incoming tide when there is an even greater danger of the boat turning head over heels, at a time when even doughty fishermen would never venture to go out – then ... but who would be crazy enough to take me out at such a time?

Cawood ... I smile wryly. Yes, my nephew with the smooth-muscled body – he would risk something like that.

We walk on slowly. There are almost no other people abroad at this time. Those on their way to the nightspots choose other, more modern routes; those on their way home are heading for the suburbs on the delta's other hills. It is just us, the little goat and I, silhouetted against the orange-silver river. We must look like an illustration in a story book: the clumsy, bearded man and the orphan kid with a birthmark.

I bend down and pick Tragos up to carry him a short way, enjoying the smell of the little body, feeling the heart beating under my hand. I scratch the little head where horns will be sprouting before long.

Once home, I first draw all the curtains and then I throw open the doors onto the patio. There I stand as I do every evening, breathing in the air for a while, before turning round and putting an opera record on the turntable, pouring myself a drink, and paging through my recipe books in search of something unusual to cook.

How long have I lived with these recipe books? Some are still in my mother's handwriting, others have entries in Sarah's hand – and how long have I followed the same routine every day! In earlier days I had to drive the distance into the city centre to the other practice. Since I have been practising down here in the poorer area, though, I seldom appear in any but the small neighbourhood magistrate's court, where the majority of cases heard are Joza matters.

Even now, with little Tragos here, there will not be even the slightest change. How will anyone else be able to adapt to the pattern of my life? If the yearning grows stronger – and it has not noticeably diminished with the coming of middle age – the patterns will simply be reinforced with the passage of time. The sediment of old habits daily settle on the bottom and there solidify.

I was born a bachelor, and am destined to die so. Sarah, probably, will be the only one to weep at my grave. 'You're footloose and fancy free,' other men always say to me – as though bachelorhood confers freedom, as though one does not become increasingly enmeshed in one's own obsessions ... Sometimes I feel like a ship's propeller in which seaweed and fishing tackle have become so entangled that the screw is now inextricably matted with things that have somehow landed in the path of the boat down the years.

I imagine I hear a knock, but then think: Who could it be at this time of the evening? It's probably Tragos, rooting about in the entrance hall.

I find a recipe which I tested months ago – a luxury which one only really finds in this part of the world. But how long will it take the porcupine skin in the freezer to thaw out in the microwave? And then the long slow process of preparation? And the side dishes? My mouth is watering. What should I add to it? Which bottle of wine should I bring up out of the cellar? How about that Meerlust which I have been saving for so long?

Yes, I will spoil myself tonight. I have decided. I will lay the main table and light candles. And after everything has been prepared I will dress properly for dinner and take my seat at the table. I will ...

But the weariness of the day settles on me. The absurdity of a lonely man sitting at a candle-lit table savouring an exotic repast! And afterwards I will be more replete with self-pity and self-indulgence than with food ...

Perhaps I should simply ring the pizza place and have something delivered – one of those pizzas with European or American names: Riviera, Dixieland ... It is as though our appetites can only be whetted if they hear exotic names, so weak is our confidence in the saleability of our own continent that even our suburbs boast French, Spanish or Greek names.

The entire fact of our being here has never yet gained a name. So many people are ready to leave as soon as there are signs that a transitional government or a new dispensation will affect our life style.

I will order a Dixieland pizza, I decide with an auto-ironic smile. Then that sound comes again – there is someone knocking at the front door: hurried, urgent knuckles.

I shut the recipe book quickly. It is not Sarah's knock. It sounds like a man's knuckles. Perhaps it is ... perhaps Seamus forgot something ... perhaps he wants something added to the affidavit by way of clarification ...

After I have put the recipe book back in the kitchen and shoved the nineteenth-century station staff which I had bought from a collector in Scotland into a wall cupboard, I go to the front door.

I flick the switch of the veranda light which illuminates the garden, thinking as I open the door that the bulb must have blown again. I stand looking out into the darkness. I know there is someone there but I can't see anything.

I close the door and hurry to the patio doors. I shut them quickly and draw the curtains. Then I switch on all the lights in the house, turn the record-player off and call Tragos.

We sit in the quiet lounge till the orphan kid falls asleep on my lap. Round us the silence of the night rustles.

I will not need to ask anyone to take me out across the bar after all: I am already steering myself into the incoming tide.

25

It is more interesting to be an uninvited guest – invisible and immune – on Fata Morgana. It is twilight. Seamus and Cawood are out on the stoep, talking. I am hovering behind them: a stoep shadow – a patch of lukewarm air, free of the light breeze rustling through the climbing roses – an absence that lingers.

'My generation,' Cawood is telling Seamus, 'simply gets bored when you old people start talking politics. We've seen it all already. We've had to hear how the whole world hated us and we've been out to your borders to fight that hate. How many of us were shot like goats in Angola? How many young men from the Kei had to sizzle like tortoises in their shells when Angola called in the Cubans with their fireworks?

'But now we're told it was all in error. Sorry, apartheid was well meant, but it was a hellish mistake ... and after all our fighting in the bush nobody tells us he's sorry. Now we are expected to bury our flag and it's suddenly a disgrace to have fought in Angola and we're not allowed to sing Die Stem when the All Blacks play here.

'We've got to swallow it all now and purge ourselves of the indoctrination as though nothing had happened. Dad, we feel nothing, but nothing, for politics. It bores us. We know Mugabe has made a greater mess of Zimbabwe than Ian Smith did. We know there's an even greater disaster looming in our own country. Apartheid is going to look like a picnic.

'Don't tell me stories, Dad. I've got my game farm and Monomotapa Safaris and my chopper and my friends, and I couldn't give a damn who shares out the oil or how it's done or who gets what ground. They must just not touch me. I'll blast the hell out of anyone who sets foot on my farm uninvited – whether he's black or white, I'll blow ...'

They are sitting on the stoep of Fata Morgana, looking out across the twilit veld. Seamus sighs: all those years of careful education, and just see how the youngster reasons. What didn't it cost me to keep him at that private school term after term. I so wanted him to learn something of the old English values, of the old school ...

Of patriotism and vigour, of a proud realisation of what right and wrong mean ... I got him to learn Kipling's If by heart before he first went to school. And did it help?

Softly Seamus begins to recite:

'If you can trust yourself when all men doubt you,
But make allowance for their doubting too;
If you can wait and not be tired by waiting,
Or being lied about, don't deal in lies;
Or being hated, don't give way to hating,
And yet don't look too good nor talk too wise ...'

Beside him Cawood gets up. 'Dad,' he says bitterly, 'you made me learn that shitty little romantic verse and you sent me to a private school so I could sit there among other rich men's sons and imagine that Cecil John Rhodes was still on the loose and that Jock still roamed the Bushveld and that everything was hunky-dory with the Empire ... But then you also sent me to university, Dad. And there they taught me all about the mythology of British imperialism. It's not much different from the nationalism of that bunch of Boers, Dad.'

Seamus smiles. Little squirt. You know you're going to inherit it all: the name, the stud, Fata Morgana, the position in a stable community that ...

'I know what you're thinking, Dad. You think I'm spoilt. You think I've had it all given to me. Well, I ...'

Sarah comes out onto the stoep. She has interrupted Cawood and now stands there hesitating. 'I'm sorry ...' she says.

'Come,' Seamus invites her. 'Come and sit down, Sarah.' He notices how attractive she is, how she can transform herself. A woman for sunsets, he thinks, for the charm of the deep blue hour, the mystical moment when day and night merge. She is wearing the antique diamond earrings she inherited from Seamus's mother; they glitter in the light on the stoep.

Standing behind them, I feel a little prick of envy in my heart; here is Sarah now, free of me and the old home, among them, because they require her to be present. I can not be here with them; but, softly, I am there anyway.

But their conversation seems happier than it actually is. There they sit waging the everlasting conversation of misunderstanding between ancestors and descendants as though they really do not know it is a ritual which may be avoided – which can be ignored without being denied. Why expose the natural distances between generations when everyone knows they are there?

Seamus looks at Cawood, who is staring sullenly at the goats coming home.

'Yes ... and?' Seamus asks. He does not want to hear what his son will say, but for politeness' sake feels obliged to ask.

'What do you mean: yes and?'

'You were saying?'

Cawood looks straight at him. 'You think I've had it all, don't you?'

'I never said that.'

'It's what you think though.' Cawood's eyes flash. What hardness suddenly, Seamus thinks, with a slight start. Where could it have come from?

'I've always given you more.'

'That's only because you thought there wasn't any other way to keep me tame.'

'That's your interpretation, Cawood ...'

Sarah sighs. 'What is it with you two men tonight? I thought we were going to sit here happily, watching the evening goats and enjoying a drink as if the world was still whole?'

'As if,' Cawood snorts. 'As if ...' He gets up and pours another sherry from the crystal decanter. Seamus notices the strong, determined hips, the fine curve of the body. You may not have my brain, Cawood, but you've certainly got your mother's fine body. It will take you far in your business. An attractive big game hunter looks good on trophy photographs.

He is bitter about his own child. Envy? Of Cawood's easy, guileless nature? From early on, Seamus realised that Cawood would not be like him, Seamus. Mercifully the boy had escaped the tendency to weak nerves. But he's lost out on intelligence. It had soon become obvious – as Cawood's marks for athletics, gymnastics, woodwork and target shooting rose higher and higher, his abilities in mathematics and languages were woefully wanting.

So every blessing has its shadow, Seamus would always tell Sarah. This little fellow would never commit suicide, but on the other hand he would never develop the capacity to understand suicide either.

Seamus becomes aware that Cawood is talking to him.

'... just as I never had a father either ...'

'What?' Seamus sits bolt upright, drawing a hand across his face.

'Haven't you been listening?' Suddenly Cawood looks uncertain – the little boy trying to impress his father with his shooting skill. And Seamus realises that Cawood has said something important.

'I'm sorry ... these new pills ... Prothiaden ... I oughtn't to take them with alcohol. The stuff knocks me out ...'

Sarah interrupts them. She has her hand on Cawood's arm, restraining him.

'No, Cawood, I don't think it is necessary for you to repeat it. Your father ...'

Cawood smirks. He swings his sherry glass up to his lips, spilling a couple of drops on the stoep. 'Oh, you always protect him. You've always done so. And that's the way you have kept me away from Dad all my life. I … '

Sarah leans forward, her eyes shining, the sherry on her lips glistening. With flashing diamonds swinging from her ears, she says: 'I couldn't do otherwise, Cawood. And just be glad that I spared you your father's anguish. Be glad that I took it upon myself to bear it alone without unloading it onto you.'

Seamus is feeling light-headed. It must be the pills. And Sarah's sudden openness with Cawood. This conversation ought not to be taking place. It is out of order. 'I ...' he begins. He wants to get up, but Sarah pushes him back into his chair.

'It's time you heard it,' she says. 'It's high time Cawood heard.'

'Ma … '

'Sarah … '

She watches them, her eyes shining, her cheeks glowing.

Seamus stares at her, confused. She looks triumphant.

But then, slowly, she shakes her head.

'Ma ...' There are tears in Cawood's eyes.

She speaks softly, in measured tones. 'You don't want to hear, do you, either of you?'

Seamus closes his eyes. The blood is exploding in his skull. He feels a shot blowing his brains out. He is falling with his face against the cold leaves of the vygies. He is a coward, fleeing his wife and son. He is burdening the next generation, and even the one after that, with an impossible load.

He smells Sarah's hair, her hands.

'Don't, Sarah ...'

They hear the helicopter's engine whining as it builds up energy. Sarah stands on the stoep weeping, her lips forming the name 'Cawood'. She watches the roaring chopper raising whirlwinds on the farmyard. The dogs start barking. The geese flee to the farthest corner of their camp.

Cawood takes off and the turbulence subsides, the roaring

fades, the red light flickers farther and farther away into the night till it might be no more than a firefly or a shooting star or some nameless sputnik.

26

I am waiting in the shade of a sparse thorn tree for TaImbongi.

The police station with the gaol behind it – a mere five cells and a latrine – sits on a bend in the road. The countryside here is parched and desolate and the people lounging on the stoep of the shop across the road are ragged and weary.

I have been sent from Bisho to Peddie, from Peddie to Keiskammahoek, from Keiskammahoek to the Katberg, and so it has gone on – a long day of shoulder-shrugging officers, vague indications about the nature of TaImbongi's offences and allegations about the ANC's destabilisation of the Ciskei.

Thinking of MaNdlovu and Ayanda, I followed the trail. I had to wait for fat sergeants to finish their business before they would look up, contemptuously, at me, the attorney from the city, from the white south-west. In these parts they are the bosses, and this attitude to justice has led to a sloppy, random way of doing things – slow, as though there are no such things as clocks; naive, as though the system of precedents and common law and the statute book are something you can snort at and bark at the constable to go off and make coffee.

And everywhere, I noticed, there were guns. Young soldiers follow me with their eyes – sometimes in open mockery – as they stand around, bored and smoking, on charge-office verandas. Every car that passes by the villages and hamlets is carefully observed. I feel self-conscious about my bulky body and wayward hair, the inappropriate suit of clothes and briefcase. The day clings to me like a sweaty shirt.

In this profession you are brought face to face with Africa. It's a profession which depends on rhythmical return dates, court orders which must be strictly observed, time as an essence which can alter lives irrevocably. But here you repeatedly run into the timelessness of minor magistrates' courts, lazy officials, the corrupt smell of charge offices where files simply accumulate. Except that, occasionally, unexpectedly, such an office may be filled with a bunch of detainees, beaten and bloody, and a sergeant striding up and down behind the counter like a boerbull.

A profession which rests on the Twelve Tables, on Roman-Dutch Law, on the clear documents of the body of jurisprudence, has to confront the cynicism of people who in their lifetime had got to know only the hard hand of the law, of justice as a sjambok, as a destroyer of pride, a breaker up of families. This region has had one state of emergency after another inflicted on it. There have always been politicians with a military background in charge of things. Very often the population itself had been brought here from great distances by military transport, clutching their meagre possessions. They had had to evacuate their dwellings to make place for white suburbs and industrial sites, and had been dumped here in desolate, noisy dust camps.

What else can you expect but this calculated guilelessness if you raise the matter of the rule of law in a poky little office behind the thorn trees? Or if you ask, indignantly: but what about the audi alteram partem rule, the precept that the other side must also be heard?

I watch – from beside my Mercedes, which I'd finally had attended to, especially for the trip – how three young boys are coming round the corner of the shop. Between them they are dragging a recalcitrant boer goat ram with a thong round its neck. One boy is pulling at the thong, inching forward with his back to the goat. The second is shoving the animal's hips while the third has a reed that he is using as a prodder, poking the ram in the side, round the ears and even, to the amusement of the onlookers in the shade of the shop stoep, in the anus. The goat's pink tongue sticks out the side of its mouth – a hard, rough muscle, toughened by years of browsing on thorn branches and stunted shrubs among the stones.

The group is not making much progress. The ram is strong. It digs in its hooves, causing obstinate furrows in the dust. There is nothing else to look at, so all of us – even those in front of the shop and the policemen at the charge office – are watching the youngsters struggle.

Then a donkey cart comes slowly round the bend in the road. The boys look at the man holding the reins, shout 'Tata!' and give up the battle. The animal is no longer struggling either. It stares at the ground at its feet, its flanks heaving. If it had been one of Fata Morgana's fall-goats it would have collapsed there and then from sheer terror and tension. But this is a boer goat, a member of a hardy species, bred to survive in this terrain with little water and almost no greenery, to rear up on its back legs and nibble the tiny leaves off the thorn trees when the ground is bare of grass.

The donkey cart has now stopped in front of the boys. In a single swift movement, which shocks me out of my exhaustion and heat-induced drowsiness, the boys' father leaps off the cart, pulls a home-made knife from his belt and stands astride the goat's shoulders. He grabs hold of the horns and jerks the head back. The goat gives a strangled bleat. With a practised stroke the man cuts the goat's throat and the animal collapses in its tracks.

The folk on the shop stoep cheer, the policemen laugh at the rapid, purposeful action of the man who is clearly irritated by his sons' struggle with the goat. The goat is loaded onto the cart, its head hanging by the few ligaments that have not been severed.

The cart turns round slowly and starts moving back the way it has come, with the children now sitting on the back, smiling guiltily.

I am looking at the dark stain in the dust when someone beside me coughs.

I turn round.

The man is old, with wrinkles round the eyes and a small moustache. He is thinner than I had expected.

'TaImbongi ... er ... Mr ...?'

TaImbongi does not reply. He looks at me, bends down and puts the little bundle of things he has in his hand on the ground. I notice, folded up, the uniform of the praise-singer: the skin apron, the rolled-up strings of beads, the genet-skin and ostrich-feather headdress.

We shake hands. I feel uncomfortable about the old man's silence. We stand without speaking, looking at the donkey cart already trundling away on the grass verge beside the tarred road.

Then we walk over to my car. I help TaImbongi load his things into the boot. He gets into the car himself. I walk back to the police station where I have just succeeded in begging for TaImbongi's release. I want to try to get something in writing about the charge – if ever one had been formulated. The soldiers stand aside and let me pass. I catch the odours of their sweat and gun oil, the canvas smell of army uniforms.

At the counter I wait to speak to the sergeant in charge. The constable who disappeared to go and call him stays away a long time. He returns and goes on with his duties without a word. He is making leisurely notes in the occurrence book. Then he goes over to the filing cabinet and stands with his back to me.

I clear my throat. 'Is the sergeant coming?' I ask eventually.

Without looking up the constable replies: 'Sergeant says the two of you had better shake the dust of this place off your feet. He asks if you saw how that goat got its throat cut.'

I stand there nonplussed.

Then I turn round, and go back to the car. TaImbongi is resting with his head back.

We drive off. Far in the distance clouds are gathering: cumulus heads blooming like cauliflowers high above the bare plain.

People from more benign regions will never understand why we are always so conscious of the landscape. One moment it is proof of deprivation and spareness, the next moment there is some majestic movement, as though a sculptor with rock and cloud, soil and distance as his materials has had a violent fit of inspiration.

That is all that keeps one going: the hope that nature will achieve a miracle – a burgeoning cumulus head, a shower of pure rain to drive the flying ants out of the antheaps, a muscular kudu bull arching effortlessly over a fence as the sun reflects off the sheen on his hide.

We drive in silence over the expansive veld, past overpopulated tribal villages where children play in the yards alongside the chickens and the pigs. All along the road are hitchhikers standing astride their bundles of possessions. Soil erosion has carved out great ditches in the earth. Farming here is unplanned, poverty stricken, without resources or mechanisation. The earth is being grazed bare, trodden into dust, washed away.

Then we drive through a winding pass where formations of stone and prickly pear bushes are the habitation of hundreds of dassies. They sit basking in the sun along the tarred road and flee as soon as any car comes by. On the bends there are numerous black skid marks where the big trucks that use this route as a thoroughfare between distant cities have braked or burst a tyre.

When we reach the summit of the pass and can look out over the plain stretching without interruption to where you can trace the curve of the earth, TaImbongi begins to talk. He amazes me: the delicate, shrunken man who has sat beside me so dispirited and weary, speaks with a mighty voice that fills the car and suddenly lends his body twice its actual stature.

No wonder he was once known as DeepVoice! What a voice!

'In this country, it is easy to hate,' TaImbongi says. 'But then you have to remember: hate is the easiest way out. There in my cell I realised once again how difficult loving is. Those young men with their caps and guns are the children of apartheid. All they want is to destroy and to break down. As though by doing so they could undo the wrecked history of this country and crack open a future for themselves.'

I look out of the car window. Yes, it is all about the difficult command to love.

'Did they treat you well?'

TaImbongi does not answer, but turns his head away.

'They are dogs,' he says eventually, softly. 'You don't throw the Kei's leading imbongi in a cell with common criminals.'

I sigh; it is part of my daily practice to listen to clients complaining about maltreatment at the hands of the police. And as often as not they are accompanied by practically unfeasible demands to lodge a claim, to prove assault and maltreatment.

Usually my advice is simply that there are no witnesses who will be prepared to support such a charge, that the police will use the old defence about slipping on a piece of soap in the showers, or that they will assert that it was fellow prisoners who had roughed up the plaintiff. Let us rather concentrate our energies, I will advise my clients, on the most essential issues.

That is what makes the profession so exhausting: all the compromises.

'Have you heard about the oil?'

TaImbongi looks at me, and for the first time there is a flicker of life in his eyes.

'Every time they threw another bandit into our cell there was a fresh tale about the oil.'

'News spreads fast.'

'I hear everybody wants to get rich quick now,' TaImbongi answers. 'Everyone wants to make up for lost time.'

'Did you hear how the whole thing began?'

'There was a story that someone had planted a bomb against the wall of the cathedral, but another had a tale about a priest who had been smelling earth gas in the vestry for a long time, so the church decided to drill for oil. They were only pretending to look for water.'

'Those are all just tall stories,' I say.

'Oh?'

'Zola Mtuze started the whole thing.'

TaImbongi's eyes widen. 'That skelm!'

I tell TaImbongi the whole story. The old man listens, shaking his head, and when we approach the city, he sits up and strokes his moustache.

'MaNdlovu will organise that oil,' he says. 'You'll see.' That is his final comment before we turn into the streets of Joza and move, sounding the hooter, through the goats and fowls.

When we stop in front of the house, there is a great concourse of folk. Exclamations follow. 'TaImbongi!' Someone calls indoors to MaNdlovu and Ayanda to come and see.

'What's all this crush of people?' I ask, but TaImbongi does not reply. He gets out of the car in a dignified fashion and I realise that he thinks it is a reception organised in his honour.

TaImbongi lifts his hand and the crowd separates. MaNdlovu comes out of the house and stands on the stoep, the white handkerchief in her hand. Her dress is crooked, as though it has only just been hastily pulled on.

Slowly she comes down the steps, her hand feeling for the railing.

'Ncincilili has been seen,' she whispers. 'They have seen Ncincilili and Mpho together, in the Lower Kei, near the sources of the river, in the reed beds.'

TaImbongi reaches out his hands to MaNdlovu.

'Ncincilili! Ncincilili!' the women in the crowd call out.

'Ncincilili is dead, MaNdlovu,' says TaImbongi softly.

He takes a step nearer to her, but she retreats.

'It's me, TaImbongi. I am free again.'

Ayanda appears on the stoep above MaNdlovu. She looks at me and shakes her head.

'Ncincilili has been seen!' calls a woman. 'He's risen from the dead!'

TaImbongi turns to me where I am standing beside the

Mercedes. I shrug my shoulders. What can I say? TaImbongi turns back to the crowd. 'But isn't Mpho in the bush?' he asks.

'He's gone,' someone shouts.

'He's with Ncincilili!'

'National liberation!' dances a young woman on the top step.

I open the boot, take out TaImbongi's clothes and give them to him. I wave to Ayanda, get into the car and slowly drive off. Then I am forced to stop and wait, idling while a donkey cart moves past in front of me. In the rear-view mirror I see TaImbongi on the pavement putting his imbongi feathers on his head, tying the genet skin round his waist and draping the beads round his neck. Slowly, as the crowd continues to grow and move in rhythm with him, TaImbongi starts dancing with astonishing grace and agility.

Let us see if the dead will arise, I think as I drive away. And what other gifts the hard earth is going to surrender.

27

After all the people have finally left once all had made their contributions to the tale about the astonishing appearance of Ncincilili and Mpho, Ayanda, MaNdlovu and TaImbongi are left in the house alone.

TaImbongi is still wearing his ostrich-feather headdress. His chest is heaving slightly. As the crowd grew in front of the house he performed at length, exercising his remarkable capacity for improvising extended praise songs off the cuff. He praised Ncincilili the Undying; Mpho the Freedom Fighter; the Sons of the Kei who are bringing oil to Joza; the Riches of the Earth and the Fullness of Days; the Assegai of the Nation lying in wait in case negotiations about the country's future should fail; the Young Lions of Joza who are demanding a Unified Municipality and the Reallocation of Land ...

Now the three of them are sitting there, and Ayanda is pleading with MaNdlovu for the umpteenth time to take her blood-pressure pills regularly. Her intermittent blindness can of course be psychosomatic, since it is only in moments of high emotional tension that MaNdlovu's sight fails her. But in any case it is high time she has a thorough examination.

MaNdlovu, however, pays secret visits to the sangoma up in Sun City, who gives her muti concocted of herbs and Mozambican monkey guts. She's forever bragging about my being an educated doctor, thinks Ayanda bitterly, but she regularly rejects my knowledge and goes to that woman who sits among her dried baboon heads, snake skins and basins of herbs.

Now MaNdlovu is sitting watching TaImbongi with that old look of hers. 'Your sons have now decided they are going to fight for their land, TaImbongi.' MaNdlovu leans forward and asks with a venom she reserves for TaImbongi alone: 'And what are you going to do to help your people? Are you going to join the march to Cathedral Square tomorrow? We need an imbongi to perform in front of the fountain of oil. Are you coming? Or are you going to lie about drunk in the shebeen while others fight for your rights?'

'Ma ...' Ayanda sits forward in her chair. 'Come now, Mama ...'

'No, you leave us alone, my child. Let us thrash out this business properly.'

'I couldn't be bothered with the ground the cathedral stands on,' says TaImbongi. He removes the headdress and puts it carefully on the table in front of him. 'My territory is my songs and all who listen to my songs are my people. Wherever those people live, that is where my place is.'

MaNdlovu wipes her face with her handkerchief. 'Oh, TaImbongi, you were born limp,' she says acidly. 'And limp you will die. You will still be prancing around in your ostrich feathers when you wake up one day to find the Settlers and the Boers have taken everything out from under your very feet. You think life is nothing but song and dance, don't you? Where were your sons before last night when they decided that enough was enough and broke out? One was stuck up there in the Mint making money for the rich and the other ran away from the bush and went to the clinic with a bleeding foreskin. You, TaImbongi, are the rancid beestings which made the calves shy away. Luckily they have now got some sense in their heads ...'

'Mama ...' Ayanda tries to stop her, but the pent-up memories of her childhood – night after night her parents had this same quarrel – paralyses her. When they squabble like this, she is reduced to being a little girl again: helpless and scared.

Scared that they will separate; scared that they don't love each other, scared that her world is going to shatter ...

TaImbongi gets up shakily, weak from the rotten food and dirty water he's had to swallow in the Ciskei's cells, as he'd said earlier. He leans on one hand on the dining room table, holding the other to his back which always troubles him after his performances.

'All these years,' he says, 'I've been the one who has brought money home. Look at this house. Look at that TV. Look at that display cabinet. Look at that mixer-mincer.' He shifts slightly and leans over towards MaNdlovu. 'There has always been enough money. When the other squatter children went to school in tatters, Mpho and Ncincilili were dressed like boy models for Jet Stores. When the other children rioted and the school went up in flames, then I, TaImbongi, had the cash in my hand to move our children to Peddie where things were quiet and they could get schooling. Then TaImbongi the praise-singer was quite good enough for you, MaNdlovu. But now you women have caught the sweet smell of national liberation and suddenly my money stinks!'

MaNdlovu also gets up. The two old people stand glaring at each other across the table while Ayanda sits there helplessly. 'It's not about your money, you hoarse old buzzard,' she says. 'It's about what is right and wrong. And that oil is spouting through the skeletons of our ancestors, not the forefathers of the Settlers or the Voortrekkers.

'It was always holy ground, that. When the cathedral was built there, there was no power strong enough to oppose the Anglicans. But now we've got the power. Now we can ball our fists.

'It's the spirits of our ancestors that have brought that oil – for us, to put an end to the poverty of our people.'

'You say it's not about money, MaNdlovu. But what else is that oil if it isn't money?' TaImbongi points a waggling forefinger at MaNdlovu and Ayanda. 'All these years you two have never said a word about the land the cathedral stands on. But now that there's oil spouting out of it you've caught the smell of riches and you trot out your "national liberation"! It's got nothing to do with national liberation! You think national liberation is going to be a stokvel and each one of you is going to get her piece of the treasure!'

Ayanda is overwhelmed with shame for her parents here in open confrontation with each other: MaNdlovu – ponderous, wobbling, blowing through her trembling lips and focusing years of pent-up frustration on the fragile TaImbongi. At home, he is always caught off his guard by MaNdlovu's outbursts but, in public, in all the places that his blue bakkie visits, he is used to being received like a hero by people who hang on his lips and drink in his every word.

MaNdlovu sits down again. That cold look which Ayanda has so feared ever since childhood now comes over her face. 'While we sat here at home panting for liberation,' she hisses, 'while we stored up the venom in our cheeks like puffadders, you, TaImbongi, polished your backside still brighter in the service of those puppets, those bottle-fed lambs of apartheid, Matanzima and Sebe. Then you would go swanning around in that shiny car with the smoked-glass windows as though you weren't part of Joza's people.'

'But the money ... ah, you always took the money, didn't you?'

'What do you know about how women suffer? No, you don't know, you always just head for the shebeen for a ragtime in those jazz-halls down at the docks ... You had a mouthful to say about your two sons out there just now, but you don't even know your own children ... There Ayanda was, on the brink of a divorce and you hadn't even caught a whiff of the troubles in this house! You're a rubbish, TaImbongi! It's your type that has always been too slack-arsed to offer the regimes any resistance, and it's your fault that the Kei is in such a mess!

'You can gather up your goods and get out of here. Drive off to your republic, wherever you think you'll find it, wherever you'll be able to lie about with your belly stuffed with food. But we, here in Joza, we will fight for our freedom. We'll get our land back, so help me God, praise the Lord, sweet Jesusss ...'

MaNdlovu falls face down across the dining room table. First her face takes on that expression of astonished forgetfulness which she always has before one of her attacks and then with a tremendous crash she falls forward. Her thick arms slap down on the table top like bread dough and then she slides onto the floor before Ayanda can reach her.

And for the very first time TaImbongi does not hurry forward to bring MaNdlovu round with the usual clucking noises, stroking of her cheek and damp kitchen cloths. He stands and watches Ayanda kneeling beside MaNdlovu who lies shuddering half under the dining room table, her feet caught between the legs of the chairs.

'You want a paradise, MaNdlovu,' he says, 'you want heaven on earth, you want freedom and everything that is right and good ... but you don't know, God knows, you don't know ...'

Unsteadily, TaImbongi moves towards the door.

'Ta ...' With one hand on her mother's face and the other stretched out to her father, Ayanda sits there on her haunches. In front of her she sees an image of a donga ripped out between her mother and father – a rent in the earth – a scar on the landscape which will never heal. She has the sense of watching a final moment.

'Ta ...'

But TaImbongi has already gone. She hears the tinny slamming of the bakkie door.

28

The priest has come to speak to Seamus about the jackal incident in front of the cathedral.

They are sitting in the lounge on Fata Morgana. Through the windows the most distant hills are visible as varying shades of blue on the horizon. On the lawn three hadedas are pecking for grubs.

Earlier Seamus pointed them out to the priest as they came up the veranda steps: 'Birds of ill omen,' he said. 'Harbingers of death.'

The priest smiled wryly and opened his mouth to say something, but obviously thought better of it. Instead, he stopped for a moment to look at the mounted buffalo and kudu heads on the wall of the stoep.

He raised the topic of their subsequent conversation: 'You are a keen hunter.' But first they had to find comfortable seats and then Seamus had to order coffee. Seamus was still trying to win time, having been caught slightly off guard by the priest's appearance at the farmyard gate. He is by reputation an enthusiastic environmentalist.

Now they are sitting in the spacious room looking at each other. Seamus is summing the man up: he looks like a mere boy, but look more closely and you notice fine veins over the nose, lines beside the mouth, creases round the eyes: small details that point towards age forty, perhaps forty-five.

They start talking about the Butlers' unique stud farm. When each of them eventually has a cup of coffee in his hand, Seamus announces: 'My fall-goats are selflessness incarnate. They are the ones who collapse and become easy prey for predators, while allowing the flock they were grazing with to escape.' He sighs and takes a sip of coffee. 'An agricultural journal has calculated that, statistically, every night, somewhere in the world, twelve of my fall-goats fall victim to evil beasts. I think about that every morning when I get up.' He shakes his head. 'But then I remember the tens of thousands of other animals which have survived the night by the grace of Caper timidus's sacrifice ...'

'But they don't do it of their own free will,' the priest counters cautiously, running his tongue investigatively over the lip of the hot coffee cup. 'It is genetically predestined, after all.'

Seamus smiles slowly. Whenever he gets on to this topic he feels as comfortable as a fish in home waters. 'Are you hinting at the concept of predestination ...?'

The priest puts down his cup in alarm, spilling a drop of coffee on his cassock. 'Absolutely not. I would never transpose the Divine Plan for man to the dumb beasts!'

Seamus's eyes twinkle mischievously. 'Yet you offered a wily jackal sanctuary under the altar erected for the salvation of human souls!'

'I felt there was something symbolic in the way that little animal led the whole hunt to the house of the Lord,' the priest replies. 'There was a sign there for all to read.'

'Precisely.' Seamus puts down his cup. He sniffs and looks out of the window. 'There is of course an enormous symbolism in the sacrifice of my goats. To ascribe it all to mere genetics is really too cold-blooded by far. Is it not in fact a matter of a genetic memory having been activated by breeding? A dormant selflessness present both in the human race and in animals – in all creation, in fact – a willingness to sacrifice oneself for others?'

The question is left hanging in the air. The priest sighs. 'I would prefer to bring the conversation back to the Word of God,' he says.

'Precisely,' Seamus continues. 'And is not Christ the very symbol of that primal memory of voluntary immolation? A sort of suicide for the sake of others? After all, long before Christ the ancient civilisations were playing out in their rituals the idea of a sacrificial death.'

'But the goat? It is a symbol of ...'

Seamus gets up. 'God conceived both God and Satan,' he says. 'I am convinced of it. If God were truly almighty, He would only allow that old spoilsport free rein if He Himself wanted to – to make things more interesting. Or,' he looks bitterly at the priest, 'because He wanted to watch the conclusion of the game from a safe distance.'

'This is a primal debate,' says the priest. 'That is the divine mystery.' Seamus goes over to the open window and looks out over his land. In the distance white speckles show the whereabouts of the herd of goats.

'God is cruel,' he says.

'No, you are wrong there,' replies the priest. 'God is love.'

'Tripe,' Seamus snorts. 'Take a look at the world out there.' He falls silent, compelling the priest to come and stand beside him and stare out over the veld. 'Visitors are forever telling the people of the Kei that we are obsessive about the landscape,' Seamus says. 'But it is the only metaphor we know, because we are hopelessly trapped in it – from birth till death. Ask me, who was born here, to rate God's performance as a landscape architect. There is no relief built into the topography, no mercy. Here only the strongest survive. Here Satan,' turning to look the priest squarely in the eye, 'is just as furiously present as God.'

Seamus notices a shiver run through the priest's frame. The man has goosepimples on his throat! I must look like the devil himself to him, he thinks. He towers over the shorter, delicately built man. But let the little cleric feel the presence of the land. Let him realise that Africa demands surrender to both good and evil. Let him understand that the battle for our souls is never over – that it reeks of blood and gunpowder, of trampled plants and dust

– that it bears the countenance of glazed eyes and drag marks in the earth – that it carries the stench of guilt and madness. This is our world, and the rhetoric of theologians – their clichés about 'divine mysteries' – is as ill at ease here as the Oriental tourists with their clicking Nikons.

In fact, they're just as alien as the hackneyed phrases of our politicians about the 'new South Africa' and 'nationbuilding', 'non-racialism', 'democracy' ... In Africa!

'Brother ...?' the priest brings him back to earth.

Once more Seamus looks challengingly at the priest. Thank goodness he's dropped the sanctimonious 'My son' since their previous meeting. 'If God had not willed Satan, then Satan cannot be here ... Right?'

'Well, you are over-simplifying ...'

'So God deliberately brought this muddle of good and evil down upon us – or else He wasn't almighty enough to stop Satan from coming into being.'

'But, brother ...'

'Those are the only alternatives.'

'Brother, brother ...'

'The third alternative is yours. That's the one that holds that God has given us only just enough intelligence to formulate these two alternatives. We are too stupid – even though we may have been created in His image – to comprehend His plan. We have to take refuge in mystery. Here we need a little bridge to help us across the stream, and that little bridge is called faith. We have to abandon all our talents of reasoning and investigation and simply believe.'

'We need to become as little children, brother.'

'God has a strange idea of mercy. We are no better off than a bunch of ... goats.'

'You have to surrender, brother.'

Seamus swings round. 'Come, Father.' He seizes the priest by the arm and pulls him out onto the stoep. 'Wait here.' He strides off to the study, unlocks the gun-safe and takes out one of his large hunting rifles.

When he comes out onto the stoep again, the priest pales.

'Come.' Seamus strides on ahead, down the garden path, past the carefully tended flower beds. Two peacocks hurry out of the way with grating squawks, dragging their rainbow tails across the lawn. Hadedas take off and disappear flapping into the trees.

At the bottom of the garden they turn off the path. Behind him Seamus can hear the priest's breathing. The man is short of breath. Spends his days sitting in the cathedral, lighting candles and reading the Bible. Look at his delicate hands, soft from all the believing.

Seamus stops. Panting, the priest catches up with him. Before turning to the priest, Seamus closes his eyes and clenches his jaws. Why, of all people, to this nice, unsure young man? Why, of all times, now?

He turns round and sees the pale face of the priest in front of him.

'Here,' says Seamus, pointing at the ground with the barrel of his gun. The priest looks down and Seamus knows what he is seeing: an open piece of ground, trodden to powder, with a few small stones and some vygie vines.

'Yes?' asks the priest nervously.

Seamus swallows. I am confessing. I am confessing to this soft mannikin, this youngster. I am confessing out in the open. I am standing here as a grown man and for the first time in my life I am showing someone else where.

The priest has noticed Seamus's struggle with himself. He draws nearer. 'Yes, my brother ...?'

Seamus's body shakes.

'Brother?'

'With this gun,' Seamus says.

'Brother?'

Seamus spins round and strides up to the farmyard gate. The priest's footsteps follow and catch up with him as they are entering the first camp.

They walk past feeding troughs where the earth has been trodden bare, then past a windmill and a cement dam whose water overflows into a drinking trough. They stumble over low shrubs, until eventually they are out on the open plain, some distance from the homestead, surrounded by camps and thousands of grazing goats in the distance.

Seamus stops and looks at the priest.

'Let me show you what redemption looks like.'

He raises the gun, releases the catch and fires a salvo of shots into the air.

The priest raises his hands as though to ward off the evil, but he is too late: they are in the midst of the spectacle of the herds toppling over.

'May God forgive you, brother ...'

Seamus looks at the priest. 'If there's anyone who understands me,' he says, 'it is God. I think God has a rough edge.'

29

It may not seem like it, but I'm trying to keep out of my own story. I don't really like standing in front of the mirror. I mock the mistakes of others so as to camouflage my own. I carp about other people's obsessions and so conceal my own self-pity.

Even now as I look back from a distance at the bearded figure sitting talking to Ayanda Thandani on the back patio in the garden of the old house, I still cannot completely shake off that weight. I'm still the same. I'll probably never achieve the liberty, the freedom from care, which I so often see in others. I trail along like a sluggish steam engine through my story, wearily dragging the trucks from station to station.

And yet: once I've got the story off my chest, a lightness awaits me. I know it; I doubt; I hope.

From the patio Ayanda and I have a view over the river. It is late in the afternoon after a muggy day; all day the pressure has been building up, and yet the sky is cloudless. After many airless days and a lack of rain upriver, the water is a deep green.

I have served white wine and soda water with ice cubes. Dark green paint is peeling off the antique garden chairs we are sitting in. Ayanda's body is deeply and comfortably sunk in the depths of the chair which has assumed the shape of long departed figures who spent their afternoons in it, their eyes fixed on the same river, that bridge, and above the horizon in the distance the vain promise of thin, wispy clouds.

Ayanda shakes her head as she looks at me. 'I can't stand the old folks' bickering any more. The older I get, the more it hurts me.'

'I am sure they are just stuck in old patterns,' I reply. 'At that age, it is difficult to change one's habits. All that happens when you get older is that you grow more and more like yourself. You lose the ability to look at things with scales on your eyes, to wear a mask, to make a pretence of what does not exist.'

'That sounds like a healthy development,' says Ayanda, taking another sip of wine. 'But MaNdlovu and TaImbongi ... They are quite impossible ...'

After TaImbongi had left in the bakkie following the great altercation with his wife, Ayanda gradually managed to prod MaNdlovu into consciousness, wiping her face with cool cloths, until eventually she helped her to bed and made her take a sleeping tablet. Then Ayanda went out onto the stoep. There had been so many developments suddenly – it was as though the advent of the oil had forced up, spouting through the crust, everything that had for so long been pent up: the rumour that Mpho and Ncincilili had been seen together, that they were armed and ready to see to it that all the profits of the oil strike came to Joza; the planning of the mass march to Cathedral Square, with young Amanda who only darted in breathlessly to snatch some food and then hurried off again, her hands covered in poster paint, her voice hoarse from all the organising she was doing; MaNdlovu who wanted to go to court over the land on which the cathedral stood; Zola in hospital, shot by unknown men in a minibus ... What else could possibly still go wrong?

Ayanda left, once she was sure that MaNdlovu was sleeping. She took Zola's kwela and drove into town. The tension was palpable. Perhaps she was just imagining it but motorists were not allowing one another any leeway. They were all driving noticeably faster. At robots drivers kept a suspicious eye on one another in their rear-view mirrors. Everywhere buildings bore new graffiti: OIL IS BLACK. GIVE JOZA ITS DUE. JOZA'S JOY? GREED IS WHITE ...

She drove past the market square where some hawkers were already packing up their wares and then found herself in front of my practice. On an impulse – or had she unconsciously brought herself there? – she stopped at my office. She would have come in, but the doors were already closed. She then drove here to the old house, but sat in the minibus for a long time before getting out and knocking at the door.

'You are looking at me as though expecting some advice,' I say, pouring us some more wine. 'What do I know about anything other than the winding ways of the law? The cobwebs of clauses? The maze of statutes and amendments?

'That is where I feel at home, as I do among the gears of my steam engines, the iambic metre of the sonnets I read, or the alexandrines of my Vondel! Or the classical predictability of my rose nursery ... All down the years I have taken refuge in safe patterns. Outside of them I feel ill at ease.'

I shrug my shoulders. 'I am just a helpless old bachelor who knows nothing of the complexities of family life, of the warp and the woof between parents and children and between child and child, with all the threads firmly entwined with the past and the future ... I should be a most unlikely counsellor for your family, Dr Thandani.' I look out across the river, stroking my beard. 'Indeed, I have so many calamities of my own that I am myself in need of counsel ...'

Improbable as it may sound now, Ayanda looks at me and thinks: He speaks the most beautiful English, as old-fashioned and other-worldly as this old house with all its strange smells and objects. 'It's a terrible time,' she says. 'It's almost as though everybody has lost their reason – as though everyone's eyes are fixed on that oil spring.'

'Yes,' I agree. 'That fountain has spewed its blackness into all our minds ...'

'I thought,' Ayanda continues after a long silence, 'that

MaNdlovu would at least have been satisfied that TaImbongi was actually in a Ciskei cell – that at last they regard him as dangerous enough to lock up, even if the locking-up was not done with any great enthusiasm. But at least ... And for all those years TaImbongi did take good care of us: I was able to go to medical school; Ncincilili, too, could get an education; Mpho will also be able to choose the field in which he wants to study. The money will be there. But MaNdlovu expects still more. She wants a hero in the home.'

'We all expect too much of one another,' I say, watching the goat kid at the water's edge. 'We want to extort ghosts from each other, phantoms of our idealised selves, alter egos to satisfy our own egos. Cruelly we try to mould others to conform to our own yearnings and fears, our own shortcomings and terrors. We want to create mirror-images of ourselves, light for our shadows.' I sigh, and Ayanda realises that I have had too much to drink. When I opened the door, she could already smell the whisky on my breath. Hence the bombastic utterances: 'No one can truly love unconditionally. No one can enter selflessly into the arena of love. Lost we are. Jetsam cast up by the river of desire and yearning, the tides of incapacity, shortcoming ...'

Ayanda notices my distress. What a strange, lonely man, hiding his uncertainties behind bombast.

'I am really rather clumsy when it comes to this sort of thing,' I continue. I take a sip of wine as my eyes follow a cormorant flying low over the river. 'When it comes to the tango of love, the dance steps of admiration and humiliation, mercy and cruelty, hate and lovableness ... there I feel quite impotent ...'

'We all feel like that,' Ayanda replies. 'There's no safe haven in love. When you open yourself to someone else, you're on the open sea: always exposed, vulnerable. But it's the risks that make it exciting ... that create that light-headed feeling ...'

She smiles, thinking of her early days with Zola, but her thoughts are interrupted when I get up, turn my back on her and look out over the river. I am still wearing my suit trousers though not the jacket. I have loosened my tie. My shirt, creased and sweaty, hangs out untidily. With my back still turned to her, I say: 'I haven't ever really loved. And no one has ever loved me either. I wonder what it feels like?'

'Have you never had a girlfriend?' Leaning forward, she feels how the wine is making her light-headed, too. When one is excessively tense, as she is, alcohol works faster. Between us the shadows are lengthening. The blooms on the rose bushes that were still a glowing red a moment ago are turning mauve, purple. A butterfly flutters past her, round my head and then disappears.

I turn round. 'I can't think why I am telling you all this. I reckon ... Oh, I don't know.' I shake my head. 'Perhaps the last few days, with everyone getting so excited about the wealth which has struck the city, and all so keen to improve their lot and the lives of their loved ones, have made me more aware of my own loneliness ... Or perhaps it's because you're a doctor. You probably have to listen to such stories all the time.'

She shrugs her shoulders. 'Do carry on.'

'You came here because you have problems of your own and now I ...'

She shakes her head. 'You need to talk,' she says. 'I can see that you have to unburden yourself to someone.'

I lower my head, standing there in my rumpled clothes. She can see my belly showing where my shirt buttons have come undone. 'I know that I shall die alone,' I say.

She looks up quickly. 'Everyone is alone when the time comes to die,' she says. 'Even when there are ten family members standing round the bed. No one can prevent the departure. And the one who is leaving leaves alone.'

I look at her with my head at an angle. Odd, she thinks, he's not drunk after all.

'I have a premonition that I am going to die soon,' I say. 'I can tell from the river.'

They look each other straight in the eye. Perhaps, just for a moment, they are aware of my presence ... The late afternoon shadows lie stretched out round them. It is deathly quiet. Suddenly she feels cold.

'Oh no,' she says, alarmed, puts down her glass and gets up. 'No, you're just overwrought. You are tired. I would advise you to get an early night.'

'I have to go to a reception tonight,' I reply. 'I must pull myself together and get properly spruced up so I can look the city's foremost citizens in the eye.'

'You're surely not under any obligation?'

'Family,' I say. 'I've got to go. It's expected.'

We walk slowly through the house. 'I just wanted to say ...' Ayanda stops in the lounge '... that love does not exclude loneliness. I have been at my very loneliest in an affair of the heart.'

I straighten my tie and smooth my shirt.

'I must pull myself together,' I say. 'And I must beg your pardon. Honestly, I have never made this sort of confession to anyone before ... Excepting perhaps my sister, Sarah.'

'I am honoured,' she smiles. 'You mustn't feel in any way self-conscious or guilty.'

'I don't know why I ...'

'Oh, forget it now.'

I laugh. 'Right. Right, I will. But come, just before you go let me show you my latest purchase. It's a genuine Garrett, made in England in the nineteenth century. It puffs away as though it had all the confidence in the world ...'

She watches in astonishment as I, stout as I am, go down on my knees on the carpet and then lie prostrate, my cheek flat on the floor. With my eyes right up close to the engine I survey the landscape of the carpet.

30

Worried, Sarah leaves Seamus behind on Fata Morgana. After the conversation with Cawood the previous evening Seamus had not been able to regain his equanimity. It was the first time that his depression had been mentioned in a conversation with Cawood – it had always been the suppressed given, the unmentionable, to which, from early on, Cawood and Sarah had had to adapt their lives.

After Cawood's departure, and on top of the sherry, Seamus had taken an Urbanol, to dampen his anxiety – and when that pill took him too deep, he had to take something else – Sarah simply cannot keep up with all the trade names any more – to give him a lift again. Now he was in bed sleeping off his hangover, after spending the whole day in the darkened room.

From time to time, when she had brought him a cup of coffee or some news about the farm, she found him with his cheeks wet with tears. She was torn between Seamus's disconsolation, her own helplessness, and her yearning for normality and a positive outlook on life – anything other than this constant teetering on the brink of the abyss – and then her concern, her mother's longing for her disturbed, traumatised son.

Guilt, too, for how could she be caught up in a situation like that without feeling herself directly implicated, without feeling that even her best was not good enough? And, of course, there is the knowledge that she and Seamus have failed in their attempt to raise their only progeny, Cawood, without the snarls, the typical fall-goat characteristics associated with the Butlers.

She wanted to telephone and talk to me, but realised that I was probably having a busy day in my office. She knew that I would have felt obliged to drive out to Fata Morgana and she did not want to do that to me. She felt, although I may not always realise it myself, that I am in real need of all the income I can get from every working day. Every visit she pays to the ramshackle old house impresses upon her more vividly the deterioration of the house, its need for refurbishing.

When it rains I simply place bowls under the leaks, but the ceilings are starting to rot and the roof and gutters are rusting from the house's proximity to the river and the nearby sea with the salt winds blowing inland from the coast every night.

The trust which our parents had left has not been able to keep pace with the devaluation of the currency. As far as Sarah is concerned, time has relentlessly eaten away at our inheritance. Worse still, she feels, it was from sheer cussedness that I abandoned my brilliant prospects with the prestigious practice in the city centre and decided to 'squat' – as legal practitioners call opening an office in a new situation – down beside the market.

So she did not feel at liberty to interrupt my working day. And in any case it is necessary for her and Cawood to talk things through. At first she had wanted to telephone him and make an appointment, because she suspected that a party of foreigners had arrived on Monomotapa. But she decided against telephoning and took the Mercedes – Seamus was so deeply asleep that nothing would rouse him – to drive through the camps of Fata Morgana.

Today, finally, she intends to lay the cards on the table for Cawood to read. All through the years she has done everything in her power to protect him from his father's profound depressions, his compulsive anxiety attacks which often leave her desperate. She had to control Seamus's outbursts to prevent the young Cawood from hearing. She had to try to confine the suicide threats to late night sessions when Cawood was already asleep.

It was only in his teens that Cawood discovered that his father was taking medication. They told him that the pills were for stomach upsets, high cholesterol, headaches – anything other than depression.

And yet she always had a suspicion that Cawood knew, that he could tell that his father was different from the other, more frivolous, farmers of Manley Flats. How could it have been otherwise? There is always a hush about the house. Fata Morgana's fall-goats assume symbolic stature. It is as though for her and Cawood life revolved round attempts to keep Seamus from toppling over.

The Toppling Goat they call him. At a church fête once, she overheard two women of the district refer to him, not knowing she was within earshot. The wealth and social position of the Butlers has naturally enough contributed to the gossip campaign about Fata Morgana: who would be interested in telling tales about the nonentities of the district? But because the Butlers and their unique stud have such a high profile, they provide fruitful material for gossipmongers who have degenerated into mediocrity and so make a pastime of trying to decry or denigrate anyone more successful than themselves.

Sarah shakes her head as she drives through the goats. Sometimes she feels like pulling out a gun and shooting at them. She feels their nervousness as mockery. When they look at her, she hears Seamus's lamentations in her ears. When they keel over at the crack of a whip, she sees Seamus stumbling down the garden to where the creeping vygies still cover the stains of his father's blood.

She wanted to have a tennis court laid out over the suicide spot. She obtained quotations on the quiet, but when Seamus heard of her plans he was nearly demented. He accused her of besmirching the Butler honour, of plotting to have him declared a State President's patient and confined permanently to a mental asylum. He snatched up a gun and, in a disgusting act which she will never forget, he shot one of the slaughter goats in the camp beside the goose run.

'Why?' she nagged. 'Why that?' but he could never give her an answer. The tennis court idea was dropped. They don't play tennis any more anyway. She had only been trying to think of some way of covering, of concealing, of achieving some sort of finality.

Now she realises that the years of maintaining silence may have had the wrong effect on Cawood. Perhaps she should have been open with him from the start. But the damage is done now. He has grown up with two realities – the one which she and Seamus have chosen to show him, and the second which lies in the sphere of suspicions and silent observation.

Perhaps Cawood now has difficulty distinguishing what is essential from what is merely peripheral. Perhaps he will have to spend the whole of his life in the frustrating experience of having things refuse to take on the appearance which he wants to give them. Perhaps Cawood will always blame life for the gaping wound that lies between what is pretended and actual reality.

And their specific business activities – his safaris and their tourist route – are not much help either. They, too, are based on a myth, an idealisation: the safari hunter, tanned in his khaki clothes; the Settler homestead with the unique, almost unearthly animals with their yellow eyes.

My son, she murmurs, as she drives, we tried to protect you, but reality has left you defenceless. And because you had to formulate and internalise your suspicions alone, a terrible gulf has opened up between you and us – and now it's too late. You could never give love; you could never accept love. You learnt early that there was a gap between what was and what ought to have been, and you could never reconcile the two. To this day.

She swings off onto the gravel road that leads up through the kloofs to the higher-lying parts of Manley Flats. As the road climbs and the bush becomes more dense, she catches a glimpse of the sea in the distance – the dome of the earth curving away on either side. Cawood always ensures that this section of road is faultless: nothing is permitted to deter the tourist buses.

Eventually she is approaching Monomotapa. The eight-foot-high game fences are immaculate, and as she drives through the gateway with its Xhosa shields it is immediately obvious that the veld is in a distinctly better condition here. This piece of ground was already well cared for when Seamus bought it for Cawood, but by dint of expert game farming within two or three years it became something quite exceptional.

The road begins to curve through the hills. She drives carefully, seeing the herds of game grazing in the distance, including the four giraffe which Cawood has recently acquired. Eventually she crests a hilltop and there, against the slope of a forested kloof with rugged rock formations behind it, stand the buildings of Monomotapa Safaris.

Already there are two small touring buses parked in the yard. She hesitates a moment, but then notices that the party on the terrace is looking up at her car. Slowly, continually braking, she drives down the hill, through the hollow at the bottom, over the low bridge across a beautiful mountain stream where the foliage on either side is so dense it almost forms a tunnel.

When the road begins to rise again she swings off on the service road so as to approach the homestead from behind. She does not want to be greeted by the tourists. And she is not sure what sort of reception she will get from Cawood either.

He is sitting in the large sitting room, a carved eagle on the desk beside him. He is writing, wearing the hat with the leopard-skin band. She is tempted to smile – he looks so 'born-to-be-photographed'! – but she walks up to him quietly. She can see that he is aware of her presence, but he does not look up. Over her shoulder she hears the tourists – a party of Japanese – chatting on the terrace. They are forming groups on the lawn, kneeling or with linked arms, taking snaps, with the tame little armless baboon in every shot.

She sits down on the chair in front of Cawood's desk. He is

going through invoices, she notices. Without meaning to look, she notices the amounts. Impressive. Then he looks up.

What does a mother say to a son like this? She carried him in her womb; she gave birth to him with the same desperate pain as the wild animals on his game farm feel when they drop their young; she protected him with the fierce jealousy of a wild animal.

She made mistakes. She knows that. That is why he is so tense, so full of repressed emotion as he sits in front of her now. But it was done in love. A love, imperfect like all loves; faulty, as affection between people always is; uncomfortable, as things just are.

She shrugs her shoulders. 'You mean everything to me,' she says softly.

He looks down. Your eyes slide away from mine so easily, Cawood. And then I can't tell what is going on inside you. He takes off his hat, mumbles 'Sorry' and puts down his pen.

They both look out of the window. The tourists are beckoning to Cawood for a photo session, but he lifts the telephone and an attractive girl in safari dress comes in. She will pose for them, a hunting rifle with a telephoto lens between her beautiful legs.

Sarah smiles. Cawood has made a talent out of a shortcoming. He will shape the world to his own will yet. He will succeed, she thinks, in making things look the way he wants them to look. It is a principle of good business.

A waiter brings her a glass of fruit juice. She drinks the liquid without tasting it. Cawood is working with his papers again. The tourist party has disappeared behind the homestead.

She does not sit waiting for Cawood to react. She relaxes instead. Here on Monomotapa there is an atmosphere which she is not used to at all – she can scarcely believe she is still in the Kei. There is a smell of well-heeled relaxation here which seems foreign to these parts.

She leans back into the cushions, listening to her son's hands moving the documents. She does not need to worry about the reception on Fata Morgana this evening – everything has already been taken care of: all it needs is to be shoved into the oven. She has two such splendid cooks nowadays that all she has to do is the final tasting and attend to the presentation of the food.

Then Cawood looks up. 'You can tell Dad that the third suicide Butler – this one – isn't going alone. He's going to take others with him.'

The glass nearly drops out of her hand. Before she can reply Cawood's hat is back on his head. 'Fuck the oil,' he says and strides out of the room. Moments later his Range Rover drives out through the gate.

Sarah sits there for a long time. The waiter returns to ask, softly, whether he can offer her anything else. Can he bring her some of the cold meats and salads left over from lunch? The kitchen will be happy to prepare a meal for her. Or would she like a drink?

She declines the offer. The tourists have now departed in their bus. The girl in safari dress comes to say, with an apologetic smile – she had watched Cawood's dramatic exit – that she has to meet another party at the tourist office in the city now.

'Since the arrival of the oil,' she says with a shrug of the shoulders, 'we can hardly keep up.'

'I am glad for your sake,' Sarah answers softly.

She sits alone among the staring eyes of the stuffed animal heads. She strokes the lion skin draped across the bench beside her chair. Then she gets up and takes her used glass to the kitchen where the staff on duty look at her in astonishment and thank her in Xhosa.

She goes out to the car and drives slowly through the drift, through the forested hills. Cawood is nowhere to be seen.

31

Seamus walks down the steps of Fata Morgana to meet his guests. He has slept all afternoon and feels significantly better. As the first car draws nearer he sees that it is the Du Pisanis. Frik du Pisani is the proprietor of Canaan Drillers and since the oil strike in their borehole the family has found itself on the guest lists of all the leading homes of the Kei.

Seamus waits patiently for the family – four lively, rather untidy children – to get out of the car. 'Good evening,' he says then. 'Welcome to Fata Morgana.'

'Mr Butler ...' Frik comes up, proffering his hand, his face weatherbeaten by sun and wind. 'Notched up plenty of boreholes,' he always says. But, somewhat improbable, under that face is a fat, flabby body – a difficult match with the face.

'Oh, Seamus ... please ...' Seamus shakes hands with Meisie du Pisani, too. 'Welcome, Meisie.'

They go up the steps, after Seamus has pointed the children round to the back of the house, explaining that a whole lot of toys and games have been set out for them on the sun porch. Sarah has dug out all of Cawood's old toys and there are cooldrinks and all sorts of games, including a TV set with a VCR and video cassettes.

'Have any trouble getting here?' Seamus asks. 'Saw some kudu, I expect. There's a smell of rain in the air.'

'Yes, I ...' but Seamus is not listening to what Frik du Pisani is saying. Standing on the stoep as he pours their sherry, he watches the approaching headlights of more arrivals.

'Make yourselves at home. Sarah is sure to be here any minute now. She has a few things to see to in the kitchen.' He goes down the steps into the garden again.

'Do you see that windmill?' he hears Frik say to Meisie. 'There ... over there ... you can just see it behind that tree ... Dad sank that one ... years ago, for old Mrs Butler ...' Seamus hears snatches of Frik's words but then his voice drops.

Seamus does not hear any more, but he feels mildly angry. His mother had that borehole put down shortly after his father's suicide. Frik is probably telling his wife about how Old Goat Butler did away with himself. Perhaps he is even pointing out the spot in the garden where the man was found dead with his rifle beside him.

Then three cars stop almost simultaneously. They are Patrick Bishop, professor of music and the cathedral's chief bell-ringer, and his friend – the man's name always escapes Seamus, but he is a biologist and chairperson of the Kei Greens currently engaged in a campaign against the oil pollution. Seamus had thought it would be a good thing if the two of them paid a visit to Fata Morgana. As a pressure group the Greens can do the city council a great deal of harm.

Then me, dressed in my white ice-cream suit, with a rose in my lapel and that awkward expression of other-worldliness on my face that so irritates Seamus. 'Hello, Seer,' Seamus says. 'Go and tell Sarah in the kitchen that the guests have arrived.' I look at him for a moment, until he realises the social gaffe he has committed by sending me, an invited guest, off to the kitchen like that.

But before he can rectify matters I have gone and the professor of drama is in front of him. This is the man who so enjoys playing the role of theatre director in any gathering. For a single dizzying moment Seamus thinks of that meeting in the hotel when he had been overcome by terror.

The man is a must on any guest list for, when the dinner

reaches the port and cigars stage, with only a modicum of encouragement, he will reel off Shakespeare's sonnets and Eliot's poetry for a solid hour, faultlessly. Some of the most beautiful moments round their dinner table, Seamus recalls, have been when George Ridge, in his Shakespearean actor's voice, his eyes closed and his head slightly bowed, has opened his mouth and allowed those splendid lines to come rolling forth.

Ridge's wife, Mary, leader of the local Black Sash, is wearing a beautiful off-the-shoulder gown and a necklace of real pearls. Seamus watches approvingly as she takes her husband's arm and ascends the stairs. One can always depend on the Ridges to lend grace to one's table, he thinks.

Once two more cars have arrived, Seamus follows the last guests up onto the stoep. Sarah is there now and soon everyone has a sherry or a small brandy in their hands. Seamus is slightly irritated when Frik du Pisani asks for Coke to add to his brandy – it is twelve-year-old KWV, after all. Soon, though, once all his guests have drinks in their hands, he too can stand on the stoep like everyone else and look in through the tall vertical windows at the beautifully appointed table: the light from the candles in their silver candlesticks flickering on the china, on cut crystal glasses.

'Beautiful evening,' observes George Ridge in his modulated voice, looking out over the garden. 'We all but drove into an antelope. Scarcely a kilometre past the turn-off from the main road – there he came, soaring over the fence, an acrobat of the veld. Fortunately,' he points at his car with a sense of satisfaction, 'the old Rover's brakes are still as good as new. An example of the best British technology.'

Everyone looks at the black Rover, a familiar sight in the parking lots outside Port Cecil's theatres, art exhibitions and the city hall whenever there is a performance by a visiting symphony orchestra. And also, people recall, in Joza during the troubles. Delicate and fearless, Mary Ridge would drive into the township to help, even though at such times cars are always in danger of being stoned.

The Rover is an old car, but it emphasises the Ridges' quiet good taste, noticeably distinct from the nouveau riche Mercedeses and BMWs so often parked beside it. The Ridges clearly believe that in a city where there is so much poverty one's material life ought to be restrained.

Later they go in to dine. Sarah has indicated the seating arrangements by means of name cards in delicate silver frames. The frames, she tells her guests, came from England in 1820 with the first Butlers. After expressions of admiration for the beauty of the table, Seamus pours wine and the steaming fall-goat liver entrée is served.

'Killed only an hour ago,' Seamus observes, lifting his glass.

'Confusion to the enemies of the Queen,' George Ridge completes the toast, seated on Sarah's right.

The guests laugh, enjoying the subtle interaction of red wine and fall-goat liver in the mouth.

'Remember the question people always ask about the assassinations of Kennedy or Verwoerd, or Mandela's release?' says Mary Ridge. 'Where were you at that moment? Where were you when the news broke that Tsafendas, the parliamentary messenger with a tapeworm in his brain, had stabbed Verwoerd in Parliament? Or when Kennedy suddenly fell sideways in that open limousine? Or when Mandela took his first steps to freedom?' She lifts another bit of liver to her mouth. 'Now our question here in the Kei is just as dramatic: where were you when the oil began to spurt out on Cathedral Square?'

The guests smile. Seamus makes sure that everyone's glasses are filled. 'I know where my goats were,' he jokes, sipping his wine. 'All flat on the ground – like corn stalks after a hailstorm has devastated the land.'

'Could you hear the explosion all the way out here?' asks the biologist. When it comes to the oil, he is a classic example of the best of British indignation.

Seamus nods. 'Loud enough to frighten the wits out of my goats.'

'Yes,' Sarah continues, 'it was as though a huge hand had

simply knocked all the goats out cold with a single blow.'

The guests are quiet for a moment as they consider this personification of the explosion. The officer commanding the army base to the north of the city now leans forward. He is in dress uniform, the insignia of rank glittering on his epaulettes. He is young to have such elevated rank. The professional defence force officers are getting younger and younger. Seamus leans forward and fills the officer's glass. They are a generation on their own, with bitter experience of battle earned in Angola before they were properly out of their teens. Cawood ...

But Seamus shakes his head and listens to the officer saying: 'I hear the explosion blew that little kaffir right into Get Lucky Fried Chicken.'

Some of the guests clear their throats in disapproval. Mary Ridge draws in her breath and glares, red-faced, at the officer. For a moment it looks as though she is about to say something, but then thinks better of it.

'It was a Mr Mtuze from Joza,' I say. 'He was standing right beside the borehole when it exploded. He was only slightly injured. A detonation of that nature frequently has a blind side – a man may be quite close to the point of explosion but still have the worst of the firepower deflected away from him.'

'The still point of the turning world,' suggests the professor of drama. 'The eye of the storm.'

'Precisely.'

Frik du Pisani looks at his fellow guests over the rim of his wineglass. 'Well, even if he hadn't struck the match, we would still have hit the oil a day or two later.'

'I thought you were on the point of giving up hope?' says George Ridge. 'I heard that you thought there was no water table above the bedrock.'

'Rumours,' Seamus comes to Du Pisani's rescue. 'It's the Joza Civic trying to make a hero out of a kwela driver. There is even some doubt about whether he ever flicked a match into the borehole at all.'

'Cultural engineering is hell itself,' jokes the bell-ringer, trying to defuse the situation. He, too, has obviously noticed that George Ridge is getting into his stride.

Everyone is now watching the brilliant Professor Bishop with his slightly insane eyes, recalling the relentless zeal with which he raised hundreds of thousands of rands to restore the cathedral bells to their original splendour. Magna cum laude at Oxford, the highest scores ever obtained in musical theory, the city's loyal music community whisper about him. And apart from his gift for playing the piano, the violin and the harp, he is also – surprisingly – an expert on that African instrument, the marimba.

He is highly strung, unfortunately, and has a tendency to stutter and repeat himself, so he does not command much respect. The students, Seamus once heard, apparently call him Tinkerbell.

At the precise moment of the explosion, the bell-ringer now says, he had been high up in the cathedral tower, tapping his little hammer on the massive dome of one of the bells in search of weak spots in the metal – which, as a result of the radical temperature fluctuations in the Kei, have a shorter life span than similar bells in England.

An infernal wind, he says, had come surging up the hollow column of the tower and struck him on the chest. The next moment the bells began to vibrate, producing the weirdest, most terrifying sound. It seemed as if the wave of sound had been trapped in them for eternity ...

The guests feel something of the bell-ringer's terror. By now they have finished their first course, neatly put down their knives and forks, and are dabbing the corners of their mouths with embroidered napkins.

He would never have thought, the bell-ringer continues, his eyes glinting as he twists the wine glass round and round in his hands, that the bells would have been capable of producing such a sound. What a remarkable sound, was his last thought before the ladder gave way beneath him and left him hanging entangled in the bell ropes like a mousebird in a noose.

His weight in the ropes set the bells ringing and he hung there for hours. 'For hours,' he repeats, and again: 'For hours!' Until one of the cathedral clergy, coming to pray about the great act of providence which had befallen the city, saw him swinging there and called the fire brigade. The firemen were engaged in crowd control and hosing down oil-covered cars, but eventually they came to his rescue.

'Well then!' Seamus stretches and gives Sarah the look which he always uses to indicate that he thinks it is time to serve the next course.

There is silence round the table. The bell-ringer's tale has forced all the guests' thoughts back to that day and the days which followed. They remember the frightful mess round the cathedral. Oil slicks very soon began to congeal and harden on the stone walls, covering even the stained-glass windows on that side of the cathedral with a layer of grease. They recall the foul furrows and blocked pools in the river, which had to be hastily dug out by caterpillar tractors in an effort to contain the stream of oil.

At times each of them had been part of the crowd which was constantly there, standing and staring at the oil as it spurted rhythmically into the air. Like the stream from a fall-goat's pizzle, thinks Seamus, not for the first time. As though controlled by a massive sphincter, the stream gives a tremendous spurt every five seconds, some higher even than the bell tower.

At that first council meeting the city fathers resolved to call in a bulldozer immediately so that the oil dammed up in the square could be channelled away. A ditch was hastily dug beside the cathedral, past the statue of the angel and the dead soldier, down two blocks farther into the foul old drainage ditch running down from Sun City, where the dirty water was forever filled with floating plastic bottles, old shoes, empty tins and even the occasional dead dog or donkey as it moved sluggishly along.

The river of oil now joined the foul water to form a thick stream. Slowly the porridgey mess pushed its way down towards the river, to First Delta, the easternmost of the delta's legs, where caterpillars were desperately throwing up dam walls to contain the mess.

The department of chemistry at the university hurriedly introduced counter measures – balls of white foam from the chemical treatments they experimented with blew across the city on the wind. When one of the oil dams caught fire the sticky smell hung over the entire city.

It was reminiscent of the smell of a garage workshop, an oil rag held near the nose, or a car engine when the bonnet was raised and you brought your face close to the engine block.

The smell pervaded everything. Visitors to city restaurants – particularly the small Italian and Portuguese eateries in the narrow alleys near Cathedral Square – could taste it in the food. There was a rumour that the oil had formed a spray which was blown across the veld by the night wind and that plants and animals were absorbing it into their systems.

The trout which had made the upper reaches of the delta so renowned began to taste like tinned sardines. The trout anglers who spent their days flicking their flies up there in quiet pools between dense undergrowth were the first to predict an ecological disaster.

Lovers suddenly found evidence of the oil in the armpits of their beloveds – a heavy, suffocating smell which seeped into people's dreams and filled their nightmares with rivers of oil.

Seamus shakes his head and looks at his guests, who are now chatting to one another again. He takes a deep breath and considers going out onto the stoep for a while for some fresh air, but decides against it for fear the guests will think it odd.

During their protracted business lunches every day the business community looks out at the spectacle from the windows of the restaurants on Cathedral Square with great satisfaction. With continual glances at their gold wristwatches, they discuss their plans over tall beers.

Hoteliers have already begun to register mortgage loans with a view to adding wings of luxury suites to their establishments. Legal firms have hastily contracted junior partners to handle the flood of litigation, contracts, property transactions and transfers, and general fraud which everyone knew would follow.

Nightclub owners instructed talent scouts up north to recruit strip-tease artistes from the mining towns, while from the mother city in the south-west came masseuses and aerobics instructors.

'All of a sudden everybody's avarice has come to the fore,' says the biologist, jerking Seamus's wandering thoughts back into the present. 'And with such covetousness rampant, everyone has forgotten our city's principal asset – our beautiful river, the unspoilt coastline, the Atlantic Gulf, home of the coelacanth which has brought our city so much renown.' He does not look at Seamus because, as everyone knows, the Greens have accused the city council of turning a deaf ear to warnings about pollution.

'Oh, people always complain about everything,' is Seamus's rejoinder. He does not feel like arguing with the little professor, but he does have his loyalty to the council to maintain. 'Those feminists you've got at the university keep going on about the phallic symbolism of the drilling machine ...' There are smiles as he continues: 'I'm not joking – I am told it was actually referred to in a seminar! And now the ecologists have woken up out of the tedium of their idems and their op cits and they – you ...' he looks at the biologist, 'are trying to assert that we are destroying the ecosystem. Which ecosystem? The bats in the cathedral gutters? Or that gaggle of old monks in the monastery at Stones Hill?' The guests grin. Seamus senses that he has their attention. 'And then there are those Thandanis who have corralled my brother-in-law into acting for them at a pauper's fee because the cathedral is now supposed to have been built over old Xhosa graves. And ...'

Seamus is startled when I – who have so far held my peace – bang my wine glass down hard on the table. The guests look at me in surprise.

'Where did you hear that?' I ask sharply.

Seamus shrugs his shoulders. 'The council has to see that it keeps itself informed.'

'Keeps itself informed? But I only received those instructions yesterday! I have not discussed them with a single soul!' Seriously upset, I hold onto the edge of the table with both hands. It looks as though I am about to push myself away from the table.

'We have our ... informants ...' Seamus smiles apologetically at his guests. He was attempting to show the council in a favourable light, but now the conversation is taking a direction which he did not foresee.

'Informants? What sort of a word is that? They are nothing but ... a gang of ... spies!' I am just folding my table napkin when Sarah emerges from the kitchen followed by her two helpers, each carrying large silver serving dishes. Sarah stops, her eyes darting nervously from me to Seamus.

'Come now, Seer.' Seamus gestures with one hand. 'Don't get so emotional ...'

'Emotional? Now that we know, finally, that it is true that the city council has spies on its payroll? So all the rumours which you have so strenuously denied are in fact true? When you said the Civic's accusations were all just propaganda?' I get up. 'So Joza were quite right when they said you knew everything that happened at their meetings about a unified municipality!'

'Seer ...' Sarah has put down her dish now. She wants to go over to me, but is hesitating. I throw down the napkin I am still holding onto the table in front of me.

'Come, brother ...' from Seamus.

'It is unpardonable.' My chest is heaving. The candle flames flicker. I stride out, and by the time Seamus follows me out onto the stoep it is too late. The yard is suffused with the diesel fumes of the battered old Mercedes as the red tail-lights splash through the gate.

Seamus watches my departure. 'Dammit,' he says. 'Damn, damn, damn, damn!'

In the shadows behind him, I grin contentedly. When he goes back into the house, I raise a metaphorical glass to the tail-lights of the Mercedes.

Well done, Seer.

32

You learn to listen to your child's moods even when you are no longer carrying him in your womb and even when you don't see him very often. Standing on the stoep at Fata Morgana in the early morning with a cup of coffee in her hand, looking out over the wisps of mist in the hollows, Sarah knows that in his own way Cawood is now succumbing to the Butler passions.

She puts down the cup on the low stoep table and starts doing her breathing exercises, growing slightly light-headed from all the fresh air she is drinking in so deeply. The food last night was rather rich, she thinks: I must not be so heavy-handed. We are not getting any younger, and nor are our guests. The body's self-cleansing capacity is no longer as effective as it used to be.

The telephone rings in the passage, but she leaves it for one of the servants to answer. Ever since the oil-fountain started its spurting there have been more and more bookings for tourist visits to Fata Morgana. It is as though the Kei is suddenly brimming over with the entrepreneurial spirit. People from far up-country are streaming into the delta city. Tourists are descending in swarms on the whole region. Even the private schools, she has been told, are already being overwhelmed by applications for the following year.

The table talk the previous evening decided that millions and millions were waiting for the people of the Kei if only everything was handled correctly. 'If only people don't lose their heads and expect everything just to fall into their laps without careful planning and hard work,' Seamus said, raising his glass to the waiting millions. Round the table everybody raised their glasses with glistening eyes and drank a toast to the fruit of the earth. 'To the millions!' they sang out in chorus.

Although Cawood had been invited to the dinner, his chair stood unoccupied all evening. He had not telephoned to apologise either. This morning Sarah woke with the certainty: she had to go to Cawood; she had to rein him in; she had to convince him that they meant only well towards him – that Seamus would not sell Fata Morgana out from under his feet – that they loved him.

She quietly completes her toilet in the bedroom and leaves a note for the sleeping Seamus. It is the freshest hour of the day when she drives out through the farmyard gate and into the landscape opening up before her. The Kei can look so gentle, almost naive, in the morning. One would never suspect that in a mere couple of hours the sun would be blistering down in fury.

It is just as well that Seamus is still asleep. He is unwilling to let her drive alone on farm roads in these times. Only last week a farmer's wife and her two children were shot in a neighbouring district. Sarah slips her pistol under the seat, though, and fully intends to drive cautiously. If she notices anything untoward she will turn back. And in any case, Seamus has had the Mercedes fitted with a radio, so it would be possible for her to contact Civil Defence headquarters at Salem at any time.

As she drives, she is thinking of my actions the night before – how overwrought I was – how such actions are uncharacteristic of me: I prefer to consider an issue carefully and comment later, if necessary. She realises that I had been furious because Seamus – and behind Seamus there looms the city council and the city's white business interests – was interfering in the affairs of my practice.

She would have to telephone me, too, today – to keep the peace and get Seamus to give me a ring later to apologise. Sarah sighs, shaking her head as she drives. If she, too, were to start behaving like that, instead of always being the one who tries to bring about reconciliation – where would they all be then?

The closer she gets to Monomotapa, the stronger grows her premonition that Cawood is about to do something irresponsible. Ever since his army service there has been an increase in his unpredictability: sudden whims – wild trips in the helicopter – hunting expeditions at night followed by bakkie loads of meat being offloaded at the homes of friends, relations and business acquaintances in the early morning. And always, that bunch of rascals who go around with him: young farmers from the district, a couple of unimportant businessmen from the city – always buzzing round Cawood to enjoy the flamboyant safari evenings, the helicopter, the hunting rifles, the free venison, the pretty girls ...

As she crests the rise above Monomotapa she notices that everything round the homestead is deathly quiet. That's odd, she thinks. He's so busy nowadays – he said he couldn't keep up with it all.

She draws up in front of the house. The front door is locked. She rings the bell. The same waiter who served her the previous day opens the door. He invites her in and explains with a shrug of the shoulders that Cawood has cancelled all appointments, that he telephoned the tourist office to say that the business would be closed for three days. He has gone off in the chopper, the man says, with a strange man who had been here once before – an officer from the army base.

He invites Sarah to sit down and fetches her a drink. She sits pensively sipping the chilled pineapple juice. It is prettily served, with a twist of lemon rind, and a red cherry on a cocktail stick bearing the legend 'Monomotapa. Discover Africa now.'

Where on earth could Cawood be? The unwritten rule still applies – and he never breaks it – that they let him know whenever they go away, and he does the same with them. There has never been any difficulty with this and it is a sensible arrangement: he keeps an eye on Fata Morgana when they are away, and they look after Monomotapa for him.

Sarah is convinced that Cawood's mysterious departure bodes no good. When the waiter returns, she cross-examines him closely. What clothes has Cawood taken with him? Where is the girl who helped him? Which direction did the helicopter take? When is he coming back? Have there been any other telephone calls for him?

She gets no satisfactory answers. She rings Seamus from Cawood's desk. When he answers, he is still confused and sleepy.

'But where on earth are you, Sarah?' he asks. 'You know I don't want you driving around alone in these times. That shooting ...'

'Seamus,' she interrupts, 'I'm here at Monomotapa. Cawood has disappeared. He's gone.'

'What do you mean?'

'He's gone away for a few days. Without telling us. He's never ever done that before.'

'No, he's never done that before,' Seamus repeats. He is silent at the other end of the line and she knows he is thinking back to their conversation with Cawood on the stoep.

'I've got such a bad feeling about it,' she says.

'Oh come now, Sarah,' replies Seamus angrily. 'You and your premonitions!'

'I had a premonition the night before the oil strike, too, Seamus. Do you remember?'

'Yes, yes, that's true. But where can the little bugger have got to? What's up with the child?'

'He's not a child any longer, Seamus. Can't you get that into your head?'

Seamus sighs and is silent for a while. 'What do his staff say?'

'There's almost nobody here. And he seems to have left without saying where he was going. He's taken the chopper and he's gone off with that colonel who was supposed to have been involved in smuggling ivory out of Angola in Savimbi's time – the one with the Porsche.'

'Oh, God. The boy has never been able to choose the right friends. Now he's flying around with a corrupt officer.'

'Seamus, I've got such an awful feeling ...'

'Sarah,' he says now in a determined tone, 'you've got to see if there isn't anything lying around which might give you a clue. He wouldn't simply leave without telling us if he didn't have something to hide.'

'Do you think I really ought to search? I mean, he's grown up and left home already, after all.'

Seamus snorts. 'Search! Rummage through his underpants if you have to. He's your own flesh and blood. And he's not supposed to clear off without telling his parents. He must expect us to try and establish his whereabouts. We're worried, after all.'

'Yes. Yes, OK.'

Hesitantly, Sarah starts scratching about on the desk. There are only accounts and invoices, some uncashed cheques, stock lists for the kitchen and the ammunition store. She averts her eyes from the actual amounts – she does not want to know what Cawood earns.

Then she goes into his bedroom. Everything is shipshape, as Cawood always is. The objects on the bedside cabinet have been placed there in an orderly fashion: a book on East Africa, five revolver bullets in a neat row, an electronic alarm clock, a packet of cigars.

On the wardrobe there is a khaki shirt on a hanger, above the pocket the word Monomotapa. Should I open his wardrobe, she wonders. No, that I really can't do. She leaves the room, but then turns round again in the passage, stops, and thinks: Is it really any of our business if an independent, grown man decides to go off for a while?

Then she goes over to the tallboy and pulls open the top drawer. Only clothes, in neat piles. The second drawer: more clothes – socks and handkerchiefs. She closes it. Then the third. She hesitates, the wood cold to her touch. In this drawer, she knows, there is something that she should rather not see.

She does not open it. She turns away and goes out.

33

I wait with Zola for the nurse with the medicine trolley to move to the next ward. He draws the curtain round his bed and bends down to retrieve his clothes from the bedside locker. The rest of the things – the daily paper, the tissues, the packet of sweets, the tote lists – he leaves just as they are beside his bed.

He walks down to the toilet in his dressing gown, his clothes bundled up and concealed under his arm. There he dresses as quickly as he can. His arm is heavily bandaged and the movement makes his shoulder wound bleed again, so he has to clench his teeth and pad the wound with toilet paper to absorb the blood oozing through the bandage.

He shoves the dressing gown down behind the toilet bowl and waits with a beating heart. Foreseeing that it would be painful, he had asked the sister who handed out the medicines for an extra painkiller, but the pills have not yet taken effect.

He sits on the toilet waiting for the pain to subside. You think Zola Mtuze is a joke, but you don't know half of what he is concealing ... You think because he's always striving to get ahead that he is a frivolous character.

He shakes his head. And it is as though their lightweight opinion of him has been transposed upon their view of the danger he is exposed to. Whoever or whatever the balaclavas are, they will be back. That much he knows. And he has no intention of being a sitting duck for them.

When the pain abates and all is quiet in the corridor, he goes out. He knows where the nearest exit is. He only hopes that he will not run into any of the nursing staff from his ward – or Ayanda herself, of course!

He goes outside through a side door, one normally used by the nursing staff. He makes it to the pepper trees beside the hospital without being seen. He will have to hurry now, because in five or ten minutes the doctors on duty will be doing their ward rounds and when they find his bed empty they will immediately search the bathrooms and then summon the security staff.

Where it is he is going, Zola does not know. He has spent a long time in his hospital bed considering the problem. Obviously a decision to return to his home would be a mistake. If the balaclavas do not get him there, it would certainly not be long before Ayanda and MaNdlovu arrive on his doorstep.

His years of hard work and long hours have so isolated him from other people that now he does not have anyone else he could visit.

Then he has an inspiration: Amanda! She would understand – during the emergency she supplied safe lodgings for various activists on the run from the security police and set them on escape routes to other cities.

Zola stands on the stairs, flattened against the hospital wall, trying in vain to catch the eye of a kwela driver waiting for passengers under the pepper trees. Perhaps this is the ideal opportunity for my daughter and me to draw closer to each other. I'm only a simple taxi driver. My generation didn't have time to get an education. We had to grit our teeth and get stuck in if we wanted to break free of the squatter camps of apartheid. It took everything out of me: getting work with Dunlop, keeping my job in the days of strikes and dismissals, doing the diploma course to qualify as a fork-lift operator, later being able to buy my own minibus, and then another one, building a house, marrying above my station and getting Ayanda Thandani as my wife ...

The younger generation do not always understand these

things. They enjoy the luxury of going to university, of reading books, of thinking and reasoning, of formulating their thoughts about politics, economics and culture in the space we created. They are able to keep up their resistance with a clear prospect of victory – all the signs are there already. In my youth, apartheid stretched out ahead of us interminably.

It is we, my generation, those whom they now vilify as bourgeois sell-outs, who created all their opportunities for them. Zola signals again towards the minibus. He knows the driver – they are members of the same taxi association.

Then the man sees him and responds to Zola's urgent beckoning by walking over towards him. Zola takes his arm. 'I'll pay you the price of a full load to Joza,' he says. 'But then you must pull up your kwela right where I'm standing. I can't get in there in front of the security guards at the entrance. And you'll have to keep your mouth shut afterwards.'

Shaking his head, the man walks back to his minibus and backs it up to the step where Zola is waiting. Zola gets in and lies down flat on the second row of seats. Past the gatekeepers they drive and soon they cross the arched bridge.

'I'll fix up with you, bra,' says Zola when the man drops him in the fishermen's quarter near the commune which Amanda shares with a bunch of other young people.

He knows from experience that they do not respond to knocking, so he turns the doorknob and walks in. He will never get used to these young people's habits. All the doors of the bedrooms opening onto the passage are open. The beds are unmade and there is music blaring from almost every room.

Zola does not find anyone in the kitchen either. A blonde girl is sitting on the back stoep, chatting to a black student with a rasta hairstyle. They look at him for a moment or two without saying anything. 'I'm Amanda's father,' he says then. 'Do you perhaps know where she is?'

'She has gone to buy poster paint,' says the girl. 'She'll be back soon.'

They offer him a cup of tea while he sits in Amanda's room, waiting. He looks at a couple of the books that are lying around. The photograph beside the bed is of a smiling young Indian. Would you believe it! Once last year she brought a young white chap to a meeting in Joza.

He sighs: the things these young people take for granted are things we had to fight for. How will they ever know to give us the credit for them?

Suddenly the front door swings open and Amanda's voice fills the passage. There are some other young people with her. She stops, astonished, at the door of her room, her arms full of shopping bags.

'Daddy!'

Zola gets to his feet uncomfortably. How odd that he should feel so strange, so out of place, in his own child's digs!

'I hope I'm not disturbing ...'

'Of course not – not at all!' she says, her voice a shade higher than usual. She hesitates, then drops the bags and comes over and gives him a hug. 'Did you run away from the hospital?'

He nods, smiling.

'And what's Mummy going to say? And MaNdlovu?'

He shrugs. 'Have you got any painkillers?' he asks. 'This wound is like fire.'

Suddenly the room is filled with young people. 'They all want to meet the oil hero!' laughs Amanda. Embarrassed, Zola looks at them. The oil hero, he thinks. What next!

When they are gone again, she tells him they are preparing for a march that evening. Various groups are going to carry placards, she says: the Youth League is going to demonstrate about the land rights issue, and so is the Joza Environmental Association, of which she is an executive member and which usually works for better conditions in the squatter camps.

'You can help us think up slogans!' she says. 'Come!'

He goes out onto the back stoep and sits down among them. They are all hard at work. In the midst of laughter the best slogans are painted onto huge placards.

No Joy for Joza, is Zola's contribution.

As the afternoon progresses, the atmosphere grows more serious. Tension is mounting.

Later Zola calls Amanda aside. 'Have you heard anything about Mpho?' he asks.

She shakes her head. 'All I've heard is that he's not in the bush any more, Daddy. And MaNdlovu of course thinks he and Uncle Ncincilili are about to do something miraculous.' She shakes her head, takes him by the arm and leads him away from the others. 'I've heard a story that Uncle Mpho has been seen with an AK-47. But there are so many stories doing the rounds.'

'And you?' he asks. 'Will you feel safe tonight?'

'Feel safe?' she asks. 'Have any of our people ever felt safe in this country?'

'Can you hide me?' he asks then, sheepishly. 'I'm afraid.'

34

The Leap Year Ball usually brings a flock of cars onto Cathedral Square. It is, of course, also traditionally the dance to which the women of the Kei invite the men. I always find myself a convenient spot in one of the restaurants from where I can watch the arrival of the guests.

This year, with the oil spray causing a thin slippery layer all over Cathedral Square, the cars have to find parking in side streets leading off the square. In the narrow winding streets lined with the double-storeyed Settler houses of the university quarter some of the most expensive cars in the district vie for space in the safe pools of light under lamp posts, before brightly illuminated restaurants or even in front of houses whose inhabitants are sitting gossiping behind the potted geraniums on their verandas.

All are aware that, according to the statistics published regularly in the Government Gazette, approximately ten per cent of these cars will end up in Joza tonight, stripped of their radios, hub caps and even their wheels. Some will be smuggled through to the Ciskei or Transkei or even farther, to Swaziland or Mozambique.

The Butlers – Seamus in the dress uniform of the Eastern Cape Highlanders, his old regiment, and Sarah in a cream coloured evening gown with glistening pearls – park their Mercedes in front of a large old house with lights in all its windows. On the second-storey Victorian balcony which leans out over the street below a group of students are sitting round a flask of wine, chatting. They whistle mockingly at the Butlers, now carefully getting out of the car, smoothing their clothes and making doubly sure that everything is locked and secure.

Seamus would very much have liked to ask them to keep an eye on the car – the city councillors' parking area has been ploughed up to form a run-off channel for the oil. Instead, the wolf-whistles of the frivolous youngsters make him and Sarah walk away self-consciously, angry about allowing themselves to be so embarrassed by a bunch of students. Once they turn the corner and the oil smell is stronger and more cloying, they relax again. 'Slowly, Seamus,' Sarah pleads. 'My dress has a very narrow skirt.'

Seamus feels in his pocket for the notes for his speech. This is a great evening for him and Fata Morgana, because it is at the Leap Year Ball that the Fall-Goat Trophy, sponsored by the estate, is presented to the person who has made the most important contribution to the economic progress of the region in the past four years. The trophy, in the shape of a ram of the Caper timidus species, is a coveted object among the businessmen, agricultural leaders and economists of the Kei.

They round the last corner and see other elegant couples moving towards the brightly lit entrance to the city hall. As they pass me, I catch the scent of Sarah's perfume. I look up to the balcony of the restaurant where I am waiting for Seamus and Sarah to arrive. Above the entrance hangs a large banner proclaiming in red letters: SKRIKKELJAAR/LEAP YEAR. On Sarah and Seamus's left gleam the helmets of the soldiers who have been positioned right round the square. The fountain is so brightly illuminated that the jet black arc of oil seems almost silver in the beams of light. The cathedral looks schizophrenic: the side facing the city hall and the fountain of oil shines black and glutinous, which lends it the appearance of having been built of coal, though a closer look shows the oil moving down the walls in long continuous trickles.

The other half of the cathedral is shrouded in shadow, its grey walls grim and morose.

As Seamus and Sarah enter the city hall porch, noticing with approval the massive floral decorations, each with an aloe as its centrepiece, and the beautifully polished floors and chandeliers, Seamus has a carnation pinned on to his lapel by the wife of the town clerk, while Sarah receives a posy of veld flowers from the nervous young man who had given Seamus the news of the oil strike over the telephone some days before.

When Seamus and Sarah move on, Sarah complaining about the fellow's sweaty hand, Seamus growls under his breath: 'Nerves. Worse than a wether.'

They enter the hall. The band is already on the stage playing a Viennese waltz. 'Beautiful!' Sarah calls to the mayoress and Seamus, overcome for a moment by his sense of self-satisfaction – perhaps he has taken a milligram too much of the sedative Pax? – is shaking the mayor's hand with enthusiasm.

Greeting various people, they move past tables covered in white damask, decorated with beautiful flower arrangements and laid with the council's best cutlery, to the main table, set crosswise to all the others, where the trophy has already been set up on a small plinth behind the mayor's chair.

The sculptor had succeeded, Seamus notices once more as they move towards their places at the main table, in capturing not only the dementia and pride but also the tragedy and anarchic terror of Caper timidus.

In a chorus of polite greetings, Seamus and Sarah take their seats.

'Have you heard, Seamus,' asks the mayoress, 'about the march that bunch of activists are planning for tonight?'

Seamus nods his head to the woman with the enormous grey coiffure and the heaving bosom glittering with baroque jewels. 'I wouldn't be worried if I were you, Dorothy,' he says reassuringly, gesturing to a black steward behind them to pour a glass of wine. Waiting for the steward to move away a little, he continues: 'Our information is that it will be a small group and that it will probably be postponed. You are aware that the radical core in Joza is actually very small.'

'Oh, these blacks,' sighs the mayoress, sipping from her glass. Seamus notices the narrow line of perspiration on her top lip. At the corners of her mouth there are tiny, barely perceptible black hairs. 'They're always wanting more, more, more,' she continues. 'But they never take any initiative and do any real work. Look how we, the Settlers, built up this city out of nothing. Look at this building, look at the tables, listen to the glorious music! Tonight is a high point for our community – and now they choose to stage a mass march!'

Seamus clears his throat. All the city councillors are aware of the mayoress's scarcely concealed right-wing sentiments. The poor mayor – go the whispers – can only keep his spouse quiet by a stream of gifts: jewels, time-share weekends, overseas trips ...

'Nothing is going to happen,' he closes the conversation. 'Our police force will see to that. All we have to do now,' he says, laying his hand comfortingly on hers and feeling the knobs of her rings under his palm, 'is just forget all about it and enjoy the evening. It's leap year, after all, the year of wonder and magic, and it's the Leap Year Ball to which you, the lovely ladies of our city, have invited us men ... It's a special evening for our whole district, because our real wealth is still ahead of us.'

But he is not able to finish his sentence because the mayor has ascended the podium behind the main table and is tapping the microphone with his fingernail to make sure that it is working.

'Friends,' he begins, and the hundreds of guests prepare themselves to enjoy the ceremony. There is an extraordinary sense of expectation in the air, since the oil strike has set the whole district buzzing. Business enterprises are shooting up like mushrooms and many unknown entrepreneurs have suddenly sprung into prominence during the last few days.

There are already – so gossip has it – a handful of potential instant millionaires in the city, even though so far these are only on paper.

This year, everybody knows, the award could go to just about anyone.

Seamus sits back, content. He squeezes Sarah's hand, pours a little more wine into her glass and feels to see whether his speech is still in his breast pocket. Here, under the sign of the fall-goat, surrounded by the foremost citizens of the district and their spouses, he feels at home and content. The Leap Year Ball is the climax of recent events. He can forget about the terrors and depressions. Here no doubt is possible – only honour, respect, appreciation and applause.

'Friends ... tempus fugit ... time is flying ...' The mayor clears his throat, leaning on the lectern. 'Our city is once again caught up in the marvellous events of a leap year. You don't need me to tell you what the possibilities are ... you have just walked past the fountain outside and your own eyes have shown you the black oil glittering like diamonds.'

The mayor, obviously satisfied with his own words, is silent for a moment, waiting for each word to sink in. At Seamus's side the mayoress sighs. 'He always speaks so beautifully,' she whispers.

Seamus is not listening any more. He is enjoying the play of light on jewels, faces, all of them known to him. Almost all are from families who have been building up this part of the country for generations. Their surnames are all to be found on the toposcope at Bathurst where the original Settler families and their farm names are recorded. And all their eyes, he knows, are on him, the breeder of fall-goats and guardian of the trophy.

Eventually, after the main course and a couple of turns round the dance floor with Sarah – and how she laughs and enjoys a lively tiekiedraai! – it is his turn to speak and make the presentation.

Seamus draws himself up to his full height behind the microphone, aware of the imposing figure he cuts, dressed in full regimentals and with the trophy beside him. And he is a seasoned orator.

'Friends,' he begins. 'When our ancestors arrived, they found here nothing but rocks and aloes. The jackal and the lion and the springbuck held sway. There were crocodiles in the river and elephants bathed in Third Delta.

'Through sheer hard work our forefathers tamed this land, laid out a city, built a cathedral, founded a university, opened schools, planned splendid residential areas. Our farmers took over the land, cleared fields, ploughed and planted.

'One of the reasons why we are gathered here tonight is to honour their labour.' Seamus raises his glass and proposes a toast: 'To our forefathers. May they rest in peace.'

'1820!'

'Of course it was not always easy. Lives were sacrificed. Terrors had to be endured. We may never forget that. But in this special year of exceptional fulfilment and blessing, it is a particular pleasure for me to declare that we are once again foregathered here in the presence of the fall-goat.

'And it is in humility in the face of the complexities of history and our own lives that we now prepare ourselves to announce the Entrepreneur of the Quadrennium.'

Seamus looks out over the faces. There are old, hardened businessmen, cynical after decades in commerce. There are agricultural leaders, grey-headed farmers who rule over thousands of hectares of land and know the country to its very fibre. There are the fresh young faces of the city's yuppies who have started up new businesses in the past few years, particularly in tourism and the entertainment industry.

Seamus reminds them of the blessings of dedication and hard work. He quotes his favourite Kipling:

'If you can fill the unforgiving minute
With sixty seconds' worth of distance run,
Yours is the Earth and everything that's in it,
And – which is more – you'll be a Man, my son!'

Applause. He pauses for a few moments. Someone drops a knife. '1820!' Laughter.

'And now, on this leap year's night, it is my privilege to

announce our Entrepreneur of the Quadrennium ... the man who by his business acumen and entrepreneurial spirit and creative thought has led the city into a new era of prosperity ...'

Slowly Seamus opens the envelope. He exploits the tension, looking out over the tables. Here and there, in among the pious silence, there are some nervous giggles.

Seamus takes a deep breath. 'Frik du Pisani, driller, for the discovery of oil in our native soil and the massive injection which this has given our commercial life ...!'

'Canaan Drillers!' yells the mayor, quite overcome.

As Frik du Pisani struggles up out of his chair, dressed rather untidily in evening dress (hired for the occasion, and in any case the poor wretch would never realise that he is just a pawn in the battle with Joza), the guests all rise to their feet. They clap their hands as the driller with his weather-beaten face crosses diagonally towards the stage. He moves sideways like a crab, his face contorted in an incredulous grin.

On the podium Seamus congratulates him and places the trophy in his hands. They stand there for a few moments as the cameras flash, and then Frik has an opportunity to say a few words.

He stands behind the microphone, swallowing hard. He looks out across the tables to his wife as though she could offer help. Tears trickle down his cheeks. He shakes his head, gestures with his hands that he has nothing to say, and makes his way back.

The mayor seizes the microphone and asks the band to strike up a waltz straightaway. Traditionally it has to be, he says, the Blue Danube, for is not that waltz a tribute to this lifegiving river on which our city stands, the river which maintains us all and brings stability and prosperity to our community?

'A waltz!' he cries. 'In celebration of fulfilment and peace! And everybody must join in!'

The band strikes up the Strauss tune, chairs scrape backwards and soon the floor is filled with couples. Round them stand the deserted tables and empty chairs, candles flickering in the currents of air stirred up by the whirling couples. Then, at first barely perceptible but gradually swelling in volume till clearly audible above the strains of the music the dancers hear the chanting of thousands of voices.

One by one the couples stop. Eventually the band stops playing. The conductor indicates to his bandsmen to lay down their instruments. In dead silence everyone stands listening.

Suddenly there is an earth-shattering explosion outside the hall. The resulting air current lifts the ladies' dresses and hair-dos and thrusts its hot hand into men's faces. The candles splutter and die, and because tradition dictates that there be no electric light at the ball but candles only, suddenly it is pitch dark.

Screaming, the guests surge towards the front door. 'Order!' shouts the mayor from behind the microphone, but the dancers are pushing and shoving their way out. Seamus takes Sarah's hand in his, takes the mayoress by the elbow and calls to the mayor to follow them. There may be a second bomb inside the hall.

With contained fear but as quickly as they can they move outside. By the time they reach the foyer they can already see the flicker of flames. When they suddenly find themselves out in the open, their perspiring bodies cold in the chill of the evening, they look up, dumbstruck, at the giant flame.

The oil-fountain has disappeared and in its place flickers an infernal torch, dominating the entire square, casting splashes of light on surrounding buildings and at times shooting up into the night sky higher than the cathedral spire itself.

Someone has detonated a bomb on the gusher. It is an act of sabotage. Seamus looks across to the opposite side of Cathedral Square where thousands of black marchers are standing with their posters, their shining and equally astonished faces all turned to the flame.

In their tens of thousands they have come. The next moment brings a burst of machine-gun fire.

35

Talking about our country today is like trying to paint a moving train. That is what the Kei is like.

When the first shots stutter out across the square, a giant hand seems to shove the crowds back. People surge away from the fountain of flame.

Sitting on the second-storey balcony of the Malay restaurant looking out over Cathedral Square, I hold my hand to my heart.

I would never have thought that I would witness a great tragedy such as this. I had ensconced myself on the balcony restaurant because the arrival of the leap year dancers is always such a pretty sight.

I suppose we should have been expecting a tragedy of some kind, really, but we are so punch-drunk from all that has been happening that we are incapable of making an accurate assessment of the forces building up around us. Perhaps others could have foreseen it. But me? As always, old Seer just climbs the steep staircase up to the restaurant, sits down at a lonely table and picks up the menu.

With its view of the oil gusher, this restaurant has become one of the most sought-out spots in the city in the past few days. One has to book a table by early in the morning. The dishes have also improved radically – a chef specialising in Indonesian and Malay dishes was flown in on the day after the oil strike.

The owners concocted new names for their dishes and hired pretty little waitresses with oriental features. This is a place where the entrepreneurs descending on the city can look out over the arc of oil and discuss their plans. Its rhythmic pumping is the erotic rhythm of their own ambitions.

The gala dancers are thronging the illuminated foyer of the city hall, the women dressed in shining, flowing gowns; the men in kilts, evening dress or full regimentals of the Border Infantry.

The driller, Du Pisani, stands with one arm round his wife's shoulders, the other clutching the Fall-Goat Trophy.

So he won! They are still clinging stubbornly to the idea that Canaan Drillers and not Zola Mtuze discovered the oil!

The soldiers who had fired fall back in alarm as an officer charges down at them. The soldiers look at their machine-guns in astonishment: has there been some misunderstanding?

The force of the foremost crush of folk has been so great that people are being forced up against the buildings surrounding the square.

People are pouring out of the restaurants and clubs round the square like red ants out of an antheap. There are so many shouts and screams that they merge into a single sound. Something terrible is happening. With the napkin still tucked into my collar, I half rise, wanting to help, but knowing myself powerless.

When the vanguard has retreated, driven by a terror powerful enough to shove those behind them back as well, hundreds of shoes are left lying on the square. Only then – as though my mind at first would have denied it – do I see the bodies.

Shapeless as hessian sacks.

Suddenly there is silence. No blood or movement is visible.

Then one of the fallen starts to move – leaving a shining trail of blood as he moves, a young man is beginning to drag himself to the entrance of the city hall where the gala guests are standing with their hands to their mouths.

Fascinated, I watch the scene. The man is making slow progress, dragging himself along on his elbows, his head pumping up and down. In disgust or perhaps from sheer obstinacy the guests remain unmoving. The man has come to within two yards of one woman's skirts when vehicles burst onto the square.

Fire engines, yellow police vans and a bunch of Casspirs bounce across the paving and the low walls round the cathedral, scattering potted plants to the winds. A lamp post is knocked over and snaps in a rain of sparks. Soldiers and policemen with Alsatians pour out of the vehicles.

The flame spurting from the oil well is only a couple of yards high one moment, then suddenly shoots up as high as the cathedral spire the next, releasing fireballs to tumble over the roof of the city hall. The escaping gas has the same rhythm as the oil. It is like the blow-flame of a flame thrower.

The marchers are still trying to get away, along the narrow streets leading away from the square. As far as they go, youths smash windows and overturn cars until soon there are smaller versions of the great flame flickering in all the little streets off Cathedral Square.

I look at the other guests around me in the restaurant. They too sit as if turned to stone. The flames flickering in the tiny glass saucers placed on each table themselves become reflections of the great flame outside now audibly bubbling with the release of natural gas.

Policemen storm into the front ranks of the crowd, forming a cordon of truncheons and dogs, as the wounded on the square now begin to moan in pain and the taunts from the marchers become more insistent. The barking howls and the splintering of glass sound louder. Soldiers are gathering up the placards abandoned on the square before the ambulance men have even reached the wounded.

An officer standing with the dancers in front of the city hall is in conversation with the mayor, whose golden chain of office gleams in the light of the flames, and with Seamus, who towers some inches above the other heads. At Seamus's side – I am watching her in concern – stands Sarah, her fox fur with its sharp little face round her neck.

What horror! To be sitting here at a neatly laid table, with fine silver, a delicate vase of wild flowers and the flickering candle, and to be looking out over this carnage.

Not to smell the blood, nor the terrified cold sweat of the huddled bodies. Not to experience the flight, nor any of the pain, none of the pressure of other bodies up against your own, their panic and distress.

But to look out on it, as though it is a film at the cinema.

Somewhere there is something terribly wrong with the Kei. The region is terminal. Its history is being shaped without reference to us, the white population, and it does not look as though we will be able to have any part in it. We can only sit here watching, dumbstruck and afraid: we are already part of the past.

Nauseous and dizzy, I rise to go, to flee. I am about to vomit. The corpses are being picked up, the glistening pools in which they had lain visible from up here.

'Oh, how frightful!' exclaims a woman at a table next to mine, and hides her face in her hands. The restaurateur pushes me gently back into my seat.

'The police have announced that all exits to the square have been blocked. Please try to remain calm,' he requests quietly. 'We shall have to wait until everything has been cleaned up.'

'Cleaned up?' But the man places his hands on my shoulders again. 'I cannot be forced to look at something which I don't want to see!' Again I try to rise, but the man keeps me in my chair until I have calmed down a little.

It is an impossible situation! The news reports on the evening's TV news – trapped in glass while you sit surrounded by your familiar furniture – are being played out live here before my very eyes. The marches and faction fights in the townships, the massacres on the trains – everything so distanced and served up to us in small, careful doses in our living rooms – has suddenly been exposed to us right here. Split open, like the belly of an animal, for its liver to be ceremonially ripped out at any moment, to expose the country's innards; the stench.

Only now do the first ambulances start moving off. Soon all of them are fully laden and on their way, leaving medical personnel to deal with the remaining wounded.

The restaurateur places a brandy beside me. 'Take a swig,' he says, resting his hand on my shoulder once more. He stops at other tables, too, pours wine into the glasses of his guests, leaning over them, encouraging them to light up cigarettes and promising that each would soon be able to enjoy a free drink in the small foyer, as soon as the message is received that the square has been cleared.

A man gets up, staggers against a table and faints. People exclaim and huddle round him. A searchlight from down on the square shines for a moment full on the balcony.

I feel myself being baptised in white light: unmasked and pilloried, exposed to the world. From down there anyone can look up – as TV crews with cameras on their shoulders are at this moment doing – and see us, the comfortable class of the Kei, sitting here protected behind crystal glasses and candles and flower arrangements, as though these might deflect the inevitable.

36

It is in the wee small hours that something wakes me, but it is not one of those dreams which have been allowing me no rest recently. At night nowadays I feel like a knight buckling on his breastplate (striped pyjamas) and preparing for jousts with the subconscious, where I have to do battle with figures from the past, present and future, in an arena where there are no valid rules; where I find myself facing disconcerting images: elephants standing around bored in shopping arcades, the cathedral spire being carried by on a single shoulder, the primeval fish crawling up out of the river to lie motionless on my patio – and when I stop in front of the mirror, my mouth is a bell, open, laughing: a clown with lips of sounding brass.

What was it that woke me ... Oh yes, suddenly there it is: the roar of an engine. I lie in bed listening with increasing terror, thinking of the figure sprinting and ducking ahead of the police van as the engine whines high in bottom gear one moment, the next rapidly accelerates to swerve round a corner with squealing tyres, then comes to a sudden halt, reverses again, gears grating, and swings about, screeches forward once more, hurtles round a bend, and then with a high-pitched roar rushes down a slope at reckless speed, round another corner, reverses again, screaming, incessant, remorseless.

Who is it that is being hunted so relentlessly while everybody is asleep? Could it be a figure escaped from my dreams, a nightmare thief now terrified and breathless, ducking and sprinting along garden fences, flattening himself behind dustbins at the approach of the vehicle and then, when it has passed, running on again? Or perhaps crawling along the kerb in the lights of the police van, elbows and knees bleeding?

Then there is a sudden screech of brakes and tyres, doors banging, feet beating across the tarmac, shouts. I feel the blows raining down onto my own body; smell the sweat on the young constables, taste the salt blood on the lips of the nightmare thief; it is my own head bouncing on the floor of the police van when they throw him in like a sack of mealies before hurtling off down the river drive again, revving their engine in triumph.

I lie still for a while, thinking that I will not be able to fall asleep again, dozing off anyway, fitfully, waking again to think: Fragility; is there anyone in Africa who does not know the concept?

Eventually, exhausted, I fall into a deep sleep.

Hours later I wake again, my body stiff with tension. I had not thought I would get to sleep again after the noise in the street, but somehow I had dropped off after all. My sleep was filled with nightmares and phantoms – I could feel their poison in my stiff limbs, in the cold sweat and the faintly flu-like feeling in my muscles.

I get up and wander about the house. I do not feel like making coffee or even drawing the curtains. Listlessly, I stop in front of the glass cabinet in the lounge, looking at the noses of my steam engines. Ordinarily this would have been the best therapy: throwing open the patio doors, carefully, lovingly preparing the little steam engine for its trip, then the mounting excitement as the steam pressure builds up in the tiny boiler and the room fills with the smell of benzine.

Then the redeployment of station staff, water tanks and tiny signals, the rearrangement of yesterday's farms and towns, as I crawl around on hands and knees after the toy cars, before at last – with one cheek to the mat and an eye at the same height from the ground as the eyes of the toy people round me – I could launch the locomotive.

But this morning all this seems a childish game, and not even an innocent one at that. Out there the city is abuzz with excitement, and here am I, sitting like a young child playing quietly while his parents are still in bed.

Because that is the feeling I get when I am busy with my trains here every morning: my mother and father are still dozing dreamily in the bed that I have just got out of; Sarah is fiddling with her hair in front of the tall mirror in the bathroom; and the dogs, their muzzles to the thin crack under the back door, are already sniffing loudly, knowing that a long walk along the river bank with the family is waiting for them.

Finally I get round to dressing. I switch on the BBC and am just in time to hear their news report on the Cathedral Square massacre. Forty-two bodies were carted away, reports the creaking, other-worldly voice with the British accent; an infernal explosion (the work presumably of either saboteurs of the shadowy Third Force, or else operators to the left of the government) had blown up the gusher. The event had blown to shreds the community of the far-off city, a community already split in two by apartheid.

I make coffee. Standing with my head over the aroma, I throw open the shutters. This is not a morning like any other; the garden is quite silent. Normally the early morning is full of small birds hopping about and silvery insects toing and froing in the flowers and trees.

Even the small flocks of sea birds forever dipping and diving above the water and moored boats of the river are absent. It was terrible; terrible to see people snapping like flowers on their stalks; to see human beings bursting open like watermelons on the pavement. The bullets had torn through their muscles, exposing splintered white bone and sinew, intestines slithering out onto the ground. Oh, God ...

I dress quickly: khaki trousers and a cotton shirt. I put my old straw hat on my head and smear my neck and forearms with mosquito repellent. I know with certainty now where it is I must go; to gain reassurance; to try to find a still point in the hectically turning world of this week.

I go out into the garden and am astonished once again by the contained tension in the day. Then I see what the cause might be: a dense column of smoke is rising above Port Cecil, the billowing black smoke of burning oil. At a certain height the column levels off, drifting in every direction across the city and the surrounding landscape. For as far as the eye can see there is a hazy grey cloud.

I turn back again and lock up the house properly. Then I walk down to the jetty where the skiff is drawn up on the bank. It is a long time – a year at least – since last I went rowing. I have been so busy getting the new practice established and now, with all this business, it feels as though those early days are lost for ever.

Something has moved across the face of history; a shadow so compelling that when we look back over our pasts they suddenly look different.

Our past is being rewritten day by day. History is in the grip of the unexpected present, the unpredictable future.

That is why I must now seek out something of the certainty of the past. Groaning – my hat falls off into the mud once and the rushes scratch my legs and stab their sharp points into my groin – I drag the boat into the river. I wait for a minute or two as I rock the vessel in the water, checking for leaks.

But no, the pitch which I myself applied to the leaking spots years and years ago, is still sound. Clumsily, I try to get on board; two or three unsuccessful attempts and then – comically! – there I am, seated on the thwart, gripping and spreading the oars.

The familiar smells of wet wood, rushes and the troubled bubbling in the muddy shallows fill me with an unlooked-for elation; I want to look up at a little girl running down the river bank with a white sunbonnet and streaming ribbons in her hair, and behind her the fair-haired woman with the single long plait and the picnic basket, and then the man with the pipe and a book under his arm and his bird-watching field glasses.

But then I remember: all that is past. I am a prisoner of my sentimentality. I shove out of the shallows and feel myself gliding into the river. The current tugs gently at the skiff, but as I give my first pull on the oars, I feel the assurance of my strength. I bend and stretch, feel the sweat breaking out with the rhythmical working of my body. My thigh and shoulder muscles feel it, but soon the initial stiffness passes and the peaceful composure of rhythmical exercise comes over me.

I row up river. The water is still. Not a boat moves and even on the river banks there is no sign of life. I am the only person left alive in the city, the only boat moving is mine. I take off my hat and shake my sweating head in the light breeze blowing in from the sea. I breathe deeply. Why don't I do this more often? It brings back so many fresh memories.

I take care not to row too deep into the river, keeping about fifteen yards from the bank. I make slow progress, noticing after a while that the cloud of smoke is hanging lower. As though the oil flowing into the sea at Fifth Delta were not enough! It is clear now that all of nature has sensed last night's massacre – as though that black cloud were a mourning garment cast over the Kei. It will drive the bird and animal life of the delta away to quieter estuaries and lagoons farther north.

Halfway to my destination I turn aside to the bank, resting a while in the boat, rocking gently between the rushes. My arms hang loosely across the oars and I am amazed at the degeneration of my body. It is hardly a year since I last rowed like this; then the exercise had called for hardly any exertion at all. Today I have to stop halfway and rest, my arms lame.

Then, before my muscles get cold, I set off again. At last I see the row of cypresses sticking up behind the river trees and I steer for shore. There is a low jetty where I moor the skiff, making sure that the oars are safely shipped.

Breathless and sweaty, I take the steep pathway up the slope to the knoll overlooking the leg of the delta. I push open the rusty old gate, almost covered with climbing pink roses, and notice how much the stone walls have deteriorated since my last visit.

This graveyard is the oldest in the city. My parents were among the last to be buried here. The gravestones date from a different era; the rococo angels are overgrown with lichen and many of the graves have subsided. Most of the children and grandchildren of these dead are themselves dead. There is no one left to take regular care of the graves any more.

And there are unmarked graves, too, from the battles of the past; clean open stones, bare of inscription. It would be men, in the main, who lay here – some from as long ago as the frontier wars, perhaps, when British soldiers and Xhosa warriors fought battle after battle here on the banks of the Kei.

Only the graves of officers bear names and other details, and even some of these are very sparse. Other ranks of the British garrisons were often buried in great haste and their graves left unnamed. The Xhosa dead were simply left for the vultures and the water creatures, left to decompose in the river reeds, eventually becoming part once again of the grass and water and mud. When Sarah and I were children we often came across human bones on the river banks.

I walk slowly over to my parents' grave. Years ago I planted rose bushes round the graves; they are now in full bloom. I stop at the grave and read the familiar details.

What would they have made of these times? How would they have acted? In their own way they were two people who also kept aloof from the social life of the city; the great occasions in Port Cecil in those times had an elegance that cannot be duplicated nowadays. All there is now round Cathedral Square are clubs with their go-go dancers, take-away joints and massage parlours, and intimate cinemas that sometimes screen clandestine 'art films' late at night.

Photographs in my parents' album bear witness to a different era: people with hats and parasols in the daytime, on the terraces of tearooms, and wearing flowing gowns at the great gala occasions in the city hall at night. Whenever Seamus and Sarah attend such functions nowadays, they resemble nothing more than a vain attempt to bring back a colonial past that is gone for ever. Or, more correctly: they were always a phantom, because, concealed behind the same hills over which Joza's squatter camps are now encroaching ever closer with each passing week, were the huts of those who maintained it all: the labourers and servants, the maids and waiters, the stable boys and grooms; the silent humanity that never reached the pages of the history books, nor the social register of the city, nor the front pages of the newspapers.

Their history is the great unknown tableau, while our ancestors' attempts to make a living here were petty reflections of another place, a different civilisation. Our memory of Europe is a stubborn one, but it is only a memory.

I look up, seeing a movement among the graves. I recognise her immediately – it is Ayanda Thandani, in her white doctor's coat.

'Doctor Thandani!' She is startled at the sound of my voice. How is it possible? What is she doing here?

I walk across the crackling gravel on the path between the graves. 'You are making a habit of popping up out of nowhere!'

She laughs, palpably embarrassed. She, too, I realise, has come here to be alone, just like me. And here we stand, awkwardly facing each other.

I shrug my shoulders. 'Forgive the way I look,' I say, embarrassed. 'I rowed up here because I could not see my way clear to taking to the streets. I thought it would be like in the old state of emergency days: road blocks and soldiers round every corner. I could not face that.'

She nods. 'You are quite right. I must have gone through ten road blocks to get here. Fortunately' – indicating the doctor's coat and stethoscope – 'these do help.'

'Oh, yes ... Yes, I'm sure ...' I stop, uncertain: 'And, um ... '

She smiles. 'And what is a black woman like me doing in a snow-white graveyard?'

I make a meaningless gesture. 'You put it that way. What I was actually wondering was about your family; if any of you were injured last night ...'

She shakes her head; something that I have not noticed before flashes momentarily across her face: rage, frustration?

'I don't want to talk about last night,' she says. 'That's precisely why I have come here to ... well, to ... try to find some clarity.'

'What a coincidence,' I reply. 'So have I. My parents ... are lying over there.' I point to a spot behind me. 'I have booked my place here, too, next to theirs.' Her eyes show no reaction to the deliberate frivolousness in my reference to my own grave, but they follow my gesture. Then it is her turn to shrug her shoulders.

'And you still want to know what I am doing here?'

I shake my head and smile sadly. 'Not at all. I have to worry about motives enough in my working hours. I will entrust your reasons to your privacy.'

She smiles. 'You speak just like the language in those law books.'

'An affectation. Lawyers have a kind of language which they hide behind. There is no shield as impermeable as the shield of learning; the grandiloquent phrasings that create such an impression of dignity ...' She laughs. 'And then you must also remember that I live alone. Whenever I speak to anyone, it is almost always in a working context. I, um, don't ... often, um ... just chat to people. I have somehow unlearnt the language of ... the language of idle chatter and small talk.'

She turns round. 'Come and I'll show you the spot I have come to,' she says softly. I follow her through the rows of graves to an older part of the cemetery. Here some of the gravestones have collapsed and we have to pick our way across chunks of marble; the fallen heads of cherubs and pieces of marble wings are strewn about. Clear evidence that the desecrators of graves have frequently been active here too.

She stops at the head of a simple grave covered by an old, cracked marble slab. There is no inscription.

I stand beside her looking down at the namelessness of death.

'Who lies here?' I ask at last.

'I don't know,' she answers softly. 'But I always come here. I always stop here.'

37

A huge black flag has been raised in front of the Civic. In the small Roman Catholic church next door the pews have been carried outside and the coffins set down in rows. On each there is a candle burning.

Weary, MaNdlovu sits behind her desk. The umpteenth journalist – this time from France – is seated in front of her. She feels she just cannot take any more questions from naive Europeans. The faces of the dead keep floating past her eyes: those whose names she does not know are known to her through their families.

When the man had finished taking photographs – he used a wide-angle lens and made her stand under Mandela's portrait – he asked whether they could walk across to the church alongside, for more photographs.

MaNdlovu stands among the flag-draped coffins, weeping into her white handkerchief. She does not want to reveal her emotions to avid pressmen, but she cannot help herself.

Outside on the stoep of the Civic she stops and leans against one of the pillars. It had been an impossible night. First the wounded and dead had to be attended to; straightaway road blocks had been set up all over, and during the endless trips which she and TaImbongi had made between the hospital, the morgue, Cathedral Square and various homes in Joza, they had been stopped countless times and made to get out and wait for soldiers to search the bakkie.

They had been a good hundred yards from the oil well, the front rows with tightly linked arms, when the bomb went off. With an audible sigh a flame had immediately exploded above the fountain of oil. She could feel the heat scorching her face, but could not prevent it because of her linked arms.

The next moment the machine-guns stuttered into action and she heard the marchers behind her drawing in their breath, like a single gasp. And then ...

MaNdlovu wipes her face with her handkerchief. She looks up at the column of smoke rising above the city. Then she turns round and almost walks into the young man standing quietly behind her.

'MaNdlovu Thandani,' he greets her.

She looks at him cautiously, realising immediately that he is bringing news.

He says no more, merely watching her. 'Who sent you?' she asks. 'Was it Ncincilili or Mpho?'

'Mpho, MaNdlovu. He wants to see you.'

'Where?'

'He asks if you can come to the crossroads at Salem at eleven o'clock. In the blue bakkie.'

'I'll be there, my boy.'

She goes indoors and sits down at her desk.

It was Mpho's bomb, she knows. Mpho, that's who it was. A mother knows things like that. He had come out of the bush to prove himself. She sighs, goes inside again and calls TaImbongi. He sounds sleepy – had probably been dozing.

'Bring the bakkie over here immediately,' orders MaNdlovu.

'But I'm trying to sleep,' he protests.

'Wash your face and come right now.' Irritatedly, MaNdlovu puts the phone down. True, TaImbongi had joined the march the previous night, and he had agreed to open the proceedings on Cathedral Square with a praise poem or two, but she could see that his heart was not in the demonstration.

Even the excitable young Amanda, who had tried to shove a placard into his hand, could not inspire him.

She waits for him on the stoep and then slowly walks out into the hot sun to the door which swings open for her.

Here we are now, driving along, two old people almost at the end of their journey, without any idea of what is waiting for our children. What are we leaving to them?

'If he planted that bomb, I'll tan his hide for him,' grumbles TaImbongi. 'We'll lose another child yet. Is that what I've spent all these years shouting my voice hoarse for?'

'It wasn't the bomb that killed the people, TaImbongi,' replies MaNdlovu. 'Just remember that. It was the soldiers.'

He sighs. 'I don't know if the Kei is going to survive last night,' he says.

'The Kei will survive everything. Look out of your window. Everything still looks exactly the same as it did yesterday.'

TaImbongi rolls down his window. He shakes his head, saying: 'You are hard, MaNdlovu.'

'I'm not hard,' she says with unexpected bitterness, 'but I'm not soft.'

With a dense cloud of emotions between them they drive out onto the plateau. They are stopped at a road block where the security officer recognises them and asks where they are going.

'We're fleeing from the journalists,' replies MaNdlovu. 'We're going to buy slaughter goats for the funeral.'

The man waves them on. 'And if we return without any goats?' asks TaImbongi.

'Let him dare arrest us!' says MaNdlovu. 'The whole world is watching them today. And they know it. Did you see how well he behaved towards us?'

They crawl slowly down the pass to the plain below. It is already stiflingly hot and when they reach the crossroads TaImbongi stops under a thorn tree.

There is not a single movement on the whole expanse of the

plain. High in the sky two eagles are circling, their calm unruffled by any wavering.

MaNdlovu opens the door and sits thinking of her childhood. The smell of dust and the thorn tree bring back memories of children's games in the hot sun. How quickly the time had sped by! Just a moment, the twinkling of an eye, and today, suddenly, I feel I am nearing my end.

She glances at TaImbongi, sitting there with his head back and his hat over his face. She wants to say something to him, but decides against it. Perhaps he was simply born superficial; perhaps he is not to blame for not feeling things the way I do.

Perhaps I have been too hard on him all these years. He is no hero, he is no Mandela – he's an ordinary praise-singer, a loudmouth, a man without vision.

Even now – facing the possibility that his son has detonated a bomb on Cathedral Square in the presence of thousands of witnesses – he does not seem to have any clear idea of what is going on.

She wants to put out a hand and touch him – she does love him, after all – but something prevents her. That so much love and bitterness should nestle together in a single heart!

Then she hears a vehicle. They get out and wait on the spot where the four roads meet. The car comes down the dirt track from the nearby hills.

The driver, in dark glasses, remains seated when Mpho gets out. Uncertainly he walks over to his parents.

'Is this the way you want it?' MaNdlovu bursts out, starting to tremble, unable to control herself. She feels faint. Where could Ncincilili be?

'Mama ...' She sees him stretching out his arms towards her and feels TaImbongi's hand on her arm trying to restrain her.

'Why haven't you brought Ncincilili with you?' she asks. 'Where have you left Ncincilili?'

'Mama?'

The ear-splitting singing of cicadas surrounds them. The eagles have disappeared; the countryside is unbelievably empty, baking in the sun.

MaNdlovu feels herself trembling. My child, my Mpho, she wants to say, I love you and I was overjoyed for a whole day when I heard that you had taken up arms in the struggle for liberation. But after last night I realise what such arms can do. Walk with me through the church when they unscrew the lids on the coffins; look at the absence in the dead before you, the gruesomeness of wounds.

'You are hopeless, you and your father,' she hisses. 'You men are worthless; the Kei is crying out for leadership and you and your father are ... are ...'

She swings round, but TaImbongi has walked off a little way. He is standing with his back to them, looking out across the veld.

She turns back to Mpho. 'Where is Ncincilili?' she asks softly.

'Mama ...' He comes one step closer.

She hears TaImbongi's footsteps approaching at an unusually rapid pace. His voice is hard, biting. 'Ncincilili was hanged by the neck until he was dead.' MaNdlovu feels faint. 'He is dead and buried. He is just bones. You'd better accept the fact.'

She takes out her handkerchief and wipes her face. Mpho holds her tight as she begins to sway. They remain like that until she is able to walk again and he can help her into the shade.

She strokes his face. It is wet – it must be sweat: no son of hers would shed tears.

'There's only you, Mpho,' she says. 'There's only you.'

They stand like this for a long time, until she calms down. TaImbongi gets back into the bakkie. She can smell his pipe. He is used to domestic drama. He lets it pass him by, as he thinks out his songs, dreaming, with his eyes on the horizon.

'You'll have to get out of the Kei, Mpho,' she says. 'Until it's all blown over.' He nods. 'Do you know of a safe route?' Again he nods in affirmation.

She looks at him; he seems older, she thinks. He has indeed become more of a man.

'You have done a brave thing, Mpho,' she says. 'And I think it has so shocked everybody – even the whites – that we'll find peace sooner now.'

They say their goodbyes and then he goes to take leave of his father. TaImbongi holds his son close for a long time. The parents wait as the car drives off.

They sit in the bakkie, weary and dejected, as they start the tiring journey back. The pass is steep and the bakkie's engine is not up to much.

Her yearning aches in MaNdlovu's breast. Her longing for her handsome son, for Ncincilili.

'Now take me to Seer Wehmeyer,' she says eventually. 'He's got to get the Civic and the city council together. We owe it to the dead to make a last attempt at reconciliation.'

38

I am distressed somewhat by my reaction out there in the graveyard. I have always had a sense of the dramatic, a feeling for sadness and mourning. But the earnestness with which Ayanda Thandani listens to my reference to my own last resting place disturbs me a little. The one time I make a joke, it is taken seriously ...

Look at me standing there beside her, shoulders slightly bowed, clothes creased, beard wind blown. As though I might stumble over my own shadow – take fright at my own ghost!

I want to walk over, to shake hands with me. I want to say: Relax, Seer; just relax and you will find it quite easy to love, other people won't seem so unattainable, you will be able to reach out; simply let go, Seer, and you will cease your wandering.

And to my other characters I want to say: You have all become me; I have quite shamelessly absorbed you into myself. Forgive me.

But I say goodbye to her formally. Self-consciously, I walk back to the boat, stumbling over a stone. I feel her eyes questioningly on my back. I realise that I will remain un-free until I make contact with someone – anyone.

When I take up the oars again, I feel even more depressed. The day is turning hot, with the sun tucked away hazily behind the curtain of smoke. The river water looks grey with dark shadowy streaks.

Ayanda Thandani's remarkable presence is concealed by the more dramatic figures surrounding her: the talkative materfamilias MaNdlovu, her tragicomic father TaImbongi, that unlikely hero Zola the oil-discoverer, and young Mpho. And of course – and suddenly I see her standing at the nameless grave again – her brother Ncincilili, the necklace murderer without a grave.

While we were wandering round the walled graveyard she told me how she and her little playmates used to play here in the old cemetery. In those days there was still a full-time caretaker who spent his days dozing in the little hut beside the lych gate; he had forbidden black children the site, but they loved the risk in the enterprise of creeping in here while he nodded and dozed, and then they would hide among the gravestones and pretend their names were Mary Dorothy Heathcote and Catherine Schreiner Cawood ... they would imagine themselves with wide hoop-dresses, driving in carriages and holding on to their hats against the wind.

'And all the time,' Ayanda told me, smiling, 'MaNdlovu was keeping our memories alive, telling us our own history, the history of the Xhosa. But it was a struggle for her, because she was having to compete with the films we saw in the Joza community hall from time to time; with the magazines which domestic servants brought home to the township from their employers.

'To us, the white life across the river was the life we were striving for: we wanted to order the creams which would lighten our skins; we dreamt of hair without kinks in it, of cheeks as pink as peaches ...'

She shook her head and looked at me. 'It was only in my early teens that I looked at myself in the mirror one day. And it was then that MaNdlovu's stories – I thought I'd forgotten every one – started to play back in my ears. It was all in my head: the stories, the dramas, the pride in what we are. It was all just waiting for something to happen to open the floodgates.'

'And that was ... ?'

She smiled. 'Nothing dramatic. It happened over there.' She pointed to the unmarked grave we had just been standing beside. 'I was here alone. The old caretaker had died and been buried over in that corner, I believe. We could come here freely because there were virtually no families who came to pay their respects any more. You whites,' she added sharply, compelling me to look up, 'don't honour your ancestors.' I shrugged, thinking: Yes, except the defenceless ones. And then it is more out of weakness and inability than from filial piety.

'I stood here,' Ayanda went on, 'looking at the gravestone and thinking: you have buried yourself and your past under a blank gravestone just like this one, Ayanda. You've used the disgrace of TaImbongi, Matanzima's spaniel, to bury your own self – to bury what you really are.

'So I decided to write my name on a gravestone; even if it took a very long time. I went to MaNdlovu and I said: MaNdlovu, I am going to be the Kei's first black female doctor.

'MaNdlovu looked at me for a long time and said drily: That's not news to me, my child. And then straightaway ...' Ayanda laughed, '... she asked: Do you know how to stop yourself falling pregnant, child? Because if there's one thing that will put paid to your plans, it'll be the ruttish seed of some Joza kwedin ...'

She looked at me, suddenly shy: 'Oh, I beg your pardon ... Some commonplace things in my line of work may embarrass other people...'

'Don't worry: in my work, too, I have to cut right down to the bone. Your mother was perfectly correct.'

She looked at me slightly quizzically and then said: 'Well, in twenty minutes' time I have to be on duty. I'd rather not think of what is waiting for me. The hospital will be bursting at the seams. They'll be lying in the corridors again today.'

We said goodbye; faintly embarrassed about the unusual encounter, but both rather glad. For two quarter-hours or so our separate lonelinesses had been set aside.

Now I am rowing into the wind. I have the sense that

something is coming to an end. The river, which had been caught in the stillness of the morning an hour or two before, is now restlessly moving. The wind is gusting more strongly and choppy low waves are making the skiff bump about a bit. To make any headway I have to exert all my strength. Eventually I row deeper into the current; the outgoing tide will carry me until close by the old house I can simply swing in towards the bank.

I look round me: days like this fill me with a nameless terror which I prefer to suppress and relegate to my subconscious. I don't know whether other people have the same experience – a premonition of a fathomless pit, an abyss right at my feet; an indescribable sense of abandonment and rejection.

But I have never been close enough to another person to be able to ask. Not even Sarah, although I suspect she is so busy trying to keep Seamus from toppling over the edge that she never has an opportunity to confront herself.

Suddenly I hear the growl of a powerful outboard motor. I look up and stop rowing, but the wind and the current combine to drive the skiff sideways across the stream, so I have to keep rowing. The boat comes round a bend in the river – it is one of those modern power-boats, streamlined and fast.

It is heading straight for me and only when it shears round me in a tremendous arc, leaving me bouncing in the wake of its powerful engines, do I recognise Cawood at the wheel, accompanied by a couple of other youngsters. Shirtless, holsters at their hips, they look at me, faces flushed with excitement.

'Uncle Seer!' Cawood mocks, as he throws the engines into reverse and the boat drifts closer to me, roaring. 'Where is my old uncle rowing to? Haven't you ever heard of the power of octane?' To the guffaws of his mates, he gives the boat's accelerator a quick push and they shoot away in a wide arc across the river. A hundred yards on he swerves back again and circles me a couple of times. The engines are more peaceful this time, but I am rocking dangerously on the waves caused by the antics of the motor boat.

'Stop it, Cawood!' I shout. 'Go home! Your parents are looking for you!'

Cawood stands upright behind the wheel. 'Where are you going?' he shouts back.

I do not answer. I don't need to give account to you, Cawood. Young stallion, irresponsible little bugger.

I try to start rowing again, but because my boat is being bounced so violently I can hardly get the oars co-ordinated in the water. Bastard. Bell wether!

Cawood steers his boat closer. 'Can't we help you a bit, Uncle?' he shouts.

I shake my head. 'Just clear off!' I shout. 'Leave me alone!' thinking: And that, Cawood, is the motto of my life: leave me alone – that has been my greatest desire all my life. To be left alone; but at the same time the terrible yearning: don't leave me alone; understand me; is there anywhere anyone who'll ...

But I am not allowed to complete the thought because now Cawood has a rope in his hand and casts it towards the bows of the skiff. The first cast misses but, to loud cheers from his mates, the second secures the noose round the bow-knob.

'What are you doing?' I shout in alarm. I try to loosen the knot but almost lose my balance. In any event the rope has already drawn taut between the boats and I am powerless; the knot is too tight.

'What are we doing?' Cawood shouts as he takes up position behind the wheel again. 'We are patrolling the river to make sure the kaffirs don't come across from Joza.'

'You're what?' I pant, shipping my oars as Cawood slowly moves his boat forward, dragging the little skiff helplessly along behind.

'And my uncle is a kaffirboetie, don't you know!' Cawood yells. 'Let's help you back to your old shack so you can play with your trains!'

He opens the throttle of his boat and I fall backwards into the skiff. One of the oars disappears over the edge and when I look back it is already lost in the foam. Cawood accelerates even further, dragging me along at a terrifying lick.

The humiliation! The little brat! Seeing myself there in the skiff so helpless enrages me. I don't like to attack characters in my own story – given enough rope, they should hang themselves – but that young Cawood! I am pushing as hard as I can to intervene; I can smell Seer's terrified sweat, feel the water splashing in his face, I ...

'My God ...' I mumble in the boat. I have to cling on as tightly as I can. My straw hat has long since been lost; likewise the shoes and socks that I had so carefully placed under the thwart. I see the bubbling screws of the outboard motors as the boat in front of me cuts its capers, and I think: This is the final humiliation. Sarah and Seamus will hear about it. It is high time that somebody ...

Taking a wide curve along the river in front of the old home, Cawood drags my boat in such a way that it heads straight for the bank. One of the other youngsters stands upright holding a panga and at exactly the right moment he slashes through the rope. Their boat shoots away boisterously, leaving mine sailing straight at the bank.

The rushes break my speed and, astounded at the youngsters' skill (does Cawood ever do anything that does not create the impression of having been endlessly rehearsed?), I come to a halt with my boat's nose in the mud.

I look back: they have already disappeared round the bend. Soon there is nothing left but silence and the gentle lapping of water against my boat.

A terrible weariness comes over me. I clamber out and barely manage to drag the boat up the bank. My muscles ache; I can feel the tension building up inside me again.

Slowly I trudge up to the house. My keys are lost in the confusion, so I have to break a window pane to get in. I spend a long time under the shower, and soap myself thoroughly.

Then I put a bathrobe over my naked body and close the

shutters. Outside it is full daylight but I draw the curtains, too, to drape the house in twilight. To hide my shame; to ward off the attacks. Hell is other people. I take little sips of whisky as I lie on the double bed.

Later my hand finds it way between the folds of my bathrobe. I draw the cloth aside and slowly start massaging my member. I think of the comfortable, loose motion of Ayanda Thandani's young body under her white coat.

When I take hold of my member, a second before my climax, I recall Cawood's naked body diving gracefully into the water. I see his penis bounce and then, alone in my darkened house, convulsively, I come.

39

Sarah is standing on the veranda at Fata Morgana, supervising the maids as they serve tea and sandwiches. There is a vast shoal of bakkies and Landrovers parked in front of the house and even beyond the farmyard gate and all along the farm road. Some farmers have come armed; others have brought a few chops, a piece of boerewors and some beers in a coolbag, in case the meeting goes on long enough to degenerate into a braai.

I am there too: in the unexpected shadow thrown by the pipe smoke, in the inexplicable restlessness moving through the dogs. I am also the shape of Sarah's anxiety: she knows, my dear Sarah, she knows without realising it.

Once the news of the previous evening's massacre on Cathedral Square had spread overnight, the local commando unit telephoned all its members in the early hours to call a crisis meeting. Those (like Seamus) who were not commando members were drawn in anyway through the invitations extended to the Manley Flats Farmers' Association, the Seven Fountains Cricket Club, the Foxhunt and the Historical Society, as well as the people from Civil Defence, the Bathurst Ex-Servicemen's League and the Dick King Club from Salem.

A request had been received for the meeting to be held at Fata Morgana because of its central position. Reluctantly, Seamus agreed, and he and Sarah had hardly a wink of sleep all night.

There was a constant stream of telephone calls – from anxious neighbours, from journalists, fellow city councillors, businessmen – all wanting to know what exactly had happened: Had the black marchers thrown hand-grenades? Who fired first? The soldiers or the marchers? When had the bomb in the fountain exploded? And every time she put the phone down, that scene on the square was replayed in her mind: women crawling about in bloody stripes, screaming for their children; men trying to thrust their guts back into their lacerated bellies ...

Seamus offers the first of the stream of bakkies a surly greeting. He has only just emerged from the shower and his wet hair clings to his head. He looks old and wan, as though he had come face to face with the arch-horror. 'There is a curse on the Kei,' he says. 'For how many hundreds of years has it not been a borderland, this eastern frontier? For how many generations have there not been wars raging black and white?'

Sarah pours pineapple cordial into glasses and listens involuntarily to what is being said round her. The farmers are standing in groups; some look anxious, kicking the points of their shoes in the dust. Others screw up their eyes to look at the horizon, not saying much. But a big bunch are hanging around joking and laughing exuberantly. They are the ones I approach, these virile young men in khaki clothes, they are the ones I listen to inquisitively, as though they might be able to divulge to me something about Cawood. They are the youngsters who until recently were still fighting in Angola or taking part in regular township operations. They keep checking impatiently that the pistols at their hips are still in place.

Sarah's eyes seek out Seamus. God be merciful to us. The officer commanding the commando – Bill Heathcote's son – has asked Seamus to open the proceedings by giving the farmers a sketch of exactly what happened on Cathedral Square. Some of the farmers with copies of the morning paper turn to pages of photos showing scenes of the massacre. The paper also reports on attacks on farms bordering the Ciskei and massive veld fires started – once again – on farms in the Upper Kei.

Suddenly Seamus is nowhere to be seen. Anxiously Sarah goes into the house. I follow, unwilling to let her out of my sight. I must hold on to her; she is the only one. She finds Seamus in the bedroom, sitting on the edge of the bed, looking at the photograph of himself and his father with the two fall-goat rams. She sits down beside him. 'Seamus? The people are waiting for you.'

He makes no reply, but takes her hand. They sit there, listening to the noise outside. I move into their body heat, then recoil.

Outside, more vehicles keep arriving and each new arrival is greeted by a cheer.

Eventually Seamus says softly: 'Listen to that. Just listen to them. They haven't the foggiest idea about what's going on.'

Sarah sighs.

'You will have to go out, Seamus. They are starting to ask for you.'

'I want no part in any declaration of war by that bunch,' he says. 'This isn't a cricket tournament or a jackal hunt.'

She speaks urgently, her hand on his wet hair. 'Then you must go and tell them, Seamus.'

'They won't listen. Look at that young Heathcote. He can't wait to take up a loaded gun.'

What about your own son, Seamus, I want to ask. There's a rascal for you. Sarah gets up. 'Seamus, if those are your feelings about things, you've got to go out and tell them so. You've got to.'

He sighs. 'I'm tired, Sarah. I've had enough.'

'But Seamus! If the Butlers don't ...'

He draws himself up to his full height. 'The Butlers ...' She notices his whole body trembling. 'The Butlers ...'

'Take a hold on yourself, Seamus. Be strong.'

Voices are calling: 'The Master of the Hunt! Where is the Master of the Hunt?' The mood outside is clearly pretty jolly.

'Just see where force has brought us,' says Seamus. 'To the very brink of the abyss. Nothing in our lifetime is going to be able to heal the wounds inflicted last night. You know that as well as I do, Sarah.'

'Then I will.' She gets up angrily, looks back at the hunched figure of her husband on the bed and goes out onto the veranda.

After asking a servant to remove some glasses, she gets up onto a low veranda table and looks out across the assembled farmers. The faces turned towards her at first make her want to turn round, to flee back into the house: they are not used to being addressed by women.

Turn round, Sister Sarah. They are not worthy of you. Let's go back. You know ... You know what the fireflies look like as they come across the river; you ...

'Seamus is unwell,' she says. Her voice sounds shrill. A few farmers who have been standing chatting in the garden come closer. 'We couldn't hear?' they say, their hands cupped behind their ears.

Sarah! I need you. You are the only one who can release me; you're the only one who can prevent ...

'I said: unfortunately, Seamus is indisposed. He has asked me to speak on his behalf.'

'Well, bring Cawood on!' calls out a ringleader at the back.

'What happened last night?' asks a young farmer close to her.

'I ...' Sarah shakes her head. She is seized by another overwhelming urge to flee indoors.

Come now, Sarah, come. The river is wearing its night colours; we are running, laughing, through the grass. Look at your hair ribbons; look at my little lantern. We're never going to die.

'Who fired first?' a farmer calls out.

'It doesn't matter who fired first,' Sarah replies. 'Something terrible happened and we shall ... We shall have to try again to heal the wounds ...'

'What?'

'Whose wounds?'

'They've blown up the oil well!'

'They want to burn out our farms! They want to chase us off

our land!'

'Nobody's going to chase me off my land!'

With Sarah standing there, I realise the train is hurtling downhill. Neither I nor she will be able to stop it. She waits for the noise to subside. They are like a bunch of schoolboys. As Seamus says (does he know men better than she does?): these men do not have the capacity to grasp the wider implications.

'They blow up restaurants!'

'They shoot innocent women and children!'

'Yes, yes, yes!'

She becomes aware of Seamus standing beside her. Although she is on the table he is still a head taller than her. He has a gun in his hand. When the farmers see him, they send up a cheer.

Seamus cocks the rifle and sends three shots through the roof of the veranda. Sarah gets such a fright that she slides off the table and almost falls. He helps her up again. She sees on his face the terrible rage that she has feared all these years.

The farmers are suddenly deathly quiet. Seamus looks out over their heads towards the slaughter kraal. All the goats have keeled over following the gunshots.

'I hereby declare,' he announces in thunderous tones, 'that Fata Morgana will not be part of any new frontier war. The Butlers of Fata Morgana will seek peace. And we are going to start today.' There is no answer. 'If you had seen what Sarah and I saw last night, you would not get so excited about retaliating.'

Some of the farmers shake their heads. Someone opens a coolbag and cracks a beer. Laughter. Another shouts: 'Cheers!' I almost smile. Yes, the old master-breeder.

Looking at their faces, Sarah realises they are not hearing what Seamus is saying. Seamus looks at her, then back at them. 'Come,' he says. Angrily he strides down the veranda steps and along the garden path. I follow. 'Come!' he shouts to the farmers, who have turned hesitantly to watch him.

Sarah shudders for her poor flower beds as the crowds of men stumble across her rockeries and borders in pursuit of her husband.

She does not even know where he is heading – then suddenly she realises. She wants to run after him and stop him, she wants to scream to the men to hold him down, to prevent him from doing something irresponsible, to bring him back to the homestead – violently, if need be.

But Seamus has already reached the bottom garden and is waiting for the men to gather round him. Some of them know where it is they are standing, because years ago as children or teenagers they were present when a memorial service for Seamus's father was held there.

Seamus waits till everyone is quiet. Then: 'Here, on the spot where I am now standing,' he says slowly, 'my father committed suicide.' He waits, looking round him. 'He came here one night, put the barrel of his rifle to his head and blew his brains out.'

Slowly Sarah moves closer. Her lips murmur softly. God preserve us. May he please not ... Oh, God, please don't let ... I come up behind her. I recall how we used to walk through the riverside grass with my lantern and how my mother would call us. She would call and call, but we believed ourselves to be king and queen in another country. We walk into the dark. The little oil-flame goes out. We no longer hear my mother calling. The house has disappeared. We stand, trembling, beside the black water. We can smell the bulrushes. Sarah whispers: Don't go away. Don't leave me alone. I don't want to die. I hold her tight. We'll never disappear, I promise. Never. We'll become fishes, you and I together. We look at the water.

Seamus fills his great chest with air. 'There have been many nights when I, too, have thought I should follow my father's example. There have been nights when I have come right here, with my gun in my hand. This same gun.' He holds up the rifle for all to see. 'I have often sat here waiting for the right moment to take my life.' He looks at them. 'But every time I have realised that I have to rip myself out of my father's patterns; that if I should take my own life as he did his, I would be handing a victory to something which was less than ... than the strength to carry on ...'

He wipes his arm across his face and strokes the rifle. 'In the worst nights of my life this gun has been my companion. In my deepest depressions I have had it beside me, this fine instrument of steel and polished wood. But I have always recoiled from it. I have looked into the abyss. I have stood back, and clenched my teeth, and turned my back on it. It would have been much easier for me than carrying on ... than trying to walk the path of peace ... with myself.'

Sarah has now threaded her way through the silent throng. She stops at Seamus's side. Through all the years they have tried to conceal Seamus's depression from the farming community. They thought it would be a disgrace to admit it.

And now? Well, there he stands, the most experienced of all.

'Don't let the Kei commit suicide.'

Seamus turns to Sarah. He holds out his hand to her. They walk back to the house, in between the mute farmers. I follow.

40

I am back, knotting the cord of my bathrobe and bending over my track. My muscles are stiff and sore. After rowing back from the graveyard, I fell asleep for a while. When I woke, my body was sore. I had got a touch of the sun and my face was red and glowing when I stopped in front of the mirror to comb the sleep out of my beard. It was as though my body was wanting to affirm its presence one last time; my old body wanted to remind me of its fragility ...

I first listen to a news bulletin and then put on a record of Richard Burton reciting Coleridge's Rime of the Ancient Mariner. With the voice caressing me I take out my new Garrett, carefully polish the engine, fill it with benzine and now I am waiting for the boiler to build up enough steam for the game to begin.

I lie with my head on my hands, talking quietly to Tragos: 'It was terrible, kid. It was like a hailstorm sweeping across a corn field. You could see people screaming; their faces were contorted with terror. But you couldn't hear anything above the clatter of the machine-guns. It went on and on; the machine-gun fire created a sort of silence and people snapped strangely and collapsed, without a sound ...'

I wipe my cheeks. 'This country has finally gone mad, kiddo. When I was small, like you, my parents thought we had been struck by lunacy. They looked at the smiling photographs of

Verwoerd and said: madness has a charming face. They should have been living now …'

Before I put Burton on the turntable, I listen to the late afternoon bulletin on the BBC's Africa Service. Somewhere between me and the transmitter there is an electric storm, but the news report about the massacre on Cathedral Square does manage to reach me; also a flash that a restaurant has been blown up somewhere in the city centre and that APLA, the PAC's military wing, has announced their Operation Shock and Scare. The operation would be aimed at making the protected white community aware of the waves of violence that continually engulf the black community.

The restaurant explosion, an APLA spokesman says, is the first of a series of attacks on soft targets in the white community. The Settlers, the spokesman explains – according to the newsreader – will be made to feel for themselves just how painfully violence can scorch.

The next news item is about the drought in Zimbabwe and the Victoria Falls which have completely dried up. I switch to the national news service. The newsreader reports that swarms of locusts are devastating the north of the subcontinent along the Tropic of Capricorn. And a team of researchers have declared that they have discovered the site of the Kruger millions and are going to mobilise funds to exploit the collapsed shafts of an old gold mine in the fever-stricken east, since that is where the bullion in the form of golden ingots was concealed before President Kruger departed on board the Gelderland on his last journey to Europe, there to plead the cause of the Boer Republics in their struggle against the might of British imperialists.

Irritated, I turn off the radio and go over to my record rack. Burton's voice always provides a rescue.

I hook a number of coaches on behind the engine. I make sure that the patio door is open and prepare to launch the train. Bending over the track, I look over my shoulder; fascinated, I look at my fat, weary back, the folds in my neck, the details of hair and earlobe. I cannot protect myself any longer. My story is slipping out of my hands; it is predestined. The train sets off with tremendous enthusiasm as soon as I release the tiny lever on the engine. There it goes: all the trucks loaded with supplies.

A blow strikes the front door. A second blow follows, with the sound of wood splintering. Alarmed, I try to rise. Tragos flees into the corner of the room and in so doing knocks over the little houses in the model town. Before I can get up – while I am still struggling on my hands and knees because one corner of my bathrobe is caught under my knee – heavy footsteps come in through the open patio door. The two men are dressed in black with balaclavas. The front one kicks the engine and coaches right off the track, splashing water on the carpet and sending the loco hissing in under a chair.

The front door gives way under the attack and bursts open. Another three men – also with their faces concealed – storm into the hallway. By now I have managed to get on my feet. I remember that I have nothing on under the bathrobe, it is hanging half open, grotesquely revealing my belly. One man hits me in the stomach with his truncheon. I fall forward, vomiting brown fluid onto the little station buildings. I crouch on all fours, shaking my head as threads of slime drip from my mouth.

The men jerk the record off the turntable. One breaks it across his knee and gives me a kick in the side, knocking me against the sofa. 'Kaffir lawyer.' The man's eyes are close to mine; glittering ice-blue through the slit in the balaclava. Now one of the others sees Tragos and lunges at him, but the kid ducks away in alarm and slithers across the floor. The others chase after him, upsetting the furniture in their attempt to catch the little goat.

Eventually one has all four of Tragos's legs in his hand. He holds the goat, which has fainted, upside down and grins at me. Then he walks over to the engine, picks it up, shakes off the coaches and replaces it carefully on the tracks. He sweeps away the magazines which have fallen across the tracks and gets the locomotive started. When the engine is running and has disappeared through the patio door, he takes a record from the rack and puts it on the turntable. Carefully he lowers the needle onto it. Then they grab me by the arms, jerk me upright and drag me through the entrance hall strewn with splinters of the front door.

The man carrying Tragos goes ahead. He waits at the front door while the rest shove me into a waiting minibus with smoked windows. The vehicle has no licence plates. They pinion my hands behind my back and now my bathrobe is hanging completely open. They shove their truncheons into my stomach, laughing when the points sink into my soft flesh.

I look out through the windows of the minibus at the man who still has Tragos in his hand. Who will feed the kid? The driver switches on the ignition and opens the passenger door. The man holding the little goat takes Tragos by the back legs and, in a single violent movement, swings the kid's head against the lintel of the front door.

41

Seamus Butler knows when he needs to be alone. He has 1820 saddled, takes his binoculars and his rifle, and rides into the veld. The familiar motion of the horse under him, the smell of the animal, and the breeze in his face have a calming effect on his mind.

His goats watch as he rides among them. They keep their eyes on his gun – they recognise it, knowing that whenever it goes off they are overcome by despair and a brief death.

But he is not like Cawood, who enjoys taunting the goats' nerves with the fluttering blades of the chopper, or wandering about with the sheep-whip lisping in among them as though at any moment he might give the whiplash a terrific crack.

No, that is the difference between me and my offspring: I have some compassion in me. Stubborn and proud as I am, I am gentle. All my life long, I have been that little boy who took fright at the collapse of the fall-goat in the dark shed and fled past his parents and their friends foxtrotting under strings of coloured lights, running away into the dark veld, stumbling, running, falling and getting up, running and running ...

I hoped my father would leave the dance-floor and come after me, gather me up in his arms with his familiar smell of sweat and shaving cream and tobacco.

I don't look round, because I hope he's there, hard on my heels.

I keep pushing onwards, through the weeds and the ditches, because I know: he won't abandon me.

But he remained unaware of me. He was circling the antheap floor to the rhythms of music which for that era was modern and for our landscape was foreign.

He preferred, ultimately, to abandon me altogether and take his own life in his hands. I died in battle many times before that fatal shot of my father's.

Seamus gives 1820 free rein. He has left the goat flocks behind now and the galloping of the horse frees his emotions. He reaches a height and climbs down out of the saddle onto the edge of a krantz. Far away on the plateau the column of smoke is rising above the oil flame. For a long time Seamus stands looking at it. The veld round him, the trees and the homestead a few kilometres away, make him relax and feel free. Everything in the distance is shimmering in the heat – that mirage of hills, trees and a homestead floating on imaginary water was what had made his forebears decide to name the farm Fata Morgana.

Mind you, there is irony in the name, too, but then of course the Butlers have always been people who lived ironically – they are far too intelligent, far too cunning and worldly wise, too honed by their adventures as Settlers on this continent, to ignore the irony.

He smiles: the first brood ewe of the species, bred from that ram from which he as a little boy had fled in fear, was named by his father Morgan le Fay: Caper timidus Morgan le Fay, named for the enchantress at the court of King Arthur.

Perhaps my father's irony and good sense caught up with him, though, thinks Seamus, caught here in an environment which made scant allowance for stimulation – a genius who could only exercise his great intelligence here in this isolated corner of the earth by breeding a peculiar new species.

I explained my options with so much conviction to the gathering – that bunch of light-headed farmers who live their lives in terms of pineapple quotas, rainfall figures, Land Bank loans and hunting tournaments. Would they have understood?

For a moment, yes, because there were a number of hearty congratulations, expressions of friendship and sympathy.

But now, only hours later, they're back home with their bored wives, who sit on their sun porches crocheting or vacantly staring out into the distance, or else they have collected in a little pub in a hamlet somewhere with their tongues wagging about the remarkable speech by Seamus Butler, the son of the Toppling Goat.

Seamus sighs. How do you hold your own in a community where, if you keep yourself to yourself, you're regarded as stuck up, and if you lay all your cards on the table, they look at you blankly and see it as criticism of themselves?

He places his foot in the stirrup. I need to go to town. I have to consult my brother-in-law. He's got to arrange a meeting between the city council and the Civic.

Seamus rides slowly back to the homestead. Sarah is anxiously waiting for him on the veranda. 'I phoned Seer's practice to have a chat to him,' she says, 'but it seems to be shut. There was no reply, so I phoned his secretary at her home. She says he phoned her early this morning to say that he was too shocked to come to work today – apparently he witnessed the massacre – and she was to stay home, too.

'And at the old home the telephone is making a strange sound. I think he's pulled out the plug.'

'Then we'd better drive down,' he replies. 'I also need to talk to him.' He ignores her surprised expression. 'Have you phoned Monomotapa?'

'Yes,' she answers, helpless and frightened. 'There's no reply there either.'

Seamus puts his arm round Sarah's shoulders. They go indoors together. 'When we get back from Seer's,' he promises, 'we'll take a drive over to Monomotapa.'

'I want to go and see Captain Bessinger again,' says Sarah decidedly. 'I want to know how they are getting on in their search for Cawood. They've got to track him down. Things are ... things are ...' She cannot get any further, tearfully shaking her head.

'He'll keep a cool head,' Seamus tries to console her. 'He wouldn't do anything irresponsible. He's a Butler, after all.'

But he knows that Cawood is unpredictability in person. Cawood could swing round as fast as a trapped lynx: one moment you could be admiring the graceful, untamed lines, the next you would be looking into the face of fury, spitting with rage.

He goes and has a shower and dresses in neat summer trousers, his old school tie, his late father's blazer.

'What's all this?' asks Sarah when he emerges.

'Before you go to the police,' he answers, 'please drop me at Cathedral Square.'

'Oh. Are you going to the city hall?'

'No,' he replies. She looks at him enquiringly, but he offers no explanation. Once she has changed too, they drive to town.

They travel in silence until, as the car leaves the gravel road and swings onto the tarmac, she asks cautiously: 'Do you think Cawood is ... is involved?'

'Involved?' he asks.

She nods. 'Yes, Seamus. You know.'

He does not answer, but looks out of the window and sighs. 'I don't know what went wrong with his education,' he says. 'Perhaps the private school gave him a sense of elitism. You know how he would never mix with other farm children who were at government schools. Perhaps we made a mistake.'

'But it was the best education he could get,' says Sarah. 'He had the very best of opportunities.'

My goats, Seamus wants to say, also sometimes throw up a freak ram; a headstrong creature for whom nothing is ever good enough; an animal with an incurable restlessness, whose emotions are likely to flare up at any moment. With them you can never predict what will happen next.

You can run a young ram like that with the most dignified of stud rams, with the old ewes of the stud; you can give him the very best treatment, but he will always burst through the wires and go for the wrong ewes, or break down the garden fence and destroy the flower beds.

An animal like that is just born contrary. As a breeder, he has to admit it: his own son, Cawood, is no different.

'He'll come back,' he comforts Sarah, placing his hand on hers. 'It's just some passing fancy. I'm sure the phone will ring tonight.'

He gets out near Cathedral Square and she drives on. She says goodbye to him with a questioning expression on her face. Through the years, though, she has learnt sometimes not to ask questions. It is her way of trying to protect herself; in order to survive she has to allow some space between herself and his terrors and depressions.

He walks slowly across Cathedral Square. The policemen on duty nod to him. He looks at the bubbling flame, burning and gurgling. The group of firemen on duty are standing close to the flame engaged in fierce argument. You will have to fly in people from Texas, thinks Seamus. You'll have to get hold of the operators who managed to extinguish the oil wells in Kuwait after the Gulf War.

It is just typical of the Kei – because we have learnt to take care of ourselves as a result of our isolation, we think we can handle even this crisis ourselves.

He walks to the cathedral. He is surprised by his nervousness; his heart is beating high in his chest. He recalls the scene here when, with the excited, sweating hunt at his back, he had come to a halt in front of the priest.

Through the open doors he can see the priest arranging candles on the altar. It is the same young man whom he had taken to point out the spot where his father had died.

Seamus turns away.

42

I suppose it is to be expected that Sarah would sense that something has happened to me. After dropping Seamus on Cathedral Square, she cannot shake off the feeling that the city is being smothered in the seven-legged embrace of the delta. Her anxiety drives her to a riverside café on the Second Delta, upwind from the oil flame.

When she looks up, it seems that the corrugated iron shacks clambering up over the top of the hillside above the river are in instant danger of sliding down into the water, should the landscape give even the slightest tilt.

The worst of the smoke is drifting across to the other side. She tries not to notice the taste of oil and natural gas in her teacup.

It is not necessary to know the river as well as she does to realise that something has come to an end. The delta legs lose their brilliance in the shadow of the smoke cloud; the foamy water stirred up in the wake of motor boats looks grey and depressed.

Sarah looks at the waitress who has served her and is now leaning over the balustrade, also watching the water. A gentle breeze is lifting the girl's apron.

Yes, it's just as you suspect, Sarah. One moment you are standing there, looking out across the river like this girl, and then, in the twinkling of an eye, you find yourself here, at a table on a terrace, the middle years almost past, tired and alone, without anyone who really understands you. You're frugal with what you have, you cherish the tiny scraps of grace and indulgence that you know are still yours.

All that is really left to you is to look round at the struggling earth, the wretched little showers of rain, the dour rocks and aloes, the dull cycads – and if you are still in doubt, go to the museum and stare into the eyes of the fossil fish; then you will understand about timelessness and about mortality. You will know, when you pick up a stone on the open plain and you hold it to your ear and listen, that the primal silence was there from the beginning and will be there evermore.

And you? You float by like an incidental scrap of thistledown blowing across the plain.

It is all over so quickly. Just the twinkling of an eye.

I can feel you loosening the ties that bind us, Sarah. The threads are unravelling. You are still on your way to discover that I have disappeared, yet you are already taking leave of me. Your thoughts are with your son. I have come up close beside you, to breathe in your perfume; perhaps you will become aware of me? But no, you turn to the waitress and ask: 'Is there a telephone here?'

Mention my name, just once, Sarah. Let me free.

Yes, the girl says, there is a cordless phone which you can use out here. Sarah sits and watches a boat sailing past as she dials Monomotapa. The phone rings for a long time, but no one answers. She sits like that for a few moments. Please just try the old home, too, Sarah. The phone will ring in the empty house. But please try. Call me back; do you remember the night among the reeds, when the house and the trees had disappeared? Do you remember how mother's voice faded away? Do you remember the smell of the mud?

She dials the ramshackle old home by the river. But there is no reaction there either.

She hesitates, then dials the police. Captain Bessinger is a friend who often visits Fata Morgana. No, he says, there is still no indication of where Cawood might be. The chopper, too, is still missing.

'And that army officer who was seen with Cawood?'

'He is also missing, Sarah. Absent without leave. I spoke to his commanding officer this morning ...'

'So ...?'

'Well, they don't really know.'

Sarah picks up the caution in the man's voice. 'Is there anything else I should know?' she asks.

'No. I am sorry. That is all.'

She sighs and beckons to the waitress to come and fetch the telephone. Suddenly she senses my presence with her, as though I were sitting here beside her; she notices my creased old jacket, the blue circles under my eyes, and I am reciting lines from Auden to her.

She smiles and looks at her watch. She wants to wipe her eyes, to rub away the smoke, to eat a fresh fruit and get the taste out of her mouth. She sighs and gets up; it is time to meet Seamus.

He is waiting on the corner near the Victoria Club, where he enjoys going – particularly in winter – for port and cigars, and where he can page through the British newspapers that are always available there.

She is about to move over so that he can take the wheel, but he shakes his head and gets in beside her.

'So where did you go then, Seamus?' she asks. 'Mr Mysterious?' keeping her voice light in an attempt to cheer him up.

He makes no reply.

They drive on in silence. 'The whole country is chronically depressed,' he remarks later as they drive through the hotel quarter, crawling with buses and visitors. Everyone looks rather dejected; in the face of a flame that stubbornly goes on burning, the oil dream has faded; it is a confrontation with one of those dinosaur dragons from aeons ago, dragons with fiery breath that go slogging through these marshes.

'The great discovery lies ahead yet,' is what Seamus ought to say as they stop at a robot, 'and that is that guilt is non-negotiable. Guilt is part and parcel of this country. Like a child learning to take its first steps, we now have to test the unsteady motion of reconciliation.'

But he does not say it and I don't want to put words in his mouth; not today. Let me keep them for my own account.

Sarah looks out of the window. When Seamus grows silent like this, he is heading for a deep depression. Once he starts likening the Kei to the human psyche, or begins to plead that the earth is in need of therapy, or sets up a wail about the inertia of nature, the melancholy of the flora and fauna – you know he is only one short step away from the treacherousness of Caper timidus, the delusion of Fata Morgana, the transitory tenure of the white man in Africa, the ...

I wait in tense anticipation of their reaction as they near the old home. Suddenly it is terribly important to me: a test of their feelings towards me. But I also know who is already inside the ramshackle old place. As soon as they drive into the yard they notice the shattered front door, the streaks of blood on the door posts, the alien bakkie.

'We must turn back, Seamus, we've got to get the police!'

But before Sarah can restrain him, Seamus has pulled the Magnum from under the seat. No, Seamus, that's not what I want!

'You stay here,' he tells Sarah.

'Seamus!'

She sits still until he has gone through the front door. 'Dear Lord...' I have to follow him, she thinks. She sees the blood-spattered body of the orphan kid at the front door; there are wood splinters all over the entrance hall floor.

In the lounge stands a large black woman and a slightly built old man. Seamus has shoved the pistol into his belt.

'MaNdlovu Thandani,' he tells Sarah with a sigh. 'And her husband.'

Sarah looks uncomprehendingly at the woman with the white

handkerchief which she has crumpled up into a ball and is holding in front of her mouth.

'You are Max Wehmeyer's sister?' the woman asks her.

Sarah starts trembling. 'Where is he?' she asks. She suppresses the hysteria, swings round and sees the little loco standing in the sawn-out semicircle under the kitchen door. The engine had run out of steam. There is only the vague smell of steam and benzine, and of fright.

Sarah swings round and runs to the bedroom. The curtains move lightly in the draught; our parents look down at her from the half-moon frames above the double bed.

She comes back and makes as if to take off the record still hissing round and round on the turntable, but Seamus stops her. He dials the police. She goes out and stands on the patio. After a while she becomes aware of MaNdlovu standing silently beside her.

The woman is watching her so intently it makes Sarah feel uncomfortable. She turns round and stares at the chaos in the lounge. The model figures – station masters, farmers, passengers with luggage – stare at her with fixed smiles. Their painted cheeks are red and unnatural.

Sarah shakes her head. She begins to weep softly. TaImbongi goes outside, walks down to the river and lights his pipe. Seamus leads her to the sofa.

Just look up, Sarah, I am here. Surely you know I am here? Just mention my name, Sarah.

MaNdlovu sits down beside Sarah and Seamus. After the police have arrived and begun to search the house for fingerprints and other evidence, MaNdlovu quietly starts to speak.

'Look how things are going, Councillor Butler. See how everything is breaking to pieces.'

Seamus shakes his head; Sarah sees the outburst coming: 'It's your Civic that's causing the trouble,' he says, so loudly that TaImbongi, standing on the patio smoking his pipe, jerks his head. 'It's you and all your talk of subversion that have unleashed all the violence, it's you ...'

Sarah realises: he is quite desperately upset. The great hands on his knees are shaking. He has grown so old, this last while. She looks at the brown liver spots on the backs of his hands, his coarse, knobbly knuckles, his weather-beaten old wristwatch.

But nothing will deflect MaNdlovu from her course. She waits for him to calm down and then continues: 'You and I, Mr Butler, have always watched each other from a distance. You were afraid of me, I know, I have heard all the things that you have had to say about MaNdlovu Thandani and her Civic in those city council meetings of yours. But I have also been afraid of you. Here on the Eastern Frontier your forebears throttled mine until they gave in. And we are both still afraid.

'But there is one thing you must know, Councillor Butler: if you and I do not get down to talking today, then the very last chance will have passed. You may as well look round you at the destruction of this sitting room: that is what the whole Kei is going to look like in one week if we don't get down to talking.'

Sarah gets up and goes outside. She shakes her head: politics without end. We toss all our troubles over the bows of politics. Our hates and fears, our hopes and yearnings – all get political names and we imagine if we create a political paradise we may live in a state of wonderful grace.

She wipes her eyes. She will not see either of us – neither Cawood nor me – ever again. She knows it and there is nothing I can do about it. She has read it in the river. The politics of these waters are played without pretence.

43

Seamus is at the city hall, sitting in the empty council chamber. Round him hang the portraits of his predecessors – grey-bearded gentlemen of the previous century, some sporting luxuriant beards and high collars, staring down at the viewer in Victorian righteousness.

Among the more recent city fathers are figures whom he remembers from his youth – ghostly shapes who had sat on the veranda at Fata Morgana taking tea with his mother shortly after his father's suicide. They had come with offers for the farm and the stud – to ease the burden on the widow. And also, of course, to profit from the widow's distress.

Hypocritical bastards. Three of those who had so persistently driven out to the farm to take a cup of tea with the widow on the veranda had – while his father was still alive – come out to Fata Morgana in the company of a lay preacher to plead with Old Goat Butler to abandon the breeding of Caper timidus. They were members of some or other sect.

It was sacrilege and blasphemy, they asserted, cross-breeding taken to the limit, a challenge to the laws of nature – and would be answered with natural disasters ...

Old Goat Butler, the Toppling Goat, politely but firmly showed them the gate. The stud was achieving world renown; farming journals from all over the globe were sending their reporters to

Fata Morgana. Students had registered at the university's faculty of agriculture for doctoral degrees in animal husbandry to study various aspects of Caper timidus: the fainting phase and its physiological causes; the effect of fainting frequency on the animals' breeding capacity; the comparison of the genetic strands of the tough boer goat and the gentle angora with that of Caper timidus. Agricultural economists studied Caper timidus's viability on world markets and compiled statistics on the number of flocks per night attacked by predators in two hemispheres, and what the savings would be if a fall-goat were used – also what effect that would have on grazing capacity.

Old Goat Butler was sure of his project and refused to listen to the city fathers. They were townees without any idea of the demands of nature. And in any case, he declared, his nerves could take it.

Three years later he lay with his bloodied head in the vygies at the bottom of the garden.

That was only the beginning of the death agonies of colonial self-assurance. Seamus looks round him. The bunch of city fathers here on the wall – oiled like mummies for an eternity which they were incapable of imagining as anything other than English and white – would now, and in years to come, look down on meetings which would surpass even their worst nightmares.

Perhaps they would be taken down off the walls and preserved in some store room; perhaps, one day, that store room would be needed for something else.

That is how our myths are unmade. We shall have to renounce our heroes. Stripped bare, we shall have to face the future stark naked.

God help us; we are the stubbornest of all His flocks. Seamus stands up and looks out of the window. The Civic would be arriving later; also the city fathers. He and MaNdlovu had personally telephoned every one of them; suddenly, there in my ramshackle old house, they had been united in their concern.

Seamus gets up, but before he leaves he glances up at the

portraits. It is time for sentiment to give way. I owe you a duty of tribute, you with your spade beards and high collars. I am your delegate.

Watch me.

Outside, he gets into his car and drives to the Medical Centre. He takes the lift up to the top floor and arrives just in time for his appointment. Hardly glancing at his therapist, without even greeting him, he lies down on the couch. Through the glass window he can look out onto the mouth of the delta.

A luxury passenger liner floats by on the open sea. Had it not been for the massacre, they would have berthed in the harbour; they must have been warned by radio. That's the way we lose things we could have won. 'It is thanatos, the death wish,' says Seamus. 'It's the longing for death that has always driven the Butlers. The yearning for silence, for complete security, for the loss of consciousness which always comes to rescue Caper timidus from terror. When we are dead, we are safe, there is peace, there is redemption from this hurtful world, and we are immune to pain.

'And it's not only the Butlers who are overwhelmed by it either – it's the entire Kei. How fervently we desire our own extinction!'

The therapist keeps silent for a moment. It is their weekly session which should have taken place earlier but which had to be postponed several times on account of the dramatic events on the square. The theme today is Cawood.

Seamus tells the therapist about Cawood's telephone number in the hotel toilet. And mentions, too, that he has not said a word about it to Sarah.

'Why the violence?' Seamus keeps on asking. 'Why this mindless repetition of the pattern? Why couldn't Cawood, the third generation, have come to his senses?'

'We don't know what it is that your son is sublimating. It is clear that as far as his sexuality is concerned he does not feel free to lay all his cards on the table for his parents. Such things can lead to massive repression. Perhaps violence – crossbows, balaclava helmets, hunting expeditions – are the only therapy he knows.'

Seamus shakes his head. 'Thanatos. There is no escape.'

'How does that make you feel?' asks the therapist when Seamus has been silent for a while.

Seamus looks up, irritated. Always that question: How do you feel? How does that make you feel? What about your own feelings? A thousand variations on the charge to bare your soul. A thousand friendly commands to delve ever deeper into yourself until your spade strikes the bedrock under your feet, only to break through to an even deeper well beneath.

He keeps an eye on the clock. The hand is creeping closer to the hour. He will have to go soon, leaving his crumpled tissue in the bin along with the tissues of others who have been here today before him.

'I wanted to visit a priest,' says Seamus suddenly. He has held back this piece of information until right at the end of the session. He particularly does not want to discuss it today. He is not even sure why he wanted to seek out that youngster with his wax-white hands and his Gentle-Jesus eyes and his habit of addressing grown men as 'My son'.

The therapist shows no sign of surprise.

When Seamus says nothing more, he asks: 'And how did that intention make you feel?'

Seamus sighs, wipes a hand across his eyes and looks at the merciless hands of the clock on the table beside the therapist. 'The priest says the Lamb is a symbol of our yearning for death. He promises us, provided we identify with him in his death, a pain-free and everlasting life after our own death.'

The therapist is watching him intently. 'And?' he asks.

Seamus watches the passenger liner sailing past the window and disappearing behind the curtains.

'I think it's a perfectly attractive theory,' he says at last. 'The sacrificial Lamb who focuses our death wish on himself so that we can live redeemed from bondage.'

The therapist does not react. His eyes bore into Seamus's. That's his way of wringing the last drop of life blood out of me, thinks Seamus, so that afterwards I'll stumble out of here exhausted and drained, dumbstruck at what the demons within me have come out with.

'You used the word "think",' says the therapist. 'But how do you feel?'

Seamus sighs. 'I understand now that I want to identify with my father. By taking my own life, I want to return to him, to a time before that night when as a little boy I stood in the shed in front of Caper timidus primus and clapped my hands and saw a fall-goat collapse for the very first time. I want to meet my father before that loss of innocence that made me run past the tennis court that night to leave the dancers behind and head for the open veld; to stumble and fall and get up again and keep running and running ...'

Embarrassed, he looks at the therapist. The man's eyes are getting sharper and sharper as the session progresses, thinks Seamus. Perhaps he is possessed by the devil? 'And I am transposing something of that onto Cawood. I am not sure what exactly. There is a vague awareness, but ...' He waves his hands, shaking his head. 'Somewhere in there there's the reason why I must have ... why Cawood ...'

'Yes?'

'Why I must have rejected Cawood,' Seamus says softly. 'Perhaps I see myself through his eyes as if it is I who am looking at my father. And I am not content with what I see. I don't know how much longer my father is going to be with me. I see the toppling goat. I see its yellow eyes, its pointed beard, its three horns, I see it at the moment of its fainting. I am trapped in that single moment of terror just before ...'

Seamus shakes his head, visibly upset.

The therapist waits considerately for a few moments after Seamus has fallen silent and then says: 'Your time is up.'

Seamus crushes the tissue in his fist and angrily throws it into the bin. He gets up, nods, and walks out. In the foyer he stops at the lift, looking at his dull reflection in the steel doors in front of him.

I haven't any more room for melancholy, he thinks. But I always feel this way when I leave here. Drained of tears, drained of words, no more fight left. Just drained.

There is actually so little one can do to change one's life. The best you can do is rearrange the elements of your personality, encourage your temper to conclude a pact with your human charity, try to get your terrors into balance with your joys, to get your hopes to see-saw with your despair without letting either drop off onto the playground.

In the end, acceptance is the greatest gift of all. The readiness is all.

He steps into the lift and feels himself sinking into the deep pit beneath his feet. He wipes his eyes, blows his nose and runs a comb through his hair. When the lift opens on the ground floor, he walks out, greeting an acquaintance at the reception desk.

Just a routine examination, he has often said when encountering people here. No one needs to know that I visit my Freudian sangoma to have my emotional bones thrown for me every week.

He drives out of the parking garage and when the sunlight breaks on his face, he feels the white onslaught of life and the demands of the day tumbling in upon him.

And the great discovery still lies ahead of us, he thinks: that guilt is seated as deep as the marrow in our bones; that we erect cathedrals to purge ourselves of it; that we confess to therapists and weep like children, or stare down the barrels of guns to achieve an insight into death.

Guilt is as much part of the Kei as the cycads and aloes and rocks that I pass on my way to Fata Morgana. It will still be here long after I am gone.

And those who come after me will have to account for it on their own ground.

That is the story of the Kei.

44

Ayanda Thandani walks out onto the hospital veranda. There are wisps of morning mist over the river. Through the fog she notices the first fishing boats setting out.

It is an important morning, and yet it has made no whit of difference to the pain of the sick lying in the hospital behind her. In her ward two people had died in the early hours – a grey-haired old woman, in a coma for days, surrendered with a quiet death-rattle through the slack muscles of her throat; but the old man, admitted scarcely two weeks ago with an unexpected cancer diagnosis, held onto her hand with the strength of a healthy young man. Gritting his teeth and keeping his eyes grimly fixed on the dawn just visible through the open curtains, he died unwillingly, never lessening the strength of his grip.

Ayanda turns and goes back into the hospital. At about one o'clock in the morning MaNdlovu had telephoned to say that she and Seamus Butler, Seer Wehmeyer's brother-in-law, had just succeeded, after a day and a half of wrangling, in convening an emergency meeting. 'And now, Ayanda, we're going to start reconciling the Kei.'

'I've got to go, Mama, there's a patient dying. They need me.'

'Child.'

Where she was standing at the night sister's telephone, surrounded by the smell of disinfectant, the night was subdued.

As she looked down the dimly lit corridor with the dark openings of the ward doors, she could hear that MaNdlovu was wanting to ask her something important. In the room next door there was someone in extremis.

'Mama?'

'Tomorrow morning you've got to help me up to the Mint, Ayanda. I know you'll be tired, but you know TaImbongi won't have anything to do with my fancies.'

'What is it now, Mama?'

'I just want to sit up there and look out over the city, child, before the great commotion gets under way.'

'Mama ...'

'Please, Ayanda, just do it for your old mama.' Ayanda saw the nurse beckoning to her.

'Be ready in front of the house at eight o'clock. Make a flask of coffee and some sandwiches. What time do you have to be on Cathedral Square?'

And that is what they had agreed to. Ayanda sighs and walks across to the clinic vehicle under the palm trees in front of the hospital.

MaNdlovu is already waiting on the stoep. They drive up the steep street to where the road ends and the veld begins. MaNdlovu says that after the visit to the Mint she also wants to call at Amanda's commune.

She laughs so that Ayanda cannot help smiling, despite being angry that Zola had sneaked out of hospital. 'That old jackal of a Zola,' MaNdlovu grins. 'He thinks he's hidden at his daughter's place – meanwhile the whole of Joza knows he's there! Someone saw him nipping across to the bottle store opposite to buy a half-jack of whisky.'

With her arm under MaNdlovu's elbow Ayanda helps her sweating mother up to the top of the hill. They progress with frequent rests and whenever they stop to catch their breath Ayanda has to explain to MaNdlovu what she sees: whether there is a great deal of activity in the city centre, how high the column of smoke has risen, whether the oil flame is clearly visible.

Eventually they reach the earth wall thrown up all round the Mint. The veld round them still has a scent of morning to it. Ayanda stops for a moment to look at droplets of crystal dew trapped in a spider's web. MaNdlovu wants to walk all along the earth wall right round the building. Tired and dull, Ayanda obeys in silence. She has to help MaNdlovu keep her balance on the sloping earth of the wall, despite feeling so utterly exhausted herself.

At last they sit down to drink their coffee and eat their sandwiches, without speaking. Ayanda is enjoying the aroma of the coffee and the silence, so removed from what is happening down there.

MaNdlovu lays her hand on Ayanda's knee. 'My child,' she says. 'I have brought you here for a reason.'

'Mama?'

MaNdlovu nods. Ayanda sees her swallowing to control her emotions.

'My Mama?'

'This time it's not to look for your brother, Ayanda, it's something else ...'

MaNdlovu wipes her snowy handkerchief over her eyes. Ayanda waits. At last MaNdlovu is ready to talk.

'Ayanda, I haven't got many days left. You're a doctor and you know my blood-pressure is ...'

'That's because you never take the blood-pressure tablets – how many times have I ...'

'Wait, Ayanda ...'

'If you refuse to take the pills regularly and prefer to keep going to that sangoma ...'

'Ayanda ...'

Ayanda sighs her frustration away. 'Yes, Mama.'

MaNdlovu wipes her eyes with the handkerchief again. 'My child, between all people there are things which are never spoken.'

'Yes, Mama?'

'I think the talking that is due to start today is going to beat all the fight out of me, child. So I wanted to talk to you while there is still time.' MaNdlovu looks out across the delta estuary as though she can see right the way to the bottom. 'It is something I have been wanting to say for a long time.' She turns her face towards Ayanda. Ayanda sees the wrinkled, almost unseeing eyes looking at her through the thick, black-framed glasses on the lined old face. 'Your mama has noticed how much care you take of your family, Ayanda. How concerned you are about us all. How you, a big important woman who could easily move into white Port Cecil and live among the rich, still stay in the township with your parents and look after them instead.'

Ayanda looks away. She watches a flock of birds flying over the city.

'Your mama just wants to tell you, child, that I don't blame you any more for what happened that day with Ncincilili.'

'Mama?'

Ayanda smells the burning rubber, the smell of scorching flesh, and sees again the policeman crawling about on the tarmac.

MaNdlovu lays her head on Ayanda's shoulder. 'Guilt like the guilt you bear, my child, can make you forget about yourself altogether.'

Ayanda feels the heartache welling up within her.

'It's time, child, for you to start living for yourself. How are we ever going to be free if we're not free here inside ourselves?'

'Mama?'

Here we sit, two women weeping on a hillside in the veld, while the people are gathering down there on the square. Journalists are getting ready. You can imagine how the politicians are scheming.

And here sits MaNdlovu, flat on the ground.

MaNdlovu takes Ayanda's hand and places it palm down on the ground with the fingers spread.

'Feel, child,' she says. 'Feel how hard the stones are, how

sharply the dried up little plants prick. Look at the marks they leave on your palm.' MaNdlovu turns Ayanda's hand over. Her palm is covered with little dents and a few tiny pieces of gravel stuck to her fingers. 'That is the Kei, Ayanda. That is our soil. Our beloved country.'

Later they get up and struggle down the hill again. MaNdlovu philosophises: 'Going down a hill isn't always easier than climbing up one.'

They have to stop at the house to change their clothes, so Ayanda takes a quick shower.

When she emerges, drying her hair, MaNdlovu is standing there, quite nonplussed, with a note in her hand. 'Today of all days,' she says.

'Yes, Mama?'

MaNdlovu shakes her head. 'He's the ... he's the ...' She stammers.

'Who, Mama?'

TaImbongi. Would you believe it, Ayanda? He's taken his bakkie and gone off to a funeral in Kirkwood to recite a praise poem. Today of all days ...' MaNdlovu shakes her head vigorously, as if to shake off the thought. 'On as historic a day as this. On such a day ...'

Ayanda smiles. In her mind she sees TaImbongi, with his pipe in his mouth, calmly driving down the tarred road, in the face of a stream of oncoming traffic. 'You'll just have to accept it, Mama. TaImbongi does his own thing.'

'He's got an alien spirit, that old man.' MaNdlovu goes into her room, emerging a little later in a dress which she has not worn for years. Ayanda nods her head approvingly but says nothing.

There is an unusual degree of activity in the city. Newspaper headlines announce the gathering. RECONCILIATION IN THE KEI? PEACE MEETING TODAY. They buy a paper from a news vendor and MaNdlovu looks at the photographs of herself and Seamus on the front page.

'Well then, just look at that,' she says.

With only an hour to go before the start of the meeting, they drive down to the fishermen's quarter at First Delta. When they get out, Ayanda looks across the water. On the opposite bank, in among the trees and surrounded by shrubbery, stands Seer Wehmeyer's house. A small boat is drawn up on the bank and the chairs beside the jetty are empty.

An odd feeling rises up within her, a sense of compassion towards the old bachelor. During the night she had made several calls at the casualty ward, though she was not meant to be on duty there. She just had a feeling that Seer Wehmeyer might be brought in.

Ayanda and MaNdlovu decide to leave Zola with Amanda. That is just what father and daughter both need, says Ayanda. Not since Amanda had reached the age of discretion have the two of them spent time together.

As they push open the garden gate, Zola's face appears at the window. He is at the front door before they can even knock.

No, they shake their heads before he has the chance to ask. 'We are not surprised to see you, we knew you were here. We've known ever since the morning you ran away from the hospital.'

'Amanda! You're looking good!' Ayanda hugs her daughter. When Amanda brings them the Kei Herald, Ayanda indicates that they have seen it already.

At MaNdlovu's insistence they all drive up to Cathedral Square together. Crossing the bridge, when she sees the river, Ayanda remembers the dying man. She still feels his grip on her hand. As the dawn was breaking in his eyes, they had grown dull. As she bent over his face, she saw reflections of the window and wispy clouds in his eyes; and behind them, the wide open, vacant pupils as though the man himself had escaped from the body through there.

And life goes on, she thinks. How could I have explained to MaNdlovu up there on the hill that I had broken my oath, that nothing could decrease my guilt?

She pulls herself together. The city is so busy they have to park a few blocks away from the city hall. Zola complains about fearing for his safety, but they laugh. 'The gun-sights are on Granny today,' says Amanda. 'You're just small game, Daddy.'

Through the twisting alleys they walk up to the square. MaNdlovu, unusually silent, has linked arms with Ayanda. The smell of smoke grows stronger. On the square there is a huge concourse of folk.

'Where are you going to wait?' asks MaNdlovu.

'Right here,' says Amanda. 'Here, in among the people.'

'You're going to wait until we have finished?' asks MaNdlovu. It is important to her.

'Of course, Mama,' replies Ayanda.

'I'm doing it for you, children,' says MaNdlovu. She walks on, suddenly alone on the square, between the soldiers and the throng of folk crowding together behind the barricades.

45

Afterwards, no one will believe our story. I have said it before: reality is amorphous; there is no such thing as a neat dénouement.

It is early evening and Sarah is standing on the Fata Morgana veranda with a sherry to her lips. Her heartache for me is like the breath in her chest, first swelling, then deflating.

They will say it is one of those legends that get so entangled with history in this part of the country and grow with every retelling that they eventually gain a life of their own.

I follow my sister's gaze. She is looking at the fall-goat ewes in the slaughter pen. Their fleece reflects the white light of the veranda and their ceaseless movement is that of constant restlessness. That slaughter pen must be shifted, she thinks, to behind the house, or better still: to beyond the dam, out of sight. An end to this continual confrontation with the sacrificial victim.

She breathes in the aroma of the sherry. And so we have seen the dark side of the moon. When she stood here waiting for her dinner guests – how long ago now? It feels like a lifetime ... – with the suicide of the fish shoal at Horseshoe Bend still fresh in her memory, and the fiery tail of the meteor still searing its path through her mind, and that two-headed calf of Bill Heathcote's still bleating in her conscience, she sensed that there was something afoot, like the ants scurrying past her feet that must have thought there was rain on the way and were carrying their eggs to safety.

And it seems as though that light earth tremor is still vibrating through her dreams; as if the earth had shuddered at our transgressions and was trying to shake us off, like the rippling skin of a horse shakes off flies.

All the signs are there that we shall be forcibly brought to account: we shall be compelled to offer a sacrifice for the sins of the past.

The taste of sherry and tears is on her tongue. She is thinking of me. She would never have been able to think, not for a single moment, that it would be me, Seer, who would have to take upon myself the cloak of Caper timidus so as, finally, to compel us somehow to return to our senses. There was not even a body to bury.

And that her own son, her Cawood ...

She sits down on one of the veranda chairs, grateful for the dark. Then she hears Seamus's footsteps in the passage and the next moment, when he flicks the switch, the strings of fairy lights in the garden come on.

They remain like that for a moment, he standing with his hand on her shoulder, she feeling his heavy presence behind her.

'I need to go for a ride,' he says.

'At night?' She places her hand on his resting on her shoulder. I can feel the heavy blood pulsing through your veins, she thinks. I feel the weight of your mind in your hand. When will you ever touch me again light-heartedly and with joy, with that old compelling energy that found expression in your youthful fancies?

Will we ever make love again in Fata Morgana's wettest kloofs, surrounded by clouds of butterflies, and afterwards laugh, carefree, at the startled goats as we race on horseback through their camps?

Will we be able to giggle again at a nervous tourist when a fall-goat ram comes closer to sniff his camera or poke his horn at the touring bus's tyre?

She lowers her face into her hands. 'Go if you must, Seamus,' she says. 'I want to drive into town.'

'Take the pistol,' he says, matter-of-factly. 'And report your time of departure to Civil Defence.' He squeezes her hand for a moment, then asks: 'Are you going down to the old home?'

'Yes,' she answers. 'I must see the river. I need to spend a little time there.'

She sits waiting while he saddles 1820. At last he appears at the stable door and, with some difficulty, mounts the horse. He moves through the goats in the first camp – she can just make out vague white clumps parting to let the horse through. When 1820 starts to gallop, the coloured lights reflect a moment longer on his groomed flanks and then she is left with only the sound of galloping from the dark veld.

She gets up and goes into Cawood's room. She looks at the framed college portraits on the wall with him seated there, smiling and sporty. Even though Cawood left home years ago, the room still has a boy-smell about it. Perhaps she was imagining it; perhaps it was just her memory.

She picks up the catapult which still hangs over the bedpost. Could we never have suspected that Cawood's love of guns and hunting might be nothing other than the Butlers' obsession with death in a different guise? Why could we not have seen that he was engaged in self-destruction?

She wanders restlessly through the house. Should she attempt the trip into town? Shouldn't she rather stay here, wait up for Seamus and perhaps prepare something for dinner? But she really does not feel she can face the conversation that will follow. Also, she hears me calling.

She turns round, dresses quickly and goes out. She walks across the garden path to the slaughter camp, throws open the gate and lets out the startled goats, first into the garden and then farther afield, through the farmyard gate, so they can fan out across the dark veld to where the vanes of the turning windmill reflect the lights from the homestead.

‘Go on, clear off, away with the lot of you, get away from us, leave us alone,’ she shouts. And what’s more, she wants to add, if Monomotapa is also gone, I’m not going to receive touring buses on Fata Morgana either. No longer am I going to let myself be stared at and photographed as though I were a member of some exotic species.

As she crests the second hill, just before reaching the tar, Seamus is standing waiting for her in the middle of the road, holding 1820 by the bridle. His sad face gives him the look of an aloe or a cycad, but when he leans anxiously through the window of the Mercedes, his manner is all tenderness.

‘Nothing must ever happen to you,’ he says.

‘I promise.’

‘Have you got the pistol?’

She nods.

‘Drive safely.’

Sarah leaves. Seamus sits on 1820’s back watching the departing car. The tail-lights grow dull in the haze of dust. In an instant, Sarah, he murmurs, I could end it all; you just don’t know how easy it would be for me.

The oil is no more than the earth’s vomit; I don’t get excited about it any more. He shakes his head to rid himself of his depression, pulls 1820 round and digs his heels into the horse’s flanks.

Seamus is a good horseman, but it is night. I follow him, curiously, anticipating finality. It is a risk he is taking, this galloping through the dark veld. The horse could easily step into a hole and break its leg. It could stumble over a rock and unseat its rider.

Breathlessly, I manage to keep up, observing how Seamus flogs the horse’s flanks, how he digs in his heels, crouched over the neck, his cheek to the straining muscles, biting his mount’s mane. I watch how, under the impenetrable cloak of the Fata Morgana night, Seamus, the master-breeder, is sweating the salt out of his mind.

We approach the bend in the river. It is stony here where the water bursts its banks when the river comes down in spate. Sparks fly from 1820's hooves. I catch the smell of sulphur and saltpetre. The stars are leaning over us, the moon is spinning. I so want to reach out and seize Seamus, to rein him in; if he had a bit in his mouth, I would jerk him back; if he had reins I would pull him up short.

Over the plain, where only a few trees and aloes are to be seen, a firefly comes up out of the dark. Seamus, I want to warn him, come back: you are galloping now into a land which you do not deserve.

The helicopter growls above the silent land, a red light flashing at its tail. The searchlight on its mast gropes across the landscape. I notice bare outcrops of rock, crooked kriedoring trees, spekboom, smudges of grass, a dry river bed, the shining eye of some nocturnal creature.

Seamus! It is too late. Caught in the glaring white beam, on the back of his horse, Seamus comes erect in the stirrups, raising his fist at the chopper. Uneasy, the horse turns in a tight circle, straining at the rein. 1820 feels the jerk of his rider's body; the huge bird above them shudders and comes closer, then moves away again; on the slopes white goats are toppling over. I move as fast as I can to catch up with Seamus as he gallops at reckless speed over the plain, relentlessly pursued by the searchlight of the helicopter. He is caught in his last flight; he will never escape.

Seamus! Come back; pull your horse round; keep away from the river, you can still turn back. Sarah is still there, and there are other things, too – all you need to do is look for them.

Seamus does not need to steer 1820 through the underbrush round the watercourse. The horse under him knows the night; knows that he has to rely on himself as he threads his way through the flotsam and pebbles. They come up on the sand bank above the bend in the river, and the helicopter prods them in the back. Cursing and beating 1820's flanks, Seamus urges the horse into the water. They advance until the water is girth deep. 1820 whinnies, lifting his head above the water which tugs angrily at the tree roots and ledges of rock here at its bend.

'Hey-hup!' Seamus urges. He looks up. The helicopter swings off again, sweeping defiantly across the river, then closes in once more. Seamus shakes his fist. The searchlight running across the earth has become a white animal chasing, trying to catch him, flashing past him, turning back – there it comes again, the white spot, flickering across treetops, over the sand bank, sliding into the water, just grazing Seamus as it flashes by, moving away, illuminating the riverine reeds.

Seamus!

Seamus shakes his head. 'Cawood!' he wants to shout, but from his mouth comes 'Dad', 'Father', 'Old Goat Butler', 'Seamus'. He crouches over 1820's neck and when the horse stumbles through the shallows and staggers up the sand bank, Seamus falls onto the wet sand. He looks up to see 1820 galloping off and disappearing into the night.

He lies on his back. Cautiously, I come closer, listening for his breathing. His chest is heaving. Oh God, Seamus, we are all sacrificial victims, prey to so many things. Get up and walk back to Sarah. Just remember that you have what I had to forgo.

Come now, my master-breeder. Up! You, more than any of the others, are the wounded one, dragging your aching past through this mean year. Bear up! You must ...

'Are you Cawood?' Seamus mumbles. I recoil. He pushes himself up on one elbow. The helicopter comes closer; bushes whirl about wildly in the vortex, moon and stars slice and splinter in the blades. The glass cabin is the shining face of Cawood walking across the sand to his father, stretching out his hands, calling: 'Dad! Dad! Dad!'

Seamus gets up. He holds his riding crop out in front of him. 'You,' he says. 'You. You have broken your mother; you have rejected your father. You flit around as if you never had any roots. Trees like you I chop out of my life, I am not prepared to ...'

Seamus! I get between Seamus and Cawood. I see Cawood's

sweat-soaked body, his shirt clinging to his torso. I see the veins on the forearm stretched out to his father. I withdraw. The river rushes by. The smell of water and wet sand is the odour of fertility. I groan, turn round, leave them behind me, leave them caught, frozen in that moment of reaching out and of everlasting rejection. I flee.

I tumble across the plain. I am nimble. I am free. I have never loved like those who share one blood. Or have I? Did my father and mother, didn't my Sarah ...?

Sarah drives through the darkness without fear. Although driving in the evening is officially discouraged, the dark plain, familiar, closes round her. She has nothing to fear. At some time or other her flesh will have to become one with the flesh of the Kei. She will become a stone or a succulent. Or a fish. Sooner or later. The prospect holds no terrors for her.

As she nears the city she catches the reek of smoke and natural gas. Ever since the gas had caught fire people have been waiting for the oil to return. She decides to avoid Cathedral Square and its seething masses. They are all gathered there; it had begun in the early evening already, when Seamus had to call at the city hall in connection with arrangements for a follow-up meeting between the Civic and the city council.

Those incorrigible Victorians have set up tables and gay umbrellas in front of the city hall. They are serving sandwiches and lemonade to officials standing about in earnest discussion round the flame. The city engineer is also there, likewise the university's geologists and the explosives experts from the army base ... all wondering how the oil is to be enticed back.

You would make any occasion at all into an opportunity for a garden party, thinks Sarah.

Farmers have gathered round portable braai-grids with their coolbags and packs of meat. On one hand they are wanting to demonstrate their presence so that city politicians can take note of their dissatisfaction. On the other, they are driven by an inner compunction to gather and discuss the flame and the prospects for oil, just as they spend their days speculating about the likelihood of rain, locusts or failed crops.

They have driven in from Manley Flats, from Lower Albany, from Addo, from the Upper Kei, even from as far afield as Katberg, the Bitterveld and Golden Valley. Dressed in khaki and with beers in their hands, they do what they always do when there are serious matters to discuss: they make fires and throw chops and boerewors on the coals.

A line of minibuses have brought in the Civic's representatives to take part in the vigil. Maintaining their distance, they watch the farmers round the braaivleis fires with undisguised mistrust.

It's getting like a church bazaar, thinks Sarah, a public auction, a tournament. The world will laugh at our clumsy bunch of Keiers, confronted by forces so much more cunning and powerful than ourselves. Those journalists will write about us as the victims of a freakish natural phenomenon: layers of the earth's primal rock had moved and forced oil upwards, and that oil has now sunk back again into the depths from which it sprang.

She feels bitter. You have forgotten the tragedies of even the most recent past; you're already looking forward again. Am I the only one who has lost so much? From the rhythms of nature you know that drought is succeeded some time or other by rain, winter by spring. Grace and mercy are ineluctable – that you have learnt through bitter experience.

What you lack in sophistication and self-criticism, you make up in stubbornness. You are archetypal pioneers – your greatest faults are simultaneously your recipe for survival, your greatest asset.

And like it or not, I feel myself a part of you. I just don't know whether you will have the ability to reach out across the frontiers and make peace with those who have always been there but who have been shut right out of your minds for generations.

She drives through the quiet city. There is almost no traffic. Port Cecil has come to a virtual standstill. The only ones left are the die-hards on Cathedral Square. The fortune seekers and magnates are all sleeping off their hangovers of the past few days, or lying low and calculating their expenses. Perhaps, if nothing happens within the next day or two, they would quietly depart, take the long straight road over the plains and seek new prospects in more rewarding parts of the country.

She turns down beside the river. The deserted old villas set back deep in their gardens stare at her with empty eyes. She remembers them with families, children playing on lawns, visitors coming and going.

Now this ramshackle old house will sink into oblivion, just like all the other vacant houses. If things start looking up in the Kei, if the peace talks succeed, then in five years or so the old villas will be knocked down and replaced with cluster houses like the ones at Fifth Leg – shiny, modern townhouses with river views, all inhabited by black and white yuppies.

But if things go wrong or drag on interminably, these houses will gradually become overgrown with creepers and start to crumble – leaving only a memory of the time, over forty years ago when families of all races used to live here, before the area was devastated by apartheid legislation.

An era will die, and there will be no regrets or sentiment about it.

She walks past the front door, which the police have had boarded up. I watch her, sensing her yearning for Cawood, her hope that he will not do anything thoughtless, and also her feeling that she will never see him again. She walks round the house and lets herself in with the back-door key which she has always kept on her keyring. The overwhelming smell which strikes her is mine: old books, benzine, asparagus, cigar smoke and the smell of mud and bulrushes that always blows into the house when the patio doors are open.

She throws open the shutters and doors, puts a record on the turntable for us – one of our parents' favourite tenors – and then pours herself a sherry. I wait; she hesitates – then pours another, in my favourite glass. It is quite dark by now, so she switches on the patio lamps which cast their light across the garden and right down the slope to the river shallows.

Leaving my sherry in the house, she takes hers with her down to the water's edge and stands beside the little jetty. She notices the skiff and realises that I must recently have been out rowing. Then she looks up at the house. Light and the warm sounds of the music stream out through the open windows. She imagines she sees my silhouette for a moment, framed in a window. She looks again, then turns her eyes away. She walks right down to the water and kicks off her shoes. Mud squeezes up between her toes. The water is like a mirror. The smoke of recent days has blown away and the river has reacted in joy. On the opposite bank, in the fishermen's quarter, lights are flickering.

Sarah wades in a few steps deeper until the water reaches her knees. Her dress is clinging to her calves. She takes a sip of sherry.

I haven't lost you, she thinks; I'll preserve you in my memories.

She hears something behind her. She spins round, startled. It's so quiet here, the nearest human being is probably across the water.

The figure that comes round the corner of the house is making its way hesitantly down along the river bank. 'Who's there?'

'It's Ayanda Thandani.'

'Doctor Thandani!' Even I am surprised!

'Who is that? Is it Mrs Butler, Seer's sister?'

'Yes, it's me.'

'I ...' Ayanda comes to the edge of the water. They stand looking at each other. Sarah is taking the measure of Ayanda.

Embarrassed, Ayanda gestures in the direction of the house. 'I was driving past on my way from the hospital. I recognised your Mercedes because it was parked here a couple of days ago, too, and I ... I thought ...'

Sarah knows that the route from the hospital to Joza lies a good few blocks farther, but she smiles. 'Just look at my dress: sopping wet. It's ruined.'

Ayanda makes no reply, but looks at her quietly. Then: 'I hope you don't mind my coming here to your brother's house. I ... His disappearance has been a terrible shock to me ...'

Sarah shakes her head. She stands for a while, looking out across the water. Ayanda undoes the straps on her shoes. Slowly she walks into the water and stops beside Sarah.

'Do you think they're going to entice the oil back tonight?' she asks in an attempt to conceal the heartache that is threatening to overwhelm her.

Ayanda smiles. 'I hear they want to give Zola the chance to rediscover the oil. With him anything is possible. He was born with a golden spoon in his mouth.'

They look out across the river. 'Sherry?' Sarah offers.

Ayanda takes the glass and swallows a small mouthful.

'He so loved the river,' Sarah says softly. 'We had such fun here when we were children. We played like otters.' I edge closer; stretch out my hands to them.

'So did we.'

'Really?' Sarah looks at Ayanda in surprise.

'Yes, just a bit farther up. I learnt to swim here – also with a brother.'

'I have heard about your brother,' says Sarah. 'I keep imagining that Seer is here with us. I hear his voice, his shadow is there on the patio.'

Ayanda makes no reply, but takes Sarah's hand.

'We must go forward,' she says. 'There's nothing else left for us.' I come still closer; I love them both. I ...

'Yes,' answers Sarah. 'Hope is an instinct.'

A noise, like the sound you hear when someone casts a handful of pebbles into water, makes them look round. The wriggling bodies of hundreds of little fish skitter round their legs in a silvery shoal. For as far as Sarah can see, the dark waters of the river are alive with fish. She imagines she feels a tremor under her feet, but thinks: it's only in my mind.

At first she wants to wade back to the bank, but the experience has quite overwhelmed her. She looks up and calls my name.

'Seer!'

Then suddenly, as though something has startled them, the fish are gone.

GLOSSARY

abakwethas: initiates in Xhosa circumcision school
ag shame: oh, shame
APLA: Azanian Peoples' Liberation Army, armed wing of the PAC
Assegai of the Nation: the armed wing of the African National Congress
bakkie: small pick-up truck
Bay, the: Port Elizabeth, in the Eastern Cape
Biggie Best: chain of fashionable interior decorating shops
bra: brother
Casspir: police combat vehicle used for crowd control
Christmas beetles: cicadas
Ciskei: independent 'homeland' under apartheid laws
Civic: township organisation involved with political mobilisation and community projects
dagga: marijuana
Die Stem: The Voice; national anthem during the apartheid years
donga: gully
hamba: go!
Ibayi: The Bay; Xhosa name for Port Elizabeth
imbongi (plural iimbongi): African praise-poet or praise-singer
impimpi: traitor
Immorality Act: apartheid law prohibiting sexual contact between races
incibi: initiation officer performing circumcision during initiation rites
jackrolling: the practice of gang rape in the South African townships
Jock of the Bushveld: classic novel about the adventures of a dog in the bushveld
kaffir: pejorative term for black person
kaffirboetie: little brother of black people
kwela-kwela: get in, get in; name for minibuses used as taxis in townships

KWV: wine and brandy-making company; brandy
My Sarie Marais: melancholy Afrikaans folk song
mampoer: illegally brewed spirit with very high alcohol content
MaNdlovu: Elephant Mother
Meerlust: wine estate; specific wine
Mongrels: township gang
muti: powerful, magic medicine, often used to cast spells or ward off evil spirits
necklace: execution by setting car tyre alight round the neck of victim
PAC: Pan Africanist Congress, political organisation to the political left of Mandela's ANC
President Kruger: Paul Kruger, president of the Transvaal republic at the turn of the century
rondavel: circular hut with pointed roof, one room only, with door and one or two windows
skelm: crook
stoep: veranda
stokvel: informal township club whose members pool money for parties or the purchase of expensive items
shebeen: township drinking hole; usually unlicensed pub in private home
TaImbongi: Father Imbongi
tata: father
Third Force: shadowy formation, rumoured to consist of disgruntled police and army members, who, in an effort to derail negotiations, were responsible for many violent acts before and during the first democratic election
tiekiedraai: dance movement; to spin, to turn on a tickey (coin)
tsotsi: township gangster, usually a jobless young man
tokkeloshe: evil spirit, usually manifested as a tiny old man
Twelve Tables: ancient record of Roman Law
usana: baby
voetsak: bugger off
Vondel: 17th century Dutch poet and dramatist

vygies: small, tough succulent plants

Western Deep: a mining complex in the northern regions of South Africa

white pipe: mixture of marijuana and crushed Mandrax (an opiate) pills